More advance praise for *Survivors Said*

"Matt Pavelich has given us a brilliant new collection of short fiction. Each of these beautifully rendered yet unnerving stories—filled as they are with characters who yearn for connection with other people and the world around them— defy our expectations for pat resolutions.

Matt's characters, who so often seem out of place, no matter where they are, insist on living. They work, they seek, they try to grasp whatever possibilities they can imagine. And it's in that trying where they make discoveries that are central to their lives."
—**Ralph Beer, author of *The Blind Corral* and *In These Hills***

Praise for *Beasts of the Forest, Beasts of the Field* (Owl Creek Press, 1990), winner of the Montana Arts Council First Book Award

"Quietly and competently, many fine fiction writers are developing into what might finally be described as a Northwest Tradition. One of these is Montana native . . . Matt Pavelich, whose *Beasts of the Forest, Beasts of the Field* is a slim collection of stories worthy of a much larger audience. . . . This is wonderful stuff, made all the more wonderful by the discovery of a truly good writer." —**Paul Pintarich, *The Oregonian***

Praise for *Our Savage* (Shoemaker & Hoard, 2004)

"*Our Savage* is an extraordinary book, more Continental than American. The startling perceptions remind me of Jean Giono. I don't know anything like it in our literature. . . . Matt Pavelich is uncommonly vital and original." —**Evan S. Connell, author of *Mrs. Bridge* and *Son of the Morning Star: Custer and the Little Bighorn***

"This tale of a gentle giant is a rapturous and remarkable look at both the failing of European power and the settlement of the West in the early twentieth century."—*Booklist*

"[Matt Pavelich's] prose has the formal, deliberate cadences of a work in translation without the characteristic stuffiness—instead, Pavelich sears each line with acid wit. . . . Some authors can master domestic scenes, and others are successful at handling sweeping, historical tableaux, but Pavelich is the rare writer who can skillfully combine the two." —**Lizzie Skurnick,** ***Washington Post***

"We published what is in my opinion the best novel to come out of the West since Ken Kesey's *Sometimes a Great Notion*—a book called *Our Savage* by Matt Pavelich." —**interview in** ***Narrative Magazine,*** **Jack Shoemaker, publisher of both** ***Our Savage*** **and** ***The Other Shoe***

Praise for *The Other Shoe* (Counterpoint, 2012)

"Matt Pavelich is a native Montanan, he knows that world inside and out, and *The Other Shoe* is rich with details that convince, insights that amaze. His prose is among the most impressive now being written, elegant, nuanced, rough when needed, the high and low of language. *The Other Shoe* is a brilliant novel of crime, love, and the American West, and it deserves a wide readership." —**Daniel Woodrell, author of** ***Winter's Bone*** **and** ***The Maid's Version***

"Pavelich's haunting, beautifully observed second novel . . . even surpasses the allure and charm of his first, 2005's *Our Savage*." —***Publishers Weekly,*** **starred review**

"Pavelich's novel is an accomplished and affecting story of love and loyalty, accountability and honor. The powerful concluding scenes race like thunderstorms across the Rockies in this arresting work." —*Kirkus Reviews*

"Sometimes you know immediately where you are—a phrase from Charlie Parker, a Jackson Pollock seen across a room. That's the way it is after a sentence or two of Matt Pavelich's. The writing is nimble, mordant, witty, each of its many characters rendered with a generosity and insight that make them hard to forget. *The Other Shoe* is a remarkable achievement."
—**Ehud Havazelet, author of *Bearing the Body***

"The people in *The Other Shoe* are haunting and memorable characters, bound tightly to their past by local history and folklore. Pavelich unwinds his intriguing plot slowly, reflecting the pace of life in rural America. By the last page, anyone who has ever lived in a small town is likely to think, *This really could have happened.*" —**Chérie Newman, *High Country News***

"[*The Other Shoe*] is a book that resists, one could say defies, categorization. It is a story about love, sacrifice, resiliency, a sense of responsibility and accountability, and perhaps most of all, integrity. . . . This is a haunting, harrowing, horrifying, and, ultimately, heartbreaking story that will stay with the reader for a long time." —**Stormy Weathers, *West of the River* blog (http://westofriver.blogspot.com)**

SURVIVORS SAID

STORIES

MATT PAVELICH

OTHER BOOKS BY MATT PAVELICH

Beasts of the Forest, Beasts of the Field: Stories
(Owl Creek Press, 1990)
Our Savage: A Novel (Shoemaker & Hoard, 2004)
The Other Shoe: A Novel (Counterpoint, 2012)

SURVIVORS
SAID

STORIES

MATT PAVELICH

DRUMLUMMON INSTITUTE
Helena, Montana
2015

Survivors Said: Stories
Matt Pavelich

Drumlummon *Contemporary Fiction Series*

Published by Drumlummon Institute, Helena, Montana.

Cover image: Untitled. Photographer unknown.
Collection of Matt Pavelich.

ISBN-0976968495

ISBN-13: 978-0-9769684-9-8

Cataloging-in-Publication Data on file at the Library of Congress.

Drumlummon Institute is a 501(c)(3) nonprofit that seeks to foster a deeper understanding of the rich culture(s) of Montana and the broader American West through research, writing, and publishing.

The publication of *Survivors Said* is made possible through generous contributions from the many supporters of Drumlummon Institute

Design: DD Dowden, Helena, Montana

Manufactured in the United States of America.

10 9 8 7 6 5 4 3 2 1

Distributed to the trade by Riverbend Publishing.
To order, write to P.O. Box 5833 • Helena, MT 59604–5833
or call (406) 449–0200 • www.riverbendpublishing.com

DRUMLUMMON
INSTITUTE
418 West Lawrence Street • Helena, Montana 59601
www.drumlummon.org

FOR MARNIE

If it ain't scary, it can't be but so much fun.
WILLIAM GRANT JOHNSON

"Himself, Adrift" is available as a chapbook from The Territorial Press

"Aim High Olongapo" appeared in *Narrative*

"Empty Lot" appeared in *The Northwest Review*

"Tacoma" appeared in *Sequoia*

"Another Quentin Houlihan" appeared in *Drumlummon Views*

Earlier versions of the following stories appeared in Matt Pavelich's 1990 collection, *Beasts of the Forest, Beasts of the Field:* "Punta Coyote," "Tacoma," "Gray Kitty," and "The Melodist." The story entitled "Their Beast Lay in the Road" for the purposes of this collection began life as the title story of the previous collection.

SURVIVORS SAID

CONTENTS

MY DISTANT YOUTH

There was a time about twelve thousand years ago when I could run from one end of the known world to the other. I was *Homo Somethingelsus*, child of a parallel line of evolution. The little group of beings to which I belonged were pack hunters with clever paws and shoulders hinged for throwing, we were at least that human, and we roamed a territory along the south ledge of the retreating ice shelf in the mammal's paradise now called North America, a bracing environment for furry things. Initial me, I came swaggering along in my auburn coat, sleek and glossy as an Afghan hound.

I doubt there were ever many of our kind. By my time we were reduced to a few packs, and every member of that species was known to every other member, but because we couldn't count beyond two or three we had no sense at all that we were few or vulnerable. Snouted things, upright, bipedal, we shared our territory with huge swine and the various bears to which we must have been closely related, and of course the mammoth. Our names and all our words were as bird song, fruity bursts of melody, of pure emotion. For detailed information we relied on the odors we knew in common, and with a language incapable of capturing the past or painting a future we lived in a succession of perfectly ripe moments full of scent and tune and clean horizons.

I, if anything, would have been the idol of that era—we certainly weren't in awe of our milky sun. A bringer of good things, I had reached sexual maturity without having been maimed or sickened or starved, and I liked to be alone as well as I liked the reassuring stench of the pack, a rare quirk that made me our wide ranger, our meat scout. Essential me. In that life I ran these ridges when many were only islands—ice comes and goes, water rises and falls, valleys are lakes, then valleys again. I've seen what an age will do to a mountain, and if the bones of my many bodies are now vapor, my beginning holds whole in memory, shimmers there, and often and easily I find myself returned to that wakening time, to my place in a hierarchy of big predators and big prey, stalked and stalking, perpetually exhilarated. I'd trot for days and never tire, never hunger, and I knew to make fire, to use it as a weapon, but I rarely bothered to spin the sticks. When I traveled alone, I traveled trippingly; when in camp I was nightly sought for breeding and never slept cold—needy, yeasty females front and back, scenes predating even innocence. That creature, of all the creatures I've been, was best pleased by its contract with nature. Younger than young then, I assumed this primordial splendor was only my due, and that it would never end.

Our two seasons were winter and a short, urgent spring when grass surged up on the prairie and grew until it was in dialogue with the wind, and on the highlands, in the timber, mammoths calved during milder weather. No modern hope compares with the seasonal yearning of my first youth when in spring, right after the year's final blizzard, I would set out alone, tongue lolling and reverently running. Greed, for all I know, was born in my own splendid breast. The mountains wore a spare arctic forest, something akin to heather, lichen, but on this poor forage many improbable animals thrived. I went out to look for the main chance, and in the end days of that particular ice age, I was certain to find it.

In the year of the flood I ran without a spear or even a hand axe but only the leather straps I wore corded round my waist; I ran scouting the steeps that have since become the Bitterroot Mountains. My gift and mission were to go light and quick, to sweep the countryside until I'd discovered a doddering bull, a young bull recently gored, a stillborn calf, a cow in labor. We lived under their hides all winter, and there is nothing as succulent as suckling mammoth; they were the wealth of that time, but it never occurred to us to stand before them flinging our light artillery. A mammoth's battened hide was better than armor, and its tusks were scythes cutting great murderous swaths much faster than we could ever run away. With respect to the mammoth we were only scavengers, and I was chief scavenger, assigned by my own inclination to go and to stay gone until I'd found one of the big beasts recently enfeebled or dead, and then I'd lead our hunters to harvest. How we loved our work in those days; I was special and specialized and of great practical value.

This was an edge of the habitable earth, a borderland that was then, as it is now, steep country. To the north lay the great lake, and north of that the ice shelf, unfathomable as the sky. Then as now, bright green pine tips grew on the mountains and the volunteer seedlings that the mammoth loved beyond all things. Their manna never grew in an abundance to sustain them in anything like herds, so they traveled singly or paired in springtime. They were everywhere, but widely dispersed and in dangerous good health, and I had run for weeks without finding the right mammoth. But anxiety, in that wide world, was unknown to me. I was descended from many generations of successful meat scouts and I'd never yet failed in my own career. Nothing remains to contradict me, so I'll boast: I was a fine specimen of a promising race that should have done very well on this planet.

Our paws, for instance, were easily superior to any hand. Our six digits were arrayed around the radius of a palm like a small catcher's mitt. Fingers and thumbs, I suppose, and they were opposed upon closing, two against four, and in these vises we could crush friable stone. Powerful and deft, I'd knap a useful face on a piece of raw rock in a matter of moments, and every terrain through which I passed contained my arsenal and my tool chest. I owned my dozen crafty fingers and a compact pair of fangs. When fine weather came, picnic weather, those of us made for the cold would necessarily pant and drool—still, I did adore to run, and was delighted to run as far, and for as long as possible.

. . .

They wanted what I wanted. Additionally, they wanted me. I'd been some days crouched in the highest crook of a juniper tree. The tigers couldn't climb the slight trunk, so they waited just below, and at times they would swat at me recreationally, their paws passing so close I could feel them pushing air. They must have thought me quite a treat because there was much game at hand that balmy year, stupider beasts who were more easily to be had, but the sabertooths waited under me. There was a bog far below where the tigers would go, one at a time, to water, and where, in almost any other circumstance, I'd have watered, too. I was thirsting to death. I'd gotten myself treed on the south side of a mountain.

I thought the tigers, as cats, would be intolerant of boredom, and I expected I could wait them out. I expected I would continue to live, because I could never remember doing anything else. To conserve energy and reduce my slathering, I slept in the tree, and deliberately I dreamt of the cool encampment at the base of the ice dam, water like diamonds leaking from under its foot and fanning in rivulets out onto a green plain where the packs would be gathered now, birthing and nursing new ones. Some of these pups, cubs, babies, whatever they were, would be mine, slick and mewling in their mothers' arms. To be of the packs, that was universal love, something I've never remotely known as any kind of man. I dreamt of my dreamy community and the satisfactions of the green plain, but whenever I woke I was once more alone with the sabertooths.

My kind died with some frequency—I'd seen many smashed, several eaten, but I could not be convinced that any such fate awaited me. Often cornered, often small game myself in my lonely profession, it was a useful flaw in my imagination that I found my own death inconceivable. I had things to do. As I weakened on the juniper, and as I neared the limits of my patience, I calculated an attack. It was the bigger cat's turn to go to water, and when he'd gone, I thought, when he was well gone, I'd pounce on the other. And ride her. And fang her spinal cord. Such an optimist then, the anatomist and strategist as well, I was more than ready, though the cat was as big as a mountain goat and built to bowl you over, and then with her claws clinging and ripping, to quickly gut you. All the advantages would be hers if I couldn't land very precisely on her back and ride there somehow until I'd killed her. One slim chance, however, was all I'd ever required, and my tongue was swelling.

At twilight the bigger cat, the enormous tom, strolled down toward the bog, its shoulder blades sliding up and down, its hips rolling, and I didn't want him coming to anyone's rescue, so I watched him out of sight and still I waited. The she cat paced lonely, and I contemplated my jump and saw myself doing what I needed to do, and I waited, trying to somehow restore feeling to my lower limbs, I'd been crouched on them so long. She sank to her haunches, and I listened to her breathing and to my own. Her eyes closed at last, and after a while I told myself that she must be sleeping and not just in feline repose. I stood in the crook of my spindly tree and the juniper shuddered violently so that I fell as much as leapt, and I failed to grasp the she cat at all but bounced off her sleeping head. I rolled away and around, and there we were, blinking at each other. Her eyes were amber and rather metallic.

She stood and lifted one forepaw to cripple me, or so I thought, but then that paw came down, and the other forepaw lifted, and then she was prancing on burning ground, but I felt heat only in my jowls and belly, and maybe this was her feeding behavior, a waltz for four paws, and I thought perhaps I should attack during the preliminaries; it was improvident to try and run away, to ever show your back to a tiger, and I prepared to lunge, but then I felt it too, that it was not the tree but the earth that had been quaking. The tigress yowled as if in heat, and she bolted off toward the bog, off to where her mate had disappeared. Upon palsied ground I ran the other way, up the mountain, for on its other side lapped the shores of the lake, a universe of tossing cold jade. The ground kept trembling. I heard an angered hive somewhere, very insistent, and this became symphonic as I climbed. At the top of the mountain I ran into a clearing from which I could see down into the valley beyond, a valley containing a vast bay of the lake, and I was reproached by a roar—the lake was emptying, tearing away its banks wherever there was a narrows in the bay, and I knew at once that the ice dam must have broken.

As it drained away, I saw the sea had concealed nothing but a bed of gray silt. All these currently lively valleys, that was their dubious start, they were only sterile bays of the lake, the Clark Fork, the Flathead, and the Mission, all these contained one body of water that would by tomorrow be a half continent away, having swept everything before it, having removed all my kind but me.

We had not in those days conceived of miracles.

I drank at stranded ponds, and I drank often, and I made nothing like my usual pace. The other animals I encountered were traveling south and away from the pounding water, even the frigate birds and the terns flew away, but I followed the sinking shoreline. Something overbore my reluctance, and I followed the water west toward the shattered ice, to bear witness, to make certain of what I already knew, that the green plain was churning under the broken dam's spillway, and that I was the last of my kind on earth.

• • •

I die, but I can't stay dead. I am memory untethered, recording centuries of bad choices and worse luck, but after all this time and all my incarnations, I've always remained essentially of the pack, and I've spent much of several lives looking for some talisman to assure me I hadn't only dreamed us. Apparently we did not fossilize, and the stones we shaped in their thousands are sunk or swept away as are the portraits we carved of each other in tusks and in teeth. If I am, as I seem to be, immortal, then it must be to serve as the repository of that love I've mentioned, to recall the singing that was its source. Our chief artifact was ephemeral. We sang under the hides throughout most of each endless winter, sustaining harmonies like the northern lights, close harmonies in six, eight, twelve parts, everyone under the shelter joined to it. We had learned to build enchantments against the impossible seasons of our time.

LEST YE BE JUDGED

Shunted by chance onto a siding near an abandoned depot, he'd come to a scoured prairie town in a boxcar with seven thousand sacks of manure. Pheelson Junction. Bitterly, Kline chose the place for its resemblance to nowhere, and in nameless cash transactions he rented by the week a room near the switching yard where in time he ceased to smell diesel or to hear the low, close thunder when Burlington Northern's rolling stock coupled in the night. His building's only tenant, Kline learned to drink rusty water rather than complain to his landlord.

Pheelson's few businesses were across the river, and in winter the wind flowed like refrigerant up the frozen channel to make it a fierce crossing for foot traffic on the bridge, an accordingly rare occurrence. Kline bought himself a stocking cap, and boots and gloves cartoonish in their bulk, and he hoped the town's merchants wouldn't notice how often he tendered hundred dollar bills for his purchases, that he had so many of them, that he had nothing else. It was a town without a bus station or a newsstand, and only one small grocery where he shopped as often as not for a fix of country courtesy from a distracted clerk, for human contact. One morning he went into a coffee shop. He sat at the counter and eavesdropped on retired farmers who had gathered round a table to stare out at the horizon beyond the grain elevators and to argue about it. The old men held strong opinions of the sky and its implications, and at least one of them would be shrewd; Kline thought he'd better not become a curiosity among them.

In cold weather he had regular employment as his own boiler engineer, knocking on pipe in the basement and shoveling coal, and some days he'd simply bundle and go walking to stay warm, but he dared not walk out at night or at any time along the railroad's right of way. A police cruiser sometimes toured his side of the river, a town cop with nothing better to do than to wonder at strangers, to marvel no doubt at a strange pedestrian in the industrial fringe of his jurisdiction. Kline was darling, however, in his bloated winter wear, and he'd not yet had occasion to chat with the police.

No one is born expecting to become a hermit. He accustomed himself to make his own coffee on the hot plate, and for company he bought paperbacks from the candy aisle, confectionary books full of air and corn syrup and sweated bodies, and these adventures were piled in party-colored stacks all around the paper and wool pallet that was his bed. Except in friendship and creature comforts, Kline was, at thirty-six, a fairly wealthy man. Ecuadorian oranges came to the market's produce section, and because he could afford them and because they savored of a brighter season, he bought these by the dozen. He ate them so exclusively for a time that the acidity began to give his stomach fits. If he couldn't somehow overindulge, what was the point? The fruit was so sunny and well bred that he often ate rind and all—food for the faithless pilgrim, and in solitude Kline was having the overvalued experience of knowing himself well. Something, he knew, must change.

On Valentine's Day the water main froze and burst in his building, and he was forced across the river to find other quarters. It was much too cold to try and catch another train, and he was in no position to stand by the road with his thumb out. Prospects were few. Pheelson was very little older than some of her older citizens, but having been largely left behind or overlooked by big wheat, she was already a withering village. The Masonic Temple here would pass for a corner bar in any other town, and the townsfolk when you saw them, were moving furtively at their fuel pumps or wandering around at half speed behind streaked windows.

Signing himself Baxter Berrigan on the register, Kline took room six at the New Dawn Motel, and though he'd gained a real bed and a television and ready electric heat, he couldn't see that he'd made any progress. The New Dawn rented just three of its rooms, his own and rooms seven and five on either side of him, the other fifteen units being beyond repair. Rooms five and seven often served roughnecks coming through on their way to and from the oil patch, and meth dealers, or worse, their noisy women. Kline was given to shielding his ears with pillows and reading his Gideon's—were you expected to read the thing or just hold it in your hands? The type was so fine it began to blur at a moment's inattention; there were so many unsatisfactory story lines. Between the old and the new testaments of this bible there was a richly inked plate illustrating Israelites on asses, fording the Jordan, a moon silvering the palm fronds all around them. The Jordan? Such a lot of life had occurred on the banks of what appeared to be about a ditch by American standards. Were they driven out again, or returning? Either way, it seemed so romantic and right to make your move by moonlight. Kline favored getting out of town, favored it more by the hour. What could he risk that was worse than this?

Every evening at five o'clock he watched the most local news that his television could summon, a newscast from a city where he'd probably been a bit of a celebrity not too long ago, but if he'd been on the news, the news had moved on, and now the broadcast was only a tepid little taste of the forbidden city where his mother and brothers and sister lived, and his fiancée. The News at Five and its reports on waste treatment facilities and the dogs of stricken children consoled him very much against the fact that he could never return. Kline tuned in hoping he might yet hear mention of himself as a daring man.

He had vaulted the counter, hadn't he? Sprung right over it in a rapture of adrenalin, his bag of loot and his necktie flying, and wouldn't the deed have been captured on a security tape? Wouldn't they have played that a few times for their viewers, shown them his picture? Employee of the month. Have you seen this man? But if he had ever been, he was no longer in the news. Kline was in room six, and very ashamed that he'd somehow made life on the run even more tedious than his life as a bank teller had been. Was boredom the yoke of his personality? In room six then, in March, he convinced himself he must steal a car.

New to thievery, Kline lacked the lore and technique of grand theft auto. He couldn't hot-wire an ignition if someone were to give him a wiring diagram, and he certainly wasn't going to hijack anyone, so he supposed he'd be reduced to a crime of opportunity. He pressed his pillows to his ears and tried to think his way through it. Some scouting would be necessary. In a town like Pheelson someone would be sure to leave their keys in their car—it was the town's only charm, really, that it might be capable of such innocence. He'd have to look around. The weather was milder, but he still needed to somehow conceal the wad of cash he carried always on his person, and he'd bought a duster at the feed store, a long canvas overcoat that swept around his legs when he walked and made him odder and more dubious than ever, and he didn't think he could cruise the crumbling streets for very long in this get-up before someone would wonder, someone would take exception.

He picked midnight as the most auspicious hour. Kline walked the several streets there were to walk, and, as if he'd been assigned to do it by the mayor, he tried the door handle of every vehicle he encountered. Trust was nowhere to be found. Things were locked as tightly here as in any city, and he was having no luck. There were, at least, no lights in the windows. He walked down to the cluster of homes fronting the near side of the river, and as he turned onto that road he heard an engine idling. He came upon a van so darkly blue he didn't know it for a van until he was very close upon it, and it was idling luxuriously, and the door opened under his incredulous hand, and it occurred to Kline to hesitate, but he did not hesitate, he got in. A leather seat received him. Freshly forged instinct guided him at once to the emergency brake, which he released, and he idled away. He'd gone an eighth mile before he accelerated at all, but then he hit it hard and he was over the bridge and on the highway, and the stars were shining bright, and shards of glass coursed in his blood, not unpleasantly. What next? The van smelled like Kline's idea of apple blossoms. Let's find the headlights.

That was the problem, wasn't it? That he'd had so little practice at charting his course. He'd been to the community college that would have him, and he'd taken the first job that had been offered afterward, and that had been that. He didn't remember choosing any of it. Nothing in this end of the state was familiar to him, but for once in his life his fuel gauge showed full. The fields and the roads to either side of the highway were mud or mud under ice and they ran for as far as the eye could see with nothing else on them but moonlight—as if he'd planned it. Kline touched the dash and happened to call forth Otis Dietz and His Hot Treats galloping through the Omaha Polka, and the radio's volley was only a slight and premonitory thrill compared to what he heard next, the liquid rip of a throat clearing just behind him. The human something. A face appeared in the rearview mirror, a small face on a large head, and Kline thought he saw a particular, detached kind of curiosity there that made him shriek briefly. Having been examined like a bug, he composed himself and said, "Gawd, you scared me."

"Stay on the road."

"Who are you? I mean?"

"I think that would be my question, wouldn't it? Pay attention there, I'm not belted in. Since it is my rig and all, I was kind of interested to know—Who are you?"

"Oh," said Kline. "Oh, Christ. Oh, oh, oh, oh, oooh. I made a mistake, okay? Phew, my chest. You should feel. Just *ham*mering."

"We were in Utah this morning," said the rider, complaining. "Came all the way up from Utah. I was trying to catch a little nap, if you don't mind. If that's okay with you."

"We?"

"My wife and I. She'd gone in to pick up our granddaughter. This is our vacation. We thought we'd squeeze in a little skiing and then have some granddaughter time. We planned on taking Amelia up to the farm. She loves it up there."

"Amelia? That sounds very nice. I hope I didn't screw that up too bad. Look, I'm shaking like . . . I've never shook, shaken . . . shaked like . . . man, I'm just *trembling*."

"So you'd probably better turn around. Rosalie is naturally going to wonder what's happened to me. She'll phone it in, and they'll put some troopers out on the highway, and there's just the one highway through here." Miniaturized and shadowy in the mirror, and with an old man's soaring eyebrows, the rider did not seem a skier so much as a scientist. Or a prophet with his sepulchral voice. "If this was a mistake, here's your chance to fix it. Right now."

"Well, it was, but. No. At this point it's more than one mistake, it's several now, and I think we're getting into that desperate category a little bit. Odd, you know, but it's been so long since I talked to anyone, anything like a conversation, this is almost kind of pleasant. I mean, if I wasn't so scared, this could be very pleasant. You'll have to accept my apology."

"I'm sure it's not as bad as you think. Just turn around now and take us back to Pheelson."

"Can't," said Kline, "and believe me, I really am sorry about that."

"Not as sorry as you will be. Well, can you at least get that stuff off the radio? I doze off for two minutes, and Rosalie dials in her oompah music. Just push that big knob. Yeah, turn it off." The face was gone from the mirror, the man had moved right behind him. Old man? He had a granddaughter. The owner, passenger, voice of reason was riding right behind in that fine strategic position, and Kline felt the back of his head tingle with possibility, the coming thump. He got instead the silent treatment, to which he was highly susceptible. He'd been taking the benefits of being alone for granted; it had been months now since Kline had been anxious little Aaron, hoping so to please. Alone, he'd been his own man. How long did the farmer plan to stay sullen?

"You're a farmer, did you say? A?—Are you?—You sleeping back there?"

"No."

"You could, if you wanted. Might as well just relax if you want. This is quite a, quite a nice form of transportation you've got. I mean, this thing has every last gadget. It's like you're in the cockpit of a jet. And you're a farmer? You must grow a lot of crops."

"We've got sixteen sections under tillage, son. We do all right."

"I'm not your son."

"Yes, that's accurate."

"I mean," said Kline, "there's nothing wrong with farmers. I wasn't trying to convey that impression at all. Not that I know any personally. But I do like to eat, so they're all good by me."

"Just so you approve. That's everything."

"Aw, come on. Let's at least try and be pleasant. I mean, I don't even, what's your name?"

"Ostrovsky," said the rider.

"First name, if you don't mind."

"David. Middle name, Derwin. Or—the Honorable D.D. Ostrovsky."

"The what?"

"I'm a district court judge. And you're kidnapping me."

"Judge?" Kline could now hear something in his breathing like the rattling pea in a whistle. A bead of sweat slid from behind his ear to his throat. "I thought you were a farmer."

"I stay busy."

"Oh, man," Kline braked hard, and the van slid to rest at once, and he turned to get a better look at this Ostrovsky nightmare. "That's it," he said. "I thought you looked like somebody. It's Mark Twain. Without the moustache. Without the wild hair."

"Without the moustache?"

"It's the eyebrows," said Kline. "Your eyebrows. Look, this kidnapping thing, I want no part of that. You have to get out."

"Step out of a warm rig, out into the cold? *My* warm rig? No."

"I can't say half the things I'd like to say right now." Kline calculated. "I don't know what I'd say. But how about this? We're turning off the highway. There's a zillion miles of dirt roads out here. They can't keep their eye on all this, even if they're looking for someone. Could you, uh, would you possibly ride in front with me? You make me nervous back there. Behind me."

"If it'll keep your eyes on the road, sure. Let me guess, you've got a real short attention span." The judge, a lithe man as it happened, climbed easily over the console between the seats. He had the look of a small dog bred to hunt large animals, that heavy and underslung jaw.

"I want you to know I am very, very sorry how things have worked out," said Kline.

"How have they worked out?"

"Well, you've been inconvenienced. Your wife is possibly worried. I don't think I could go as far as kidnap, though. I don't see how you could say that. But then you're the, I guess you'd know the technicalities."

"Do I want to be here?" asked the judge. "No. Are you the reason I'm here against my will? Yes. That pretty well covers it, a *prima facie* case of kidnap."

"I didn't think of it that way. I tried to, I tried to let you go. Didn't I? Wouldn't I get some credit for that? No. Forget it. So what do I do?"

"Turn around," said the judge patiently.

"Ah, yeah, I'd like to, but, are you? Would you be my judge if I got caught here?"

"I'm recused already, as part of the *res gestae.*"

"Which means? Sorry, you'll have to stick to English. I'm only like semi-educated."

"Means I'd be a witness against you."

"Oh. But if you were my judge. Say you were, and I got caught, what do you think I'd get? A sentence?"

"For kidnap? What's your record like?"

"Clean," Kline beamed. "Clean—clean, you wouldn't believe it. Not one traffic ticket. Nothing. I've been quite the model citizen."

"Sentence would also depend a lot on whether you turned yourself in. If you don't, then an arrest has to be made, guns drawn, things like that. Unfavorable things."

"Oh, no," said Kline. "I don't see that, no, not even worst case scenario, I can't even imagine. No. I mean, how would I kidnap you when I can't force you to do anything?" He'd said too much, thinking with his mouth open, and Kline began to consider a point he hadn't previously considered. He had nothing with which to threaten this man, and the judge's voluntary cooperation was going to be very limited. As soon as they stopped anywhere, or came upon any little pocket of humanity, then the judge could pretty easily stall the whole exodus.

"Let's make a pact," said Kline.

"I don't believe I care to."

"Sure, I see. You've got your big farm, and you're a judge and everything, and things go your way, don't they? That's actually what you're used to."

"I've given you the best advice you can get."

"But here's another little wrinkle you don't know about. I robbed a bank. So what's that worth? How many years would that be worth?"

"No idea on that. That would go federal, so I haven't sentenced on that."

"See, though? It just gets deeper and deeper, doesn't it? Worse and worse. One minute I'm standing there dressed for mid-level success, bored out of my mind, and I was getting this ratty, no-pay overtime assignment, year-end reports, and my boss is blah, blah, blah, and he's holiday this and the holidays that, big deal office party—and then there's this bag. And this money, and I happen to know it's non-sequential bills, big ones. So I lose it. For about half a minute, but that's all it takes. I was *so* careful 'til then. But then I see that money, and a good way to carry a lot of it, and *bam*, I'm on my way out the door. I'm on a dead run down to the stockyards, the closest trains. So, I mean, I know you're saying, 'Turn around,' but really, what should I do?"

"Turn around," said the judge.

"What we ought to do is just keep going every whichway on all these dirt roads out here, it's like infinity. I'm almost at the point now where I don't even know where I am. How would they find us, if I don't even know where we are?"

"Yeah, but I know," said the judge. "Never been able to understand how anybody could get lost on the prairie. You can always get a fix on something out here; almost impossible to get lost if you pay attention."

"Well, I am. Lost. I was paying attention to a lot of other things. Like a guy who jumps up in the back seat—my big time cardiac emergency. Anyway, why am I explaining? I want to be lost. I *need* to be lost, it's my only chance."

"It's good country to find your way around in, you can see so far, but for the same reason it's a bad part of the world to try and hide."

"I couldn't agree more. So, are you trying to help me now? Is that what I'm hearing?"

"You'll have to help yourself. There's only one way to do that."

"For a guy as smart as you seem to be, I'd think you could come up with at least one other idea. You know the thing—I'm sure everyone would have said, 'Oh, he's a good person' back home, 'He's a really good person.' But I wasn't; I was too much of a coward to be a good person. I stayed out of trouble, that's all."

"Was that so bad?"

"It was," said Kline. "Terrible. But I have to say, your Honor, this van of yours handles like a dream."

HIMSELF, ADRIFT

While memory persists a man must choose to live with what he has and has not been: I stepped off at midnight to end myself in mortal sin, and though the fall from a sternwheeler's upper deck is only brief and mild, I cannot swim a stroke, and I fairly expected the Missouri to claim me. But mine is a certain kind of luck. I happened at once to find an empty cask afloat on the water, and, my bitter impulse spent, I clung to it, dressed for the occasion in neither boots nor trousers, nor even a proper shirt, but only the pistols I'd strapped to my nether garments, and these only for anchors. I sent my Colts one-by-one to the bottom. I continued. I was. I am. One survives and survives, and every survival exacts its price. My God, I am hard to extinguish.

Long ago, when I possessed more than the necessary quotient of courage, the crown promised to have me drawn and quartered. Under sentence of death, the loftiest platform an Irishman may attain, I spoke of a new insurrection on the old sod, new sovereignty for an ancient nation. Thus, I plotted my martyrdom, but before I could seize it, the empire, cruelly citing my youth, commuted that large fate I had planned for myself and transported me instead to Van Diemen's Land to be paroled there upon my suddenly precarious honor. An early ambition so pure and absolute will render dross all that may follow. Still young, I was in exile with an inexhaustible life ahead of me and the certainty that I was already being forgotten at home, and that the "new" insurrection was already in the ashbin with all the previous ones—Young Ireland, indeed. I had thought that surely death was to be preferred to boredom and irrelevance, but soon learned in the antipodes that such choice was not necessarily mine to make. I married the farmer's daughter and passed my banished days listlessly poling our punt out on the small Tasmanian lake where we settled.

I have escaped danger, obligation, and ennui, escaped by land and by sea, and in these many flights, regardless of purpose or circumstance, I have found nearly all the sweetness to be had from a life too long.

Away on the back of the river then at five English miles an hour, and I checked myself before I might call out; for would not my plaintive cries be repeated all through the territory and the war department? I had no taste for rescue or to hear told yet another tale of the bibulous Meagher, reeling disgrace even to a race of supposed drunkards. Also, there were the bands of assassins I'd sensed behind me all along the trail from Helena—these would be Judge Munson's craven crowd, and my creditors' representatives, and perhaps that foul Indian agent, and surely joy would surge unrestrained in all those poxy breasts should they learn that I was alone in the river, disarmed and as near to death as a man may be without ceasing to breathe.

Long was the darkness. The moon was now in my face, now at my back—I was caught in a succession of horseshoe bends, rounding meanders and making very little progress cross-country away from Fort Benton. I made my passage mostly submerged, hidden, cramping with cold even in fair weather, and wanting whiskey or only just the solace of my own voice, but I kept my counsel all through that night of wheeling stars as animal shadows shifted constantly along the banks. Skulkers. I might at any point have steered to ground but I wanted first for my enemy to show himself.

Burnside's experiment taught me something of strategy, Mr. President. If you can wait until your enemy shows himself, he will by all odds be less terrible. The whole Confederacy awaited us behind that wall, and Irishmen among them, and my brigade of boys who should have formed choral societies or sailed home or built a thousand houses in the territories, my men went forward, and now so many of them abide only in my heart—all of an eternal winter's day in old Virginia, my blasted blue heaps, my still and my writhing lovelies there on the slopes of Marye's Heights. My command with its many high tenors, and wasn't it I who only an hour before had urged them in my stirring way to their glory? Of what avail are we, my chief, in this age of dangerous eloquence? A hole in your head, Mr. President? A neat, deep hole? I should happily pay such a price to atone for my part in it.

As I was upon that grand shelf of North America that drains to the Bay of Mexico, it seemed reasonable to drift, and as I was carried along I resigned without a word of ceremony or farewell my several offices and another marriage, and for full measure thought to quit my very name. Let the good folk of Waterford enshrine Meagher of the Sword—in bronze or in verse—but let this new traveler go unencumbered. Me. At first light, I kicked for the south bank where it conveniently turned to me, and I waded out so far as my numb frame would permit and repined on rounded rocks that were no warmer than the water had been but were solid. An egret stood watch on its stilts, some other bird stuttered nearby. For all my vast trembling I slept, and I dreamt apologetically of poor Elizabeth who'd soon be learning of my death, and of her sad estate, my miner's stove and a sheaf of speeches advocating an invasion of Canada. My debts. Meagher, we were well rid of him. The sun was high when I knew the day again, and I found myself in a holy land of cedar and small pine, sage on the cut banks, bulrushes in the backwaters, every manner of fleeting beast. I lacked desire or means to hunt, but in curiosity I stumbled out of the bottom, scaling a high wall of white clay. There I crested the cut, and a plain rolled out before me in the very shape and likeness of eternity.

I did not think to attempt the prairie afoot, no more than one might swim an ocean, I only stood at its margin for a moment, reduced to an atom in my tattered socks.

So my way must be the river, chief thoroughfare through that wilderness, and I expected a period when it should not be easy to pass furtive along its channel; until such time as the lack of a razor and my constant exposure to the elements should provide my disguise, I must necessarily creep about. My feet are tender. I am by habit and station a horseman, and I minced from one place of concealment to another. Day and night and past and present twisted into each other so that I could not now accurately remark the passage of time, but I recall that I'd an unquenchable thirst and drank constantly of the river. I remember desiccated berries that tasted altogether like chalk and were probably no more nourishing. During that time I starved at my leisure, beyond hunger and all common care, and I slept in bowers where other beasts had bent the grass before me. I was in fitful communication with the distant and the dead, many of whom seemed to think I should explain myself.

One morning down on the strand I glimpsed a figure hunched on the bluff above me; for all the world I thought her a bird of prey, a bird big enough to carry me away. On longer attendance, though, this vision proved human, a thing rocking at the precipice and seeming, as per the current fashion, to contemplate working its own destruction. I climbed to it, and the figure was not naked as it had first seemed, but dressed in skins of no distinction, of no discernible tribe. A woman whose nose had been sacrificed to an infidelity or contagion, her face contained a great crater of knubbled flesh resembling the meat of a pomegranate, and this pulsed as she breathed. She was just at the edge. "Halt," I told her. "Halt, miss. That cannot be good for morale. I am Governor . . . Secretary . . . General Meagher, and I forbid it." Like me, she was not shod. "Are you abandoned? Cast out? I'm Meagher; except for the mutilation I am quite of your set. Believe me. Stand up."

My first wife died bearing me a son I've neglected, and now when she came to demand that I befriend this poor primitive, it seemed little enough to ask. "Catherine," I had to wonder, "do you pass beyond jealousy when you pass beyond?"

"No," she said, "nor anger, nor shame. It is hell."

"You were never," I said, "never in life unkind, Catherine."

"Never mind," said she, deceased and therefore entitled to the last word.

So it was in part at the bidding of my departed darling that I acquired the woman I would come to call Bella, or Bella Union more formally. She happened to possess a flint and a striker and a fund of lore about handmade snares and fish traps, and she would introduce me to an invigorating diet of hare and prairie vermin and roots and grubs she dug with a horn. She was, except for her deformity, in abundant health, and she might have sprung away or overwhelmed me at any point, but instead she dedicated herself to my service—I have ever inspired loyalty.

She hadn't a word in her head, and I was never to know if she was silent by choice or by defect, but she was silent and would listen to anything I might say as if I were the oracle, and she undertook at once, and for reasons of her own, to care for me. While I might tell her anything I wished, I lacked the precise language to explain that I was unworthy of her effort, so we went on, Bella and I, forming our intentions by watching the sky. I had no designs on New Orleans, nor St. Louis, nor so much as the mouth of the Yellowstone, for I could foresee no welcome for us in even the meanest settlement. We'd be scavengers there, our place in its society but to dart at scraps and to suffer the pent wrath of every coward in every outpost. I liked better to roast a sage hen over a greasewood fire, to have my turnip, roasted or raw. It was not for the sparkle of my argument or my reminiscences, not for the luster and romance of my career that she sat back to back with me whenever we stopped to rest. We were grateful to evade for a while the wind, the complaints of our misused feet, and ours was a partnership exact, back to back and happily and comfortably seated on the ground; I had never yet disappointed her.

Winter ended that ease. When the weather turned we had traveled no distance south and our slight raiment was not suitable to the season. From such small game as we slaughtered neither collar nor cuff might be manufactured, and we derived no fat for our bones; needs be I built us a hut in the Bannock manner, though more porous I think, and we made a small fire—our life's work to feed it—and here we whiled away another portion of time, long enough to be cured as hams in that hut. I recalled and recited of Ovid and of *Plutarch's Lives*. I intoned a mass one morning, blasphemy, all of it, *now and at the hour of our death.* We crouched at our little flame. A tiny economy, the woman and I, the smallest possible society, we developed, when rooted like this to one encampment, the usual set of civic problems. Soon we had overharvested the ground close around us, and we were eventually beset by our own wastes. In time all Latin came to sound dull in my mouth as the thump of the regimental drum. Bella was avid after any spirit, any tale, they were all the same to her, and I was overawed by her patience. She would assent to any scheme. One luminous morning when I could no longer tolerate myself at such close quarters, I told her, "No more can I huddle here." Have I mentioned that her eyes and her mouth were very fine? Have I said how this heightened the tragedy of my Bella's poor, excavated face?

We set out under a sun whose radiance was only another piercing expression of the cold, and we walked at intervals upon crusted snow, and before our expedition had been underway an hour our feet were bleeding and turkey buzzards circled overhead. "I cannot," I calculated, "return to that shelter for any reason." But there was no use in explaining my ruminations to Bella, who only waited to follow whatever I may actually do. I had been a first in rhetoric at Clongowes Wood, but I was never so persuasive, I found, as when I could not make myself understood. The cold that day was not astir, there was no wind at all, so we walked along the height, looking to the prairie and to the canyon below for we knew not what, but walking because to stop would be to freeze. The cold worked fantastic patterns in our flesh, and I expected we'd be losing fingers and toes at least to my restlessness, and we hurried on.

These were the extremes that prefaced our association with Blankenship and James whose raft as we found it had ridden in on high water and gotten beached, grounded on a bend and had come to wear a thick collar of lacy ice all around it; they'd made it their home and their store. We followed for some miles the tendril of smoke that issued from the stovepipe that issued from their shelter, and we came to it from above, and their raft's decks were heavy with cargo in hogsheads and in crates. We climbed down to it, and as we could ill afford caution I simply called out, "Upon your mercy, sirs, you there aboard. Take us in, will you?"

A negro of alarming dimensions emerged from under the timber wigwam, followed by a younger man so heavily freckled he seemed to comprise some new race of his own. The negro proved mild of manner, "What happen to dat po' woman? How you feel, mizz?"

"She is hale," I said. "Who among us is truly intact? She is stoical as one may be, and a boon companion. Let us in, won't you?"

They acted as one, removing their pipes from their mouths and aiming the stems at their home by way of invitation, and I thought we were met with men of few words, a theory they would shortly disprove. Their wigwam sat on dry deck, and was only just big enough to contain a table and four chairs, their stove and several lamps; our hosts, who very fortunately lacked the purer commercial instincts, gave us blankets, trousers, and even ill-fitting boots from their stores. We sat face to face in a close redolent of leaf tobacco and oil and kerosene in various stages of combustion, and most vividly, of ourselves—in this manner we waited all through what I judged to be January for the killing cold outside to abate. Our only real hardship now was each other, the company we kept, though almost any company would have been less congenial. The raftsmen were a pair of philosophers and they'd been in dialogue a long while.

Blankenship said that as a boy he'd been the ward of a woman whose sister had owned James, and, "We started right off misbehavin', well before the war, and we been dodgin' one thing and another ever since. But business, wouldn't you know it—business might be our worst idea yet. Hey, James? Well, we'll call it New Cairo and see what happens. Call it Riverside. It is your town, ain't it, if you land on it and nobody was there before?"

Theirs was a barge made to be towed upriver, and their misfortune as they recounted it had begun with a deckhand axing a hawser line, a boiler leaking at its seams, losing steam, and the tug they'd hired to tow them going past them downriver, the doughty deckhand calling on the way by that they were on their way to St. Joe for repairs and that they might return as soon as next spring.

"Barge this big, we was helpless, two men on two short sweeps. We just washed right up, and was lucky to light pretty here, lucky to've settled down nearly level as we did. But James seen it in a hair ball, didn't you, James? Saw it way back when. Said I was to stay away from water, which I haven't did. Hair ball also said I was to get hung, which hasn't happened, either, though there's been some that wanted it. One thing leads to another, and lately we get to thinkin', why we may as well be traders, much as we get around anyway. See what come of that? Here we are hunkered down on our inventory. Come spring though, once the ice breaks up, we'll put out a bully sign, won't we, and we'll sell this trap up and downstream. James used to be merchandise his own self, right about eight hundred dollars' worth, but we're free men now. Or at least he is, and I will be as long as I stay out of Nevada Territory. Free men, except for all these dry goods that owns *us* now. We got to tend to it all, which is a thing I somehow never thought of as we was throwin' our hand in. Store *keeper*. Never thought of it that way 'til we was stuck with all these goods."

"De river," in James's opinion, "you don' git free'a dat no matter how many war dey fight. River do what it want wid you. But if my daddy who never see me, see me now, his eyes bug out. My own sto'. My own moonisability—what I say we call it Jamestown fo' de high tone dat's in it. Jamestown. Don' you ever think I ain' glad 'bout what I's become. *Hair* ball? When you a slave you ignorant, you *got* to be."

"The Irish," I observed, "are as literate as anyone in Christendom. There are many methods and styles of subjugation, sir."

But Blankenship would have no pessimism among us. "Not here," he vowed. "There don't need to be none of that in our town. I've always said it, you got to be peaceable on a raft. Peace. That's all I'm ever after, and it is so hard to come by. Our very first time downriver, and I fell in with a feudin' family, and I see what the quality does to each other for entertainment, how when they get to killin' each other they just keep at it as long as they can. So I remembered that, and later I figured, well if that's a feud, what must war be? Two weeks in the militia was plenty for me. We lit out west. James and me made for the mountains, made for the gold fields. We've always traveled light, ain't we, James. But it's best to stick close to the river, 'cause the river's been good to us, if anything has. A body can just put out in the river, on a log if it's all you got, and you're gone from whatever needs left behind. Only rule is, you got to stay peaceable on a raft. That's how we like to go."

"But I say dey be one mo' rule: We got no truck wid dead folk, suh. I sho' wish you quit talkin' to folk what the rest of us cain' see. Give me de *fan*tods when you go on de way you do."

James's late wife, I would learn, was an Elizabeth, may God rest, and my living wife was an Elizabeth, may God grant her safe passage back to Fifth Avenue. Blankenship's given name, as mine, was Thomas, and I thought I noted a synchronicity moving among us, as if we'd been thrown together for purposes not yet revealed. My thoughts were not well organized. I was at a constant disadvantage in this company, for the others were innocents in outlook and intent—and I the only one among us to have received Holy Communion. How I envy the easy rectitude of the heathen, the uninitiated. All in all it was the sanest company to which I have ever been privy; we were safe, and we were necessarily in sympathy and equivalence, a perfect society of generous souls.

But Meagher. He may call himself Stephen Icarus or Oedipus Next or by any *nom de plume*, but in the end he will be Meagher, the same despoiler, and though he find himself at last in a perfect society, he is never satisfied, for he has been sick so long with latent revolution that he is at his core a malcontent. It was not with malice but curiosity that my companions tore at me during our weeks at that table. What hard intimacy. They were, even Bella in her enigmatic way, a crowd of Socratic interlocutors, and in the course of our long confinement their easy but incessant curiosity would flay me down to my finest veins and sinews.

"Say you one of de main rebels wha' you come from?"

"I was a voice for the movement."

"Didn't I tell you, James? When he first hailed the raft, I said, 'There's a stump speaker or a carnival barker, one. Friend, if you could see yourself come down to it, we could likely find use for that voice in our operation. You can call 'em in off the river, tell 'em what they're missin'. We got one of everything at Jamestown-on-the-Missouri, got every useful item on this barge. Hundred pair a' boots, two hundred leather belts, got a ring they tell us the Queen of England used to wear as a child.'"

"But we don' carry what dey all want. We don' carry no liquor. Thomas's Pap, he been so bad to go to de bottle, scare us bof to temp'rance. So let me see if I got dis right, you a rebel in de country you come from, but once you get in dis country, you wanna fight fo' dem Federals?"

"I got a better question yet," said Blankenship. "Why'd you want to fight anybody at all? You've seen what comes of that these days. Folks are never so clever or brave as when they set out to slaughter each other. Them machines they make for it, it's a heavy industry now. And you say you just up and went to that? Took others with you? Brave or stupid, whatever the prime ingredient is, I wouldn't have enough to try war the first time. They line them cannon up, and I will be headed the other way soon as I know about it. Nothin' else makes any sense to me, and I guess I can stand it if I'm a coward."

"Mr. Lincoln," I told them, "has my ear, and he commends me again: the Union is preserved."

"De Union? Is dat de Federals, too? De ones dat send out dem carpetbaggers? You fight fo' dey side, suh?"

"My men fought to free you. Know that."

"De Irish? Dese be dem same Irish lynch so many niggers in New York?"

"The Irish 69th. New Yorkers. Thrown against the enemy until they were a shadow."

"De one thing don' make sense up agin' de next thing. Do it?"

"We are a noble race," I said, "not a merely logical one. The finest motives are in almost everything we do. "

"Dey move some lines on a map," James observed, "den everybody inside dem lines got to do different. Now, did everybody agree to dem rule, or how did dat come about? 'Cause to me, dat seem such a silly way to go. Dey used to say, Jim, we owns you. Dey used to say dey own me, en ever'body jis' agree to dat, too. Who decide dese rules? Why we got to go by 'em?"

"All we got to do," said Blankenship, "is sit around peaceable, and smoke, and chew the fat, and wait for our custom to make their way to us, and hope we don't use up too much of our own goods. We wait, and they'll come floatin' in."

"Where there is commerce," I reminded them, "there is dispute. And that will mean law."

"No, that's only your brown study, friend, from havin' not enough to do; no, I've seen the law at work; we don't need that any more than we'd need a plague of influenza. Not here. Don't we know how to behave decent enough so's no one gets hurt? Ain't that enough?"

"Not even in paradise, they tell me. There is apparently some organization necessary even beyond the veil of tears."

"Dere you go agin', Mr. Tiberius, or whatever you call yourself today. Beyond. Ain' nobody wanna know 'bout dat. And de law? Ah don' like to argue. Some does, some don't, en' I don'. Upset me som'n terrible to spat wid anyone. Tell you what I like better. What about a onion? Sweet onion, some fresh green, das what I mind about. Long ol' time since we ate som'm came outta de groun'. My *teef* fixin' to fall out."

My companions were natural utopians and effortlessly kind, and I aspired in vain to their stout decency. I had only hoped to do well by them as they had done so well by me, and I recognized in them a morally superior species whose favorable opinion I coveted. My poor consolation now is the thought that we were all of us highly nomadic beings in that wigwam, and one of us would eventually have done something to upset the putrid perfection of our long symposium. But it was I, I who pleaded one day, "Let me go abroad, why don't you, with one of these splendid firearms? Shouldn't we have fresh meat if we may? Bella can surely take me straight to it. A haunch of venison, and we could char it here upon our beach. A feast, a libation to request the return of temperate weather—the woman and I wish to make some contribution to the ship's mess if we may. Allow us that dignity."

"Gun's yours, an' plug away if you got to, but de dignity, you got to see about dat yo'se'f, suh. We ain' got it to sell or give away. Nobody do."

"Take a pass," said Blankenship, "if you see any antelope. I'd as soon eat rat."

It was an arid, crystalline world Bella and I encountered when we went out to hunt, the countryside scoured by the purest midwinter, midday daylight, and any slight sound carried in silvered resonance, seemed to carry very far. Conditions were not propitious for stalking game, but we now wore trousers, and our shawls and our boots, and I had the use of a rifled musket that I expected to be accurate at a quarter mile. I wept after a fashion, for joy, tears springing easily into eyes irritated by fresh air. Bella beside me was become a presence to banish all other presences, a breathing reassurance who kept at bay those voices so hot to pursue. My hideous angel from whom nothing might be concealed, and who yet approved me, and who seemed at all moments to be saying, "Yes, go on."

Wanting the long vistas of the prairie, we climbed up to it and looked out upon a great open countryside, all the more forbidding and wonderful for having become brittle in season. Not a cloud in the aching sky. That ground of dun grass made a long, gradual ascent away from us, and Bella pointed to two presences just under the southern horizon, no larger than ants but clearly equine in their movement. We were seeing them face on, and we watched them for some time before it became clear to me that these animals were mounted. They came on very slowly, and Bella and I stood transfixed. I cannot recall who I thought they might be, or what I thought was occurring, but I know that as they approached I could think of nothing but the riders on the rise. I believe I had some notion of directing them to our host's store. Having fallen into a strange state of fascination, I never once thought of retiring to the canyon or returning to the raft. I was having difficulty seeing them at this distance as more than shapes, and my curiosity lacked all caution.

"Bella," I wondered, "have I always so imperfectly known the world? My failing eyes, all my perfidious senses. Well, it is not information we seek, is it, but understanding?"

The riders were no longer coming forward. They merged until there was no separation between them, and I saw them, horses and riders, as a single brown smudge. Someone dismounted, and, even in miniature, even under a buffalo cape, this tiny figure's movements seemed quite purposeful. I watched large, complex gestures, and only later would I understand that the man was erecting a forked pair of rods for use as a rest, that he was preparing to bring us under fire. Bella, with her better eyes and purer instincts, appreciated the moment long before I, and for the first time in our acquaintance she moaned. She seized my arm, something unusually forward for her, for she held my person in some awe, and the first plume of smoke issued from that distant rifle, and we heard a rushing whine, and she flew back. I felt the shock of it transmit through her hands in the instant she was flung away from me. A massive report echoed afterward.

Dead as I knelt to her, the familiar wonderment was in her eyes, but she lay in unmistakable stillness, the life blown quite out of her, a concavity in her chest to match the one in her face, and now at last she was briefly given voice, and she said, "I was not capable of regret. That, you should know, is what you so admired in me."

"Bella," said I, "Bella Union."

"That," she admonished me, "was never my name."

With that, she was done with me, truly gone, and all in a moment all the harpies came crowding round, and anyone at all might submit his disappointed whisper into my ear and comment on man's inhumanity to man and my uncanny ability to promote it. I thought I heard Napoleon decry the disadvantages of occupying the low ground, of remaining within reach of the enemy's superior weapon. "It will be a Sharps," said I. "I believe at this range, though I am no artillerist, that they must have a Sharps or something like it to make such a shot. Buffalo hunters. Madmen withal. It is not I, Emperor, but fate that is forever arranging these unfavorable strategic sequences. Now that the woman is gone, it scarcely matters."

Catherine was suddenly there to ask why those entrusted to my care invariably perished on account of it.

Elizabeth suggested that I return to her, to my former life where even now all might be forgiven, and where I might finally resolve my arrears by employment on the lecture circuit, and I would fill the halls again, tell a rapturous lie of my abduction and escape from captivity. It was my wayward gift Elizabeth loved, the round emanations of my peerless mouth.

The rifleman on the rise regularly set the air awhir around me, and from his prodigious expenditure of ball, and from its failure to have any effect, I concluded that the success of his first shot was a matter of enormous luck, good or bad. I rammed home a minié ball and sent it upslope if only to demonstrate that my tormentor should keep his distance. I had nine more rounds, and the rifleman on the rise was a hundred yards outside the effective range of my Springfield. The whole intervening distance swam in my sights.

So I strutted there before him, an always moving, an erratically moving target, and I hoped with this constant display to somehow announce myself, my plan to kill them now, and I must have successfully communicated this, because the gunner expended round after round, and I heard the exasperated rip of his ammunition tearing the air right around me a great many times, a protracted volley that eventually brought Blankenship and James running up out of the canyon and to my side, and now we'd three Springfields, and still we represented little immediate threat to the hostiles.

"Who doin' all de shootin', and what dey 'bout, you reckon?"

"We cannot know their purpose," I said, "only their character, and that is evil."

"Won't you get down?" pleaded Blankenship. "There's no reason to be quite so proud as all that."

"Indifference," I instructed them, "is my only tactical advantage. Let him bang away, in the end I shall I have him, or he shall have me, and it is all the same. I suggest you retire from the field, gentlemen, for this fight is mine." I loosed another ball toward our tormentor, and as I did James rose from the grass where he'd knelt beside me, and he meant to pull me down into concealment. He died as he touched me. Another terrible wallop from the Sharps. "Now see where you got me? Why you white men always got to play the fool? Why everybody got to be so stubborn and mean? And why I gots to be gone fo' spring?"

"Get down," Blankenship screamed, "or I'll shoot you myself. Good people is killed. We don't need no more foolishness at all. I said it. I said it, and I said it, and I said it, but I could never make it stick. Peace." Blankenship's features twisted all in a moment into the purest pain, and he howled and rose up, and ignoring his own good advice he rushed toward the riders, taking no precautions at all but advancing in bee line, and we ran up until we had brought them within range of our Springfields, and then we stopped to exchange. Only the Sharps was in play from our opponent, and we did not know what to expect from the other rider, but the Sharps, by itself, could match our rate of fire, Blankenship complaining all the while that they'd been sold flawed Springfields. We advanced again to decrease its advantage, and Blankenship, mad with grief, was a banshee, more heedless and headlong than I in this assault, and even when he himself had died, he continued some way forward toward the vengeance he wanted for his already fallen friend.

I caught him up and reached him where he lay. Sightlessly, Blankenship considered me, and I asked him, "Have you been granted your peace at last?"

"It don't hurt, that's all I can say so far. James tells me he still ain't keen on ghosts, even if that's what we are our own selves. He ain't accepted it, but he always has been hardheaded. You might wish to lay off these criminals, and never fret too much—I was born for a bad end, and James'd bore so much sadness about his family; he's free to look for 'em now. You ain't entirely obliged to kill these fellers."

"I believe I must. They are a pestilence."

Once more I strutted before the rifleman, and again he let fly, and that peculiar charm of old deflected his every effort, and soon enough he'd exhausted his ammunition, while I was heavy with it, Blankenship and James having come up out of the canyon with stores of fresh charges and cartridge. The second rider dismounted at last, and each of them held his horse's plunging lead in one hand while with the other they fired in sheer folly their dragoon pistols. Now it was I who was beyond their reach, and I shot in impunity, and I shot and I shot, and they were too stupid or timid to come at me and bring their pistols within range. It was a leisurely exchange, and even tedious, the better to finally slake my rage. While I shot, the harpies hovered round and they sang to me of the prodigious debt my continued existence could only enlarge, and I shot continuously until I burnt my thumb on the barrel of my weapon. My treacherous eyes. The riders were not dead. In the quiet interval while I waited for my barrel to cool, the rifleman bolted and tried to swing up onto his capering, terrified bay, and the animal squealed and shied violently away from him, and I heard his leg break as he was thrown.

The other came running afoot, emboldened at last, and in his buffalo robe he could not run very fast, but we had finally closed quarters so that he had some hope of reaching me before I might reload. His pistol, I deduced was reduced to a club, for he sought to make no other use of it, and it was so close a thing that I was only just able to raise my muzzle as he ran onto it, and I fired, and he fell.

This was a boy.

He said as much when he complained, "I was only a boy, one with no advantages, and see how you have killed me. I did not have high hopes of the world, but I thought I might do better than this. Oh, I was terrified, and this is no proper cure for it. You should be ashamed."

The other was still alive, too much alive if anything, in his agony. His eyes were open and blue and sentient. His mouth contained only its foremost teeth and his was a rodentine aspect. The man on the Sharps, the rifleman. He still had his pistol in hand, but was sprawled so that he could scarcely bring it to bear, and I walked up on him. "We are all," I said. "All that remain, so I am especially curious to know, what manner of blight are you? Are you dead?"

"Dead? Dead? What are you saying?"

"No, you live, more's the pity. Your tunic. Were you of the militia?"

"Governor? Why didn't you speak, sir. Why didn't you call to us? Oh, the trouble."

"Who commissioned you to fire on civilians?"

"Wasn't you, sir. You only provided the shirts, and we had to ride a thousand mile just to get 'em. It was the others, sir. After we was broke up as a unit, couple these ranchers get together and says they'd pay bounty on either Blackfeet or Crow. You mean to let me die out here, sir?"

"I'm. . . ."

"I know that, sir. Now. You should have spoke. Wouldn't have took but a few words, and we'd've known you."

"You have killed saints here today, and the ground so hard it will not accept their bodies."

"Do you remember? We sang at your door in Virginia City, and you praised our voices, and your lovely wife praised our outfits. The speech you gave—why we would've whipped a nation of Indians if ever we'd found 'em. You had us that aroused. Are you still in politics, sir?"

THEIR BEAST LAY IN THE ROAD

The foothills awaited the year's first snow, and Mitchell Lefthand felt the swelling sky as an embrace, a fond memory. "We'll have good trackin'," he said. His riders, hunched in the seat beside him, would not share his optimism. "I told you guys this heater was weak. You should've wore your long johns."

"I wore all the underwear I own," said Harlan Brattle. "Your wing window leaks."

"I can't sit on this spring no more," warned Vernon Birfato. "It's really pokin' up now. Why didn't you buy a Ford?"

They passed a beaver dam and a field of sunflower stalks. Mounting a high bench, the road climbed through lesser gullies into Morigeau Gulch and toward the tree line. Wool, gun oil, and Vernon Birfato's musty hair thickened the air inside the cab. They stopped so that Brattle could get out and open a wire gate in a barbed wire fence, and then they followed a faint two-lane track down toward a creek bottom choked with alder and wild rose. Lefthand drove through an opening in the tangle, and through the creek, and breaking a fringe of ice they climbed out the other side. He bounced his shifter off Vernon Birfato's knee. "This gear box is a little broke; I miss second a lot."

"What ain't broke on this thing?" At fourteen Vernon held opinions untroubled by doubt or too much information. "You got ripped off. For three hundred dollars you should get a radio that works or a seat you could really sit on. They must've saw you coming."

On the far side of the creek the old woman had her place at the edge of the forest, a place the forest seemed impatient to reclaim. There was no sign of any recent traffic to or from; her Nash Rambler crouched where it had these ten years past, the

rubber rotting out from under it, a bulbous bumper from an earlier wreck leaning nearby. No smoke from the cabin. There was
a teepee as well; Lefthand knew she liked to shift seasonally from
one residence to the other. And shift and shift. She'd got around.

"Now what's this?" wondered young Vernon. "I thought we
was supposed to be hunting."

"I have to see about my Auntie, long as we're up this way."

It was a homestead not a hundred years old but already far
into its antiquity. The cabin was of logs faced by broadaxes and
chinked with clay and joined at the corners with fancy dove-
tailing. There had been an undertaking here, ambition and
hope. The outbuildings had been made of thin, wide boards
and these were fantastically warped now around the two-holer,
the smokehouse, a hutch that had harbored by turns chickens,
goats, and swine. A gate frame recalled the fence that had once
fenced the garden, and there were the remains of an apple orchard harried nearly to death by bears. And then the forest, just
waiting. Here the forest began, and from here it ran dark and
continuous all the way to the border and for hundreds of miles
up into Alberta and B.C.

"Kind of spooky," said Harlan Brattle. "I like it. Think she'd
be home?"

"Never know with Auntie."

"Bet I've passed by this place a hundred times, up on the
road, and I never once saw it. This'd be just right."

"Forget it, whitey. This is Rose Vallee's. It's her allotment. It
can only belong to her or the tribe."

"Yeah, I spose. The better women, the better ground, somebody owns 'em. Every good thing's been spoken for. You can't
have it, and you can't have it, and that's always the first thing
they tell you. That is the news."

"Poor you."

"Poor me."

"There's nobody here," said Birfato. "Come on, let's go."
Lefthand looked into the teepee and found there a mound
of empty Butterfinger wrappers, the clean skeleton of her last
beloved Boston terrier, and some molding blankets. "Hello the
house," he called. "Auntie." A galvanized washtub leaned at her
door. There was a fifty-gallon drum on end, filled to the brim
with empty cans— pork and beans pork and beans peaches.
"Auntie Rose."

"She ain't here. I told you. Nobody ever listens to me."

Lefthand rapped shave-and-a-haircut on her timbered door
and waited until the old woman cracked it enough to exhibit
one drifting eye and a rifle barrel. "Mitch?" She stepped out,
barefoot, a Hudson Bay blanket round her shoulders. Her braids
were thin as cording and fell across her gingham bosom and
down to the vague demarcation of her waist. She went hungry
sometimes but was always stout. Her front teeth were gone,
bottom and top, and in Rose Vallee this made for an expression
of constant good cheer, of knowing the prime joke. "Yeah," she
decided. "Mitch. And who's this you brought with you?"

"This white boy's Harlan Brattle, friend of mine just got
back from the war. He claims he never killed a single baby over
there. And this other one's Vernon. Vernon Birfato. One of Clive
and Alma's kids. He's the one we might wind up killing if he
keeps getting on our nerve. Would you mind if we left his body
in your root cellar for a while?"

"Clive? I'm supposed to know somebody by that name?"

"Yeah. They're your relations. The Birfatos? Auntie, geeze."

"Some I remember," she said, "some I don't. Come in. Sorry
I don't have nothing to feed you. I did have some huckleberries,
but that was quite a while ago."

She settled on her bed, and rolled an oblong cigarette, and
she smoked it, never letting the splayed butt an inch from her
lips, dreaming between drags. She'd lived intermittently in this

cabin for as long as Lefthand could remember, but it was not slightly homey—her few things radiated a chill, the Monarch range, steel and filigreed enamel, a great heat sink with no fire in it, and an iron bedstead to bear a thin mattress, and there was a man to whom Lefthand was no doubt related; this for-bearer or precursor or whatever he had been had been captured in an oval frame about a half yard tall and hung on the wall near Rose Vallee's creel, and the man sat in a kitchen chair at the edge of a failing cornfield, his hair wound in a nest at the crown of his head, a poor growth of whiskers depending from his sharp chin. In his thick homespun and thin moccasins the man must have been uncomfortable all the time.

"Nobody's brought you any firewood?"

"Last people I seen was them Dupuis women. We went drinking in Polson. It was that Crème de Mint. They had a lot of it. Boy, that made me *sick*."

"This is not too good, Auntie."

"I could bring some things up," offered Brattle. "Stay with her. See she doesn't. . ."

"You're about six cords short of what you'd need to keep from freezing."

"You boys know an Adams?" she asked them. "What was it? George. That George Adams. He's from up around Mission."

"I told you before," said Lefthand. "He's dead."

Vernon Birfato stood from where he'd been squatting on his hams, and he said, "I can't stand this no more. I shouldn't even have to try."

Lefthand handed him a dull axe. "Go out and get some apple wood."

"Where?"

"Where the apple trees are, numb-nuts. Just get the stuff that's down. Buck it up a little, and throw it in the back of the truck. Tony Bill uses it to smoke his fish."

"This is not what I came up here to do."

"I hate to have to keep bringing this up, but we do have this trained killer with us. You should be useful for a change." Birfato huffed out, holding hard to the axe for his dignity. "He'll be about seventy-five before he ever catches on, and by then it'll be too late. That Vernon's a slow learner. Auntie, you got any boots or anything you could put on your feet? Your toes always look that way?"

Brattle offered her his socks. "Like I said, I wore extra. They're kind of tight in my boots."

The old woman nodded at a pair of rubber waders in the corner, then did something with her mouth, as if to savor her own tongue, and she recalled, "The people used to come back up the river every year. We was travelers in them days. There was none of them dams."

"I don't remember," said Lefthand. "I wasn't along."

"Remember Baptiste?"

"Only what you and Gram have said about him."

"The children," she said. "Even the children, they'd come in the spring. They knew the right time to come."

"So I've heard. It was perfect for us in oldtimes. But the only language I know is the white people's, so I have to think their thoughts, and how can you get any more surrounded than that? Oldentimes are over." Lefthand fell in and out of respect; he'd spent his whole life doing it. "All right, Auntie, we're taking you with us. Taking you down to Gram's to stay with her and Dolores and them."

"I know who she is."

"Gram? Yeah, she's your sister. Your half-sister."

"She cheats at cards. Would I have to be nice to her?"

"You'll work it out."

"George Adams, though, he owes me money. We went irrigating. Couple of places in Lonepine, couple of them cheap ranchers. And we worked all summer, and then we finally got paid, and then he run off with all our wages. George did."

"He's dead," Lefthand insisted. "Long time ago. And I'm sure he was dead broke before he died."

. . .

It came down in cupped discs the size of dimes, and looking up through it you could sustain an illusion of effortless ascent, and they were soon trying to drive up the mountain on a carpet of snow. "We could sure use some chains," said Brattle.

"I had some. Ace Dondanville stole 'em before I could ever put 'em on."

There were four of them in the cab, and four rifles clacking against each other and against their legs, and Rose Vallee's cat that had climbed in with them just as they were leaving, its ceaseless yowls drilling at their ear drums. "God *damn*," said young Vernon. "I can't see nothing at all. I could barely even breathe under her, and this spring's digging me a new asshole." The old woman rode on his lap; he had sharply rejected the chance to ride on hers.

Mitchell Lefthand had heard of a herd of elk lately to be found in a certain pocket in the woods that was known to him, a place he knew that might be approached from above, and the snow would muffle the sound of their coming and stifle their scent. This was just four or five miles from them, but almost all of that would be uphill, a succession of switchbacks. Lefthand knew they were poorly equipped to reach it that day, but he thought of those nearly defenseless elk, huge with a whole summer's grazing, and he thought he'd better get there somehow.

They were a half mile into thick timber before they reached the first serious incline. Lefthand stopped and backed up to get a better run at it. There was no good way to accelerate on the slick, so they hit the bottom slow, and he thought if he was patient they could climb slowly, touching that accelerator lightly, the brakes not at all, and they climbed a while and gained a bit, and then he felt his machine turn unwilling beneath him, and slowly they lost steam and were stopped, and then backward, lickety-split, and still he avoided the temptation of the brake, which could only make things worse, and over a Kelly hump, and finally they slammed to a stop with the rear end well up a bank. Steam issued from under the hood.

"Okay," said Lefthand. "We've got to get some weight over the driving wheels. Everybody get in back."

There was some discussion of physics and of the deference due to age and to youth, and finally Lefthand convinced them they were going nowhere until they'd made another run at the grade.

"But," pleaded Brattle, "your aunt?"

"Well, yeah. She's the heaviest one. We want the load where it does us some good. You don't mind, do you, Rose? Ride in back for a bit? Give us some traction?"

"I'm having a good time," she said. "I like you boys."

"Vernon. You been doing something nasty under there, make her like you so good?"

"What?"

"Go on and get in back. Everybody in back. We have only just begun to fight."

His cargo took a while to redistribute. It was necessary to lower the balky tail gate so that Rose could roll in, and then it had to be pounded substantially to make it latch again. A hiss could still be heard from the engine compartment.

"Ready?"

On the flat, he found, he could gather pace with this ar-rangement. They were hollering encouragement behind him. Up they went with thrilling momentum, and this time they'd climbed a full eighth mile and were well into the first hard turn before he broke traction. A bigger failure, such a long way down. Lefthand touched the brake pedal at last, and cranked his wheel, and all in a moment his passengers were flung uphill, and they were headed down frontwise, at least, but he dared do nothing else to check their progress, so they were picking up speed, and now the calls from behind were advice or misgiving, but Lefthand didn't properly hear them, and they bounced through forty seconds of something like terror before he could bring them once more to rest. Harlan Brattle appeared at his window.

"I think that's enough," he said. "Don't you?"

"How's Rose?"

"She loved it. She had a gay old time, but she's more padded. I really didn't care for it, myself. I'm convinced already, we can't make that hill in this thing."

"Yeah," said Birfato, crowding close behind. "This is why everybody else has four-wheel drive. Death trap. We was about two inches from going over the side. Then what?"

"Well, you can't please everybody," said Lefthand. "Come on. Get her out of there. You want to keep riding in back, Vernon?"

"No," he said. "It's cold, and you're crazy, way you whip around."

"What happened to the cat?"

"Who cares, man? Good riddance. See where that fucker scratched me? Look, it's four lines, one for every claw."

This was its maiden voyage, and even going downhill the truck was prone to skate. "I probably did get ripped off," Lefthand conceded. "These tires were no bargain, either. Good thing I'm not in business for myself, I try and trust people." It was a miserable retreat, punctuated here and there with slipping panic. Jammed so close together, they began to breathe collectively, and dusk was upon them at least two hours early, and there was nothing like a horizon in the still falling snow.

"Aaaah," said Birfato. "Ow. She's heavy."

To pass the time Rose Vallee told them a story concerning another legendary hag, and how she'd climbed onto a young man's back to ford an icy creek, but when they came to the other side she wouldn't get off, and she rode him until the young man was forced to bend her over a bed of burning pitch brands. This parable had been known to everyone when she was a girl; it was a way of teaching girls how to behave.

But she'd lived more instructive stories than she told. Lefthand recalled, for instance, that as a boy he had happened to be at a carnival, happened to find himself standing among a clutch of crisp tourists, when who should appear in the grass behind the generators but his aunt Rose, well past her prime already then, but not past a good brawl, and there was another old woman, and these heavyweights swung and landed and swung and missed, and Lefthand heard around him expressions of dismay, heard them turn to tittering as the pair wheezed away, inflicting little punishment. That had ended with Rose laughing, offering to buy the other a piece of pie. The tourists had applauded, and Mitchell Lefthand remembered how he had been pierced with wondering then if he didn't, after all, belong to some kind of childish race. He preferred her stories of old times to the more recent ones about fights in stale saloons and poverty and car wrecks and the misdeeds of priests and nuns.

His headlights were on and useless.

"Why couldn't I just be a caretaker? Take care of it for her? I wouldn't need to own it, I could just stay there for a while. Fix it up a little. Would there be any rules against that? Ma'am, would you mind if I stayed on your place while you're away? I'd keep it . . . It would do me a lot of good. And maybe I'm with the hippies on that, maybe owning shit *is* bad; all we could ever be is caretakers."

"We had that idea, too. We wasn't allowed to keep it."

"Ow," said Birfato.

"I do like that location," said Brattle.

"See what it did to her? Bad idea to talk to yourself too much, huh, Auntie?"

"I told you I was with them Dupuis. We had fun. Run all over the place having fun."

"I could spend," reckoned Brattle, "just about any amount of time alone. That doesn't bother me anymore. But people, most of 'em, that's another deal. People make me feel a completely 'nother way."

On the last rise before the final descent into the valley, they encountered a cow, a rheumy-eyed Hereford that someone had only half succeeded in dehorning. She swayed stupidly before them, and when she turned back to regard her pursuer she showed cockeyed. "Slow elk," said Lefthand.

"Which belongs to somebody," said Brattle.

"We'd already be in trouble if they caught us hunting the rez with a white guy. What's one more little thing when your freezer's empty?"

"I wish you'd get off this 'white guy' kick. I mean, I am, but what am I supposed to do about it?"

"What is it?" said Birfato. "What is it? I can't see. Could we finally shoot something, please? Let me out."

The cow was more bovine than might be believed, and when they stopped she stopped and turned her ugly head and looked back at them, never leaving the middle of the road. She looked back while Lefthand's riders discharged like circus clowns from his truck, and while he instructed Birfato in the harvest. "Nail her right in behind her ear. No, get away from the cab first. Know how loud that is?"

The report was most dramatic, echoing who knows how far, the cow a twitching heap. Birfato chambered another round. "Whoa," said Lefthand. "She's been got."

"See that thing? Dropped it like a bad habit."

"Yeah, you're deadly. Now you get to gut her. Knife's in the glove box."

Mitchell Lefthand was in the middle of another bad idea. Their beast lay on the road, so old and stringy that every bit of her would have to be run through a hamburger grinder with gobs of suet. The shot heard round the world. "All right, let's go, let's go, let's get her loaded."

Still the snow kept falling, and they moved as if underwater, wrestling the big carcass around to where Birfato could open it. "No, it's just one cut, Vernon. Just keep at it, it's cowhide, it's thick—you only want one cut her from her bag to her dewlap, don't be hacking away like that. Just open her up." Next he directed the boy to reach up in the body cavity as far as possible and sever the animal's esophagus near its tongue. "Get all that. That rots in there if you leave it. Get up in there. All right now give Auntie the liver there. That's the liver. You can tell, cause it looks like a liver." Finally, he told Vernon to cut a circle round the cow's anus. "Now you can lift the rest of the guts out. Take 'em over there and throw 'em on the other side of the fence."

"Me? Me? What about you guys? Look at me. Shit, did I have to get inside the damn thing? What are you guys supposed to be doing?"

"Watching. It's your kill. That's field dressing for you. That's life. And don't worry, we'll all be a mess by the time we get her up in the truck."

Truly, they were already well incriminated by gore, ghostly at their posts round the spread-eagled cow. Vernon Birfato lifted out the first load of her innards, and they trailed behind him as he took them to the fence. He kept his face averted from his burden.

Rose Vallee held her hands before her and said of the organ faintly steaming in them, "It's a pretty one. A real pretty one. Ain't it?"

SUMMER FAMILY

My Uncle Carl somehow finds out I'm a violin player, so he
asks my mom to send me out to spend some time on his farm.
Like that makes any sense. I'm supposed to finally meet my
mom's side of the family, the Mastersons, and it doesn't matter that there's a boy interested in me that summer, and they
don't care if I've got a nice job at the mall where all I have to
do is smell pretty. No, my parents just drag me down to the
bus station, and it's, "Have a great time, honey," and over the
mountains I go. But I did see a bear up around the top of the
pass, this insanely cute little cub with fur that shudders when
it runs, which was all right, but also there's a baby screaming
in back for most of the way, and I know about how that baby
must feel, but that doesn't mean I've got any sympathy for it.
You have to wonder why certain people, including me, don't
just stay home.

Uncle Carl's the only one waiting, and I'm the only one
getting off in Cut Bank. They leave the bus running, so we're
standing there in those black fumes, and Uncle Carl looks like
he does in the pictures they send with their Christmas cards,
but he's taller than I expected. In his boots and hat and everything he's like a tree; we shake—my hand totally disappears. We
get my suitcase out from under the bus, and he's carrying it for
me, and he says he's disappointed that I didn't bring my instrument, says he plays a little fiddle himself, but that's all right, he's
glad to see me anyway, and he's got one I can use if I want, if
I feel like I need to practice sometimes, and he's about to cry,
which is going overboard I think, but he tells me I took him by
surprise. I caught him off guard. Says I'm the spitting image of
his mother.

"Edna? Edna, wasn't it? She, I mean." This would be the grandmother my mom never mentions, the real dead one. She'd be my mother's mother.

"We called her 'Dutch.'"

I tell him that if I ever met her, I was too little to remember.

"*My*," says Uncle Carl, "*What* a resemblance. Course I never knew her when she was your age, and I don't necessarily believe she ever was as young as you are now, but. . . . It's wild how much . . . you sound like her, too. Same voice. Only way you'd ever win an argument with your grandma was to kill her, and nobody ever did that, so she won 'em all. She was sort of famous for it. But I bet she'd've got a kick outta you. I'd imagine you're quite the little steamroller, too, aren't you?"

"That I'd have to doubt."

"She used to say that. Word for word."

How could it be a good thing if I looked so much like this woman whose kids didn't even seem to love her very much? Mostly from what they didn't say, I got the idea she must've been mean or something. Did I come off like I was mean? I told Uncle Carl I was fairly wishy-washy. Which was completely true; it was even a problem I had.

So we're walking, and it seems like we've walked a long ways, and I'm about to ask him why he thought he had to park on the outskirts of town when we finally get to his truck, he's left it running this whole time, and we're back in that diesel smell. He's the kind of guy who buys tractors two at a time, and he's got two, great big blue tractors chained onto the back of his truck, which does not look safe to me. He says as long as he was over this way, he thought he might as well get me, too. "Hop in," he says.

You're way above the road in that thing, up in the cab of his truck, and it is fun for a while, for a little ways, but then there gets to be a lot more of this state than there really needs to be, and you just keep going. You get off the bus, and then you get in that truck, and you drive, and you drive, and you drive, and you've already been over the mountains, but it's hundreds of miles left to go, and you're riding with Uncle Carl who tells you jokes he got from *Reader's Digest,* and you try to laugh, but after a while it's really hard, and he's talking about his farm, his family, and it's cute how much he likes 'em, but we're driving and driving, and the farther we go the less there is to look at, and you're on and on, until you're out there where the only thing there is in any direction is wheat fields and silos, and you can see for a hundred miles. Finally, I had to tell Uncle Carl that I needed to use the facilities, and I'm just praying he doesn't have something in his truck that you're supposed to pee in, but it works out fine because we stop at this place that pops up along the road, it's a truck stop in the middle of nowhere, and all I want is to use the restroom and maybe have a cheeseburger, but Uncle Carl says "no way," he says this place serves the best rib eye on the Hi Line, and I might kick myself for the rest of my life if I passed on that, so I had one, and it was bloody and hot, and with the onion rings and the potato and the peas and toast and tea and everything, it was too much. And that big piece of pie I had. So now we're back in the truck again, and we keep on going, and, if you ask me, if you asked my sad tummy, it's all too much, but we do keep going.

The sun will just not go down, but we finally get there, and on the way down their lane Uncle Carl shows me where there's a graveyard behind the orchard. "Your people," he says. He tells me it's the family farm, and I'm not exactly sure what he means by that, but this sort of explains my mom, I think, if this is where she grew up. I guess they bury their own dead people, just dig their own hole and throw 'em in, which is a little too basic for me. Uncle Carl says he's really outnumbered now, with three women on the place—that was the first time in my life anybody called me a woman—and it's been a long day already, and I've still got these relatives left to meet, my aunt and my cousin. They have some huge cottonwoods around their house which smell, you know, like cottonwoods, which I really, really like, and to have so many trees all in one place, that's quite the landmark in this part of the world—must keep the wind off a little bit—and their house is tall and skinny, old style, and *very* white, like they paint it every year. I bet there's two hundred coats of paint on that thing. They're really settled in. Got a nice fence around this actual lawn.

Uncle Carl's women. This is where they have their outpost or whatever, and I think they must be quite something if they can keep this up. Way out here. It's like living on an island. And I'm wondering, what do they need with me?

But I get there, and they've made a million cookies because they knew I was coming. So me, in the morning I'm the biggest nerd girl in Kalispell, and then I take a little drive with my Uncle Carl and all of a sudden I'm a big production, like I'm a holi-day or a new puppy. I'm kind of a Goldilocks, too, 'cause Uncle Carl's so big and loud, and Aunt Sissy's so quiet and neat and small—and then there's Vivienne, my cousin. She was just right. We were fourteen that summer. They told us we were born three days apart, and Vivienne says we have a lot of things in common, but she's only being nice, because she's ten times prettier than me, so we're living on different planets, but was there any good reason to bring all that up? No. Instead I go ahead and embar-rass myself, and I tell her I loved her even when all I knew was her name. From their Christmas cards—and her picture. I tell her she's got a name that is so, so much better than mine. I tell her it suits her perfectly, and I even say it, "Vivienne Masterson." I'd feel silly saying it that way, but I think she must hear things like this all the time—she's about six feet tall and she has these shoulders, and she's got, what?—could you call 'em, sapphire eyes? Real bright ones; and these nice pink cheeks, and she just blooms and blooms, and she's probably used to having people come unglued when she's around. They must all fall in love with her, or all the ones with any sense would.

So I was very relieved.

I mean, I *had* to be there, which in many ways sucked, but these are the nicest people in the world—to me. They just hover around, treat me like I'm something special; and who gets much of that in their own house? Not I, *mon cherie*. These Mastersons are the nicest people by far, and here I am in their very modern and shiny kitchen, pile of cookies in front of me, and a big glass of milk they got out of their own cow, which is, like, rich. Basically it's just cream. They were so nice, and they acted so excited to see me, and to be honest I never even dreamed I could possibly screw this up.

• • •

So, finally it's bed time, and Aunt Sissy grabs my suitcase, which looks like it's quite a load for her, and she zips off up the stairs, and I follow her, and Vivienne follows me, and Aunt Sissy's got a room for me up there; you can tell she's put a lot of effort into it. She's too proud when she opens the door, and she's already told me I'll love it. But this room's—I swear—it's Pepto-Bismol pink, large amount of stuffed animals in it, too, the kind you'd win at a carnival, and these porcelain things—I think they were supposed to resemble angels—and she's sprayed it with something that smells to me like bad fruit. "Voila," she says, "the guest room."

But Vivienne comes to my rescue. "Mom, come on, you have to let her stay with me. Please?"

And Aunt Sissy makes me decide, she's, "Whatever you say, you're the guest, sweetie."

Now, who calls me, "sweetie"? Only Aunt Sissy. So this means I have to choose which one of these people I have to

disappoint? How are you supposed to be polite? To everyone?
And Vivienne's in my ear, "Come on out with me."

"Out?"

"The bunkhouse," she says. "Don't you want to farm it up
and stay out in the bunkhouse?"

I knew they plowed at times, that plowing was involved,
but what else? I wasn't interested in doing farm things. Was
it harvest yet? I don't like heavy lifting, and I don't like their
scary machines, but if it came down to that, it was still better
than Aunt Sissy's pink room, which would be like going inside
someone's body, and I'm sure Aunt Sissy could see me cringing
a little bit, and I probably hurt her feelings, which was the last
thing I wanted to do, but I had to choose the bunkhouse. I kind
of had to go with Vivienne, I liked her so much already.

"Farm girls," says Vivienne, like it's us against the world.

"Farm girls," says Aunt Sissy, "who are going to be giggling
all night long and then regret it in the morning."

"No we won't, Mom. We won't regret it a bit."

I have to say, my cousin thrilled me. How Vivienne formed
the opinion I might be fun, I'll never know. But she did. And
who knew? Maybe. Under the right circumstances. Around the
right people. Did I absolutely have to be dull all my life? Maybe
Vivienne had spotted some qualities in me that everybody
else had missed so far, and that's what I mean when I say she
thrilled me, it was really through and through, but not, you
know . . . that. She's just the greatest person I ever met, and she
likes me, and that's a miracle in my social life. She was such a
huge upgrade over any friends I had before. But wouldn't it be
horrible if I disappointed her? I mean, Aunt Sissy has already
had her feelings hurt, and now if I also. . . . I'm telling myself I'd
better just *be* fun. Starting right now.

Their bunkhouse is a house with one room, way out in a
dark part of their barnyard and out away from the trees—walk-

ing out there you get that loneprairie feel, and you can hear every cricket on earth—there are two beds in it, and that's all, and they've got these wild bedsteads, iron that's shaped like plants, or plant life, and a couple mattresses from hell, and somebody has stuck a car window into the wall, and this window's just at the right height to catch the moon cruising by. No electricity. All these strange shadows. Your imagination just goes ape in there. And I'm wondering why I ever worried about entertaining my cousin, because Vivienne, I find out, barks like a seal when she's feeling satisfied—and she's got a lot of little routines like that—this girl's been out here by herself a lot, and she knows many ways to keep herself amused; she's this wonderful person, and she wants to know if my town is bigger than Bozeman, and I tell her I don't know, I've never been to Bozeman, and she says she went to a basketball camp there, "So it was mostly just the gym and the motel, but I could see some mountains from where we were, and we went uptown once, and there's all these different food smells. Different kinds of cooking. I liked that *so* much. I liked playing against some size, too, some kids I could really bang into."

I told her I was usually the girl with the nosebleed in gym class. "If only," I told her, "If only I was that sturdy. That must be the best. That sounds like a riot—banging into each other. When you put it that way, I . . . but it wouldn't . . . not quite for me."

"Sturdy? Well, that's the last thing you want to be when you're refined. Like *you* are."

I'm too flattered. I know she'll eventually see through me, though, so I admit right away, "Weird, is more like it. I mean, I am in the civic orchestra and everything, and I *am* the second chair . . . or soon *will* be second chair violin. Which is pretty, that's pretty good, I'd say, for my age. In fact my parents were happy to send me here, because they think I'm unhealthy. They say I need to take a little break from it. They say I used to be disciplined, but now I'm compulsive, but seriously I think they just can't stand to hear me play anymore. They're still okay with some Vivaldi, but—refined? No. I mean, that's it. That's it. That is almost all I do at home—I play. Play and study. So, I'm considered strange, which I can't exactly deny."

"You?"

"I am a very extreme geek. A *little* fashionable, but . . . you may be the first athlete who ever actually spoke to me."

"You're a doll," says Vivienne. "A complete doll. Wait 'til we get a little sun on you."

Then we're doing girl talk, which is odd for me, but I like it, and right away I'm telling her about Deaf Ted the cellist—the boy I mentioned, a boy who seems to pass the perfume counter a lot, and I'm almost certain he's getting up the nerve to say something to me, maybe try and be nice. She tells me I should just call him over, whistle him on over, and I'd never even considered this; and she tells me a funny story about how, at a Christmas party no less, her principal's son put his tongue in her mouth and it tasted like beer and grape gum, which she did not enjoy. "But let's not talk about boys," she says, "the hell with boys. You like horses?"

"I might. I'm sure I would."

"Yeah, I bet you would, too. We'll ride tomorrow."

"Oh? Well, that sounds. . . . I'm sure."

"It's easy. They do all the work."

"Where do you ride *to*?"

"Just out and back. At least we'll get over the rise for a while. You'll like it. You can use Gerty."

Of all people, it's this one person who knows me. Sure, I'm in love. I mean, she actually thinks I'm interesting. What a night it was. We tell each other how we're both misfits: I have to as-sociate with some of the strangest people in the world just to be a musician; she has a hard time getting good grades, because she's so active. She said she got in trouble a lot for being overactive, and it was embarrassing, but I couldn't honestly think that anybody would ever be too put out with Vivienne. She finds out I work in a department store, and she has me walk her through it, department by department, and we bought everything she liked. This went on 'til the birds were singing.

So when I conked out at last, I conked hard, and I wake up and it's a hundred and ninety-five degrees in that bunkhouse—Vivienne's gone, her bed's already made—and I've really slept in late. I'm groggy and sweaty, and as happy as I was last night, I'm feeling that bad today. What did she say? Was it this morning? It was when I couldn't hold my head up anymore, she was telling me about this guy who'd been to the war, comes back and he's a regular at their church. "And you should see his poor eyes," she says. This guy has left two fingers over there, but really a lot more than that. He's *so* lost, she says, and she felt *so* sorry for him, and finally she just did what she could do—and he was sweet and gentle.

Like I say, we were fourteen that summer. Wow.

• • •

Her kitchen is the cleanest place I've ever been. She seems to kind of live in it. And I'm, "Just an apple, please. That's plenty for me." I've had my shower, and I feel a lot better, but I am definitely *not* hungry.

Aunt Sissy won't hear of it. "How do you keep going on just that?"

"I ate enough yesterday to last me for a week."

"Would you like some orange juice or grape juice? Buckwheat or buttermilk?"

"Pancakes? Please, no. That's way too much trouble. If I had pancakes I'd have to take another nap. How do you guys stay so trim?"

"*They* work it off," she says. "I'm more like you. I just don't eat as much. But, sweetie, you do have to eat breakfast on a farm."

"You do?"

You can't say "no" to her food or her advice, so she scrambles me some eggs. "Water, never milk," she says. "In a buttered skillet." She asks me if I know that she and my mom used to be big friends. They were best friends from grade school on, and she's *still* her best friend even though they're not in touch as much as they used to be, as much as they'd like, and she tells me my mother was a lady even as a child, and I'd never thought of her that way, but I can kind of see it. Mom is very proper. "You two are just alike," she says. "Elegant. You have that elegant air."

"What? Sorry, but I'm a klutz. As you'll probably notice."

"Serene," she says.

"That's very nice of you to say, but . . . well, okay."

They keep making these improvements on me, but what am I supposed to do about it? Aunt Sissy feeds me her eggs, and they're much better than I ever thought eggs could be, and I can see where I might be a little heavy for a while. At this rate. I don't even know to ask where the others are, where they might be, and real, real obviously it's just the two of us. Aunt Sissy and me, and this is all afternoon we're together, and she's nervous about something, so it's a lot of work to be with her, and I hope she doesn't notice how I'm hoping one of the others will come along; at last I think we both understand she wants something from me. Which is good, because I've been trying to be sophisticated for her, and it's wearing me out.

"I've got a favor. . . ," she says. "Or maybe you can shed some light, but. . . . If you can, would you? I know it's a lot to ask." She acts like she's known me my whole life. In a way, she has. She's known *about* me, which is almost the same.

"Can I? If I can, I'd like to."

"It's Vivienne," she says.

"Oh."

"I'm worried."

"Oh?" I feel now like I need another shower, and I even ask—I go, "I know it seems silly, but would you mind if I took another shower?"

"That *is* silly. There's something . . . new? Something new."

"Hm."

"And I can't put my finger on it."

"I wouldn't be able to compare," I tell her. "Before and after. I've just known her this short while."

"But does she seem a little . . . off kilter to you?"

"*On* kilter," I say, "if there even is such a thing. She seems great to me, and I mean it."

"Oh, don't get me wrong, I'm not criticizing your friend. You girls are already thick as thieves, aren't you? It's no wonder you're bushed, but, no . . . she has been—what? Something. I don't think of myself as old yet, but I'll be darned if I can accurately remember how it felt to be young. You lose touch with that pretty fast; you just get on a different wavelength. But these coaches, and her dad a little bit, they put so much pressure on her. Now that she's into high school they have all these plans, all these things they want her to do. It may be too much. I'm kind of thinking it's taking a toll on her. She's not herself lately."

"I wish everyone was like Vivienne, or at least *more* like her. I think she's absolutely great."

"Don't we all? Never worry about that, sweetie. She's got all the fans she'll ever need. And I'm the biggest one of all. Don't worry about that."

But I am worried, and she's worried; we're both worried about Vivienne and neither one of us knows exactly why; but I've probably got a better idea. I've been let in on something. No, I tell myself, I don't know anything—for sure—so how can I say anything? About that.

Then Aunt Sissy's telling me about these magic times before

I was born, before we were born, Vivienne and I, and I find out for instance that our mothers drove to Calgary once in a wired-together Dodge. Aunt Sissy tells me how they liked to barrel race and drink beer, how they'd been half milers together all through high school, how it usually came down to a race between the two of them. They swapped clothes and boyfriends. Aunt Sissy was the maid of honor at my mother's wedding, and vice versa, and now I'm remembering—I've heard all these stories before—but for some reason I didn't listen when my mom told 'em, and I'm wondering, Why not? Now Aunt Sissy's telling me she married Uncle Carl, probably, because it was as close as she could get to marrying my mom. Which, though it's very weird, I can understand; but it's hard, and it's not very pleasant to think that your mother was ever anybody but your mother—for me, anyway—so I was not unhappy when Vivienne and Uncle Carl came home, and they're smelling dry, like dust. They're talking about other things, thank God.

Vivienne's had maybe three hours' sleep, and now she's been out with her dad fixing a grain bin all day, and she's covered with stuff like from a granola bar, and she's dipped her head in this deep sink to clean up for supper, and she looks fabulous. I swear she just cannot look any other way, and I'm also thinking that I must be the only wussy woman in this entire family. I wouldn't know a grain bin if I saw one. Aunt Sissy feeds us again, and mind you, all I did was watch her make it, and compared to people like this you feel useless, especially when you slept most of the day, but it's riced potatoes, which I didn't even know existed, and pork roast, some greens from their garden, and I'm eating like I worked hard all day myself, and the Mastersons are so nice they wouldn't have it any other way.

After cake, my Uncle Carl tells me, "I'm on strict orders from your mother—'Don't even let her near one'—that's what she told me."

"I know. I heard her say that on the phone."

"But, why couldn't I at least get your expert opinion on my instrument?" says Uncle Carl.

"If you want, I'd be happy to." Here's one thing I can do for them. "But I'm no expert."

"That's not what we've been hearing," says Aunt Sissy.

Uncle Carl's violin is in a good enough case that I'm expecting something maybe a little fancy, a little nice. Case is real leather. Old leather. "This was your grandfather's," he says, "and I'm not sure exactly when he got it, but I know it came out of a Sears Roebuck, and we've always had it around, been fascinated by it ever since I was knee-high, but about all I've ever played on it is *Smoke on the Water*, and *Ironman*. The old man never played it at all, I don't know if I ever saw him touch the thing. So I've always been kind of curious to see if she'll do anything else—bet she will if you knew what you were doing."

The bow is warped or something, frayed. The violin—first thing I notice is the very dull varnish, which can't be good. It feels too light when I pick it up. I'm tuning it, and here are the Mastersons all around, just fascinated. It's kind of distracting. I can't make the G-string stay at one pitch, it keeps going flat, so really there's just no tuning this thing at all. I try and I try, but I cannot tune this fiddle, so finally I just scrape on it a while to see how it sounds—better than you'd think, soundwise—but I do a few arpeggios, a little bit of *Alison,* and with that stupid G-string it's sort of middle ages. It's quite ugly in spots.

"Man," says Uncle Carl. "That is unbelievable."

"Very polished," says Aunt Sissy.

Vivienne's, "Do something else. What *you* like. More."

Usually I'm not appreciated this much, and here I am with this whack violin getting rave reviews. I play a little reel, and it sounds like some space-age horror show because of the weird tuning, and I play, but after awhile I think it's only merciful to stop, because I know it can't be exactly ear candy, but the Mastersons are so polite they think they have to watch me the whole time and smile.

"Now that's quite something," says Uncle Carl. "The old girl didn't know she had that in her. Why don't I just . . . better than leave her in the closet another forty years, why don't you just take her on home when you go? You might say in fairness to the violin."

"You should keep it," I say. "You never know when it may come in handy." For firewood, I'm thinking.

"Very smooth," says Aunt Sissy. "That's what I like about your style. It's soothing."

"Out—raageous," says Vivienne. "I don't know anybody who can do anything even a little bit like that. Or that good."

It's a bad violin. It was bad music. But I tell myself I don't have to fess up about every little thing. You try to be pleasant, or at least I do.

"I don't care what my sister says," says Uncle Carl, "you play whenever you want. It'd be a shame to keep you away from your . . . your muse, I guess it'd be. Be a damn shame, in my opinion. I'm only an agronomy major, myself, but even I can see who's got a gift and who hasn't. You just play whenever you want, steamroller, as much as you want in my house, and if it has to be, it can be our little secret. You have to keep at that same high level, don't you?"

"Carl," says Aunt Sissy.

"It's all right," I say. "I really don't need to. For a while." But now Uncle Carl's hurt, so I'm, "I guess some would be all right. I could play just sometimes, for a little while. You can do a few things with three strings if you have to. If you wanted, I could."

"Let's take that ride," says Vivienne.

"Don't you *ever* get tired?"

• • •

I live just as far north as they do, so their days shouldn't seem
so long to me. A lot of things seem to happen during one of
their days out here. Vivienne's been up so long without sleep
she's got the giggles, and she's on this prancing steed. "Jolt," she
calls him. My horse has a condition, she's swaybacked according to Vivienne, which means it's very easy to stay on her, and
she doesn't like to move any faster than she absolutely has to,
so we're getting along fine. We are riding, though. And I *do* like
it. It's very late in the day, and there's a little breeze up, and you
can hear it in the wheat, and the sun's quite low in the sky so
the fields are red gold right now, and right now I'm glad I came,
glad they got me out here. I tell her that.

"Me too," says Vivienne. "It was just ess*en*tial you came when
you did."

"You think?"

"I needed somebody. I guess I needed you."

This is scary talk, no matter who's saying it. "What for?"

"I just did. I think I needed somebody who might understand."

"Well, I'm, I might be able to. . . . Understand what?"

"Me," she says.

That was the exact second I knew I didn't understand her
even a little bit, I mean, who was I kidding? How could I? And
I'm thinking I might be in over my head, but we're riding, and
the whole country's sighing, seems like, and I'm, "Do you know
how I know we're going east? Because of how we're following
our shadows. See how long we are? What a neat effect."

"You know what I mean?" she says. "About knowing me?
About how I need that?"

"I have to warn you, I'm not that wise or whatever. I might
not understand you as well as you'd think. Or even at all."

"But you'll at least try," she says. "You'd try, I know."

"How far are we from your house? I can't believe we can still see the trees from here."

Vivienne's on this peppy horse, and it goes sideways as much as anything, like it just can't stand the pace my horse is setting, and Vivienne's holding it in, and she's so tall and straight on that Jolt, and she points to her heart, and I don't know anyone else who could do this and not look like an idiot, but she points to her heart and she's, "We know. You and me. We just do. We have to."

It's kind of like being addressed by a general.

"You think?" I say. "Yeah, probably. We probably would." I have no idea what we're talking about. I don't know anything, and I'd like to keep it that way. All I know is we're riding, and even on my nag I'm feeling like the prairie heroine, and I like it that I can see so far. These fields are just breathing, whispering, and it's the time of day when you feel some warmth coming off the soil, and we're clop-clop on the country road. "I like this," I say. Our saddles are creaking.

There's something in the middle of this conversation that's not there yet. I don't think we're talking about what we're talking about. So what I do is just ride along quiet and hope she doesn't decide to fill me in. You get to a point out here where any talking seems pretty much beside the point anyway, so you don't talk, and that's where we are now, and we're riding along, and you could say I'm happier than ever for the many, many things I do not know.

• • •

The next day was Saturday, and we dug a short trench for some reason, and then we butchered some chickens. I am not kidding. Then we ate those same chickens, which was quite a bit easier than I thought it would be. If you're up early around here, they put you right to work, but they'll also literally feed you to your heart's content. By about seven o'clock we're asleep in the main house, on the floor in front of the television, fan's waving over us, and I am like unbelievably comfortable. So that was Saturday.

And then it was Sunday.

Sunday morning I find out Uncle Carl has called up the guy at their church, calls the pastor I think it was, and he says I'll play for the congregation. But he didn't ask me. And I'm, "No." But he's, "These people don't get a chance to hear anything like this. This might be the last chance some of these people ever have to hear *good* music. At least in person. Believe me, I know. If you've got something like what you've got, it's only right to share it, and I don't mind the chance to brag about you, either. You can bring us rednecks to the light."

I should've given him the whole story on that violin right then and there, and I should have said I absolutely would not play it in public. But I just whined. I'm whining, "It's *only* those three strings. The one's useless, and the others are pretty vague."

"You could probably tear the house down," he says, "on just one."

So, another big breakfast, and we all get in this huge sedan of theirs, and we're off to the Skyview Methodist Church, which is a ways. Miles are nothing here. I'm starting to have a thing in my stomach. It's a cramp to say the least. Out here where the bathrooms are far apart. I do not solo much. Never, actually, but now I've got this crummy thing, and I hate to hate a violin, but it's about to humiliate me, I feel it happening before we're even there. Here we are driving again—it's quite a long way to their church, and Vivienne's in the back seat with me, rolling her eyes. She thinks her parents are eccentric and we're not.

But you should have seen her that day. Vivienne Masterson decked out for church. She wore a white summer dress—really white against her tan, and an obsidian necklace. Her hair was up, and her neck was quite white compared to her face, and her neck seemed very long. The girl's a swan. I can't believe I actually know her, I'm related to her, she's my friend. I cannot believe how goofy she can be in the car. So I'm looking at Vivienne, and I'm laughing at her, and I feel a lot better.

Then we get there.

It's this metal building with nothing around it but a parking lot. A place of worship? They do it humble here, but that's okay. At home I don't do it at all. We're not churchgoers at home. So I am really a stranger here, *and* I'm carrying this awful violin, wearing jeans which is all I thought I was going to need, and I'm very red from yesterday, but fortunately everyone else is sunburned, too. They're windburned, whatever—chapped. And we're in this building, and the first thing I notice is the acoustics, which could not be worse, but it's pretty dressed up inside, the candles and stuff, and something in here smells nice. I like the way the people talk to each other. They smile more than cool people do, and they even laugh a lot, but not very loud.

At some point, I'm supposed to play this violin. I feel this coming. Horrible. It *is horrible*. And Aunt Sissy's introducing me to all these really pleasant people who are all so interested to hear how I'm the cousin from the city, the niece, and I'm going to be playing something for everybody. They're, "How nice." And Aunt Sissy's, "Got any requests?"

Requests?

So the pastor finally walks out in front by the piano. Everyone stands up. I remember he said something that made me feel pretty good, but I don't remember one word of what that was. Then he's, "Take out your hymnals," and everybody's singing, and I lip-synch, and even that's pretty bold for me, and it's, He shall abide or We shall abide or something like that, kind of stirring actually, and at the end I even pitch in a little bit and sing. Sang, which I never do.

Then we're praying again. Then we sit down and the pastor's

talking about youth camps and retreats and things, and my mind
wanders, and the next thing I know, he's talking to me. What did
he say? I vomit a little bit in my mouth, but I keep it in. "Sorry?"
"Would you like to come up?" he says. "Like to favor us with
a song?"
It's burning in my throat. "Uhm, I'm not really..."
"Don't be shy."
"It's not exactly that. I...."
"Come on up here and praise Him."
"Well ... okay." I am trying to tell myself that one day I
will have a good laugh over this. If I ever had a boyfriend, this
would be a good story to tell him.
They're watching me. All these healthy people in their best
clothes, and me with this thing that is the dullest, saddest, worst
instrument ever made, and my hands are stiff from digging yesterday, and I'm going up, and they're watching me while I take
it out, and I don't even bother to try and tune, lift my bow arm
and there's this great big pit, I'm soaked under there. "What
about *Blue Moon*?"
"I'll bet that would be perfect," says the pastor. "Sounds very
relaxing."
So I do that, and I'm thinking about my armpit the whole
time. It's not like I'm blind. I can see the kids out there laughing at me. But I do it. Verse, verse, chorus, verse. And I'm done.
Pretty little ditty, and I'm done.
"We're blessed," says the pastor. And they're all clapping.
They seem to mean it. I can't tell you how healthy this crowd
was, how decent.
Then, and I've almost got that violin back in its case, almost
had it closed up—Vivienne says, "Hey, play that other one."
She's making a face at me. Enjoying herself. Then somebody
else, some man's, "What about, *Danny Boy*?"
"I'm sorry, I don't think I could...."

"Praise Him," says the pastor. "All praise to Him. Go ahead. With your heart."

I'd rather have a decent bow.

Does no one but me see these faces Vivienne is making? Uncle Carl's out there beaming, and he's nodding, "go on," and Aunt Sissy's looking around, smiling, but her smile's getting a little tense. I stall. Maybe I'd play *Air on a G-string* if I had a G-string. It's such a funny sounding thing, this thing, and I don't know what to do. But I happen to think that when I sit down again, between my breath and how much I'm sweating and everything, I will really, really stink. So I might as well just. . . . I don't even try for a recognizable tune. I just play.

• • •

So afterward, of course, we ate. It's a pie social, which should be a pretty great concept, but I'm there with my plate in the corner, and people keep coming up to me and telling me how fantastic I am. I'm only trying not to breathe on them, and I overhear one of the ladies tell Aunt Sissy how impressed she is: I'm talented *and* humble.

Then Vivienne brings over this guy, the one with the missing fingers. I hadn't noticed him before, or I didn't see his hand so I didn't know who he was.

"This is Derrick," she says.

She tells him he already knows who I am. Her completely outrageous cousin.

You get the impression from Derrick that he doesn't want to be caught stinking, either. You do feel for him. "Hi," he says, but that's all. He's the palest person in this building, though he must have spent some time in some desert. His eyes *are* a mess. What to say?

I'm, "Hi."

Then we're standing there, and I'm eating my pie so I won't have to say anything else. Derrick is not a boy, that's the thing.

He's not a boy at all. He's a man already, a ruined one. Vivienne treats him about the same way she treats her dog, which is very nice. He's old. That seems to be his main problem now. He got old pretty early, and standing next to Vivienne, he's kind of done-for looking. Now I'm completely relieved, like when you wake up from a nightmare. She takes care of him, just like she'd take care of anything else. Any*body* else. If they needed it. That's all. Now I feel terrible that I ever thought it was anything else, and I am completely impressed with how kind she is. I've got Derrick sort of in the corner of my eye, and he's wearing a lime green sport coat with sleeves about three inches too short, and these real clunky shoes. If he's got any expression on his face, I don't know what it would be. Lost cause, I'm thinking. But that's way better than some of the other things I was thinking.

Vivienne whispers in my ear. "What do you think? You like him?"

I don't *dis*like him. "Yeah," I say, but it sounds a little fake. I mean, how enthusiastic could you be? Poor guy. He's embarrassed. I bet he's embarrassed most of the time. It's like he was thrown in the wash with some bleach.

"We're gonna try to. . ." and she cocks her head at the back door. "He's got a van."

"Oh?"

"Okay?"

"What?"

"You think it's okay?"

"What?"

"Kind of cover for us. It won't take long."

"You're. . . ?"

But he's already leaving, and she's watching him. She waits a couple minutes before she follows, but in the meantime I can't catch my breath and I don't know what I'd say anyway, what I should ask her, and I'm jamming pie in my mouth, and then she winks, and she's off, she's following him, he's out the back, and she's headed that way, and she's in no hurry, she's just moving through these nice, these real pleasant people, smiling, and they smile at her as she goes by, which is easy to do because she is beautiful without trying, the most beautiful girl I've ever seen, and she's going through this crowd of people who I don't know, and she's going to that door.

AIM HIGH OLONGAPO

Gray was a seagoing marine and a good one in that he disappeared into his duties whenever he was at sea. It had been difficulties ashore that had kept him these three years at the same rank, a rank entitling him to a bottom rack in the enlisted men's berth. Aboard the USS *Mansfield* his was an ant's routine, scurrying to distantly issued commands, calling fools "Sir." On orders, he might go prowling the steel passages in body armor with a scattergun, or running and ducking through watertight hatches, all in the pretense that some plucky enemy had stormed a nuclear aircraft carrier in the middle of the Indian Ocean. Stand by to repel boarders—sure.

It had been a long, long enlistment of polishing boots and brass. He had in his time polished the big shell casing the senior NCOs used for their ashtray. He had performed close-order drill on the hangar deck, slapping smartly through his manual of arms. Gray had walked guard around disabled aircraft, stood at parade rest behind visiting dignitaries, served at times as a human flag stand, and from the moment he understood that he was being used ceremonially he'd been overwhelmed with a resentment for which there could be only one cure. Reaching the end of this final float, his last WestPac, he craved that day, five weeks hence, when he would check his shotgun and his sidearm back into the armory, walk out onto the brow to salute the bridge, and be on his way with an honorable discharge. By enterprise, and more recently by vast discipline, he had accumulated enough money to let him leave Oakland on an American-made machine.

Because the better moments of his life had all involved leaving, and Gray knew this was probably not as it should be, he did sometimes wonder if he might be a malcontent or even a species of coward, but he had never for a moment questioned his desire to free himself from the United States Marine Corps. Junior in rank to all his friends, he shared a cube with them where blue smoke curled in a wan red light, and they lived in near dark, not knowing if their quarters were above or below the ship's waterline, frequently not knowing where they were on the ocean. They were like rats in a cupboard, and fancy thinking was unwelcome among them.

"A fun-filled vacation," said Corporal Sano, "for six thousand—in love-leee Subic Bay. First, I hit the Hi-Life, pound some San Miguels, then I have Corazón make me some adobo, and then we do the deed over and over. We've got two fans rigged up in her room. It's actually cool in there when you run 'em both. One hundred and fourteen days. So far. Haze gray and under way—I got the haawngrys."

"Not for nooky, man," said Sergeant Thibodeaux, "I never leave the base, and I'm sticking to that. You can swim on base— in a clean pool. You can drink on base and never get ripped off. Eat way better than you can eat in town. That's one ville I always try and avoid. Of anybody, Gray, you should know what I'm saying. You of all people."

Gray, on his first visit to the Philippines, had been riding through Olongapo, a passenger in an indigo Jeepney, when a long-legged island boy ran up alongside and tried to twist a Hong Kong Rolex from his wrist. Gray had punched the lad in the head. "A month," he now reflected. "I got a month out of that, and you wouldn't believe what they use for their brig on the *Ranger*. They locked me about a month in a closet so there'd be no trouble. That other thing was just a regular fight though; could've happened anywhere. That was Pitts. Edison fucking Pitts and the shore patrol, those nancies and their batons and their whistles, and—*wheet-wheet*—I'm busted again, got another knot on my head. So this time I'm finally smart—this time, shipmates, I do not leave the boat. I'll walk everybody's guard the whole time we're tied up to the pier—for money, honey. Then go home and buy some leathers."

"Wait and see," said Sano, "when the exec offers you your little bonus, you'll re-up. What else you gonna do, once you been out sailing the seven seas?"

"What else would I do?" Gray consulted his always-expanding list of options. "Get above deck. Stand on solid ground. Not breathe fifty farts a night. I will do what I want to do for a change. Also, you know what? I still get seasick. Even on this thing, got a keel on it like the Empire State Building, and I still have some bad times in the chow hall—"Mess mate, hand me a pail." Laid up in your rack, green at the gills? Fooo. That's a . . . and the smell of salt water? Which everybody claims they like so much? Not me. Not me, troopy. I am headed inland. Short, I'm a two-digit midget, and I know places in Nevada where water's only a rumor. *Vrrroom-bah, buhm-buhm-buhm-buhm.* Winnemucca, here I come."

He dreamed of this while the others played cribbage on their footlockers and tortured a small guitar. In truth, he had no exact destination. He was a drifter. Panhead, knucklehead, Gray didn't care, even a little Sportster would do, anything running strong; and then there'd be no more of their silly announcements and pronouncements and solemn horseshit, and no more of their claxons, their tired rules, their shattering ordnance firing at empty sky. Fighter-interceptors had been bouncing off the flight deck without interruption these past several months, and they had outlasted his patience. Gray was not absolutely opposed to noise, so long as it was noise of his own making, and he was mild enough, so long as he was left alone. He was mild aboard the *Mansfield* too, but in a some-what coiled way.

Steaming toward Subic, the *Mansfield* had suspended flight operations at last, and most of its aircraft had been flown to various strips on the beach. One evening after chow the whole marine barracks was turned out for a five-mile run on top. At about two miles the steel became very hard underfoot. Gray felt that his friends, with their cigarettes, had corroded his lungs. There was a new lieutenant with them who was still enthusiastic about sounding off—*I don't know but I been told, a man in need is a man who's bold*—Gray was too salty to do more than mouth counting cadence, but he ran with a will. The detachment ran in column counterclockwise around the half-mile circumference of the deck, and the eastern coast of Palawan lay to starboard, steaming, brooding, primeval jungle, and to port pink cumulus towered far off, dumping plumes of rain onto open sea. There were some things oriental, Gray conceded, that he might miss. But from the elevation of this flight deck he could see halfway home, wherever that might be.

• • •

Gray would sometimes inflict strange hardships on himself. He had been standing the most despised post on the ship, waiting at a hatch to come to port arms whenever anyone came through the passage, and allowing entry to those with a certain red placard. Gray didn't know what he was protecting, and apart from fellow marines the only person he'd ever seen in the passageway was a round civilian with a Ben Franklin haircut and the right red credentials. The civilian had gone past him several times now with no sign of recognition. The danger of this watch was its nothingness, the long uninterrupted hours in that long steel corridor, all white, dimly lit by the Navy's cheapskate light, pipe and cable snaking overhead. This watch was often assigned by way of punishment, and Gray had stood it voluntarily now all day and all night.

The new corporal of the guard wasn't happy at this news. He'd come to inspect post with a fresh PFC. "You know what happens," he reminded Gray, "if you fall asleep. Especially in a high-security area."

"I'm not falling asleep. I'm standing up."

"Big deal. This is like watch number five, right? In a row? How'd you get away with that?"

"You know how much money I'm making?"

"Sixteen hours? No. Twenty hours? Definitely not."

"Is this some regulation?"

"What it is—you fall asleep, then that's my ass too. You're relieved."

"I've been paid already. Rainey paid me to stand this watch for him."

"You're relieved, Gray. What did I just tell you? You can work your own thing out with Rainey."

Gray had lived on the ship longer than he'd lived in many of his boyhood towns, but he still sometimes got lost on board. There were miles of similar passages and hundreds of identical ladders, and sometimes when he wanted to find his way to a chain locker or to sick bay, he found himself caught in a maze. Starting from far aft and deep in the vessel, his route to the hangar deck that morning was up and forward until he arrived at last at the vast, open bay. He went across to look out on the pier—not the usual bustle. Artificial light and first dawn contending, the big cranes throwing long shadows, and, as ever, the ominous heat.

He went below to secure his weapon, then to quarters, where he got undressed and lay in a bed that wanted no part of him. An image much like the white passageway was imprinted on the backs of his eyelids, and there was no rest in closing them, so with his body mildly humming and his thoughts all astray, Gray happened on a decision, a mission. It was good to know what to do. He showered and put on some jeans and a flowered shirt. From a bottom corner of his footlocker, beneath socks neatly folded and stacked for inspection, he took a tiny ziplock baggie containing a dark stone. He put it in the fob pocket of his pants. Lance Corporal Fralic was also astir at that hour, dressing in his summer tans. They went to breakfast together.

With the ship at dockside their mess had new stores of fruit, and Gray ate a good deal of cantaloupe. There was fresh-made coffee in the urn, doughnuts warm from the oven. Fralic wore his tie very tight, which resulted in an overripe face, and he'd heaped his plate with peculiar dark bacon. "You were down there how long? I heard 'em talking about it. You never made a head call that whole time? Never ate or anything?"

Gray flicked his thumb across the palps of his middle and index fingers. "Paid," he said. "That government check, by itself, that's sad-ass if you want to hit the bricks running. Gotta supplement. It is Sunday, isn't it? You going to chapel?"

"Mass," said Fralic. "In town. They do a really beautiful one."

There was no line at the gate, only helmeted marines on the one side, helmeted nationals on the other; tired, bored soldiers waving them through. They crossed the fetid river to where cocks were still crowing intermittently and shoeshine artists and cigarette vendors had slept on cardboard pallets awaiting their arrival. They did not buy a shine or a smoke. They were approached by a man on an ill-tuned motorcycle with a sidecar, who said, "You neber hab to walk. You marines, I know. High and tight, man. Get in."

"How many p," asked Fralic, "to take me to the Shrine of the Holy Virgin, honcho?"

"Por you, pipty. Special price—marine-only price."

"Yeah, that's what I thought. St. Columban's is right over there, isn't it? See? Right there. Why would I want to go all the way out in the boonies to worship? Tell me that."

The cabby was shaved everywhere but in the hollows of his cheeks, an odd effect for an almost toothless man. "Tirty-pibe."

"We don't need you, buddy," said Gray. "Thanks."

Fralic invited Gray to join him for first mass, said that it wouldn't matter what he wore or what his real religion was, as long as he was sincere, and it really was a beautiful service, an unbelievable choir, and Gray might benefit by keeping some decent company for once, but Gray said he was decent himself, that his own company would suffice, and he went his own way. Along Magsaysay Street it was not Sunday morning but post-Saturday night—shuttered nightclubs, slinking cats, and thousands of flattened paper cups. Those few Jeepneys running carried cargos of starched, church-bound children. Spent fireworks were everywhere on the sidewalk and in the street, and the air still smelled rancidly of small explosives. The climate was infection here; Gray walked with his eyes often downcast, alert for broken glass or standing water. Apart from a few street vendors, the only business open in Olongapo at this hour was a twenty-four-hour pharmacy.

Gray turned down an alley too narrow for any but foot traffic, windowless cinder block on either side, feminine wash strung overhead, and he began to hear the gurgle of a Tagalog ballad, a lonely bar girl singing with her radio. He startled and was startled by a pair of small ocher mongrels bursting from a broken crate. Running head down, they shot away from a Styrofoam tray of fried rice. Bonanza of waste. The fleet was in. Where the alley intersected another alley Gray turned, and he came to a barred hole in the wall, and he looked in through it. Inside, a woman and her daughter lay like nesting question marks on a mat on the floor.

"Belen," he whispered through. "Hey, lazy."

The woman propped herself on one arm, swept hair from

her face, and smiled by stages. "I had nice dreams," she said. "I know you were coming."

She let him in through a wrought-iron gate so narrow that he had to turn sideways to pass through it, and they were in a tiny courtyard where cabbages grew, and then they were in the room where the little girl still lay sleeping. "She gets taller," said Gray, "every time I see her. Better be nice to her, Belen; by the time she's ten she'll be looking you right in the eye." Belen crouched at the hot plate to put the teapot on. She demanded that Gray occupy the room's only comfort, her cane rocker, and she informed him that she knew when the *Mansfield* came in, and she knew that he was still aboard, and why had it taken him so long to come around?

"Good-bye," said Gray. "It's good-bye. I do it all the time, but I don't know how to do it. That and, you know, I just cannot afford to get jammed up at this point. But I thought maybe I could run in and see you in the morning without. . . . Wanted to bring you something, too."

He took the ziplock baggie from his fob pocket and gave it to her. Belen finished preparing the tea, and then she made a ceremony of opening the baggie and tipping it over her cupped palm.

"Oooh," she said, assessing. "Oh. So this a . . . it's a rock?"

"Emerald," said Gray. "Uncut. From Sri Lanka. It's for you. For you to keep, or sell, or do what you want with it. They tell me it's a nice piece. It'll facet up nice, lot of carats left when it's cut, and I just know somewhere in this town there has got to be some guy who can cut it, some jeweler." Now that he was saying it, the whole proposition sounded dubious. The stone or anything else he might give her would be swallowed at once by her poverty, and it was very unlikely she'd ever find the means to make it beautiful. He should have contrived to give her cash. "I wanted you to have something, anyway, 'cause this is my last time through."

"You said before," she said angrily. "I already know, so you don't keep saying."

"I knew I had to come in and see you," he said. "But I thought. . . . It's hard. I barely know anybody anymore but you. What am I supposed to say?"

He believed it would be their last time together, and Gray had come to visit, but instead he slept, and in time their conversation sounded in his dreams. Though Elvie was only three, she spoke her mother's provincial dialect, a tongue more musical than Tagalog or English. He smelled an astringent meal—Belen with a plate under his nose, urging him to eat, but Gray's sleep was without hunger or, for that matter, any desire at all. When he woke, he was alone in the room, and out in the streets motors were firing again in all their profusion, and elaborate horns sounding, and music throbbed from a hundred sources. Four o'clock in the afternoon. Once again he'd overdone it. The chair had hurt him, and his neck was kinked. Gray extracted himself from the rocker and toured the room, a journey of a few steps—the room of a homely whore who worked in a city of pretty ones—they had their fan, the hot plate, mats, and a tiny television from the PX. He was leaving, and they would go on this way. It was all they knew, and it was therefore their way, but Gray didn't find this consoling. Mother Mary mooned at him from a grocer's calendar, one hand tipped palm out as if to propose an alternative.

Elvie at this hour was with Mrs. Padilla in another part of the compound. Her rooms had no door but a curtain, and Gray called in to see if he might have a moment with the little girl. Mrs. Padilla ushered him in at once, saying sure, oh sure.

She was one of several little girls rapt on the floor before a television. Elvie tried to ignore him but could not resist one last killer grin. "Elvie!" said Mrs. Padilla. "Come."

"That's all right," he said. "I think she's mad at me." Gray pressed some paper pesos in Mrs. Padilla's hand, and he went out of that warren of rooms, and out through the same rusted gate through which he'd entered.

. . .

From its founding, the Fouled Anchor had passed through many hands, but with every change in ownership its principal custom had always remained marines, Semper Fi; war after war they passed through, and they came during the occasional peace, and theirs was a gentlemen's club with strict decorum and amiable girls; it was an open-air honky-tonk with a level pool table and a rack of straight cues. The beer cooler was kept a half degree above freezing, and except for some novelty tunes from the marine band, the jukebox offered only rhythm and blues. Ceiling fans slowly paddling, bar girls rattling through bead curtains, the peacock patrolling the patio—over the course of many deployments the signature click and clink of this place had suited Gray very well. Until now. His current idea of a good liberty was no longer served by the slightest confinement with other marines, enough being enough. He'd heard everything these boys had to say, and he'd heard it many times. The Anchor had become a faded paradise where he went only to pass time with Belen. His smarter impulses overridden, Gray went there now.

Belen had thick lips, a thick nose, and even somehow thick eyes, but in sum, a most expressive face. She was behind the bar when he came in, and she registered joy, then dismay, then sympathy, all in the time it took him to cross the floor to her. "Sad, huh?"

What to say? He was on his way back to the ship. Since he'd known her he had always been on his way back to the ship, and until now it had made for such an easy acquaintance. "I didn't even bring anything for Elvie this time."

"You," said Belen. "Just you. You come and snore so much, and that make her laugh. She like it better than the cartoon when you snore. We laugh and laugh."

"Good."

"I'm miss you all the time," said Belen. "Miss you more than most guy, eben you don't make lub to me. It's okay. I know you like me."

"Yes, I do."

She could not lie in word or deed or manner, and it was plain to him that her sorrow at his passing out of her life was already over. She stood not three feet from the place she'd been standing when they met. "You want ginger ale? You want seben and seben? Oh, and the new boss, I didn't tell you about him yet. We got a new boss and he tell me you hab to pay bar pine. You were in my room. He's not a good guy, this Herman—Herman he say, but we think maybe it's not his name. And *mean*. You mind? The bar pine?"

Gray pulled his wallet from the shaft of his right boot and began to spend money. The girl who called herself Honest Asia was slow dancing with a new hire, and while their dates leered on from their table, the girls slowly orbited the room. As they rounded toward the bar, Gray bought them a drink.

Honest Asia instructed her young trainee, "Old friend, Gray. Some guys they treat eberbody so nice all the time. Gray one. Almost always."

"Hey," called Asia's date. "Keep dancing."

The new girl, mistaking his intentions, tipped her chin and her glass at Gray. She had other, unfinished drinks at her table, a previous understanding. Freshly fascinated with her power as a commodity, she wore a yellow jumper. Honest Asia waltzed her away.

"That one," said Belen, "maybe no good. We hab to wait and see about her."

A man Gray took to be Herman came in at the back then
and accosted Belen at the bar. She handed him the bar fine that
Gray had only just paid her—Herman seemed to scold her
anyway, but Tagalog always sounded like scolding to Gray, even
the mildest conversation. Herman would not look Gray's way.
The proprietor carried himself with the weight of his shoulders
over the balls of his feet; he had a face incised with many thin
scars. He settled at the far end of the bar, where he sucked at a
lemon wedge while manipulating a calculator and filling a journal with figures. Had this furious little businessman ruined the
Anchor's atmosphere, or had it always been so dismal?

"He think," said Belen, "you should buy me drink."

"He thinks? He thinks, but he doesn't think for me."

"No," said Belen, "but you don't mind? It's easy. No problem that way. One Shirley Temple, okay? See, easy?" Under her
breath she added, "Mean."

Gray bought a round for the house, including the boss,
whose choice was Chivas Regal. When Belen had distributed
all these, she returned to Gray and said, "Bad time, I know. But
eben we hab to say good-bye now, better if you go, honey. It
good time, okay? You can go, okay? Please."

Gray had a lime rickey in front of him, and he'd not been
raised wasteful. He also wished to stare at Herman, whose eyes
cut everywhere but to Gray. The man wasn't shy in his own
establishment, and he wouldn't give the first thought to who
held him in what regard; so this was some other reluctance,
something sly. Gray, for his part, could not bring himself to
look away.

"Honey," said Belen, urgent now.

A young marine from Honest Asia's party slid onto the
bar stool to Gray's immediate right, and he said, "Hey." He
looked like everyone who'd ever been through a recruit depot,
jug-eared and stupid. "Sounds like you really know your way

around. We just got here, Strein and me. Marine barracks. All we do, we just walk a lot of guard . . . So . . . you know what's going on? Here in town?"

Gray could not think of an insult blunt enough for the boy, so he asked him, "What do you want?"

"Little more excitement."

"This isn't enough for you? What—cockfights?"

"You know what I mean."

"Well, they got women and booze here, so no, I don't know what you're after. Spit it out, boot camp."

"I mean, come on. You a narc?"

"Are you?" Gray parried. "What do you want?"

The young marine lowered his voice and delivered it through the side of his mouth, "I just want to get high."

"They've got buses," Gray said, "that go almost all the way up Mount Pinatubo."

"Fuck you. You know what I mean."

Herman watched this exchange, looking always at the young marine, who eventually returned to his table and to the girl in the yellow jumper, who appeared to be making a joke at his expense. From the jukebox, Sam Cooke told Cupid to draw back his bow.

The other young marine, Honest Asia's date, got up and came to Gray and said, "Pardon my friend. Kid's from Mason City, Iowa, so . . . I'm Strein. I mean, Gary Strein." He seemed to think he was somehow different than the other.

"So I heard."

"You heard about me?"

"Hasn't everyone?"

"Hasn't. . . ? Oh. I get it." There wasn't a thought in the boy's badly barbered head. "We just need some information. That's all we're asking you for, man, and that ain't much."

"You're wearing me out with this."

"Anything, okay? Just anything. We like to party."

"You're in Olongapo. Walk down the street. Whatever you want, they got."

"You don't want to help us?"

"All right," said Gray. "Guy down there with the adding machine—ask him."

Belen had been hovering near. She gasped, "No. Oh, no. That Gray joke. You don't go him, okay? *Wrong* guy."

"Why not?" said Gray. "He can only say no."

"Oh, honey," said Belen, "Why you didn't leabe already? Leabe now, please."

"You didn't show me any respect at all," said Strein. He was wearing the ugliest shirt Gray had ever seen, a geometric pattern with sweat stains. "If we're supposed to be from the same . . . I'm as good as you are. Better."

"Congratulations," said Gray.

"Maybe I will try him," said Strein. "At least it looks like he's serious."

"No," said Belen, "*No.*" Strein went back to his table to sit there staring malevolently at Gray, while Gray stared at Herman, who stared in turn at Strein. The girl in the yellow jumper got up to dance alone; her dance amounted to closing her eyes and swaying in place. Gray might have left the Anchor then, he meant to, but at that very moment all the girls, including Belen, took a chorus with Smokey Robinson—*Baby let's cruise awaaay*—and Gray lingered for the high harmony, and while he lingered, Herman finally returned his gaze. Herman removed a bank pouch from a cigar box, and from that he removed a rolled swatch of velveteen. He unrolled it on the bar, and spread there on its surface were three engagement rings and a familiar dark stone. He petted these items with his fingertips, and Herman did all this without once looking away from Gray's face.

Gray was only aware that he was on his feet when he heard

Belen behind him, "Five hundred mile a day. Remember? You ride. Ride that much if you want. That soon, honey. That you, honey, and you almost got it. Ride way up in mountains, smell the star?"

The other marines were also standing now, looking around confused. They had identified ill will, but not what it was about. They were accustomed to confusion, liked it.

"You—Herman," said Gray, who felt once again that he had come to set things right, "she give that to you, or did you take it?"

Herman looked well satisfied with himself.

"I gib, I gib," said Belen. "You know that. He get what I get, and he don't talk American, not one word. Say he won't—he say why he should? But everything okay—honey? *Honey.*"

The other girls were still singing.

Happy at last, the owner wore a dreamy smile.

"Hey," said the repetitive young marine to no one in particular.

OUT ON A FIRE

A fire crew was hired one afternoon through the employment office and word of mouth, and some hours later they were loaded onto a DC-3 to make a night flight into the Idaho panhandle where it was, they were told, hot. They sat along benches bolted to the fuselage; in high summer the hatch had been left open and the near drone of the propellers cancelled idle chat among them. They were strangers anyway. Some of them could see out through the hatch, but there was nothing to see in the dark sky around them. Some were already back home in their minds, spending the money they were about to make on this fire. Cyrus Clift and Sarah Flynn faced each other from across the aircraft, their eyes avoidant. By holding her chin very high and breathing deeply Flynn could just manage her mistrust of the old airplane; her elongated throat was the most feminine thing Clift had ever seen.

They felt through their tail bones the plane's steep, skidding descent, felt it rolling out on a grass runway. They transferred from the plane and into the back of a forest service cattle car. It had been cold in the airplane; it was cold on the truck. They rode for a long while on washboarded roads; the dark was abetted by smoke so they couldn't see the glow of the fire as they approached it, but the smell became harsher and stronger as they went along. They breathed charcoal. "What a fantastic recipe for boogers," someone said. "Crunchy and creamy style. Jesus, couldn't they've found us a bus?"

Their ride ended in a meadow where they were given paper sleeping bags and pointless instructions about making camp. When the truck's headlights blinked out, there was no light at all, so by feel they made pillows of their fire shirts, and got into their rattling bags. Clift had been acutely aware of Flynn's location since he'd first seen her on the tarmac back in town, and he believed that even now he could distinguish her particular rustling. Taste of ash.

Flynn, shivering in the cold and dark, wished that it had been silent as well; she felt she was obnoxiously loud in her wrapping.

They had warmed a bit, and had slept some, fitfully, when the camp cook called daylight-in-the-canyon; forest service reveille and a recent fact, dawn. "Get up. Drop your . . . get up. Five minutes to breakfast." There were plastic buckets of water set out on the tailgate of the truck so that they might wash their faces. Their clothes had been impregnated in the night with smoke, a smell that accompanied them where they went. Sullen and sleepy, they ate government pancakes.

This would make the fifth summer that Clift had gone out on at least one fire crew, and this was the first of those crews to include women. They were into everything anymore. Weren't there natural divisions of labor? He knew he'd make a fool of himself if he couldn't somehow avoid this particular woman for as long as they were on the crew together. It was too hard to look and then to look away from her. If any part of what he was thinking should be apparent in his eyes—What was he thinking? No. Shy was best. Very shy. Tools were distributed, and the crew left camp walking in file up a narrow drainage.

Through the dewy stretch of the morning their climb was gradual, but then they broke from the trees and were confronted by ground they'd been warned about back in town, "steep as a cow's face," alternating timber and scree, and the crew leader traced with his finger the route they were expected to take. Straight up. Flynn, here on another ill-conceived lark, realized too late that she had overlooked how little she liked being told what to do. The urgency of the order, of the whole operation, made no sense to her. Were they going to be late if they took an easier way up? Where was the fire?

As they climbed out of the shade of surrounding mountains, the talus beneath their feet was sun struck, and the radiant rock became hot underfoot, and she wiped and wiped at her face with her sleeves. This was authority. This was the kind of insanity people in authority were always promoting, and she'd let herself in for it. For money. Flynn would hold up her end of the deal, but that didn't mean she didn't know it was a bad deal. They pay you, and because they pay you they think they can ask you to do any stupid thing. Why should everyone have to wear the same shirts, and why such an awful yellow? What was the purpose? She was not a convict or a soldier or a wide eyed school child. She was, however, following orders.

They reached a small bench, and the crew leader, a lean and overburdened boy noticeably younger than most of them, called the day's first break. They settled in a semicircle, in a stand of bear grass, the crew leader asking his radio, "Yeah, but can this be right? Over. Do what? Over."

There was another woman with them who was sick as soon as she sat down. She had lacquered nails and a web of vomit hanging from her chin. Her hollow eyes happened to fall on Clift. Did she want sympathy? Help? Someone fit was going to have to take her back to camp, and the crew would be short two hands, and she was a grown woman who should have better known where she did and did not belong.

Flynn wasn't having it; she came to the stricken woman, settled beside her, and said, "I'm Sarah," as much as to say that everything was going to be fine. She placed herself between the sick woman and the sun, and pulled her head onto her lap. She wetted her kerchief from her canteen and mopped the ruined face until it was clean, and until, as if she'd applied a thin wash of water paint, there was color in it again.

"I'm Bev," the sick woman said at last. "Good lord. What I did on my summer vacation."

"Take it easy, sweetie."

"My two weeks. I thought this time for a change I'd make some money on vacation. Put something extra by so the kids could have a decent Christmas for once. So here I am. This is what I get for thinking in advance."

"You'll be okay, Bev. Here, drink."

"Better go easy with your water," Clift heard himself say. "You don't know when we'll see our next Lister bag."

"I *better*?" said Flynn. "You think I *better*, do you?"

"The day," he said, "can get long. Hot."

"You don't say."

"Well. . . ."

Bev claimed to be feeling a whole lot better, and thank you, thank you, thank you, and then the break was over, and Sarah got behind her in line and willed her up the mountain. Clift came following next, enjoying the view, that long, free stride working right there in front of him. She did nothing about her beauty but live in it. Probably too much woman, but he thought he'd be all right so long as he never risked another word her way.

They reached the ridge, and the view of the other side of the mountain was very different; they looked down into a hanging canyon, a big cirque. Fire had been at work in the bottom and was still burning. It moved in rivulets over the ground, and whenever the wind came around to pour through the canyon's throat, flames would ride the treetops. There was no place in front of this fire where a crew might work in safety or with any effect, so they were stationed to watch from high above on the ridge. The fire could only climb so high on the amphitheater before it ran onto a wide collar of barren ground and out of fuel, and that would occur more than a thousand feet below them, so they watched in dull safety from a post commanding a grand sweep of pine forest and finger lakes, perhaps the Priest Lake that had given its name to this fire. The ridge was rock and the rock was an oven. In time the crew was arranged in column on the ground, lined up in the shade of a lonesome bull pine, the only shade to be had.

"You think this is hot?" There was a misused veteran among them. "That can mean only one fucking thing, people—you've never been to the Mekong Delta."

A pair of elk burst from the timber, and someone wanted his rifle, and their veteran, a '13' scrawled in grease pencil over the pocket of his fire shirt, had a little episode of the shakes and told them they didn't understand, they just did not understand. Clift hoped he was correct. Hard sleep could be had in the enervating heat. There was talk of trick exhausts and cam shafts, tales of impossible accelerations. Drugs and sex were mentioned competitively, bad jokes badly told. The fire flared, subsided, flared again, and it ran through the high valley, sparing some, burning some, and deer in their arrogance or foolishness kept bounding out of the woods just ahead of the flames. Bev wondered how her kids were doing, what they might be doing now, and how her parents were doing with the kids—they could be quite the handful, those two. The crew leader's radio squawked perpetually, a hateful crackle, and every hour or so he spoke to it to assure someone that their sector was secure, fully contained, which was true, but the crew leader, embarrassed by it, never mentioned the destruction they could not prevent. He was very young and very serious.

Clift would have preferred to dig fireline. To pretend so hard, for so long, that she wasn't there, or that he wasn't, was more than he'd signed on to do. For most of that day she was near enough that he might have reached out and touched her, and they said nothing. Sarah. Mother of nations, and wouldn't there be generations just aching to spring from her loins? But he was getting ahead of himself.

. . .

In a twilight swimming with millers they had steak and sweet
corn. Camp, in their absence, had established itself like a mid-
way on the meadow, lights, big generators humming, and several
clean new crews sitting around with plates in their laps. There
were pockets of fire, they learned, all around them, and crews
were to be sent off in every direction in the morning. Winds
aloft had scrubbed the sky clean just in time for early stars,
and in the deep confine of this valley there was no evidence of
the fires said to surround them. Flynn's neck, her face, and her
hands were sunburnt. She drank small cans of apple juice, one
after the other. She drank water until her stomach distended.
She took her sleeping bag into the outlying dark to be away
from the rumble and glow of camp, and she came upon a patch
of marsh grasses, dry now and standing in tufts. Someone had
already settled on it. "Is that you? My eyes haven't adjusted."

"Is it who?"

"Who do you think? Is that stuff soft?"

"Featherbed compared to last night."

She cast her bag beside his, and fell on it. "How are your feet
doing?"

"Good," he said. "Yours?"

"Not terrible. I inherited these boots from my grandmother,
and I think they were mostly for riding. Oh, this is better. *Way*
better."

"Did you hear anyone say anything about where we're going
tomorrow?"

"None of these guys," she said, "has ever said anything useful
in my presence. If I have to spend another day listening to those
fucking idiots. . . . That is uncalled for, to be that dumb."

"It'll be better when we've got something to do."

"Be better if they lost the power of speech completely."

"That's what you get when you traipse around with the great unwashed."

"You think I'm being snooty?"

"No," he said. "We've got some real specimens with us."

"Is there any reason for us to be here?"

"Us?"

"The crew," said Flynn. "All these crews. What can we do? Throw a little dirt on it? I'm sure that would really slow it down. You look at that fire, even the puny one we had today, and you know you're just nothing, or just a human being. I mean, is this even a legitimate thing, this firefighting? Or is it just some made-up government gig?"

"Usually, you don't have to wonder if you're earning your paycheck. It's not usually like this."

"My problem," she said, "is how much I hate to have anyone waste my time. When that starts happening I sometimes lose control. I get pissed off, and . . . that losing control, that's my biggest weakness."

"Your weakness?"

• • •

In the morning their crew was marched up the same mountain and posted on the same ridge as the day before, and to no better purpose. The fire below had burnt itself out and the valley floor was figured in black and green paisley. Today they could see smokes from other fires, other places they might have been. Once again they aligned themselves in the shade of the bull pine to wait, and once again it was not clear what they were awaiting. There were complaints and some crowing about easy money. There were stories dull and implausible of other jobs, of concerts attended, game taken or missed. One of the young bucks told in detail of the women who had wronged him, and of the woman who was wronging him now.

Clift approached the crew leader. "They want us to sit here?

Again?"

"That's how I understand it."

"You explained what this is?"

"Over and over," said the crew leader.

"We should at least go down and take a look."

"They want us on lookout. Up here."

"All of us?"

"You want to go down and see it?"

"Anything," said Clift. "I'd do just anything but this."

"Anybody else? He says he wants to go down there and take a look. Anybody else want to go?"

Sarah was the first to volunteer, and Bev the only other, and then one of the boys said, "*Ooooh*, it's a picnic, girls."

Crablike on their backsides they went down a face of scree, and they heard laughing on the ridge. Their tools were of no use and were much in the way while they were descending. Expecting Bev to tumble, Clift tried to keep himself just downhill of her in case she should begin to fall or slide.

"Picnic," said Flynn. "I hope they picnic on shit and die."

"Aw," said Bev, "now it's not that bad, is it? They're just having some fun."

They went down a steep of rock and then of gravel, all of it very uncertain, unstable ground, and when at last the slope conceded and let them walk upright again, they were at once into soot. The very bottom of the valley was not in view from the ridge and had been under snow as recently as June; it was boggy and not too flammable. Just above that, though, was a tier of high-altitude pine where the fire had feasted; these trees weren't consumed, but very many seemed seared beyond recovery.

"Is that a. . . ?" Bev thrilled. "That looks like a lily pond over there. Is that what that is? It's the hidden garden."

"A spring," said Clift, "I think."

"I'll tell you what it is," said Flynn. "That's our reward for coming down here. Let's soak our feet."

"*Yes*," said Bev.

A puddle in circumference, and wrapped all around with a slick of new moss on rocks, it was artesian water up from the depths to burble gently here, and they knelt for a drink of the cold and sweet, and then the women removed their boots and plunged their feet in it.

"What about you?" said Flynn. "If you're worried about polluting it, we already did that."

"But air pollution," said Clift. "That'd be me. I've had these socks on two days straight. You wouldn't want to be anywhere close when these socks come off."

Bev paddled her feet in and out of the water, her olive face having been flattered by the sun, and there were angry places on all her toes; she spread and flexed them. Her head lolled back, eyes closed. "You know what I've been wondering? I know we're doing something, but what are we doing? Us firefighters? I know we've been really working hard and everything, going up and down. But, what do we *do*?"

"We have to stay ready," said Clift.

"For what?" said Flynn.

"If things should change."

"Which things?"

"You never know," he said.

"So you have to stay ready all the time?" Bev was incredulous. "Ready for . . . anything? Everything?"

"I guess so."

"Well that sounds horrible. That just sounds like anxiety to me. I hope that's not what we're doing, because I can do that at home. I am soaking my feet, and that is all I want to think about."

"As long as we're down here," Clift said, "we should really try to do something. Maybe we could tamp down some smokes, see if there's any hot spots. Something. At least we'd go back to camp tonight looking like firefighters."

"Is that important to you?"

She had him in a bad way. If this Sarah was a shrew, and she might be, Clift was afraid it wouldn't matter.

"We're here," said Bev, "so let's just enjoy ourselves."

He was infatuated, or worse, and he wouldn't be enjoying himself any time soon. Clift went into a stand of charred scrub pine with his pulaski and bit into some blackened bark with its blade, and white wood was revealed, glistening with sap, a tree with every intention of living. The valley was only slightly violated, it had been a healthy little burn, and here was Clift, useless again, feeling late to the dance. A borate bomber passed over, and soon after it flew out of sight he heard the lugging groan it made making its passes to drop retardant on an active part of the fire. He envied the easy pleasure of the women lounging at the pool. Forces of nature, the big labors of big machinery; why did everything conspire against his significance? A troll lived in Clift, writhing in envy of everyone and everything, and if not here, where might he go to escape the petty gnawing?

• • •

"There is always some Dudley Do-Right around," Flynn observed, "and his only purpose in life is to make you feel like a goof-off."

"Don't let it bother you," said Bev. "Are we hurting anything? We could have just stayed on top like the rest of 'em. They've done even less than we have, so. . . ."

"I still think a shovel is a joke," said Flynn. "In a place like this—what is a shovel? But here we are again; it's everywhere, everywhere, you just have to go through the motions, don't you?"

"*You* go through the motions? I don't think so. You don't strike me that way at all. Just go talk to him. I'm *sure* he wouldn't mind."

"I mean the silly shit. Like digging where it can't possibly do any good. Like what I am about to do."

"Knock yourselves out," said Bev. "I'm happy right where I am. Until we go back up, this is where I'm gonna be. I *really* like this. Wait 'til I tell Tad and Polly what their mom's been up to. It's not like I usually have that much to talk about when I come home from work, so this is kinda neat."

Flynn was in familiar territory now, not sure why she was doing what she was doing, not even sure what she wanted. To pull her right boot on, she stood on her left foot, which was naked, and which slipped between two slick stones to be clamped there as she tipped sideways. She fell and heard her ankle break even before she'd finished falling. Her mouth became a cave to try for a scream, but she could only manage to grunt— —to breathe either in or out would tweak an already impossible pain. Flynn grunted as Bev came crawling toward her.

"Oh . . . oh . . . ooooh, *hunnney*."

Her foot was cocked at a new angle to her shin, a vision she glimpsed in a swimming field of black dots, through a sudden damping down of color and time. "Hahnh, hanh, hah."

"Hey," called Bev. "*Hey!*" And Clift came running, and when he reached them he said, "All right. First thing, we've got to make her comfortable."

"Comfortable? Are you out of your mind?" Flynn had found her voice.

"We have to treat you for shock," he said

"Shock? No. I am not into that."

"We have to be careful and not make this any worse."

"Get me out of here. No more talking."

"Helicopter," he said.

"Can't land."

"We could clear a landing."

"No," she said.

"Then what do we do?"

"No more talking." She extended her arms to him, and nodded and grunted until he understood that she intended for him to carry her out. "Come *on*," she said.

"You," Clift told Bev. "Go up and get us some help down here. Run ahead and tell 'em what's happened."

"No," said Bev. "I'm not leaving you guys. Out of the question." She helped Sarah mount Clift's back, and then because she didn't want the Forest Service to charge them for their loss, she gathered up all their tools, and Sarah told her to take her grandmother's boot as well, and rattling like a tinker's wagon, they started out.

Clift carried Sarah over the first easy pitch, through the scrub, and at first she was light enough that there was still room in his thoughts for the lascivious ones. She was astride him and he'd never hoped for more. Like any boy he believed that someday his heroic nature would happen to shine. He listened in lust and solicitude to her breathing in his ear, and he walked on, somewhat impressed with himself.

"I wasn't sure," said Bev, "if I was quite cut out for this. Even, you know, before. But it's okay. I'm sure we'll be okay. Aren't you?"

Flynn breathed and tried not to wrap her arms round his neck, to choke him; she hung on as best she could. When the climb turned more vertical and the ground to gravel wash, she felt him working harder under her, his legs churning at times just to keep them from sliding downslope and backward, and it would have been hard to say whose gasping was whose, and at last she said, "Okay. Okay. Put me down. Rest."

Clift arranged her with her legs uphill, then sat under her with his hip at her back to brace her on the slope. "Bev," he said.

"Now will you go? Will you please go get somebody? You'll be able to see 'em in just a couple hundred yards. You can't possibly get lost. Get us some help now. Or I will."

"No," said Flynn.

"This isn't working," Clift told her. "I can't do it. I can't get you any higher than this. This stuff won't hold our weight."

"No," said Flynn.

"No—what?"

"Rest first," she told them. "Rest a minute."

Clift rested but without benefit; he was about to fail her. Whatever happened next would be bad. Bev had arranged their tools gracefully in her lap. "Isn't it odd?" she said. "We hardly know anything about each other. And here we are, huh? You're Sarah, but where are you from? Not from around here, is it?"

"Mmhnh," said Flynn.

"Where?" Bev pressed.

"Fuck," said Flynn, "I'm from the rosy-fingered dawn. Okay?"

"Yeah. I like that. That's me too. The rosy—fingered? Cool. That's where I'm from, too. That's where we're all from, huh? Some women are women of mystery; that's not me to the least little degree, but it must be sort of fun to. . . . "

"We *do* have to figure something else out," said Clift. "I'm going up and get some help."

"No," said Flynn. "Not them. You. Us. We can do it." She told Bev to forget about the tools and then with gestures she directed the pair of them to come to either side of her so that she could drape her arms across their shoulders. "Upsy daisy," she said, "but *easy.*" They moved out three abreast, and with their five good feet working they had just enough purchase to make their way upslope. They didn't crawl, but were so deeply and awkwardly stooped that crawling would have been easier, and for all their effort and traction they still slid back occasionally, and

Flynn would cry out at this and other shocks, and she hated to be the source of such pitiable noise. They made no more than thirty short steps a minute, and even that pace was often interrupted.

Bev told them, "My mother comes over every Thursday. It's casserole Thursday, we call it. This is actually easy, compared to that."

She told them, "My manager is a homosexual, which is quite the blessing in disguise."

She said, "The first thing I do when I get home, or the first thing after my shower, I'm gonna jump on the scale. Can you imagine how much weight we're losing?"

And she asked, "Is that just blisters popping, or is that blood in my boots? Tell you one thing, I bet I don't wear heels again in the real near future."

Clift's hips, back, and shoulders were in agony under their unbalanced burden, and his lungs were insistent: stop, stop, stop. Where did the women find the breath to make the sounds they made? If not for these women beside him, Clift would have quit early on, but they were suffering more and better than he was, so he was obliged to keep going, and he came to despise, among other things, their courage.

"I'm gonna pass out," said Sarah, "if you let me."

Clift blew in her face.

"Stop that. *Talk* to me. Dudley. *You.* We just got to paradise—tell me about it before I pass out. No, don't stop. Talk."

"There's water in it," Clift improvised. "Hot and cold running water. Quite a bit of fruit. Fresh. There'd probably be a few more second chances, some room for error."

"Where's this?" said Bev. "It's like an agency?"

"Lions'll lay down with the lambs," said Clift. "There's gonna be lilies of the valley on top when we get up there. A ride out of here. They'll take you somewhere and feed you a milkshake."

"It's just my kids," said Bev. "That's my whole package,

heaven and hell and every other thing to me, and *darn* it, I wasn't gonna cry."

They stopped to rest again when Sarah became too weak to object. Once again Clift arranged her head-down on the mountain. Her eyes were clear and focused, but seemed set in a death mask. "*Now*," Clift said, "Bev. Come here. Get under her here, and support her. Here. Now. Please."

"I'll go," said Bev suddenly. "I'm . . . I'll go."

"They're not far now," he said. "Soon as you get above that rise they'll be able to see you."

Bev climbed away from them, silent at last and glancing back frequently, clumsy with exhaustion.

"Let's get your feet a little higher."

"Let's not move me at all," said Sarah.

"You need more blood in your head. We'll have you up on the ridge in no time now. They should be able to pick you right off the top of the ridge there. There are a couple places up there where they could come in and get you."

"You've got a lot of faith in *they*," she said.

"One way or the other, we're getting you out of here."

"You are," she said. "You did. You and Bev."

"You're the toughest person I ever met—which wasn't the first thing I noticed about you, I have to say. I mean it was unexpected. You're holding up great."

"Yeah. Or dying, which would be more my luck. I am really going in and out here, like woozy wise. Tell me something so I don't dim out. Anything."

"Well, you're not dying," he said. "That much I can tell you."

"Never?"

"Never," he said.

"You ever wonder if you'll run into something you just can't stand? Something that's too much?"

"You haven't hit it yet. You're holding up fine, and it's almost over. The worst is. Just rest."

"Quit telling me what to do."

They could see Bev above them enacting a pantomime, and something in this dumb show suggested first that she was having trouble being noticed, and then that she was having trouble being taken seriously by the boys on the ridge. Then she called out, a call she invested with such alarm and sorrow that Clift and Flynn expected help was already on its way.

"I could have been nicer to you," said Flynn. "It would have been just as easy. But I am a terrible judge of character."

Bev came down to them in a barely controlled slide. "They're coming," she said. "They're on the radio, and they're coming, and I should've before, but... They're coming now."

The crew came all in a rush when it came, and they made a litter of shovel handles and briskly finished carrying Sarah Flynn up to the ridge where the ranger district's on-call helicopter was already being directed. Clift and Bev lagged far behind, unable to climb any faster than they had before.

"Wow," said Bev. "That was ... you must think I am the ditsiest woman in this entire universe."

"No, ma'am," he said. "I do not."

"Her foot didn't look too good."

"They can do wonders anymore. They can bolt you back together if it comes to that."

"Sure. Sure. She'll be all right, she'll have to be, because it wouldn't be. . . . God, listen to me talk, and I know you'll never believe it, but I am not usually a very talkative person, but, oooh. . . . I, I'm going out on that helicopter, too. I mean, even if I have to hold onto its leg thingy. Like they did in Saigon. I'm going out. Why do I have to learn everything the hard way? This is what I hate so much about being an adult. This is what always happens with your hidden garden."

• • •

Clift was with the crew two more days before they were taken off the fire and driven all the way back to town in an olive drab school bus. He had never quite recovered from the climb out of the cirque, and he slept for many hours in the punishing right angle of his seat. They were let off on Broadway, across the street from the Palace Hotel, and his intention had been to hike home to bed and doses of aspirin on the north side, but when his feet hit the sidewalk an impulse turned him toward St. Pat's.

The hospital's lobby was cool, and flat, and hushed except for the elevators' coded bells as they traveled up and down. He knew it as a place where very serious people wrought miracles and very sick ones died. The nun at the information desk wore her order's long-visored wimple which required her to tilt her head well back to look up at him; her sleeves were fantastic, her face doughy.

"I had a question," he said to get himself started. "Uhm, how do you find out who's being treated here?"

"Have you been in an accident?"

"No. I was on a fire with some people who were hurt."

"When?" asked the nun.

"Day before yesterday."

"Where were they injured?"

"One with a broken ankle," he said, "and the other was just. . ."

"No, dear," said the nun. "In what lo*cation* were they hurt?"

"Oh," said Clift. He knew then that he'd never find them. "We were in Idaho."

"I believe they'd be treated in Idaho, then. Wouldn't they?"

"Probably, but the crew was from here, so I thought maybe. . . ."

"I'm sorry," she said, "there's a new policy. We couldn't tell you even if they were here. There have been some lawsuits. Were you related to these people?"

Clift thought to try a middling and useful lie "Their names

were Sarah and Bev. I was their crew leader."

"I'm sure they'd be very pleased with your concern. That's good leadership, young man."

"Thanks. So?"

"We couldn't tell you if they'd been admitted," she said. "But, it doesn't seem very likely, does it? From over in Idaho?"

"No. I'm loopy, but I just thought. . . ." He thought that faces from the past do recur, but never the ones he wanted to see. He knew everything he might need to know about them except how they might be found, and they were gone. "I just wondered. Could you even tell me. . . ?"

"No," said the shadowed nun, "but I'll pray for them, and I'll pray for you, young man."

HOW I GOT CONNECTED

Well, to begin with, I'm in industrial sealants, which pretty much says it all. Got a boss half my age who calls me her road warrior, like that's all the motivation I need, and I'm still out here flying tin-can airways with my plastic belt buckle, and a plastic identification card I wear on a cord around my neck; out here selling gaskets to my manufacturer pals, the red meat and whiskey crowd. I'm an engineer, an expert, so go ahead and ask me anything you ever wanted to know about heat and resistance. It's a living, but let's face it, not exactly what you dreamed of for yourself. Gaskets.

So, one night I'm hungover in the airport, alone with my thoughts and that poor old Kodiak bear they keep under Plexiglass—cancelled meeting, canceled flight, and I'm all night in the Spokane airport, and to add insult to injury I get moody and stumble into a bad thought. I happen to recall how I've loved in my life, and I've been loved, but I've never quite managed to do both at once, have I? No wonder a person feels funky so much of the time. The janitors are tooling around on their riding vacuum cleaners, and here I am, the guy without a backup plan, poor mutt trying to use the sports page for a blanket.

Morning finally comes, as they do, and my flight's still a long way off, but every other plane in North America is going through Spokane that morning, and the brats start really infesting the terminal—do people have any control at all over their children anymore? The gal finally comes in to open the Sky Box Lounge, and I was never so happy to see a bartender in my life. She turns on the televisions and builds me a vodka tonic, and, thank God, we're in the middle of basketball season. Tag on her vest says she's Cecile Desilva. She's got a hairspray afro, pretty bad, but she does give you the impression that she has no life outside this bar, and I like that kind of professionalism. She tells me she is and always has been a Syracuse fan. "But do you ever see the Big East out here? You just don't get power basketball when you're this far out in the sticks. Cable? Worthless. Satellite? Worthless."

I could only agree. "When's the last time you saw the University of Washington play? Wake Forest?"

"Bad programming," she says. This had bothered her a long time, and I shared her pain. "It's down to a few teams anymore," she says. "I mean, Notre Dame? For basketball? You have got to be kidding me. But they're on television all the time, and my question for the Pope and the cardinals is this: Why can't you put out a decent team? Except for Gonzaga? Why do you have to saturate the airwaves? People might begin to question their faith."

"It's all salesmanship," I tell her. "What's a salesman but a shill with a shiny bauble? "

"What?"

Right at the moment I don't quite understand what I'm trying to articulate, but I keep talking, like I might pin it down. "Who plays this game? Who watches it? Look at your demographics, look at the advertising, it's a lot of investment brokers. Realtors. So, you see what I mean?"

"No."

"Who buys, and who sells?"

"Is this about basketball?"

"Basketball is just an example."

"Of what?"

"Of everything," I tell her.

"You could've said that in the first place. Of course it is."

Cecile has some fine qualities, and here we are in her nice

gloomy bar, and maybe it's nine in the a.m., and maybe I'm looking like a bag lady, but who knows what lurks in the hearts of men?

See, I'd been thinking that I had to take more risks. I've got a spider plant in my apartment that's been at death's door many times. Of neglect. That's how much I'm out here, and I can be away for weeks at a time, come back, and all I've got is some flyers the Jehovah's Witnesses have stuffed in my box. I'm out here in every blipville and podunk in the West, and what I really latch onto is these sports stations. Broadcasters, commentators, the actual athletes—that's my society. They go everywhere I go, and they'll talk to me all night if necessary. I know what some of these people will say before they ever say it, and here's one thing they all say, "One game at a time." You hear that so much because it truly is the whole program. I try to take it a sales meeting at a time, a trip at a time, and that way I kind of trick myself into feeling like I'm anxious to get home.

Lately I've been thinking, if this is where I'm living, then this is where I have to live, and here's Cecile Desilva, fixing her garnishes, a genuinely pleasant person. She's making zest. She wears a turquoise pinky ring, and I couldn't begin to guess her age, which makes me feel a little sorry for her, but she's old enough. What did I even have in mind? What did I think I could ask her? "So, what do you do for fun in Spokane?"— "Shall we spend our twilight years together, dear? I'll be back through town again in six months, and we can discuss it." What did I even hope to accomplish? You just want to say something. To somebody. And here's Cecile, trying to be professional, me nursing my yellow seltzer.

They're having an argument on television about the best of all time. It's a morning show, all talk, and these guys who make a career out of arguing with each other are debating who was the best to ever play the game, and I think they're both wrong, so this is where I decide to inject my two cents, and I say, "It's Kareem. Hands down. He owned the sport for years. Remember?"

"When he lost all his albums in that fire," she says, "his jazz, that was sad, but that's really the only time he ever connected with the public."

This Cecile is probably my soul mate.

She's the kind of person who comes to work, and she works, and she's pleasant. These are not minor accomplishments. They are also not the kind of compliments you usually offer. We're in this lounge, and what do you say?—"Cecile"—No, "Ms. Desilva, I don't actually know any people, so would you be my friend?" I mean, how do you approach these things? You don't, and that's the problem, and, mind you, I was still quite hungover, but I think I had almost got up the nerve to make a massive fool of myself when in comes another lost soul and plops down a few stools away, lays this aluminum briefcase on the bar. I probably owe him for saving me some embarrassment, but gratitude kind of escapes me. He's in a blazer, creased khakis, and I can't see his feet, but I'm sure he's wearing tassels. He wants to know if there's any espresso or coffee, and I'm thinking, yeah, at the Starbuck's two doors down, but Cecile brews him a pot and he drinks it with brandy. Then it's the three of us, killing time.

Whenever you set out to impress a woman, there are so many ways that can backfire, you kind of come to expect it, and you tend to quit trying after a while, quit exposing yourself, but I must've been desperate or inspired or tired or something, because I started bragging a little bit. There we are at the bar, the whole day ahead of us, and, I don't know, I start feeling kind of competitive, and I just throw it out there for general discussion, "Lost two hundred last night in the ACC," I say, "but I made five hundred in the Pac Twelve."

This does get Cecile's interest. "You bet on these things? You put your money in the hands of teenagers? I could never afford that. That's exactly why I follow the college game, it's so unpredictable."

"I've got a system," I tell her. "I always beat the spread."

The guy with the aluminum briefcase says, "Nobody beats the spread. Not in college basketball."

"I'm ahead. Four straight seasons, season in-season out, week-in, week-out, I'm ahead. Ever since I devised the system."

"You're a handicapper," says the young know-it-all.

"I'm a scholar. Student of the game. It's all analysis. I beat the handicappers." This is me, strutting what little stuff I've got to strut. I do have Cecile's full attention, though. "I'm funding my retirement out of my hobby."

"You do that good?" says our third wheel.

It's always creepy to me when somebody's grooming is a lot more upscale than their grammar. "It's like anything else," I tell him, "it involves a certain amount of work."

"Percentages?" he says. "How much are you ahead?"

"That's personal."

"No, it's business. You're in it for the money, right?"

"Oh, I don't know. Maybe just the thrill of the chase."

"To win?" he says.

"That's almost a non-issue," I'm still bragging at this point. "I win. I just do."

"And you know you won because you made money." He's out of a men's wear ad, he's one of these blue-jawed guys. Too handsome. He says, "Money's how you measure, isn't it?"

"It's a clear indicator."

"And you're ahead with your bets?"

"So far," I have to admit, "I am."

"How much? How much you making?"

Sometimes people's manners are just so bad, you don't know

what to do. "Cecile," I say, "give this gentleman another one of those, whatever-he's-having. Fix yourself something, too, if you're so inclined at this hour."

No man is an island? I think we all are. I'm around people all the time, crammed in with 'em, and you'd think it would be physically impossible for me to be lonely, but you talk to people and you see their eyes go blank whenever you're not talking about them. You're out there, and you make the first move, try to commiserate with your fellow traveler, and what do you get for your trouble? Bored to death. There are so many of these people anymore who can spend half an hour telling you about a half-hour lunch they had with someone you've never met. It's better not to let them get started.

But for once, I've got a captive audience, fanatics like myself, and I usually do not elaborate too much on the system—a trade secret if there ever was one—but now I've got Cecile's ear, and I'm flattered. Simplicity is not the system's strong point, which means I can spend a long time talking about it, and I probably pontificated. I know I did some computations where I could have just said, you-win-some-you-lose-some. That's my underlying principle. Or don't-put-all-your-eggs-in-one-basket. The rationale isn't that complicated, and neither is the conclusion—the best way to win is make a lot of bets, but I just have to do some fancy math to plot it all out. And I'm thinking as I go through it, you know this might have worked in your private life, you'd have done better if you'd taken a few more chances.

But then there's variable two. Your better bet is obviously your informed bet, and how do you make an educated guess on three, four dozen games a week across ten or fifteen different conferences? Is this impossible? Almost.

Probably by now I'm kind of gloating, because now I'm getting into the meat of the system. I talk about the five

weighted factors, but I don't reveal the factors, or the weighting system. It's informational, I say. If I know five things, five discrete things about any game, I'll beat the
spread like a red-headed stepchild. It's a steady return. It's like an investment, but way more gratifying. I go so far as to say elegant.

"Five things?" says the guy. "Five things the people who set the betting line *don't* know?"

"They see, but they don't know what they're looking at. Or how to look at it."

"You still need to know those five things about all these different games."

"I said it was some work."

"Sounds like a job to me," he says.

"I wouldn't mind a job like that," says Cecile, "if I was smart enough."

That was the high point. Her enthusiasm. I'd gotten used to that hairdo. Everyone is entitled to one mistake. I'd decided I liked everything about her.

Since then, I've been through Spokane several times, and I always check the lounge, but she's history. No one who works there now remembers her. People are not friends anymore, they're associates. She's not in the phone book. Who is these days? The guy with the aluminum briefcase, though—he's another story. His name was—is—Andrew Scales, and no one calls him Andy. He isn't very smart, but he knows smart people, aggressive people, wealthy people who like to diversify a portfolio. High rollers, really. Mr. Scales is number one on my speed dial these days; in a couple months he's got me set up as a tout to the too-rich and the semi-shady, and we've all been making money ever since. Don't get me wrong, what *I* do is perfectly legitimate. Still, it's a long way from what I wanted, which was a friend or a frolic.

Now I'm talking code to Dan in Dubuque and Pete in Peoria, and my wisdom is wreaking havoc with bookmakers all over our glorious republic and Tijuana. I'm talking pretty often to Mr. Scales who doesn't go for idle chat. I have acquired apartment complexes in Mendocino and Medicine Lake, and I'm talking to my property managers, and I don't know if I even believe in the system anymore, or if the system can survive so much traffic and greed, but I will say I am always on the phone these days, talking with people who want something from me. People who at least know I'm there.

EMPTY LOT

Seasons passed, and years, and still the Canadians would not fill our vacancies. Eventually the old man lost the Maple Leaf Motel. He was bartending at a bowling alley that summer, and my folks, never all that guarded in their despair, were always holding forth on how far and how fast we'd come down in the world. As if it needed mentioning. We had moved to an apartment complex that was sided in teal Masonite and situated in the ugliest block of our town's only industrial neighborhood. It hadn't escaped my notice that our rooms there were sweatboxes, or that bacon, cookies, and real milk were now nearly absent from our diet, but for a long time my family's misfortune remained obscure to me, for I was only rarely to be found in my own body or my present predicament, a lad completely devoted then to making himself a self-made man. This was when flights of fighter jets roared over every picnic or pet show, a time so replete with masculine example that I was often busy and always moonstruck, and even if the folks were pissing and moaning and rolling their own cigarettes, I delivered the *Lake City Ledger* to more than a hundred homes, so I usually had some money in my pockets.

You force yourself to it every morning. A boy never wants to leave his bed. But then you're up, a wedge of dry toast in your mouth, and you're on the Commander, and fifteen seconds later the NuVue Apartments are completely at your back, and you pick up your papers, learn once again to accommodate the misery of that canvas strap over your shoulder, your neck, and you ride out, your legs pulsing, and when you've breathed enough grassy air to get your second wind, then you're loose in the larger thing. Battle sounds appropriate to the various centuries erupt from your mouth, bronze thuds on hide, steel rings on steel, muskets chuff, machine guns trill, you reproduce the tympanic rolling of ack-ack from the depths of your throat. You bomb Nuremburg. You ride, if you care to, with Achilles against the doomed defenders of Troy, and you may die in these encounters, but you must never lose.

I knew this much about the man I intended to be: No shift work. He would not detest himself. There'd be no hesitation or doubt for this guy, and I must never suffer a moment's misgiving about my personal appearance. The specifics of my eventual self were not, however, well filled in, and I was wide open to suggestion and moving fluidly from any ideal to any other.

I was briefly smitten, for example, with the example of Sonny Liston. Because the folks needed more culture than they could afford, I bought us a *Life* magazine, and this happened to be the issue with a life-size picture of the challenger's fist; I followed that thing from the toilet tank to the coffee table as it migrated around the apartment. In those days any success story stirred me, and here was he, a sharecropper's twenty-fourth child who'd learned to fight in prison, been discovered there by a priest, and now, his troubled past behind him, was redeeming himself with a string of knockouts. I liked the challenger's glamorous prospects, and I coveted his bearing. There was a shot of him sitting on the ring apron at his ease, his back bowed under the weight of tremendous shoulders and arms. He stared out from under a hooded sweatshirt with his face still dripping from some effort now entirely suspended, and he offered the camera the level and leveling look of one who clearly does not care. Hands like mallets and a barely detectable soul—this seemed a very sound formula, and I yearned for Sonny Liston's uncomplicated emotional life, but I was plagued even then with elements of pity in my character, of pity and of light. These have always given me trouble.

In the morning, by the time I'd finished my paper route, the old man would be up and having his coffee, and we'd sit on the couch together watching the *Three Stooges Hour*. He liked to see me laugh. He'd been in the war that everyone still called The War though others had intervened by then, and he'd acquired a hole in his heel. He would lounge around and watch me laugh and suavely ash his cigarette into that hard old scar the Japs had given him at Hollandia. Shrapnel. He told me it took seven significant scars to make a man, scars and a deep appreciation of beauty. I thought he would probably know. He read *Moby Dick* and the poems of A.E. Houseman. He worked at what he called a street bar and did his own bouncing, and I was given to understand he did this efficiently. He called himself a zoo keeper. The old man could squeeze more compound pleasure out of a nickel ice cream cone than anyone I've ever met, but he was too obviously heartsick, and there wasn't much I wanted from his life.

As for my mother, she would bring us fruit. For years she professed amazement at how much of it there was to be had for free, and she'd bring us spotted apples and pears, saying she liked her boys regular, she liked them happy. She made us happy, too, and for that and other reasons she was the best person I knew. But Mom was a woman.

I shared a room with my brother Curtis, the most extravagantly wounded member of our family, whom I envied relentlessly. The summer before, at a dance in the city park, someone had broken a bottle against his eye, and now that eye could never close, so he slept with it open. Girls called for him night and day. He smoked even more than the folks did, and he ran long distance races for the high school. He flayed blond bongos

with his thumbs, keeping time to forty-fives he'd stolen from
the drug store and Jacques Penné's. He wanted me to leave him
alone, wanted it so much that sometimes I found it impossible
to pry myself from our room. Leave, he'd say.

Make me.

He claimed, accurately, that I did not understand him, and
so Curtis went to work for a landscaper and bought his first and
worst Chevrolet and was essentially, from that time forward,
gone. I liked to think of myself as a loner, but I could not be
alone in that horrible room. It was as long as an ordinary room,
but no wider than a closet, and it stank of us, and I believed it
to be a little haunted by the ghosts of tenants past.

There was a scrim of gravel and oil tanks and clotheslines
behind the apartments. I avoided this territory because of
the boy I would soon come to know as Randy Creamer. From
my bedroom window I had estimated him to be of about my
age, to be the kind of kid who keeps goldfish or a lazy cat. He
moved like Howdy Doody and never seemed to stray from the
crummy grounds. There were tees of steel pipe set in concrete
for the clotheslines, and he'd try to chin himself from these. He
disgusted me. If he hadn't come to my back door, if it had been
solely up to me, I suppose I'd have kept clear of him forever.
But there he was with a brand new baseball and no mitt. Do I
want to play catch? Mom's right behind me: How nice. Now, go
on. Get out there and play.

We were not too far out that door before I set him straight:
I made it very clear—excepting Home Run Derby, I detested
baseball in all its forms. He seemed relieved. He held his nose
bunched and his head cocked back like a rabbit's, said he wasn't
seeing very well because he'd lost his glasses, or at least that's
what he'd told his mother, and he wouldn't be seeing well until
he'd learned the value of things. She couldn't be buying him
glasses all the time.

Did he have a bike? He did, but he couldn't safely ride it right now.

Did he want to go over to Tugg's Hill? We could run. He said he'd have to ask his mom when she came home from work. Ask her if he could go that far.

Leave her a note. No.

Had he had polio? Scarlet fever, he said, he'd had scarlet fever as a baby. He said it made him fast. As I later demonstrated, I could almost outrun this kid going backward. Could he at least go to the store?

He had no money.

Come on, I told him. Come on. I was becoming a leader of men. He needed my leadership.

Randy Creamer's toes turned inward as he walked, and his elbows turned out, and he had a girl's eyelashes. The kid's lack of confidence made me queasy. I took him to the corner store and got us some bubblegum cigars, and he embarrassed me by selecting the yellow. Mine, as always, was chocolate, which looks quite like the real thing, and you can chew half of it and clamp the other half, the stub, attractively at the corner of your mouth like those GIs you'd see on the cover of Argosy—you'd have your cigar, your heavy stubble and your submachine gun, companions vile and voluptuous. But Randy Creamer had put this yellow thing right in the center of his lips with no concept of how bad it made him look, and he'd been real impressed with the fact that I owned a wallet. I had to wonder if my guidance would ever be enough to snap him out of it. Then I happened to think, Why not hop the train? As an American citizen, I knew what it took to bring a guy around. You'd have to go bold.

There were railroad tracks embedded in the asphalt of our street and our traffic included the Good Humor cart, the usual cars and trucks, and a freight train. This train rolled by three times a day, almost always at walking speed, almost always emp-

ty—four or five empty, fugitive boxcars from the Soo Line that
seemed to serve no purpose beyond tempting me. You could
just make out the engineer's head in the cab of the engine, a
man who had nothing to do but lay on his airhorn from time to
time, a man with a nearly perfect job, though he'd be no Casey
Jones.

We awaited the train on my observation post, the roof of
an abandoned garage. From this favorable location you could
lean over the façade and spit, and your spit would fall thirty feet
to the sidewalk, wonderfully sinuous and globular in its flight.
Once you're a hobo, I explained, wherever you hang your hat is
home. We don't have hats, said Randy Creamer. Once you get
the knack, I told him, the world is your oyster, because you can
ride for free, and by now there must be trains running everywhere—you could go from the Everglades to the Arctic Circle.
He'd already been to the Arctic Circle, had a hamburger there
for his birthday, and he could hardly wait for next year to go
again. Did I really think I was going to jump that train?

Didn't I already say? We both are. That's our mission now.

You first. What if you got your leg cut off? Or you got just
completely crushed?

Crushed?

By a train? Are you kidding me? Sure.

It was as if this kid had never seen a decent Western. If you
fall, you roll in between the wheels. You lay flat on the tracks
and the train goes right over you. What are you worried about?

I don't think that thing even leaves this town. Do you?

From the moment you're certain you'll do it, from that
moment the waiting becomes hard. It's a tarpaper roof, and
the tarpaper gathers heat through the afternoon until it burns
underfoot. And you're thirsty, but you don't come down. Randy
Creamer is becoming sunburned. You dance on the angle of the
roof, and he sits astraddle of the ridge, saying, stop it, and then

you hear it before you see it, and the train is finally coming, the orange locomotive shrieking at every startled intersection. Now you scramble down, come on, come on, it's almost here, and it's coming up the street like a land mass, and you try to stand indifferently on the sidewalk so the engineer won't glance down and guess what you're up to—what could he do, anyway?—and it comes on grudgingly, this is a slow train, and those cars are empty again, doors grinning open. The engineer never looks back to see where he's been. If he ever noticed you at all, he's already forgotten you were there.

Now, you say, and you start running, though running may not be strictly necessary.

You wish you'd retained a little of your cigar for this, for confidence and for dash. The floor of the boxcar is shoulder high to you, the wheels, on closer inspection, seem quite inescapable, and as you become more intimate with it you hear how a freight train, even a very slow one, speaks from the bowels of the earth. The situation wants no further study. You jump. You glide. You are aboard, and at once you scramble up and turn to summon Randy Creamer. Come on, I'll grab you. You are not surprised when he backs away, waving like a lady in a beauty pageant. He will not follow—but he admires you. Who wouldn't? You ride the train.

It was going along just great, too, until Randy Creamer's mother pulled up, home from work, and there's her skinny kid out in the street, gawking at the train and at me on the train. She spilled right out of her Volkswagen, and she jogged a little to catch up to me and walk alongside with that same weird gait her son used. She wore a maid's uniform, white shoes. There were probably occasions when she was pretty, but at the moment she had a little linen coronet on her head. Which I hated.

What are you doing?

It's a mission. Kind of.

Do you want to be killed?

I did not, not unless it was absolutely necessary. How long would this woman be bothering me? Would the engineer notice her and stop the train? She was ruining everything.

Stay on there, she said. Just hang on tight. You'd better stay on there now until they stop this thing. This is really not safe at all. She blinked and blinked as if I were a proximate sun. Was this the face of the voice of reason? She wanted to know who I was. I shrugged, and, inspired, I dashed to the other side of my boxcar, to yet another open door, and I leapt and landed running. I hadn't run more than three blocks before I was once again in a handsome part of town.

I thought I might be done with Randy Creamer then, that with any luck I'd be off limits to him; he seemed so comfortably hopeless that I did not see how I'd find any more fun in feeling sorry for him. By the time I'd circled back home I'd ceased to think of him at all. I settled in to watch *Popeye* and *Captain Cy* and to inhale the siren scent of Velveeta bubbling in the oven, my mother's enchiladas, and I was so very young then that I still expected such mystic moods and moments to persist. But of course there came a knock at our back door, just off the kitchen.

This was Marge. Randy Creamer's mother, calling herself Marge. She had changed into slacks and removed the item from her head and was wondering if she might have a little chat with me; I noted all this flashing up the stairs where I intended to lock myself in the bathroom and fake a lengthy bowel movement. My mother spoke my name, however, and arrested me in midstride, ascending. Get down here, she specified.

Mrs. Creamer would have learned by now all the details of her boy's afternoon with me. I knew she would misinterpret these as my attempt to lure her Randy to a messy end or a maiming, and I wondered if I should even try to explain my plan, the sheer need I'd seen to take action. But no, I'd never get a word in edgewise. In such debates a boy never has the floor. Now I would hear, at the very least, that I'd been disappointing once again. There would be an appropriately severe and exotic punishment—the old man still threatened from time to time to use his belt—and I entered that kitchen very keen to read the weather, and very surprised at the smile Mrs. Creamer had prepared for me. I might have been her long-lost dog. Suspecting a trick or a trap, and mired in poor luck, I took little hope from her beatific regard. The women looked at me and looked at me, as women will do, to extend the anxious interval.

At last my mother told me that the Creamers had asked if I could have supper with them. She told me that it would be more than fine with her. If I went. That I should go.

Yes, Mrs. Creamer said, because I'd been so nice to her boy, and generous, and they just wanted to return the favor if they could.

You mean, right now? I mean, for a piece of gum?

He'd be delighted. Wouldn't you?

But. . .

Delighted. Now . . . you . . . *get.*

Mrs. Creamer walked as if she were forever picking her way through some detailed mess. She continued to smile at me. She wanted to know what grade I was in and about my paper route. Did I like it? Sort of. Randy, she said, had had one for a while, a nice little route. He'd earned some really decent prizes, too. In fact he'd been trying to win that trip to Washington, DC, when he got beat up, and then they'd decided it wasn't worth it anymore, but he missed those little extras a lot.

That's a shame.

It's a crime, she told me. An actual crime, I think. But what can you do? She wasn't really asking me.

Mystifying odors vied with the basic undertone of mothballs

in their home; Randy Creamer was far too pleased to have me
there, and he whispered, I hope you like cream cheese. Afghan
blankets were everywhere. Mounds of variously colored wax
covered their kitchen table, and I saw that television trays were
set up in the living room. Mrs. Creamer apologized for this, but
I thought it was the best thing they had going for them. Randy
Creamer took me upstairs and showed me his ant farm; the im-
mobile ones, he insisted, were not dead. He had stacks of comics, mostly Archies, some shitty Huckleberry Hounds. He had
a miniature hari-kari knife, but when I tried to cut some paper
with it he said we'd better not. His room was identical to my
room, in a building identical to my building, and I was already
depressed when Mrs. Creamer called us to supper and fed us
some bologna she'd fried in margarine. She gave us celery sticks
with pink paste in them, and she added some magenta powder
to our water that tasted, even in solution, like dust. She was so,
so happy now that Randy had a decent friend. But one thing,
she said, and I knew she'd just have to bring it up: You need to
stay away from that train, young man. You wouldn't try that
stunt again, would you?

Nah, I'd already done it.

You're basically a pretty good boy. Aren't you?

"Good," it seemed to me, was a very small attainment in a
nation of heroes, so I thought that I might say that, yes, I was
pretty good, without bragging. They had a painting of a grief-
stricken clown and another of a boat stove on a stony shore. I
told Mrs. Creamer I'd never have guessed these were paint-by-
number, and it was only the truth; she'd done a fine job with
them. Did I do any kind of art? I had a trumpet I might play
for her sometime, if she wanted. I could do most of the national anthem. We ate with their television left mute and dark
to make way for what Mrs. Creamer was calling a nice conversation. Everyone, said Mrs. Creamer, needs a friend.

Not necessarily. But I didn't contradict adults, not even tiny ones, and I did not wish to hurt Mrs. Creamer's feelings. I had secreted much of my meal in a pocket of my jeans and dreamed of escaping undetected before the mess might seep through to touch my leg. Meanwhile, at my own home, they were eating every last enchilada.

The next day Randy Creamer declared in my presence that we were almost best friends, and I had worried that something like this might occur, but I didn't want to hurt his feelings, either, so I never said otherwise, and it seemed that every morning after that I'd look up from my Malto-Meal, and there he'd be, rattling the screen door. What he wanted to do, absolutely all he wanted to do, was sit in one of our rooms reading comics. It's Randy. Randy's here. Come on in, Randy. My mother thought he was very polite, and he was, but he feared my firecrackers, my football, his own bicycle. I had a hard time ever to coax him out beyond the chainlink fence that ran along our alley. Every time we went up on the garage again he got a fresh sunburn.

Finally one fine morning I said I was going to the beach.

With your dad?

Just me.

That's the other side of town.

This is not Tokyo. It wouldn't be all that far.

Why the beach?

You don't know?

Myself, he said, I can't swim.

Me neither. That's all the more reason.

I'd settled on this adventure mostly to make him beg off and leave me alone, but no, Randy Creamer just had to come along, and because he was coming, and because he couldn't or wouldn't ride his bike, we walked the whole way. He wasted a lot of this hike explaining himself, which frustrated my design to march through Algeria with my real friends, the Legionnaires. We are not Frenchmen, I explained. We just work for the French. It's the *Foreign* Legion. Randy Creamer was not interested in these distinctions nor the whole notion of wandering the desert with the lighthearted Lost Patrol. No, he said. No. Without his glasses, he said, things were murky for him, things came up on him too fast; his feet felt funny sometimes. He said he didn't like to complain. He said he tried not to bump into things, tried not to let his mother know about the headaches; she already felt bad enough that he had to wait around until pay-day-after-next to really start seeing again. He'd never met his dad, and he didn't know why, and he was a big expense because his teeth were bad, and his mom wouldn't let him buy a lot of the comic books, the ones with too much violence in them, not even when he had some money of his own—and so forth, and by the time we'd reached the beach I was gagging on his life as he told it, so I rushed right into the lake, shirt and all.

It was a wader's paradise, City Beach, a stretch of the city's sifted sand embracing the lake's shallowest bay, its waters warm as piss. So we waded, Randy Creamer and I. We were among timid children at first, venturing only a little farther out than the diapered ones. This embarrassed me after a while, so I walked out on the sandy bottom and kept walking until I was treading water, in over my head. Spastic as a wet cat, I was, however, intentionally afloat. I thrashed around for a moment before regaining my footing, completely spent by my ten seconds on the high seas.

See?

See what? You better be careful. I couldn't save you if you started going under.

Save me? I'll be Tarzan, the way I'm going. I'm getting this. This is easy. It's easy. I'm gonna go out there.

There was a plank platform anchored out on the lake, a

platform from which to dive and upon which to appear golden. People stood on it, glistening.

You said you couldn't swim.

I couldn't, but I think I can now. Just about. I'm really getting it. You can splash around with the kiddies, if you want. I'm swimming out there as soon as I can figure out how to steer a little bit and kind of go where I want to go. Look at all these people. They're doing it. Girls. Old people. That little, little kid over there. Come on. It can't be that hard.

I'm getting a cramp.

No. Come on. You just walk out there until you can't really walk anymore. Or you lay down, and you wiggle, kind of move your arms— like this? See, see how that guy does it? That's the way. Does that look so hard to you?

While I was learning to dog paddle that afternoon, Randy Creamer taught himself to swim. Once I'd talked him out into it, that deep water was for him an amniotic fluid, and he soon developed a sidestroke that let him slide along like a clipper ship, back and forth and back and forth from the platform to the shore. Instinct had him swimming at once, and he could even swim and talk to me as he swam. Even laugh, which I'd not heard from him before. Just relax, he said. Once you relax, it's like whip cream.

My method was bad; I was always in a small storm of my own making, and water was not a frothy element for me, but clinging and heavy, and the slightest progress through it exhausted me. I was not noticeably buoyant. Come on, come on, he said, swimming alongside. Once you relax, it's not bad at all. It's great, huh? You just float.

I could not answer because I could not answer, I couldn't spare the air, and because I couldn't in any case accurately say what might happen when you relaxed. For me that would be an advanced technique. I held my chin so high off the water that a knot tied in my back, and my legs worked like a Chihuahua's, and still I felt myself always just at the point of sinking. It seemed to do Randy Creamer quite a lot of good to swim alongside and see my eyes so big.

We were at the beach often after that, and in time he could breaststroke upon the choppiest lake, while I continued all that summer, and have continued ever since, to swim like I'm having shock treatments.

School rolled around. I was the new kid in class, the new kid who was friends with Randy Creamer, the worst possible set of credentials. On the first day, at the first recess, I got into a pickup football game, and when I saw him standing on the sidelines, watching me, I knew that I was to have no peace and no popularity at Midvale School, that Randy Creamer and I were about to charter a small chapter of the deeply unwanted club. Of course he would happen to be in my class, more than ever the tumor on my ass; I was at school with him all day and had begun now to hear his voice in my dreams at night, his voice and a mocking laughter, to include perhaps my own. He often got into trouble with Mr. Gray our teacher because there was nothing in his file to confirm that he should be so blind, and Mr. Gray wasn't buying that excuse, mister, so don't even try it, and sometimes when Randy Creamer was being chastised this way I would laugh very hard at him. No one liked him, least of all me. I was his only friend, and to be his friend would mean I'd have no others here.

All the great ones are outcasts sooner or later, so I accepted that, but I often found myself at the edge of the school grounds with him; he was a gossip who had particularly bad things to say about anyone who got up the nerve to have a moment's fun in our presence. We stood apart, well above that kind of thing; we condescended to those who never noticed us—everyone. His appreciation of every other child on that schoolyard was dreadful and fouled with longing. He knew who was strong and who was weak, and, as if I couldn't see it for myself, he knew who was cute. He graded them in all things and for all purposes, and no one but me I suppose was quite up to his standards; he measured these people who so rarely glanced our way in very fine increments, and he shared with me his hushed appraisals, and I never drew a truly fresh breath of air in his presence. I was beginning to adopt the general opinion: We were unwholesome, he and I. It no longer mattered to me that he could swim so well. That season was over.

Something had happened involving his mother and his mother's Volkswagen and the bank, and so as late as October he was still without his glasses. One day I could no longer stand to hear how we'd go riding bikes when he had them, how maybe I'd let him try my bb gun again, how we'd take his black compass out into the big parking lot and really get our exact, true bearings. I had come to believe that Randy Creamer was a bit blissful in the cocoon of his bad eyesight, and it made me feel unkind. I told him I could already find magnetic north, and that was enough for me. I told him the price of bbs had soared, that I wasn't shooting much these days. I said these things and felt I'd been insufficiently hard, so I said, When you get those, when you finally get those, you better strap 'em to your head. You better get yourself a real strong strap, a springy one, and just strap that thing on. Tight. Because I never want to hear another word. I couldn't stand it if you lost another pair. Could you?

Though I'd fallen well short of how mean I hoped to be, I had hurt his feelings. He confessed himself on account of it and told me he hadn't lost the others, that he had given them to a kid named Clyde Fuhr. A strap wouldn't have made any difference.

Why?

Because they didn't fall off or anything, I just. . .

No. Why'd you give him your glasses?

He said he'd pound me if I didn't.

Why'd he want to do that? I asked, though I thought I might know.

Because he could, that's why.

Yeah? So, what then?

What do you mean?

You gave him the glasses, then what? You tell somebody?

And get really pounded? No. He lifts concrete and stuff. I am not out of my mind.

So he's had those all this time?

I guess. He couldn't wear. . . . I doubt he could sell 'em.

So you handed your glasses to him? You just handed 'em right over?

You would, too, if you ever saw him. You'd give him your lunch card, your . . . shoes. Whatever he asked you for, you'd give him.

I don't think so.

He's the toughest kid in town. By far.

So what? Why haven't I heard about him?

Ask anybody. He's finally up in junior high now, but you ask anybody who was at this school last year. He's got his own gang. He broke a kid's finger, and the kid wouldn't even tell on him for that, and then the poor kid had to transfer because he was so scared all the time. That was Steven, poor old Steven Idling. I guess there's this place where Fuhr goes and plays pinball for hours and hours, 'cause he's using everybody else's money. He steals cigarettes, throws rocks at you, everything. I'm glad he's gone.

But he's not. You'll be in junior high next year, and so will he.

That's next year.

He's got your glasses? Your mom's trying to save a couple, a few . . . and all this time he's got your glasses?

I don't know if he still does. He might, I mean, for all I know. I shouldn't have brought it up, I guess. I needed a new prescription. It was no big deal. When he took those. They're no good. I was pretty ugly in those frames, too. God, if I'd known you'd get so excited—Relax your slacks, all right? I didn't even mean to bring this up.

I was new to outrage and found it exhilarating. I knew where Clyde Fuhr lived, I thought, if he happened to be the son of *Ledger* subscriber Harold Fuhr of 12½ 6th Street East.

Let's go get those back.

Who?

You and me.

When?

Right after school.

Yeah, but I already told you, that prescription, that's no good anymore. Anyway. So you don't need to get carried away.

They're yours, aren't they?

So?

They're yours. We go get 'em back.

You think he would? Give those back now? By now he's probably tired of 'em, wouldn't you think?

He gives, or we take—I don't care how it goes. We get 'em.

Yeah. Right. Dream on. You haven't seen this kid. He's a teenager. You know Horst Shelby? Well, he's about twice as big as Horst Shelby. And way tougher.

To see for myself I rode over to Harold Fuhr's tidy bungalow later that day; it lay on the South Side, crouched in banked rhododendrons, and I waited to see if he might have a son. I concealed myself in tall weeds, commando or outlaw style, and neither the Fuhrs, nor the Gestapo, nor anyone from the Pinkerton Agency detected me during my long surveillance, and eventually a red-headed kid—I'd been told to look for red

hair, a certain prominent mole—came efficiently out of his
people's house, and he pulled awake a 2-horse Briggs and Strat-
ton motor under a little tote goat, and he rode off on it. I had
already been very taken by this tiny motorcycle, just watching
it lean against the fence, now this must be Clyde Fuhr upon
it, stout and stylish. I felt somewhat abandoned as he zipped
around the corner.

So now it was just a matter, I believed, of arranging the
interview.

On the off chance that the Fuhrs didn't know yet that their
son was bad, I decided not to confront him near his residence.
Also, if I took a whipping there, it would be a long way home
from his house to mine. Our school let out fifteen minutes
before the junior high, and the junior high was fairly in the
middle of town, and so the junior high, I told Randy Creamer,
was where we would catch up to him. Randy Creamer thought
this was a bad idea, but he was unlikely to approve any location
for it; he was only going along with the operation to prevent
me from telling his mother what had happened with his glasses.
This way, I said, he could tell her he'd found them. So he'd better
figure on coming along with me, coming even if he had a headache at the time. For one thing, I needed to make absolutely sure
I had the right guy, didn't I? Before I started accusing him of
something? And for another thing, I said, You want to be looking him right in the eye when you get those glasses back.

Like he'd have 'em on him. That couldn't even happen. He
probably doesn't have 'em at all. Anymore. Anywhere. After all
this time? Those things are gone.

Later, after school, I was the non-commissioned officer
charged with marching my reluctant recruit over to the junior
high, and along the way I saw why the armies of yore had so
often resorted to the lash to boost morale. Randy Creamer
dragged and bitched and pitched Jeremiads every step of the

way; still, we arrived right at the bell, in time to wait by the bicycle racks as the building emptied. I thought I had lately grown accustomed to be out of place, but here they hated us openly, loudly; I was hearing names I'd never heard before. We were told to perform anatomical miracles, told to leave, and we'd already endured much ugliness before Clyde Fuhr finally came along with his retinue, a parade of swirling jackals.

That's him?

Randy Creamer said nothing, and his nod was small and ambiguous.

Is that him?

Yuhb, he said, as if he could retract it halfway up his throat.

One of our tormentors seemed to understand what we were about, and he called out, lickspittle fashion, Hey, Fuhr, there's some little kids here to see you. You know these kids?

Clyde Fuhr approached, trailing his capering pals in a vee formation. He swelled as he came, becoming both thicker and denser. Except for his boy's bad haircut and his pimples, he was a man. The mole on his cheek, like everything about him, was variegated, red and orange, and very overripe.

You bring me something or . . . what? Do I even know you, kid? Who are you?

We came to get his glasses.

His what? Clyde Fuhr's cohort stepped up. They remained behind him, but just behind.

His glasses.

You want his mittens or any fuckin' thing else? While you're here? Didn't you know possession was nine fuckin' points of the law?

His glasses, I said. You've got 'em. They're his.

Kid, he said, horrified. There was laughter around us, much like your studio audience might produce.

Forget it, said Randy Creamer, already in tears, a bad leak in my sinking ship. We're going, he said. We're leaving, okay?

No, I said. Not yet. What about those glasses? This was the funniest thing I had ever said; I was the new delight of the junior high, soon to be harmed or humiliated for their viewing pleasure.

Glasses? Oh, those. I think I put those in my terrarium. You know what a terrarium is, fuckwad?

It's not where his glasses go. You better get his glasses for him.

Now they were outraged, everyone but Clyde himself, who remained amused. You want 'em? Fight me for 'em?

That does not make sense.

Vermin catcalls; more awful names, all for me.

You wanna fight me for 'em? Or not?

All right.

Wait, said Randy Creamer. Wait. What are the rules? You guys have to decide on some rules.

We were aghast, Clyde Fuhr and I. I'd always supposed the rules were known to everyone.

But there were a few formalities. We couldn't fight just then because of his already extensive history of fighting at this school. They'd send him somewhere down south if he got caught one more time. One of his lieutenants, a blond with a cowlick proud on his misshapen head, informed me of all this and asked if I wanted to do it on a Saturday.

Saturday?

Not this Saturday, but the one after next. Did I know the place called Lonepine? That's where everybody goes. Your girl-friend there'll show you where it is, if you're not sure. So, you've got no excuses, fuck hole—toilet ring.

That's . . . nine days from now? We counted on our fingers. Ten days from now? Yes, said the booking agent. Eleven o'clock. Don't tell anybody, especially not your parents. Just show up. Eleven: Got it?

Who are you? I said to this second fiddle. His face was a

blunt wedge. You piece of shit. Operating under the assumption that to seal one's fate was the noblest thing, I told Clyde Fuhr, You just bring those glasses. I'll be there. You be there, too, and you bring 'em. They don't belong to you.

I was not accustomed to fistfight by appointment. All my previous combats had been of the brief, eruptive sort, and most of those with Curtis who couldn't afford to hurt me very much. Though I knew I could use the ten days to train, I might easily have done without the waiting. Now that I needed him, Randy Creamer proved useless; I took my catcher's mitt to his house for him to catch some punches while his mom was at work, and it was ow, ow, ow, and that was the end of training camp as far as he was concerned. So I ran and I did pushups a couple dozen at a time, more and more sets as the days ran down. I did hundreds of pushups, and threw thousands of punches into the air.

I wanted to get my stance down and to perfect at least two essential punches, a nice jab and a hook. Hook to the head, hook to the kidneys, I liked that combination very much. These, I thought, should be enough weapons for a guy with right on his side. Still, I did need to refine my execution, and to that end I stood before the bathroom mirror stripped to the waist, and I liked what I saw, was sure that Clyde Fuhr had never dealt with anything like me before. My hands, flew righteously before me and seemed to batter my own highly impressed face; this kid was a fighter, me, and I threw and I threw until I smelled very strong, and all my foes had come to regret their thoughtless words and deeds, I threw from all angles, with both hands, threw until I threw that punch that met the mirror, which splintered. I suppose I yelped.

My name drifted up the stairs, posed as a question.

Repairs were impossible, that much was instantly plain, and so I called back, It was an accident, Mom. But I'm okay. It's all right. I'm okay. I'll pay for everything.

My name again, a sharper question.

I was pleased with my progress. I had made mincemeat of that mirror with only incidental damage to my fist, and I took this to mean I was ready.

Sometimes when my mother was angry with me, and perhaps she didn't know quite why she was angry or just how angry she should be, she would go down to the bowling alley, and she could bowl for free if it wasn't league night, and if it was league she'd just drink beer. She went to the bowling alley after I broke the mirror. I was never happy when she was displeased with me, and I certainly hadn't meant to drive her out, but I did exploit her absence.

I wanted a black tee shirt in the worst way and had wanted one for a long time. No garment has ever appealed to me so eloquently, and I particularly wanted one for the fight. Since there were none to be found in my town's stores, and I'd made it my business to know, I bought one of the usual, white ones, a plain old undershirt, and I bought a box of black dye, Midnight more precisely, and that afternoon after Mom had only just got my promise not to destroy the place, and after she'd left in her taxi, I went to work.

I made a stew of it, the shirt and the dye, and I used less water than the instructions on the package called for, thinking to make my color even denser this way. It percolated, and to my nose smelled of darkness coming on. I made a peanut butter sandwich, watched the evening news, and by then my shirt was the color of deep space. I ladled it out of my dye vat, and took it dripping out to the clothesline. Instructions called for a hot dryer, but I had instead a hot day that I hoped would suffice. Randy Creamer came out and watched me hang it.

Had to have it. This is what I'm wearing tomorrow. Cool, huh? Tomorrow?

You know that . . . Lonepine? That place you showed me?

Your glasses? That asshole?

Oh. Really? You're actually doing that?

I said I was.

I wouldn't, he said.

You didn't know I meant that? That I was going?

Well . . . I already told you. About the prescription. So I can't really see why.

You're going with me, too.

Oh, no. I never said I, I can't fight. At all.

You don't have to, you just have to come.

What?

Well, you have to watch at least. I want you to look into his eyes.

That again. I've seen 'em already, and believe me, they're nothing to. . . . Oh, oh—uh oh.

Smoke billowed out the back door of our apartment, smoke from my mother's kitchen. I'd left the element on under her best cook pan and dyed its bottom black, and no cure for it but to throw the pan away. The apartment smelled as if someone had been welding in it. I threw the doors open, front and back, and ran through, fanning with a towel. The stench was no longer visible, at least, by the time Mom came home from the bar.

When she came home I explained the sequence of events, with discretion, and she, without it, explained that I had finally, completely smashed her old Irish heart. She was a little tipsy, and that should have meant some treat for me, a bread pudding, but instead her chin dropped and she told me I just didn't care, I was thoughtless and dangerous, and I was to go to my room and stay in it, except to deliver papers or to go to school. Until otherwise advised, I was to stay in that God-damned-room. She just couldn't trust me at all, could she? My father was working two jobs so I could break everything faster than. . . ?

She ran out of steam and sent me upstairs where the reek of my disaster was still particularly concentrated. This was late in the day, the day before my fight.

I could see it from my window, hanging in a breeze that would have been the last breath of Indian Summer and that I called sirocco, I could almost watch it dry. I was going to be striking in that shirt. Night fell and all the heat went out of the air outside, and though the room stayed hot, I smelled Fall through the open windows, coppery, crisp, nostalgic, and I couldn't sleep and thought I heard the moths colliding under the street lamp fifty yards off. Wheeling bats. I was certain I heard an owl. Very late that night I could still make out my shirt, my standard hanging on the line, a deeper darkness down there in the general dark. Curtis stared up at me, long since sound asleep.

I slept some myself, but not for long, and not too consequentially. It was a groggy morning for making plans, and I'd made myself very stiff and sore with training. I got up and did the paper route, and when I was done there were still hours left until the fight; I couldn't go home in the meantime and run the risk that I wouldn't be able to slip out again as necessary. That apartment was a hard place to slip away from unseen. So I didn't go home, I rode around; I went to the hobby store and looked at model airplanes, went to the library and reread the racy parts of *1984*. I went by a bank from time to time to check its big brass clock, and as the day advanced I finally noticed that I was dying myself, that the black was bleeding from my formerly superb tee shirt and the sweaty undersides of my arms looked necrotic. There were powerful sprinklers at the gravel pit and I visited these to try and rinse, but it seemed that I'd permanently printed an image like a thunderhead on my torso, and while I liked this pretty well, I was sure my mother wouldn't, and I seemed to be committing some new offense every several hours now. It was nearly eleven.

The designated place was an empty lot. Nothing there, certainly no tree, and while I waited I wondered if Randy Creamer had, by mistake or by design, pointed out the wrong battlefield. It wouldn't be the first time in history. I could say I went to the wrong place, but they'd never buy it. They'd say I chickened out, so I worried. Lonepine? It was an empty lot between two sheet metal warehouses, and there was nothing so distinctive about it that it would be the kind of place to bear a name, and where, if anywhere, was I? This was Lonepine, Randy Creamer had said, but I was having my doubts, and they were not entirely unpleasant ones.

I waited and I waited because I had no watch, and at last Clyde Fuhr came weaving down the street on his tote goat amid the bicycles of his friends, also weaving. I was left with waiting, watching, and wanting to be included in their good time. They reached the lot and swarmed across it. Clyde Fuhr shocked himself when he flipped the wire off the spark plug to kill his motor, and he said, shit, and announced that now he was in a bad mood.

The others formed a semicircle behind me. They were animated clothes to me, rattling bicycles, sounds from behind, shapes in the corner of my eye—and that was all they'd ever be to anyone, and I hated them in direct proportion to how much they hated me, which was odd as we'd only just met. I was not sure whom to watch or what to do or when to take up my stance, so I looked to my opponent for the etiquette of the thing, and he hit me on the jaw. I got up and squared before him, my left making tiny, threatening circles.

Not bad.

He swung and missed. He swung and missed. He hit me again, up on the temple to sound a ringing in that ear. I did not go down. I was tasting blood but not teeth. The pain, so far, was tolerable. I flashed my practiced jab and felt my knuckles nick him.

Are you bleeding, Clyde? I heard from behind, one of the seven sisters inquiring, That little fucker didn't. . . .

No, he said. There was blood on his lips. His truth was the truth they had to accept, and Clyde Fuhr said, No. And he said, I do, I think I really do like this kid.

Someone asked, a dullard to my left, What is fuckin' wrong with you? You look like an asswipe.

He'd noticed my mottled skin, and I thought to explain it, but this was not the moment. Clyde Fuhr drove straight into my nose. I didn't see it coming, and then I couldn't see at all, and I was terrified that my tears would be misconstrued. I threw big and missed.

I *like* this kid.

I liked him, too, as a more direct kind of person than so many. You knew where you stood with him. I weaved in and jabbed him again. He knocked me down with just a lazy blow to the shoulder. I hit him as I was getting back up. Now we would respect each other, I thought, and now we would be friends, and perhaps we would ride off together, Clyde Fuhr and I, and none of these others, his squealing buddies, my Randy Creamer, none of them could follow. No, from now on it would be Clyde and me, tough and disdainful of the others. I hit him again. He put me back down. The effects were adding up, and I was ready now to make friends, but first I just had to ask,

Did you bring those glasses?

I forgot, he told me. Ever think you might've made a bad mistake?

Someone was asking him if he was all right. Is that hurting your hand, Clyde?

These others wanted in.

I got up. You were supposed to bring those.

What if I did? Have 'em? They're mine. He knocked me

down again. He was finding my face with every punch and I had somehow twisted my ankle.

I was a mouth breather now, nose gurgling along. I did not bother to rise before announcing, as if I hadn't made it clear, I came for those glasses. I want 'em.

I was kicked from behind and Clyde Fuhr told his attendant, Lay off. Didn't I tell you I like this kid?

Here, I thought, was where we would become friends and in our mutual respect we'd render all these others obsolete, and together we would. . . . I was out of good ideas, out of alternate images from the arthouse of my mind, and so I sat where I sat. On the ground.

I saw myself through their slitted, happy eyes, and I saw I'd done nothing to amend their stupidity, to ennoble them by my example. They were winning. I would grow tired, and then fearful, and then, eventually, I would listen to Randy Creamer's craven whisper inside me, and I'd give up. I wasn't getting those glasses. I wasn't going to give as good as I got, and sooner or later I'd have to quit. But it wouldn't be in any timely way.

A boy, in his innocence, is not yet accustomed to be both frightened and bored. This had already gone on too long.

Had enough little buddy? You might as well stay down. You did pretty good.

Instead, I stood. The last thing I wanted was their advice.

THE CATERWAUL

His was the gray Toyota in the faculty parking lot; its seat, which had molded to his hams, embraced him as he sat in it, and the interior smelled much like a brand new car, but this was only the afterwhiff of drycleaning. As band director of Belle Prairie High School, Vance Howe had no tests to grade, no papers to correct or lessons to devise, and so, as usual, he was leaving the lot well before the other teachers. In this, at least, he considered himself a success. Having borne another Thursday, he let a peppermint disc melt under his tongue—never bite, never crush it, for the whole sticky reward might only be had with good discipline. Later, as he was called upon to recount this afternoon again and again, even his most sympathetic listeners would find weird the exactitude with which Vance recalled turning up Towne Street at three forty-six; "I'm quite the creature of habit," he would explain, and truly, he had at that point come to live as if driven by a metronome.

He turned up Towne Street and listened for his car's first mortal complaint—a ping had lately developed in the lifters; slowly he brought his engine up to twenty-two hundred revolutions per minute, a labored, A-flat hum. Though he was a frugal man and a man who believed in exercise, Vance never considered making this commute by foot, for his route was through a neighborhood recently thrown up along the margins of the freeway; there were no sidewalks here, none but a few saplings for trees, too slight to throw any shade or even to be distinguished yet by species. There were motorcycles and faded fiberglass boats, driveways scattered with tools and spotted with oil, small lawns littered with primary colors. Everywhere toys—but no one, neither the young nor the old, was to be seen at play in

this part of town. The east side of Belle Prairie was something
to be got through, even if you lived there, and like his unknown
neighbors Vance considered the neighborhood an annoyance to
be endured on the way to and from the snug of his home.

And he'd been nearly there. Vance would come to measure
his bad luck by the fact that he'd been just three blocks from
his door that day when he happened on Porter Hulquist. Porter, who was instantly recognizable even hunched on the curb
with his arms wrapped round his shins and his face pressed
to his knees; those chopstick legs, black denim, a black tee,
the shock of hair he greased into a blue coxcomb. Vance knew
better than to blunder into the swamps of his students' private
lives, and this Porter Hulquist was particularly apt to revel in
his troubles, to recite them given the least opportunity, but the
boy had set himself out along a long empty stretch of curbing
so that his misery might be impossible to ignore. His shoulders
were heaving.

Don't stop. What to do here but chastise and wheedle?

But young Mr. Hulquist, with all his discontents, was will-
ing to play the French horn and unique in his capacity to play it
almost in tune; his instrument was the only silken element in the
caterwaul of Vance Howe's current band, and Vance felt he owed
the boy something on that account. He braked at last and rolled
his passenger's side window half open, as far as it would go.

"Porter? Hey, Porter, is anything? Is something? Where were
you today? You know, we've got exactly three rehearsals left
until . . . Porter?"

Porter Hulquist's face, when he finally looked up, was swollen with crying and with something else. A precise line of fresh
injury ran from a corner of his mouth down to his jaw.

"Oh," said Vance. He did not want to imply any curiosity at
all, but it had to be asked— "Are you all right?"

"What do you care? What's it to you?"

"Well, if you're okay, then. But you shouldn't be missing school, unless, ordinarily you shouldn't— if you can help it. You need to be there."

"Why? So everybody can shit on me all day?" The boy's skin was drawn taught to his meager countenance except where a fold of it hung slack to his throat. His eyes were green, with something of perception in them, but these were ruined at the moment, and vainly searching.

"I didn't know you lived around here. And—language—okay?"

"Live?" said the boy.

"Do you need a ride? I could give you one if you needed. Are you sure you're all right?"

"What do you think?"

"Get in. Come on, get in. Do you live somewhere near?"

The boy came to the car affecting or exaggerating a limp. He grasped but did not operate the latch. He leaned down to look in, his upper lip glistening with clear snot and curved so as to suggest he considered this the opening of a negotiation. "You don't even know where I live?"

Why would I? thought Vance as he said, "No, but if you'll tell me, we can, come on, hop in. It's no trouble. Really." He calculated his patience to be good for one more exchange, and then he could in good conscience drive on.

But Porter got in the car. "I can't go home right now," he said, "that's for sure."

"Do you think you might need to be looked at? Some medical help? Would you like to try the emergency room?"

"No insurance," said the boy.

"They'll treat you, if you need it; I believe they have to."

"And send my dad the bill? Huh-uh. No fuckin' thanks."

"Porter—language, I mean it. Come on, now."

"Big deal. That's even how my mom talks, and if you heard the way my. . . . Could I go to your house? Not for long. Just for a little while? Please."

"Are you in trouble?"

"What do you mean, trouble?" challenged the boy.

"I don't know," said Vance. "I don't know. But, the thing is,
I just don't have any supplies to speak of at my house—those
ointments or salve or anything; I rarely get hurt myself. Looks
like you could use some, probably some antibiotics? What is
that, a scratch? There on your. . . . What happened, anyway?"

He'd assumed the boy had been set upon by healthier youths.
It wasn't hard to imagine. Sniveling—a word Vance hadn't
thought of in years.

"If you don't want to," said Porter, "okay. If you don't want
to help me."

Vance wanted his nap, the customary torpor of his day
rounding into his empty evening. "No," he said. "No, that's, uh,
maybe you could lay down for a bit. Would that help?"

"You don't care about me. Nobody does."

"Maybe if you stretch out on my couch for a while you'd feel
better. Would you like to lie down?"

The boy winced. "Ooh," he said, his head turning side to side,
testing a limit. "Agh. Just it, it wouldn't have to be very long. I
can't go home, that's all. I shouldn't go home for a while."

A husband once, briefly, and never a father, Vance Howe
drove with his eyes locked on the road, his hands at ten and
two on the wheel. He was definitely not the kind to intervene.
He had kept one irreplaceable cat for fourteen years, but since
Andy's passing Vance had been quite alone in the prefab house
he'd bought on orders from his accountant, for tax purposes.
The house itself had become his only family, his sole companion, and he was unsettled lest this stranger look upon it with
the slightest disapproval. It was clad in gray
vinyl that rattled when the wind blew from a certain direction.
At their approach, a motion sensor aimed lights onto the

daylit driveway.

"I don't do much, oh, exterior stuff. Maintenance, you know; I keep the lawn mowed, and that's about it. I keep thinking about a fence, but—come on in."

The boy advanced several steps into the living room and stood at its center with his arms slack at his sides. "Man," he said, "this is, so it's just you, huh? No wife or kids?"

Vance would not have thought it so obvious. "Dyed-in-the-wool bachelor," he said. "You get to a certain point and, well, who'd put up with you? You're so set in your ways after a while, who'd have you?"

The boy moved to the photographs on the knickknack shelf.

"My folks," said Vance. "Their wedding picture, and the other is from when they went to Hawaii. Their thirtieth, I think that was. All those shells are shells they brought back for me. Dust collectors. And that, that was my cat. That was Andy."

"Geeze," said Porter Hulquist. He fingered the mute keys of Vance's piano. "How do you keep from going crazy?"

"How do I? Are you feeling better, Porter? Would you like to go home now?"

"Why?"

"You seem like you're feeling better."

"Do I?"

"I thought. What happened, anyway?"

"Nothing." Porter Hulquist tried the piano stool and continued to molest the piano. "Can you turn this thing on so I can hear myself? I'd like to try this out."

"There's a short in it," Vance lied. "It doesn't play anymore. I thought you were going to rest. Wasn't that the plan here?"

"You got a pop or something?"

"No," said Vance.

"Any booze?"

"What?"

"I've got pain," the boy calculated.

"I'm sure you do." Vance had only just noticed a lavender medallion of fresh bruise on the boy's temple. "What we should probably do is take you to the hospital and have you checked out."

"Get me out of your hair, huh?"

"I have no training," said Vance. "In medicine."

"You know that Cindy? She's in choir?"

"Cindy Bascomb?"

"You know about her?"

"I know she tries very hard." And Vance knew her to be utterly tone-deaf.

"Yeah. What else?"

"That's all I care about," said Vance.

"She's pregnant."

"I'm not concerned with that. That's not my area at all."

"Are these dumbbells yours? What are you, a chubby little weight lifter?"

"Look," said Vance, "what do you want? Or need?"

"What do you think?"

"I don't know," said Vance. "But let's keep on the subject here."

"What's the subject?"

"I haven't done anything to you, Porter. If someone has, then I'm sorry. If there's something I can do, some way I can help, then fine. If not, I know you're hurting, but I have to say I don't care much for your attitude." Then, because he was somehow uncertain of it, Vance said again, "I haven't done anything to you."

Porter Hulquist began to cry.

"Ah, Porter. Come on."

"What?"

"This isn't getting us anywhere."

"You don't even have a pop I could have?"

"I don't drink pop. You want water?"

The boy stared past Vance into an obnoxious mystery and then, without a moment's warning or preparation, hit himself with the heel of his right hand so that his upper lip burst, and Vance Howe's first thought was of an embouchure ruined. As Porter Hulquist's fist remained cocked at his side Vance thought it best to gather him into a bear hug.

"What the hell, Porter?"

"Are you supposed to be swearing? Language, Mr. Howe."

"Stop it. Will you just stop it now?"

"Why? It feels good."

"Stop it. This is completely, I'm taking you. . . ."

"Where?"

"If I let you go, will you stop?" Vance let go his grip and stepped back and looked into the triumphant smear of the boy's face. He could remember nothing like this having been mentioned at the school of education. "Okay," he said. "That'll be enough. All right? All right, now?"

"Ow," said Porter Hulquist. "Fuck."

"See? It wasn't a good idea, was it? Do we need to talk? Is there someone I should call? Can you tell me what this is about?"

"You wouldn't understand."

"Maybe not. Probably not, but there's no reason, no reason at all, to hurt yourself. Is it because you're the, uh, are you the father?"

"The what?"

"Of Cindy's baby?"

The boy created a horrible grin. "You think she'd even let me touch her? Or anyone would? Man. Nice try."

"I'm just trying to understand."

"You don't care," said Porter Hulquist.

"All right," said Vance, "let's just say I don't."

"You don't care."

"You're wearing me out, Porter. What am I supposed to say? What am I supposed to do?"

"No one cares."

"You may be right about that. It's a hard thing to face, but for all I know, you're right."

"Fuck you," said Porter Hulquist, "you old. . . ."

"Say it. Go ahead." Vance expected he'd hear something about his weight, his hairline, his insufficient kindness, but the boy only turned petulant and rotated his shoulders and let his arms swing out at his sides like a toddler's, and he could only manage another, "Fuck you," with droplets for emphasis and a string of pink spittle. His face contracted in some new way, and then he was gone, the air vaguely spicy and the door standing open behind him. Vance did not move immediately to close it but looked for a long while out upon his own framed section of an empty sky.

• • •

His lawyer's secretary wore a light sweater even in high summer. From the beginning she had loathed him. "Did you see, Vance? We got the new *Field and Stream*. We got the new *Smithsonian*." But Marilyn couldn't quite bring herself to look at him, could she? "There's instant coffee or tea if you like." Her enameled fingers walked the tops of some files, and her eyes never left them as she spoke to him. "He shouldn't be long, and—and I hope I'm not getting carried away and saying too much, but I think it might be something good today. Finally. For once. He's in a will conference that's gone a little over, but he shouldn't be too long now."

Vance sank into the lawyer's low sofa. From a wall dedicated to Grant Hannon's many moods and accomplishments the lawyer clowned down at him; from under a fisherman's hat with its tiny hooks and hand-tied flies Hannon mugged fake chagrin, his face between two fish, one held by a woman—no doubt his wife—the other by a girl—no doubt his daughter. Vance did not find the lawyer's showy joy persuasive, no more than he trusted the man's advice. Vance in his heart of hearts could only believe that he'd been summoned to hear another pitch in favor of accepting a plea bargain before it was too late; he thought he'd come to hear once again at the eleventh hour how he wouldn't have to admit to doing very much at all. Barely criminal. If he just wanted to get this over. He would hear once more how seriously he must weigh the risk, in light of the evidence, the accusations made, the harrowing severity of the charges. Vance expected to be asked again if he had really considered what a trial this trial must be for him, and was he prepared for that much ugliness?

This morning, though, lawyer Hannon had taken a new tack and a new tone—brotherly— and he'd called very early. "Come in," he'd said. "No, I mean it. As soon as you can. You need to hear this in person, but believe me, this is something you'll like. A lot. It's real good, so come on in, and this visit's on me, buddy; there'll be no charge for today."

Vance Howe was not about to be gulled again, and he had never believed in things for free, but the weight of all this skepticism hadn't slowed him a step, had it, from coming to hear even a lawyer's idea of good news? On the principle of take-what-you-can-get, he'd come right along to find himself waiting once more in Grant Hannon's outer office. His body was electric and misbehaving, and Vance had only just started to ask, "Would I have time to use the. . . ?", when out came Hannon with his previous client, a whippet of a woman, a ringleted blond who shook her finger.

"And *only* the pound. Understood? They get everything. I want Rick so completely written out, it'll be like I never knew he existed." The woman was the youngest and by all odds the healthiest person in the office. "I want the Humane Society to get it all, okay? Absolutely all of it." She studied Hannon as Hannon walked her to the door, his head precisely cocked to convey his constant understanding of, and sympathy for, her problem, and when he'd ushered her out he turned—large, balletic, beaming, and he seemed to want to shake Vance's hand, but Vance was too deep in the davenport to readily rise for him.

"We did it," said Hannon.

"We?"

"It's over," said the lawyer.

"What is? The—everything?"

"The ambulance was called to the Hulquist house a couple nights ago. This time it was for Mrs. Hulquist. She had those same marks on her mouth—they're ligature contusions, apparently very distinctive. Looks like old Pete uses a cord, like a bridle he uses it on them. Mrs. Hulquist still won't say anything against him, and neither will Porter, though they don't think Porter saw anything. This time. No wonder the kid's such a mess. Anyway, our prosecutor looks at this for about two seconds before he decides to dismiss all charges against you. I just found out this morning."

"Now do you believe me?"

"That's not necessarily my job, Vance. But, yes, I sure do."

Marilyn stood near, one hand nesting in the other, trying hard to look delighted.

"So, what now?"

"It's over," said the lawyer.

"No it's not. It can't be. Can I sue them? Can I sue those people now? For slander? I told everyone they were lying. I told everyone. Didn't I?"

"Yes. Yes you did. But they were all lying—there were a lot of them lying. The whole family. As I've been telling you, that would have been quite a problem. They were so damn consistent, too. They'd worked it out in some detail."

"It was three drops of blood on my tie. That was it, except for . . . those people. That was slander. That had to be. Can you sue them for me? I mean, those detectives, those lab types took a sample of my hair; they took my saliva, for Pete's sake. I'm thrown in jail, and they're taking pieces of me to some laboratory. All because of those people."

"Sure, we could sue, and I'm quite sure you'd prevail, probably win a judgment worth a buck fifty in attachable assets. Nothing from nothing leaves nothing, though, that's the math of it."

"It's the idea," said Vance.

"Sure, it's the principle. If you can afford it. Better all around to let this go, Vance. You'll get back to your life a lot sooner if you do."

"Let it go," said Marilyn, soothingly, as if the idea had been hers in the first place.

Vance thought that he should rise now, struggle up out of the couch, and jig his way to poor old Marilyn and demand an embrace just when she couldn't gracefully resist. He could seize her and jape if he wanted; but he was too shy, wasn't he? He could never embarrass someone for the fun of it, for fun was not his gift. "I guess you'll prepare me a final bill, then?"

"Well, sure," said Hannon. "We'll have that to you real soon, but good God, man—Congratulations. You must be so relieved right now. Enjoy. They really did put you through it, though, didn't they? "

Marilyn shook her head in solemn wonder. "Those Hulquists," she said.

• • •

Rather than renew his contract, the school board had abolished Belle Prairie's band program altogether, so Vance Howe sold his house at a disastrous discount and moved one state north where he took work in the city with University Security. He walked foot patrol in the Psychology and Liberal Arts buildings between ten in the evening and six in the morning, six nights a week, and his new employer was content with him so long as he managed not to lose his flashlight. When Vance accepted the incessant echo of his own passage through the halls, and when he'd trained his feet and legs to bear without much complaint the hard miles on polished cement, he was at last comfortable in his vocation. Night after night and for shifts on end he might never see another soul or hear any voice but his own rolling baritone. *Alas, my love, you do me wrong, to cast me off so discourteously.* At work, he was his own hit parade, free to mumble as he liked, or shout if he wanted, and he walked his beat and pursued the topics of bad luck, poor justice, and lackluster vindication until he was bored with them, until tedium was a mudplaster on his wounds.

Home was another matter. In suite nineteen of the Northern Lights Apartments he could only assume that every sound he made could be heard by his every neighbor, for the walls were an afterthought around them, and he could sometimes hear his fellow tenants even to their most innocent sighing. A dozen creatures were constantly to be heard above, below, and to either side of him, a brimming crowd that did not care if he was a night worker or that their lives were too ghastly and wrong to be shared or overheard. Vance had listened hard for a while, amazed and a little elevated by the depravity of those around him, but in a week he was surfeit and sick of it. *Didn't I tell you, and tell you, and tell you? I told you you were getting on my nerves.* He heard many odd notions of music here, many circular and belligerent dialogues. Zinc steam registers sat cold along the walls; zinc ceilings soared above a space impossible to heat; his building breathed its hundred years of grain and grind and sweat, its memories of colognes and disinfectant, generations of disinfectants, and cigars and cigarettes and strong urine or boiled kraut, baked potato, burnt cheese, take-out Chinese. New vomit was often in the hallway.

At the Northern Lights he wore his headphones as much as he could; he went about on cat's feet and never uttered so much as an opinion to himself. Such constraint and such vivid stench made sweet the thought of the day when he would have saved enough to afford quieter, more private housing in the metro area. Vance wanted trouble-free plumbing and reliably hot showers, with water pressure; he wanted, and after all he'd been through he felt that he deserved, a condo in a trim new cul-de-sac.

But one Monday morning, the day of his night off, he stood at his stove with a blanket around his shoulders, making cocoa, and just beyond his kitchen sink, there in the next room, his most intimate neighbors were calling each other Jimmy and Leerah, which could lead to viciousness. They were prone to fight in their kitchen, and Vance had been sitting a deathwatch over their marriage.

"Do you know how disappointed I am?" he heard Mrs. Blinkman wonder. "Fucking Jimmy. I mean, why would you even do something like that? Why would anybody do that? I am real, real disappointed. Man. By you."

"So?"

"Yeah. So. So what?"

They might go on like this for some time, or they might fall silent, but in no event would they exchange information or insight. They had none. Vance Howe had reluctantly become a fan of these aimless squalls, a breathtaking emptiness that made him feel, by comparison, complete.

"We were all so embarrassed, Jimmy. I've had it. I have had it with you."

"Ask me if I care."

"Do you care?"

"Ask me if I care," he said.

"What? What do you keep saying, you fucker?"

Because they were often stupefied, there were long silences in their fights; they wore through the will to wound, or more likely could think of nothing more to say, and then there were the silences, and these were for Vance the zest in the event: What were the Blinkmans doing there at the other side of his sink? Unheard. He sometimes took up his clarinet to announce his existence or to drown them out, in a punitive mood he might play his scales, but Vance had no thought of his instrument today. He waited, listening.

"What do you want me to do?" The young man finally asked his wife.

"Leave," said Leerah. "Get out of my sight."

"Okay."

"And maybe I'll leave with you," she said.

"Okay."

"But, what do you think? You think we should?"

"Whatever," said Mr. Blinkman.

"No, I mean, really—what do you think?"

"You know me," said the young husband. "You know what I think."

"Nothing?"

"More or less. Or less."

"What do you think about *this?*"

"If you want," he said. "Then, okay."

"If I want *what?*"

"Whatever," he said.

"Fucking Jimmy. Well, let's do it. Let's just go."

"Away, you mean?"

"Don't you want to?"

"It's like I always say—whatever."

They went out into the hall, and down it, and they fumbled for a moment at the door and were gone. Vance Howe hoped to hear no more of them. They were, according to the index card taped above their mail slot, Mr. and Mrs. James Blinkman. Written in dull pencil. In the three weeks that they'd been his neighbors, he'd seen them only once, when they were moving in. They had come up the street at him, suitcases in either hand, and he'd held the door for them. Not a word passed. They came on and flowed around him like escapees, the girl was a former farmgirl, and still big-boned, but with pox and pallor on her, and a quivering sense of purpose. She came a stride ahead of her man, who seemed accustomed to follow and was short, and badly dressed for any weather.

Vance Howe thought they'd be thieves, he was almost certain of it. From that very first glimpse of them, he had wished them gone, and he tired very quickly of checking his door frame when he came home from work, of forever taking his miserable inventory to be sure they hadn't gotten in.

Night was day, and day was night in the schedule Vance was still trying to establish for himself; he'd not yet taught his body when it might conveniently sleep. When his intended bedtime came at noon, he ignored it, and he steeped successive pots of Mrs. Respbert's Raspberry Bang. He made his apartment and its contents immaculate, wrote a long, incoherent chapter in his virgin journal, and finally he gave over and paced his apartment. Their absence was exhilarating. What a thorn in his side they'd been, and when at midnight the Blinkmans had not returned, Vance was humming phrases from the *New World Symphony*.

He heard a flannel thumping then, faintly, and then a second time so that he was sure it was coming from the Blinkmans' apartment. Vance pleaded with his senses to let this be the wind flipping a shade. In the still of the night. *nung-nung-nung*

A triplet again, an uneven one, a rhythm that may have been Latin and was unquestionably human. Vance pressed his ear to the wall. A higher order animal, at least, had been left behind. *nung-nung-nung*

"Hello? This is. Hello? Is everything all right over there? I'm your next door. . . . Hello?"

nung-nung-nung

"Hello?"

The Blinkmans, at peace, had called each other "babe" or "baby," and they had also referred to their craving by code as 'the baby'. Or so he'd assumed. *nung-nung-nung* A thought shot through him. Vance had no telephone. What to report? The baby? A baby? A dog. A dog's intelligent tail, knocking a table leg. What? What? Why now? What didn't he know about the dangers of butting in? Vance was in the hall, his ear pressed to the door of seventeen. "Hello? Anyone? Hello?" He tried the door; it wasn't locked. It swung right open. Listen. Listen. Head across the threshold, he felt for the familiar light switch, found it, stopped—"Hello. . . ?"

Vance hit the light. There was an infant's car seat turned on its side on the floor of the apartment's central room, an infant strapped in it, reeking. Litter on a littered floor, the child was tipped away from him so that he could not see its face, but Vance saw how it held an empty bottle by its rubber nipple, and how, *nung-nung-nung,* it beat the floor with it. Plastic on an oak floor. A room as ripe as rotten cabbage. What did Vance know of babies? He'd been an only child and then a bachelor, and he sensed he was already in the midst of a critical mistake; he went into the apartment and righted the car seat.

"Are you? Can you? No? Well, it's okay now." Calf's liver red, its face was awash with tears and swollen with the effort of wailing, but it made no sound at all. It sought to bang its bottle but could not reach the floor now that it was upright again. Vance took it out of harness, and, holding it at arm's length, he took the baby to the table where the Blinkmans had left a bale of plastic diapers. First, he must make it clean.

It was a blocky boy child, and he'd been long untended; there were layers of encrusted dung beneath the fresher stuff. Vance called him "Walter" after Walter Piston. The baby wiggled, mute, author of a long, unheard howl, and Vance took him into the bathroom and held him under a running shower; the child was inflamed where they'd left him so long in his filth. His fat legs pedaled in the water, and almost at once little Walter, for all his burning, his abandonment and now insatiable hunger, began to pedal and to silently grin, and it was only a moment's work for the baby to break and to capture Vance Howe's previously useless heart.

AND A CLOUD OF DUST

Hinch lies in a deep and narrow valley. Between the solstices the sun rarely touches its streets and ice can be a constant. The sawmill closed some years ago, but people continue to live here in company houses, the shanties they acquired for nearly nothing when Tyrone Timber went under. They call themselves Hinchies, and if they work, they work elsewhere. Hinch High School persists, home to declining enrollments and endeavor, but this year the Hellcats have produced an unbeaten squad. They have some football players at last, and one in particular, the Strizich kid, plays like an act of revenge. The town turns out to see him hit, to see him forbid the other team his half of the field, and he takes his half from the middle. The sons of Hinch feel dangerous and vindicated when Strizich is at work. It has been a splendid fall; the Hellcats will play for a divisional championship.

A junior this year, Strizich comes off both sides of the ball at two fifteen, and he comes like a fist. As the school brute he is entitled to the perky girlfriend who has spent two excruciating years surrendering her virginity and all the predictable details of her interior life to him. Wendy Bellweather is just one of several foregone conclusions to which he has been harnessed, and he inspires a fawning if recent admiration around his town, but he hopes that this is not yet the best life will offer, for he still lives in Hinch. His mother commutes thirty miles to keep the books for a truck stop, and his father only ever comes to mind when Strizich has eaten heavily of garlic and is sweating.

To transcend the gloom of the valley, Strizich has climbed the mountain rising out of his back yard hundreds of times, and he's built a pair of legs that he hopes will eventually carry

him to some equatorial village where no one knows the shack
of his boyhood. He has recently learned of coconut milk, and
he wants to string a hammock one day, somewhere within the
sound of surf, and recline and drink straight from the coconut.
He doesn't mention such notions where he lives, where talk of
the trade winds or of any gentle breeze would be in the poorest
taste. If he were not such a hitter, he would be an outcast here.

The championship is held at a neutral site halfway across
the state, and Strizich rides at the back of the bus with his co-
captain and friend, Van Knapp. The feeling elsewhere on the
bus is that these two do not deserve their gifts. They are friends
because circumstance has long conspired to lump them together.
Knapp is also the only son of a single mother, and Strizich envies
him for having already escaped Hinch; Rapid Van left long ago
to sail the undulant seas of his mind, and Knapp, to his credit,
remains one of the more unpopular boys in town. His talent has
kept him thus far out of institutions other than high school.

They are only minutes out of Hinch when the country
opens abundantly, the valleys widen and the mountains walk
back to give them some breathing room, and they are abroad in
a state golden under the affectionate sun of that season. They
are expected to ride in quiet contemplation of the game, but the
miles mount, and in the course of such a long trip their un-
governable silliness reminds them that they are still essentially
children. Strizich is in love with the countryside, his explosive
body, his will.

Knapp gropes the air before him, a sleepwalker with a
strangely triangular face. "Stand up," he says. "Stand up, sit
down, fight team, fight. Personally, I am flights of angels, and
we always win. Why? Because we *have* to. Check the paint."

"What do we win," Strizich asks just for fun, "when we win?"

"Gift certificates. Our eternal reward. I will get what I always
wanted, whatever that was. Won't you?"

"Don't get excited yet," says Strizich. "We're still two hundred miles away."

Coming out of Hinch, everywhere, everything looks prosperous, and it is hard to be so beset by envy. Forest and prairie, fruited fields of grain, none of it theirs. The Hellcats need no prompting to roll into the championship angry. The lawns of this middling city are still green, and even its pavement seems pristine compared to the poorly patched streets of Hinch. "Tear 'em up," says their driver as they depart the bus.

In a well-lit and clean locker room that does not smell of mold, Strizich wraps his broken knuckles in athletic tape, protection the officials won't make him remove. His fingers have become mottled like cheap sausage links because he frequently makes illegal use of his hands. This late in the season, everyone has some injury, and there is pleasure in binding up for battle. Old sweat and liniment, the scrape and click of cleats on concrete; Strizich is becoming that paradoxical thing, light and dense; he feels himself becoming a missile. They run out under the lights and into the visible vapor of their breathing, and captain Strizich leads the Hellcats through calisthenics counted out in loud, simple rhythms, a virile barking. The grass smells superior to any he has known; the lime that marks the field is iridescent tonight and there is a press box high above, silhouettes behind the glass. The Hellcats gather again in the locker room for Coach Falmouth to tell them that these will be the finest hours of their lives, and that they haven't come all this way just to lose. Have they? "Team, team, team," they chorus, but Strizich is bored with the hoorah, the fulminations of lesser beings. He only wants to hit.

With Knapp he meets at the center of the field with the referee and the captains from the other team, one of whom looks to be at least thirty-five. Their banners say they are Bulldogs, and their uniforms are black with blood red numerals, and maybe these boys have also come from a bad place, not that it will do them any good. "Tails," says Knapp: When the coin falls tails, he elects, contrary to the coach's instructions, for the Hellcats to receive the ball. "Check the paint," he tells Strizich as they trot toward their places on the return team. "I had to have the pig. Had to, man. Right away."

Van Knapp will do the unexpected, which, on the field of play, is still to his advantage. Strizich will hit. They are unaware of anything more important. A potency hums in them like saw blades as they consider the black line formed downfield and then sent toward them by the crowd and a trumpet. "Aaaaah, *boom,*" the call of a toe in a football. Strizich is running, his legs instantly heavy because his excitement has him gasping. These gasps are all he can hear. Knapp waits at the end of the rainbow, and when the ball drops into his arms he looks for Strizich to batter ahead. Strizich begins to read hesitation from far away, the reluctance behind those approaching face masks, and he aches like the bull to ram them. As they close, he can see them lose heart. He is leading the interference: Follow me.

To sacrifice no speed, he waits until the last moment to lower his shoulder, and then that bravest, foremost opponent comes grunting, and then the sweet light comes on in Strizich's skull, and a shock passes through him, and he barely breaks stride trampling this first one under. Raging downfield, he senses Knapp behind him, probing, juking, and Strizich already has a taste of his own blood in his mouth, that ferrous flavor that comes of acquiring real estate in the good old-fashioned way. They bring it out to the Bulldog forty-two.

• • •

His mother was reluctant at first to let him quit his job stocking shelves at Food Mart so that he could play ball. Gloria Strizich had relented only when she decided that the game might teach her boy something useful about adversity, a condition in which he was already well schooled. Mrs. Strizich has never understood that the game is very much easier for her son than everything else has been. Away from the field, the response to anything he might say is typically "Hmm?," and he is often told he is too soft-spoken when he is in fact only too easy to ignore. Helmeted, however, he is irresistible, and football is not so much a set of rules for him as it is a haven of rules suspended, a charmed environment where he may freely punish those who oppose him and where he is never overlooked.

He has been told, they have all been told, that team is everything, that they can be a whole greater than the sum of their parts, but every game is for Strizich a series of individual combats. All the victory he needs is an adversary flat on his back—to look down at that. Team? These Hellcats were boys, most of them, who liked to mock his fashion sense not so long ago, his hand-me-down stylings. Except for Knapp, whom they had also scorned, these other Hellcats are only dutiful mediocrities on the field of play, with only such aggression in them as they might milk from the example of Strizich on a rampage. Pound by dense red pound he has increased himself, made himself useful in this way, and he feels he is more than they deserve, that he is entitled to his satisfactions just as he finds them. His allegiance is very narrow, so when it happens that Van Knapp chooses the championship game, of all times and of all places, to stage an insurrection, Strizich finds himself complicit almost by instinct.

The first play comes in from the sideline, an end around involving the wide receiver, to which Knapp says, "Bad idea. Real bad—no—Give me the pig and send me through the four hole behind Anton."

They have joined in a small circle of steaming, mutually regardant, and now generally confused faces. "We can't just run what we feel like," says the quarterback. "We run what they tell us. Come on, man, settle down. I-formation. . . ."

"Nope," says Knapp, "God did not make me for a decoy."

"We can't do whatever we want out here."

"I can," says Knapp, "which I guess everybody has just overlooked. I can make the stars swim home, unlike some people I know."

"Let's just go up the gut like he says," says Strizich.

"But we can't. . . ."

"Before we get a delay of game," says Strizich.

"On two," the quarterback concedes, "and you guys better make this good."

At the snap, fullback Strizich barrels through the slot to the right of the Hellcat's right guard, and he destroys a Bulldog linebacker, and through the resultant gap Knapp pours like mercury and is tackled only after he has reached the twenty-seven. Coach Falmouth is livid along the sideline and sends in instructions about another play, but Knapp again countermands him, calling for them to repeat the play they just ran. "We don't need any surprise," he says. "I *am* the surprise." It seems he is right, because he scores a touchdown on this, their second play from scrimmage. When the kicker comes out to kick the extra point, Knapp sends him back literally hopping in frustration, and then the Hellcats score a two-point conversion in exactly the same manner as the previous two plays.

Knapp is not a member of the kickoff teams or the defense. Strizich never leaves the field. While he attends to his duties there he also notices from time to time the scene along their sideline where Coach Falmouth is yelling at Knapp, no more than six inches from the side of his helmet. Knapp's posture is that of a court dandy, one foot elegantly forward, his hands clasped behind his back. Falmouth wears his lucky orange stocking cap. This is his first winning team. Even under the spectral lights, even at this distance, the mutations of the coach's complexion are evident.

After Strizich stops the Bulldog kickoff return near their own goal line, they send three successive plays away from him, away from the middle of their formation, and only succeed in demonstrating the football truism that running side to side is no way to advance. Strizich can feel their resolve slacken; they are about as resistant now as tackling dummies when he hits them. Three plays for no gain, and then the Bulldogs punt deliberately out of bounds. The Hellcats have the ball again near the fifty, squarely between both benches and both grandstands. Strizich realizes that a band is playing, has been playing all the while. He recognizes the *Mission Impossible* theme.

Approaching the huddle, the quarterback, who has apparently been assigned to continue Coach Falmouth's harangue, is saying something to Knapp that he punctuates with a plaintive, "Okay?" Then, when they are assembled again, the quarterback, whose name is Billy and who is of Hinch's upper crust because his father owns a gas station there, says, "Slant right, option pass, on. . . ."

"Naah," says Knapp. "Don't be ridiculous. I need carries. Gimme the pig and heaven will be yours."

"Aw, Van, come *on*. You *heard* Coach."

"Let's go left this time," Knapp tells Strizich. "Give those boys on that side a taste. Just anywhere left. Blow me a hole."

"Ah, *shiiit*," says Billy the quarterback. "Okay, okay, I fucking give up. Dive left. On one."

The Hellcats march down the field. Knapp, a sublime certainty around which chaos blossoms, continues to call his own number on every play and his team is seldom troubled with the need to make second or third downs. They reel off great chunks of yardage. Across the line the Bulldogs are complaining about the officiating, arguing with each other, already assigning blame; from the general silence along their sideline their coach's rants are easily heard, "*Hit* somebody. Contain, con*tain.*" The Hinch sideline, with the exception of Coach Falmouth, is loud and rapturous, but the team out on the field is befuddled by its success. Where is the discipline in this? The teamwork? Obedience to the game plan? They are little more than observers.

At the half, the Bulldogs have managed a total of three first downs and no points; Knapp has danced in for five touchdowns and five two-point conversions, shattering, among other things, a state record for individual scoring in a half of championship play, but there is not much enthusiasm in the Hellcat locker room. Coach Falmouth stands at the whiteboard and glances around at his team and can only shake his head. He sinks down on a folding chair with his elbows on his knees. "I don't know. . . . Just stay tough on D, I guess. That's all there is to it. I can't see how we wouldn't win." Falmouth seems relieved when several players ask his help in adding fresh tape to their ankles.

Strizich and Knapp sit apart from the others, as they have since they were freshmen. Strizich notices again how a game compresses time so that he is never able to savor it as he would like. He notices how swollen his forearms have become and that one side of his rib cage complains a little with his every breath. Though he is no fonder of the other Hellcats than he has ever been, he is a little ashamed for them.

Knapp sighs. "You know what I wish? I wish that guy with the ice cream truck still came around. Not now. In summertime, obviously. You never see people like that anymore. Remember those jokes he'd try and make? That was one kind guy."

"What?" says Strizich. "Were those the good old days?"

"You know how long it's been since I had a Dilly Bar? Since I was a kid."

"You're a kid now," says Strizich.

"I have always wanted to write a song. Many songs, I mean.

Negro spirituals. Classical songs. Like Beethoven. Like Old Man River used to write."

"I didn't know you knew. . . . You know music?"

"It'll find me," says Knapp.

Strizich is troubled to think that his friend may be right.

"Ba*soooon*," says Knapp. "Ba*soooon*. You ever seen one? You even know what that is? Check the paint, Anton. Ba*soooon*." The Hellcats kick off to start the second half, and something has happened to energize the Bulldogs. Perhaps their coach has successfully humiliated them. Strizich is caught from behind, a clip the officials miss, and the wind is knocked out of him, and the Bulldogs start with their best field position of the game. Their new offensive plan is to run right at Strizich, and he is at the bottom of one dog pile after another, thumbs groping eagerly for his eyes. Almost incidentally the Bulldogs are finally moving the ball. They begin making bold noises, observations about Strizich's ancestry, and eventually one of them manages to bite his right calf very near his Achilles tendon.

The game within the game, the game that even the most avid fan does not see. Why do people do the things they do?

To await the next play Strizich drops so far back from the line that he is standing beside his free safety. He would have the Bulldogs think they have turned the tables, that now he is the reticent party, that his fear will be an opportunity for them. "What's going on?" his safety asks him, an all-purpose question.

Into the void they push, a pulling guard and a Bulldog running back behind him. By dropping back Strizich has given himself those extra several strides he needs to meet them at full speed, and he jams the guard so hard that the lad flies up and back into his own runner, who is staggered, and all in a moment Strizich collects himself again and slams the wobbling back at his thighs. The Bulldogs have lost possession of the ball and two of their better players. Strizich has inflicted such an agony on the pulling guard that the boy can only make that sound small children make preliminary to releasing a torrent of tears. The wounded are carried off. The Bulldog resurgence is over. Their runner has fumbled.

The Hellcats' team manager, an awkward boy in high-water pants and with a towel draped over his arm like a fancy waiter, runs out with the offense as it is taking the field, and he runs importantly up to Strizich and says, "Hey, come on. Coach needs you."

"For what? We're playing a ball game here."

"It's Van," says the manager. "He says he's done. He's back in the locker room."

"Is he hurt?"

"I don't think so. He just said he's done, and he went up to the locker room. Coach says you're the only one who can get him back out here."

Strizich finds his friend in the shower, singing a song without any center or any words. "Van, you okay?" The body in question is a stringy thing and should not be capable of its historic accomplishments. Strizich is always a little surprised at the sight of it.

"Let's have a band," says Knapp. "You want to be in my band?"

"You're not hurt?"

"Why would I be?"

"You tired? You just worn out, or what?"

"I never get tired," says Knapp.

This is true. Strizich asks him, "Don't you want to score some more? Those guys, they're all over, they're done. You'd score every time you touched the ball. There's still a lot of game left. You could really make the papers. Don't you want to be the athlete of the week?"

"At home," Knapp says, "I'm always running out of hot water. I just get started and the water goes cold on me. This is wonderful. Wouldn't it be nice to have a shower like this, and say a piano? Some backup singers? Some girls with real high voices?" Somewhere in the bowels of the building a boiler is producing limitless pleasure, and Strizich can say nothing to make his friend quit it.

The Hellcats will score no more, but they are able to sustain long drives and keep possession of the ball. The Bulldogs may not want it all that much, considering what has gone before. By the middle of the fourth quarter, fans from both sides are leaving to start their long drives home. Even the teams, mutually drained of purpose, have become a little bored with a game that has devolved into such an anticlimax. When it ends, Strizich learns that he has broken someone's leg. He apologizes sincerely to the Bulldog who delivers the news, who is not in any case offended. In the locker room the Hellcats are more cold and tired than triumphant. They will appreciate their success later when they can reorganize it in their minds. Coach Falmouth offers up a sad, short speech about pride and about the story they will one day be able to tell their children. A bald man in a bad suit comes in to give them their yet to be engraved trophy. The game ball is given to the deaf mute who travels with the team.

Strizich is slow and deliberate about getting dressed. He has begun to anticipate tomorrow which he will spend in bed with a hot pad and *Mutiny on the Bounty*. His mother will build him a pot of stew to eat while he slowly regains the capacity to move. She will lovingly cluck and disapprove. It will be one of those fine days when school is not session. He dreads the ride home. Van Knapp has his ear, and already he has conceived of a new vocation. Together they will make their way to Hollywood where Knapp will be an action star and Strizich can do sound or lighting. Strizich, the eternal anchor of this friendship, reminds him that they must first endure another year and a half of high school. The others are practiced at ignoring them in their corner, and it comes as a small surprise when the coach approaches them there, seeks them out. "There's somebody here who wants to see you boys," says Falmouth with mock gravity that causes Strizich to think at first that they may be in some kind of trouble. Falmouth then allows himself a grin. He leads them up some stairs, through a huge gymnasium, and to a door with a brass plate that identifies the room behind as the lair of an athletic director. Falmouth raises a finger before he knocks on it. "Best behavior now. This could be quite an opportunity for a couple of Hinchies."

Inside they are greeted by a man in a tie and a cornflower blue windbreaker, the color alone enough to identify his provenance. He is from the Big Sky, the state university. He calls himself Coach Sharper, and says that he is *very* glad to make their acquaintance. What a game they played. The best yet, and he knows, because the Big Sky staff has been following their careers. Career seems an odd term to Strizich. He feels himself swelling like a balloon, his future has so suddenly expanded. He's seen pictures of oaks lining brick walkways, that promising campus.

"You okay, young man?" Sharper asks Van Knapp. "They didn't ding you, did they?"

"I'm fine," says Knapp. "How about you?"

"Me?"

"He's okay, sir," says Strizich. "Thanks for asking. He doesn't get hurt. Neither one of us do." He recalls the term from the sports pages. "We're not injury-prone."

"We know that," says Sharper. The coach is a big man, well fed and rosy. "We know a lot about you guys. What we don't know are your plans for the future."

"I'd like to go to school," Strizich immediately volunteers. "If I could."

"That's what we like to hear. We like an ambitious kid."

"I'm going in the CIA," says Knapp.

"Impressive," says Sharper. "A patriot, huh? Of course, you'll need a college degree first."

"Maybe *you* would," says Knapp.

Coach Sharper looks to Strizich with a question he does not ask. He says instead, "So let's get down to brass tacks, as they say. We're prepared to offer you both a full ride at the finest school in this state."

"Ba*soon*," says Knapp.

"Oh, yeah. We've got an orchestra. My wife goes all the time. Can we get an early commit from you boys? That's all we're asking at this point."

"Yes," says Strizich. He's seen a pamphlet with a tall clock tower, students in lab coats, students gathered singing on stone steps. Your Gateway to the World. "Is there something I need to sign?"

"Man," says Knapp. "I am *so* hungry. They better feed us on the way home."

"What's *your* answer, young man?"

"What was the question?"

"Now don't be cute. Have you had a better offer? I don't think so. We keep track of these things. They don't recruit these small schools much. This might be it. I mean, you want to play at a community college? Major in food service or something? That's certainly your privilege, if that's what you want."

"Oh," says Knapp happily. "I forgot. I've got a candy bar in my duffel bag."

"Wait," says Strizich.

"I'd give you some," says Knapp. "But it's just one little candy bar. Barely enough for me. Don't let this guy make you miss the bus."

Knapp leaves and a long moment passes before either Strizich or Coach Sharper can think how to remark his absence. Finally Strizich says, "You're right, sir. He hasn't had any other offers; not that I know about. I'd probably know if he did. We're friends."

"We know that."

The "we" to which the coach keeps referring seems a hovering, somewhat evil bunch to Strizich. He doesn't know what else to say.

"We know he's got a little attitude problem. We can deal with that. We deal with that all the time."

The room is full of commemorative balls. Footballs, basketballs, baseballs. There is a cracked helmet on a desk, a pen in a dusty stand. Team pictures. Strizich feels the presence of ghosts. "It's . . . you should know . . . Van's. . ."

"Your friend. Right?"

"He is," says Strizich. "But. . ."

"But what?"

"His grades are a little. . . . He has some trouble concentrating sometimes."

"What kind of friend are you?" Coach Sharper's face now reminds Strizich of the housewives examining the inferior produce at the Food Mart.

"Sir, I just don't want him getting in over his head."

"We're used to dealing with all kinds of problems. Look, we know about this kid. We do. And I have to tell you—my offer is kind of a package deal. We think he'll go where you go. We think you can talk him into it, and you're maybe the only one who can."

"How do people get that kind of information, if you don't mind me asking, sir?"

"What I'm saying is, and don't get me wrong, we'd be happy to have you, you're a heck of a football player. But we want *both* of you. Without Van, your scholarship is, well, we've got better uses for it. We want speed. Speed puts butts in the seats, you see?"

"Yes, sir."

"You're a hard-nosed kid, which is fine, which is great, but any young man with a chip on his shoulder and access to a weight bench. . . . there's just a lot of you. There's dozens of you right here in state, a lot of 'em more athletic than you are. But speed. . ." Sharper is enraptured with this topic. "We want speed, usually we have to go down south to find it. *Way* down south, if you know what I mean. Homegrown speed is very, very valuable to our program. So can we count on you to get him to commit? To get him to come? 'Cause once you're there, son, the world is your damn oyster. We'll arrange a campus visit that'll blow your minds. We'll do everything we can to help you."

"I'll try, sir. I'll try as hard as I can."

"You do understand me now?"

"Yes, sir," says Strizich. He has been given to understand once and for all time that he is as common as the dirt he can never entirely remove from under his fingernails throughout a long, long season of play.

DANINE OR NOT DANINE

Earl Strayhorn jogged across the street, frequently touching his blazer pocket to make sure the state's petition hadn't fallen out. He was winded in the foyer and deeply winded when he'd climbed the marble stair to the mezzanine outside the courtroom. He introduced himself to his newest client, a young woman wearing handcuffs, baker's whites, and a sullen intelligence. The respondent, Danine Mannon. Flanked by a sheriff's deputy and a jail matron, she looked up at him only when Strayhorn said he'd come from the public defender's office. Her glance revealed nothing.

"Why's she still shackled?"

"You know the policy. Counselor." The deputy's career was chauffeuring crazies and juvenile delinquents around the county, and he did what he could to wring just any fun from his small authority.

"I know the *transport* policy," Strayhorn said. "I've read it. But she's here now. She's not in transit, so it doesn't apply anymore."

"So you say."

"Let's call the sheriff," Strayhorn suggested. "He'll have those policies right there at his elbow." The commitment petition spoke of old scarring on Danine Mannon's wrists. She had nowhere to run. "Come on. Please. You got her right out of the hospital. What do you think can happen?"

"Okay," said the deputy. "But it's on you. On *your* legal advice. We understood? On you."

"She's not a prisoner."

"Then what am I?" Puffy in the face, Danine Mannon had the forearms of a stone mason. Clenched fists. "Can I go? I mean, if I'm not?"

"See there?" said the deputy. "See what I mean? She's *not* a flight risk?"

"You can't go," Strayhorn told her. "Not yet."

"I just want to go home."

The matron, a spare, patient little woman, was finally moved to demand, "Take 'em off, Doug. This is no good like this—because you're really not all that demented, are you, Danine?" The matron spoke as if to a freshly hurt child or to a very dull one. To Dan-eeen, as she luridly intoned it.

The young woman could only shrug. Her eyes were couched in plummy flesh and did not seem to blink. Strayhorn felt himself appraised and dissected and knew from his own instant appraisal that his client would now reassemble him for her own purposes; she wore her determination about her like bandoliers.

"This is a preliminary hearing," he told her. "We really don't get too much accomplished at a prelim."

"Detention, though. They will decide whether I can go home or not. Before the next hearing."

"You've been through it before."

"Oh, yeah. I'm thirty, so that would make it about—oh, a lot of times. I get so sick of it." The law to either side of her shifted in their shoes. "Can you help me?"

Probably not in the way she'd want, still Strayhorn felt bound to continue explaining processes to her that she knew as well as he did. "The judge will give you your rights, tell you what the state is claiming, and what they want to do about it. She'll tell you there'll be a hearing within five days, or you can have a jury trial if you want. She'll tell you that the state is saying you should be committed to the mental hospital, to Warm Springs, so you have certain rights. They say, the petition says, that you're a danger to yourself. An imminent threat. They claim you've been trying to hurt yourself. But now they'll have to examine you again and get a second opinion."

"I can't be that dangerous," said Ms. Mannon. "I'm still here. And again, I mean every time this happens, I'm asking, why do they think they have to come to my rescue? Why couldn't they just wax the ambulance or something? I would really, really, really like to go home. How unreasonable is that? Can you do that for me?"

"I can try," said Strayhorn. "But all those pills they pumped out of your stomach—the judge'll want to play it safe. If it was only a mistake, though, we can tell her. . . ."

"No," said Ms. Mannon primly. "I won't lie about it. That would make it even uglier, what I've been trying to do. I've made it ugly enough, believe me."

"Maybe if you give her your word that you wouldn't try anything else, and make it convincing, maybe she'll send you home until the commitment hearing. That's your best shot."

"I can't even do that. I couldn't even make that promise."

An excessively honest client was a rare problem in Strayhorn's work. Her escorts looked at each other, chins down, eyes raised.

"Did you get a chance to read your copy of the commitment petition? I got mine about ten minutes before I came over here, which was also when I was informed I had this case. You know what it says?"

"I can guess," said Ms. Mannon. "I don't read those things anymore. They make you sound like a lab rat. But, whatever they said I said, I probably did. Say. I was very woozy at the time. Why can't they just . . . just imagine how someone might want to lie down and get some sleep? *Sleep*, for once. I don't sleep anymore. I'm awake all night, every night. I live alone."

"Okay," said Strayhorn. "Okay, they're calling us into court."

The preliminary hearing was drone and foregone conclusion, Strayhorn lodging his usual complaint about how little time he'd been given to confer with his client beforehand. Their judge, vivacious in her concern, apprised them all of their rights and obligations, an exhausting recital, and then, in the usual course of things, Judge Friedlander attempted to appoint Danine Mannon a friend.

"Oh, yeah, the friend," said Ms. Mannon.

"Someone you trust. The law directs me to appoint someone to kind of help you through this. Someone in addition to the public defender we automatically appoint, Mr. Strayhorn here."

"For that they usually get some pastor-type to come in, somebody who *has* to come in, in the name of the lord or something. Sorry, but you'll need to get one of those kind again. Call a church. Look at me. I mean, in all honesty, would you want to hang out with someone like me? Madame Judge? If you didn't have to? I've had no friends for years, no actual ones, just these poor appointed people."

• • •

Psych was hardly large enough to qualify as a ward, and close supervision of any one patient there seriously strained the nursing rotation; Danine was resented by the staff and by her fellow patients. Curled in her beige chair, she was under almost constant observation and knew she must make a dull, grim spectacle. They watched, and worse, they seemed to think she wanted them watching. The walls were eggshell blue. She stayed to her room to avoid the television in the dayroom, the shuffling in the hall, and though she was surrounded by the softest colors, still she found those colors discordant. Sensibility? Sensitivity? Danine expected to be and was disliked.

• • •

The world, or Earl Strayhorn's portion of it, was surrendering to madness. He'd been in six commitment hearings so far this year—mental health, about which he knew nothing, or exactly as much, he thought, as the experts he'd encountered in the field. Strayhorn was not fond of his own profession's jargon, and he hated theirs. He loathed the easy diagnosis, the ready quantifying of his clients, and sometimes he also hated the clients themselves, some of whom proved far stranger than clinical or legal language could ever properly describe. The worst of them, by far, were the depressives; Strayhorn was himself no one's ray of sunshine, and if their rank despair proved a contagion he'd hardly be immune. He'd no desire to know them better.

Strayhorn removed his shoes and emptied his pockets onto a shelf in a supply room, a nurse taking inventory of his possessions. "This is getting to be second nature, isn't it? Our little routine here."

"I still don't understand about the shoes," he said. "Why the shoes?"

"Oh, it's just how we do it. As you know very well by now. I guess we like everyone padding around. They require *us* to wear rubber soles, which are extra heavy."

Because the staples had been removed from them, Strayhorn was allowed to carry with him the reports of a social worker and a psychologist. He was the kind of presence on the ward that meant some patient's situation was about to shift; Strayhorn stirred ripples of addled curiosity as he passed down the hall, a man in a suit. The nurse escorted him to Danine Mannon's door, the room nearest the nursing station, and left them to ". . . have a good chat." Danine Mannon was alone, a nautilus curled in a chair, wreathed in a giant's seersucker robe. Strayhorn was slightly ashamed to find himself grading her again—not pretty.

"Hi, Danine. I see you got the nicest room."

"Yeah, guest of honor. There's restraints in here. They haven't used 'em on me, but a person still knows they're there. Soft restraints. Which I fucking hate, excuse my French."

"Good," said Strayhorn vaguely. "You've got everything you need?"

"I need? No. I've got everything *I don't* need."

"I mean the necessities," said Strayhorn.

"I know what you mean. Looks like you got the psychiatrist's report. Which is basically what the judge will follow."

"The reports are usually pretty persuasive; they actually kind of take the decision out of the judge's hands; she has to like that."

"And it says, this latest report?"

"He says you're depressed. Suicidal. Critically suicidal."

"And Warm Springs?"

"Doctor Forn strongly recommends a full evaluation. A commitment long enough to get that done. Develop a treatment plan."

"They won't let me just walk in?"

"They don't let anyone go in that way anymore. Because people walk out five days later, as they say you did several times. So now, if you go, you can think of yourself as a member of quite the exclusive club. You'll have to be qualified for membership."

"If?" Ms. Mannon would not suffer herself to be a fool or in any way optimistic. "Oh, I'm going. Again. Think I don't know? Think I can't be embarrassed? You don't get used to this. I can't get used to anything, as far as that goes. I don't adapt much."

"The doctor's report refers to a lot of older reports, from other places—you've been through some tough things."

"Who hasn't?"

"There's no shame in it, is all I'm saying. If you need some medication, if that would help...."

"I've had 'em," she said, "all of 'em. All of 'em almost at the same time, and in every different combination, I'm a toxic waste dump. Medication does not do me any good. I have no sense of humor. Tell me if this is funny—there was a woman who felt so bad they sent her to the nut house to feel better. How is sending you over to Warm Springs supposed to make you *less* depressed? This'll be the umpteenth time they've made the same mistake with me, I've been sent away from three different counties. Really, I don't put anybody down. Psychiatrists. Nobody. You can tell they all mean well, but if they can't help you, they can't help you, and they should just leave you alone. The doctors there, some of those doctors must feel the same way whenever I show up again. 'Oh it's *her* again'; I know they're wondering why I can't get it right, just get it over with."

"Talk like that," said Strayhorn, "isn't doing you any good. Legally. If they didn't have enough to commit you before, you give them more every time you open your mouth. There's other reasons, too, better reasons not to talk about it so much. You'll talk yourself into it. Have you asked yourself lately what you really want?"

"Easy," she said. "That's easy—my apartment. Now is that a lot to ask? Leave me alone in my own apartment?"

"Some of the things you've said, they're going to make the judge wary. She's a strong Catholic, you know. So, I'll ask again, can you think of a real good reason for her to send you home? She'll need one. Something to make *her* feel safe."

Ms. Mannon considered at annoying length before she could finally offer, "I could always tell her the truth, that I'm too tired to do anything right now, because I am. Now I've got to start all over again, you know, gathering my strength."

"That's good, though. That sounds so much better. You pick yourself up, gather your strength, and you go on. Like everyone else, and maybe it isn't that great, but you go on. The alarm rings in the morning, you get up and go do something. Good for you."

"Not what I meant at all. I mean courage. To give it another try. Somebody told me once it was a coward's move, a real cowardly thing to do. I'd like to see 'em try it once. It's not easy. I'm living proof of that."

"Danine, you know they feel they need to watch you for a while. And I'm sure you know why."

"They can't watch me forever."

"Until you're out of the woods," said Strayhorn.

"Yeah, but that's my point—I don't get out of the woods. Ever. Because I have *no* sense of humor."

• • •

Most working days saw Strayhorn bearing bad news, urging someone toward a more reasonable strategy. They were at counsel table, at the commitment hearing, and Danine Mannon's lawyer leaned to her and whispered, "She's just *not* going to let you kill yourself. I can't think of a single argument that would make her even think about it. And even me—I'm not ethically bound to support some proposition that'll do you harm."

"Not gonna let me? They can't stop me, can they? If I ever get my act together, they can't stop me. So what does it matter, one way or the other? I just want to go home. I thought you were. . . . no one has ever really tried to help me before. I'm miserable, I mean *unusually* miserable in these places, so I thought maybe, thought you might be the type to at least give it a try."

"It goes against. . . ."

The hearing was gaveled to order. Strayhorn stood and buttoned his jacket just long enough to tell the Court that the Respondent was ready to proceed, a lie. Her lawyer could not decide on his duty here, much less how to do it.

Deputy County Attorney Farrier, another humble civil servant in mid-career and a wrinkled suit, started his afternoon's chore by walking Dr. Forn through his education, credentials, and experience, and qualifying him as an expert. Then, together, they plodded through the well-documented latter half of Danine Mannon's life. She'd been under someone's care, intermittently, since she'd been fifteen, and Dr. Forn had come to divulge her sad story, outrageously in Strayhorn's opinion, wearing an argyle sweater and corduroy slacks.

"She had a very traumatic loss," Forn said, "and there have been clinical encounters very regularly ever since."

"Disregarding any previous diagnosis, Doctor Forn, what is your current diagnosis for Ms. Mannon?"

"You don't disregard those," corrected Forn, "you can't. But based on symptoms observed, I can confidently say she is currently suffering from Major Depressive Disorder."

"What were those symptoms?"

"Suicidal ideation. Persistent strain."

"She wants to kill herself?"

"She wants it very much. She seems—committed, I think you could say."

"According to the earlier report, Ms. Powe's report, Ms. Mannon took a potentially lethal dose of pills and then came to her work place, which is where she collapsed. The pills took effect shortly after she clocked in. In your professional opinion, Dr. Forn, did Ms. Mannon do this just for attention?"

"Objection," Strayhorn rose to get some blood back in his legs. "Your honor, no one, professional or otherwise, can ever do more than speculate as to someone's motives. For anything."

The judge, a woman so hale and blond she might have once been a milkmaid, paused several beats, as if in thought, before ruling for the state. "I'll allow it," she said. "Mr. Strayhorn, I think I can determine for myself whether the doctor's testimony is or isn't speculative. Go on, Dr. Forn."

"If it's only a gesture," said Forn, "it's still very dangerous. A series of gestures like this, a long history of them, that has to be taken very seriously."

"In your professional opinion, Doctor, do you think she means it?"

"Yes. But either way, whether she does or doesn't 'mean' it, her behavior is dangerous. Her behavior needs to be monitored and addressed clinically."

"Major Depressive?" asked the County Attorney.

"Yes."

"As described and defined in the *Diagnostic and Statistical Manual of Mental Disorders*?"

"Yes."

"Can you state to a medical certainty that she suffers from a condition legally recognized as a mental illness?"

"Yes."

"And Ms. Mannon exhibits suicidal ideation?"

"Ideation and attempts."

"In your professional opinion, does she still pose a risk to herself?"

"Yes."

"Is this some future risk, or one she would face today if the judge were to send her home?"

"She's been clear about her intentions for some time, and her intentions hadn't changed as of my interview with her the day before yesterday."

"What were those intentions?"

"To kill herself. I think she'll keep trying until she succeeds, unless we can intervene."

"State," said the county attorney, "will pass the witness to Mr. Strayhorn."

Strayhorn stood and laced his fingers into a palm-up pouch which hung just below his belly. "Mr. Farrier," he said, "that was thorough."

"Proceed," said the judge, "with your cross, Mr. Strayhorn."

"Thank you, Your Honor. Now, Dr. Forn—you have diagnosed Ms. Mannon with a disorder?"

"Yes."

"And in support of that diagnosis you offer exactly one symptom, her stated desire to kill herself?"

"And her attempts. The attempts are more important."

"She wants to die?"

"Yes. She's quite clear about it."

"Therefore she's mad?"

"Not *mad*. That's not a term I'd use in any context." Forn had coaxed or drugged himself into a state of the flattest sanity, and he was well pleased with his own steady presence.

"*Major* Depressive?"

"It's a mood disorder," said the doctor.

"Am I to understand, then, that there are some moods you consider acceptable and some moods that aren't? Some moods are insanity?"

"Moods are transitory. Mood disorders are not. It has to do with the way you take the world in, the way you react to stimuli."

"Stimuli?"

"The things that happen to you. Random stimuli, especially one's troubles. Some cope better than others. Some cope very poorly."

"Did you evaluate Ms. Mannon's coping skills?"

"Her skills, her strategies, she has very little of that. In most ways her intelligence is at or even well above average, but she has no emotional resilience at all. That's not really a function of intelligence."

"And this is what you speak of, Dr. Forn, when you say Major Depressive Disorder?"

"Yes."

"Overwhelming? Painful? Overwhelmingly painful?"

"Objection," said the Deputy County Attorney, "where was

the question in that?"

"Withdrawn," said Strayhorn to the judge, and to the witness he said, "What's the cure?"

"For. . .? For Danine's condition? There is no cure as such. You could compare it to diabetes—it's something you have, and that the patient may have to manage for the rest of her life. Manage the symptoms."

"By manage the symptoms, here you'd mean that Danine would quit wanting to kill herself? If that is her chief symptom?"

"Sure. I think you could call that a good outcome. Don't you?"

"Your report mentioned five previous suicide attempts. Documented attempts. These were strung out over fifteen years. Those previous attempts have to have some bearing on your findings here today?"

"I thought I'd said as much."

"How does someone get so fixated on killing themselves, Dr. Forn?"

"I couldn't say. Generally."

"Are they without hope, doctor?"

"Probably. For that moment."

"And Danine Mannon has been in that utterly hopeless moment at least five times since she turned fifteen?"

Judge Friedlander then interrupted Strayhorn to ask why he had chosen to undermine his own case. Strayhorn asked her indulgence and was allowed to continue, which he did without confidence. "Are you saying, Doctor, that you don't know, in general terms, why people choose to take their own lives?"

"There are certain trends, certain personalities that are more prone. But generalities are imprecise."

"Major Depressive Disorder? Isn't that a generality, Dr. Forn?"

"It's a category," said the doctor, finally showing some capacity for impatience.

"Is it possible that we're overcomplicating this? Don't people generally try to kill themselves when the pain of living starts to outweigh their fear of death?"

"I believe you were the one," said the doctor smugly, "who just said we can never know others' motives."

"So some suicides, in your view, may actually *want* to be alive?"

"I'm not minimizing their pain," said the doctor. "I'm sure it is the biggest factor."

"And Danine suffers from a condition for which there is no cure?"

"She does, but. . . ."

"And the one terrible symptom of that condition recurs again and again?"

"We do the best we can do for people. We keep trying."

"But there are some you can't cure?"

"Many, but we manage symptoms so well now. We can alleviate a lot of suffering. We do."

"And what of those you can't help? There must be patients whose pain is so unendurable they can't mask it, or deflect it, or even cut it out of themselves?"

"Pardon me, but," said the witness, "what's your hypothesis?"

"Despair, Dr. Forn. What have you got for that?"

"Oh, certainly," said Forn, "that's a given. Despair. We don't 'have' anything for it. People self-medicate, of course, but never very effectively."

"So how do you unburden your patients of their despair?"

"I don't," said Forn. "That's not a clinical term, it's not a clinical objective."

"But you know what it means?"

"I do," said Forn, "but it's a little overbroad, a little archaic for my uses."

"But if I were to tell you patient X was in despair, you would understand me? You'd have a pretty good idea what I meant?"

"I . . . might."

"You'd recognize it as that condition you can't cure?"

"Maybe a suite of symptoms that. . . . Wasn't I supposed to be testifying about Ms. Mannon? I hadn't prepared for anything else."

"I have nothing more for Dr. Forn," said Strayhorn.

Deputy County Attorney Farrier stood, and staring all the while at Strayhorn, he said, "The State rests."

Even as he saw the argument that might be made for what his client wanted, Strayhorn knew he must make it, but he was not at all at ease with his conscience for knowing what he must do: Success here would consist of freeing Ms. Mannon to go home and drain her veins in a warm tub. Or something. The doctor's report had especially remarked the number of different ways she'd tried and failed to destroy herself and how all her old troubles were compounded now by a mountain of medical debt, debts she'd have to live several lifetimes to discharge.

"Does Respondent have any witnesses?" asked the judge, her head at a kindly, dismissive tilt.

"Your Honor, Danine will testify in her own behalf."

Danine Mannon took the stand and the oath with some polish, far less pathetic now for having had two nights' consecutive sleep. She was in her baker's whites again, but they'd been freshly laundered and smelled slightly of bleach. Her cheeks were taut and somewhat flush, her eyes clear. Her hands were, as always, working, but they were out of sight in her lap as she sat in the old-fashioned witness stand.

"Danine," Strayhorn began, "we're here today because some people are saying you want to kill yourself. So let's just clear the air about that issue. Do you want to kill yourself?"

"A lot of the time, I do."

"Is that what you want at this moment?"

"At this moment I can't feel much besides embarrassed."

"Why?" said Strayhorn.

"Why?"

"Why do you keep trying to take your own life?"

"Oh. Well, obviously they've talked a lot about that. The people I've seen over the years. I've heard a lot of theories. But me, I think it's just that I'm tired and pissed off too much of the time. What's so good about that? And lonely. I mean, why keep doing that?"

"You've felt this way since you were fifteen?"

"No," said Danine Mannon. "Before that. I've always felt this way. It's who I am, which is no great thing to be."

"Danine, the doctor mentioned something bad that happened around then. He was too discreet to go into details. Would you like to tell us what happened when you were fifteen?"

"He's talking about January. My twin sister, identical. We went out skating, my idea, and we were on the river, and neither one of us really knew how to stop, and there was a hole in the ice. She skated right into it. 'Whoops,' she said, and she was gone. I mean right out of sight, and we never did find her after that. They said she must've got carried along by the river running under the ice. They said the current underneath must've been really strong."

"Your twin sister?"

"Yeah. And we did look exactly alike, but that's all. We weren't the same. She was the nice one. The one who was fun and had the good imagination and everything. I was me. But this one time, I read *Hans Brinker*, so it was me for a change with the idea for some fun. 'Let's get some skates.' We had miles and miles of river. Yeah, it was me, 'Let's go skating.'"

"Did you feel responsible for your sister's death?"

"I did, but let's not bring January into this. Like I say, I've always been this way."

"Describe for the Court, Danine, what you mean when you say, 'this way.' What *is* your state of mind?"

"Gloomy."

"Isn't there anything you can do about that?"

"Work," she said. "Real kind of down and dirty work, that helps. It's why I like the bakery, that and the hours. I like to work at night. And I went to work, by the way, after I took the pills—I only did that because that's what I do. It was just habit. It wasn't me saying, 'Oh, look, I'm dying again.' Or maybe it was. I don't know."

"What about your childhood?"

"Nice," said Danine. "It was very nice. My dad was the vet up in Plentywood, mom was a Martha Stewart type, but sweeter. And January. Everybody loved January. My childhood was great, but I was already cloudy weather then. I had that reputation. So that's why I sometimes want to say enough is enough. Middle of the night? Sometimes? It's just too much."

"You're certain you've tried everything to feel better?"

"I just know who I am," she said. "It's no good being me. I don't know how to feel better, to feel much at all, but I can't quite get numb. Why do this?"

"Thank you, Danine."

Farrier declined to further question the witness, and Strayhorn said the Respondent would rest, and Farrier rose to say that the testimony before the court, and reports admitted into evidence showed to a medical certainty that Danine Mannon was and had been for some time mentally ill. She was seriously mentally ill in that she was so determined to die. Farrier said that only placement in the state mental hospital could assure her safety over a long period of time, or until she was stabilized.

Danine got her lawyer's ear in the moment before he delivered his closing, and she breathed, "Yeah. But I still want to go home. Okay?"

"May it please the Court," said Strayhorn, rising. "What we've heard today is a tautology, not a diagnosis. Danine is suicidal, therefore she is depressed. She is depressed, therefore she is suicidal. My client, Your Honor, very readily concedes that she takes no great pleasure in her life. She will not deny that she often considers ending it. The only legal issue is whether the state has any authority to intervene in that decision. She suffers, we are told, from a mood disorder for which there is no cure, a condition that permanently colors the way she sees the world. This is a burden, Your Honor, we cannot begin to understand until we've carried it. We've been spared that experience. We don't know how it feels to be Danine Mannon, but she knows, moment by moment, she knows, and she doesn't like it. Do we assume that, because we are so uncomfortable with her decision to end her life, her decision is irrational?

"We are told, Your Honor, by patient and physician alike, that there is no cure for her pain or her disappointment or grief or whatever plagues her. So, if the state lacks the means to make her life tolerable, can the state insist she continue to live it? Danine's occasional longing for death appears to arise out of cold calculation, and not delusion. She is not mentally ill, she is just very sad, and only Danine Mannon can lawfully say what to do about that."

He'd drawn one plausible portrait of this woman, but there were others, and Strayhorn was careful not to look at her as he sat down again beside her. He did hear her startled thanks.

They hadn't two minutes to wait for the ruling from the bench. Judge Friedlander appeared to be making check marks. "The court," she said, "finds to a medical certainty that Ms. Mannon suffers from a recognized mental illness, Major Depressive Disorder. She has repeatedly and recently spoken of and attempted suicide. She continues to contemplate suicide.

She requires a high level of supervision to secure her safety at this time, and the Court therefore commits the Respondent to the state mental hospital for a period of no more than ninety days, for evaluation and treatment. Medication may be administered during that period at the staff's discretion, with or without the Respondent's consent."

Strayhorn heard her weeping beside him, and still without looking her way he set his hand on her shoulder, where it rode rising and falling.

"Ms. Mannon," said the judge, "the Court has to believe that somehow you'll find the hope or faith you'll need to carry on. It's tough going sometimes, Ms. Mannon. For all of us."

As the deputy and the matron approached with their padded manacles, Danine Mannon hissed under her breath, "It's *hope* I'm trying to get rid of, Mr. Strayhorn. I'd be just fine if it wasn't for that little clingy bit of hope."

THE NERVE TO YOUR WING

Even before he opened his eyes he knew the air would be alive for him. "Ooh," he said, waking, and Vida said, "No." She rolled away. "Would it be so terrible to put a cooler thingy in that window? A fan? God, it's sticky in here." Her hair was coiled unattractively for bed; she'd made a fortress of her back.

"You want to drive for us later? I think we'll have big weather today."

"I have to work, Noah."

"Not *every* day. Not all day."

"*Yes.* Every day that I'm scheduled, I have to go in. That's another one of these simple little things you do not get—if you don't come in to work, they fire you."

She'd been using an aggrieved tone lately that he found, unfortunately, exciting. Noah Tenon got up, dressed, and went into the kitchen to make coffee. As he smeared a heel of brown bread with butter and honey his gloves twirled out of the bedroom and landed in dancers' poses in the hall. "Could you please quit knocking around in there and split?" This appeal must have come from on or near her pillow. "I'm still trying to sleep. Could you go do whatever you've got to do? And leave me out of it."

Tenon finished his coffee on the landing outside their apartment, looking out across the neighborhood's shingled roofs and its treetops. Maple and ash in full leaf. Summer. It was that rare morning in the mountains when the heat of the previous day has survived the night and the dawn has no chill in it, a tropical morning, a volatile promise he felt on the flesh of his face and his forearms. Vida's recent thesis was that he was not a very serious man, that he was not suited for sustained practicality, but she must be wrong, for even now, even as the valley's contained heat built toward instability in the low, brooding, slate gray sky, even as the forces of nature were aligning themselves to his perfect satisfaction, Tenon was also thinking of lesser obligations. Such as his own work. Did he not tend to business?

Their apartment was tiny and severely feminized, and so he used the back of his jeep wagon for storage. Tenon briefly inventoried through the window: He owned two clean shovels; there was a carpenter's chest stuffed with the tools of that trade; a full-length pod harness with a parachute mounted on its chest; a fared equipment array with an airspeed indicator, an altimeter, and an analog variometer; a two-pound sack of buffalo jerky; a heavily resined hash pipe; a broken nail gun and some pneumatic hose; a small oxygen tank with a rubber face mask; a translation of the *Bhaghavad Gita;* a plastic bleach jug swaddled in wet burlap and now in use as his canteen; rolls of electrical and duct tape. Above the jeep, running like a horizontal spinnaker along its whole length, rode the Roc in its twenty-foot sock, a red pennant hanging from the end.

As Tenon drove south, elders and other inepts entered at every crossroad to meander in front of him. He had contracted to pour a slab in Lolo that morning; out on a treeless, charmless subdivision they were to make a monolithic concrete slab that would be someone's foundation and their clammy floor. He operated at the very bottom of the cement industry with forms and finishing tools he'd bought for nearly nothing at an estate sale and with a crew he'd hired from among his friends. None of them held a union card. Tenon knew very well that professionals were expected to own and to wear wristwatches, and he was often haunted by the sense of being late, and now, goaded by his radio, he slalomed with illicit grace through slower traffic.

His forms were set square and level, and the dirt within

them had been well compacted, but the iron work wasn't finished. Tenon was no engineer, and so, to be safe, he grossly overbuilt everything he made. He set about weaving with wire and rebar a skeletal matrix to support the concrete to come. And he grew indignant. If Vida and the loan officers and the like should see him as he was now, all alone and diligently bending steel with his bare hands, wouldn't they have to form a completely different opinion of him?

Johnny Illich arrived in a dove gray step van driven by the immodest Genessa, his girlfriend of the moment. The step van spewed several of her children when she parked. Johnny and Genessa came to him in a cloud of fake berry odor, and Johnny shrugged his powerful shoulders and said he couldn't make it. "My arm's broke—remember?"

"Your wrist," Tenon specified. "And why'd you cut the cast off if you weren't ready to go?"

"I brought smoothies. Genessa wore a flouncy skirt and an eerie well-being that she seemed to want for everyone. "To which I've added monster doses of vitamin B and calcium. Why don't we just have those? Kids. Come over here."

"No," said Tenon. "No, no, no. We've got this concrete coming. Soon."

"Well, I can't be reefing on any shovels yet," Johnny Illich said. "Sorry."

"What about later? Would you want to go flying?"

"Fly what?"

"Driving, I mean."

"This woman," said Johnny Illich. He arched his eyebrows and rolled his eyes and let his lips hang slack. "She's got me *cleansing.* I can't get too far away from the reading room. You've got her number, though. We'll be there. Getting *cleansed,* man. I just can't make it today."

"Johnny," said Genessa, pleased, "my personal crazy." Then,

to round them up, she commanded, "Kids!" The children flocked like gulls to the step van. They were shrill as gulls, too. The party loaded and left, and from the van's open windows a breathy soprano sang of ice cream castles in the air.

Tenon was bleeding red ink on this job. He submitted bids so low that he sometimes found himself paying for the privilege of working, but without this, or some element of risk, he knew he couldn't stay interested for very long in building cut-rate foundations for ugly houses. His business was a slightly profitable series of narrowly averted catastrophes, and because he was himself so poorly organized Tenon could only be a little annoyed with Keene and Cornelius when they finally arrived in the company truck. "Hustle," he told them. "Get that two-by over here where it'll do some good."

"Take it easy with that sledge," said Cornelius. "You'll mash your thumb off with that thing. Slow down."

"You speed up. You move like an ocean liner. You're way late, and we're shorthanded. If these forms blow out, I don't get paid. We're lucky the cement truck's running late."

Laborers Keene and Cornelius wore kerchiefs on their heads. They were often together and had become so alike they might have been fraternal twins. Small and well-knit and ruddy, they were fine pilots and adequate musicians, and the two of them together did not amount to one good construction hand; he could only suffer them. But the boys were well pleased by the mud puddle portion of the work, and an hour and a half after the truck arrived, the concrete was snug in its forms, and level, and Keene was sliding a bull float out across its glossy surface.

Tenon's shirt and jeans were entirely sweated through. He drank three pounds of faintly chlorinated water, watching the concrete harden.

"Where's your kites?"

"Ain't nobody here," said Cornelius, "but us chickens."

"We don't put gliders up on that rack with lumber," said Keene. "They're not compatible. Lumber shifts around on that rack, it just does."

They also had in common very blue, very earnest eyes. "We said before," Cornelius stated, "we said if it was like this, we weren't going. Days like today are why God invented guitars. You know it'll overdevelop."

"We should drive up, anyway, and at least take a look at it."

"You wouldn't," Cornelius said, "just take a look. New site, weird weather, that's your exact ticket, Noah, but we're not aiding and abetting you this time. Why get your equipment beat up? Yourself? Look how useless Johnny Illich is since he pranged in. He's scared now; why try and duplicate that shit? You want to go down in the deep woods?"

"Or you could say," said Keene, "first there is a mountain, then there is no mountain, then there is. There's always tomorrow."

Mountain, mountain, mountain, the word ripened every time it was mentioned in his presence. "Well," said Tenon, "I think I'll catch a shower and run up the hill then. I'm taking a look at it. Since you guys aren't, you might as well stay here and finish off this slab."

"One day," Cornelius predicted, "you'll give the sport a bad name."

The mountain Tenon had in mind had stood for an age before he or his kind were rumored to exist, and it would be standing when they were long forgotten, but Tenon had teased himself into an urgency about it. Point Nine, as it was named on the Forest Service map, was home to antennae and radar apparatus, the tallest spot in a big patch of densely timbered wilderness just north of town. Though there was a road to the top, Tenon had heedlessly asked permission of the mountain's leaseholders to let him launch his glider there, and the response

was a certified letter warning him that his presence on top
of the mountain would be a trespass, and that KSTX, Inc., in
conjunction with its several subsidiaries, would, in the event of
such trespass, pursue all remedies, civil and criminal.

But it taunted him every day. Point Nine was in sight almost
everywhere in the valley where he lived, covered much of the
year in snow. On the map, contour lines flowed toward its
peak in shell-like patterns and shorter mountains crouched all
around, merely its shoulders. There would be lift above that
mountain. He had convinced himself that, almost regardless of
what the weather or where the wind, a rising body of air would
center right over that peak as often as not. In summer the top
was a great shale dome, thirsty for sun, and if ever he could get
himself over it, he and the Roc might very well circle up and
up in booming thermals, rise up on his wits and the quirky air.
Such an episode would certainly be worth a little brush with the
law. If, as was likely, he should fly this mountain only once, he
thought it should happen on a pregnant day like today with all
things in proportion and big—Point Nine and a rare sky that
promised by late afternoon to turn itself inside out.

• • •

The Angel's Rest Inn was not an inn but a roadhouse, and poor
Vida, who described her shifts as endless, was its book keeper
and day bartender. In a room full of furtive daylight and the
stale smell of dead festivities, she often did a dismal business.
Tenon was a reluctant visitor here, a sometimes unwelcome
one, and his presence alone was enough to make her suspicious.
She had once again unplugged the juke box. "If you're here for
the air-conditioning, then okay. Anything else you can forget
about." She had high cheeks and gimlet eyes, and she'd hung
a large brass disc at the tips of her collar bones to very good
effect. Just behind her a trout leapt continually upon a winking

stream in behalf of a light beer. "You hungry?"

"I had some apples and cilantro on the way, and a burrito at the gas station."

"I would've fed you something. Some bar food at least. But anything else—the answer's 'no'. And, yes, I know exactly what you're up to."

The bar's only other patron stood by with his fat foot on the bar rail, and though his eyes were open, seemed catatonic.

"What do you think I want?" Tenon asked her "How bad could it possibly be?"

"Are you still going up there?"

"I just dropped by to file a flight plan."

"A flight plan?"

The lonely customer moved a stool closer to them and suddenly realized, "Oh, he's your *boy*friend."

Vida stood with her arms folded and her mouth in a dubious twist, and why did she think she had to take such a hard line? She had the constant advantage of Tenon, who was neither handsome nor handsomely turned out, and she almost always had her way.

"Just you?" she said.

"The broadcasters, they've really spooked everyone off. The company. Far as I'm concerned, though, they only think they own it. How could anyone actually own that?"

"Aw, Noah. Who's driving? I'm not driving."

"My name's Ed," said the other patron, "Ed Plapp. What's going on?"

"I'll leave the jeep outside their property line," Tenon said, "and hike in. Come back later and pick it up. That's if I fly at all. That way, I don't think they can seize the jeep—if I should happen to get caught."

"If," said Vida. "Shit. You're going up there by yourself? I cannot leave this place again, Noah. I am in so, so much trouble already."

"I just want you to know where I'm launching from, and where I'm landing; it's a standard aviation practice. That's all I want."

"To your girlfriend? People give this information to their girlfriend? I don't think so."

"I'll be on a heading almost due west, and should come out over. . . ."

"Heading? What about azimuth? Better throw that in, too. Like I know what any of it means. Or directions. I'm very sure you know that whole language is gobbledygook to me. You and your parasitic drag, you think it's poetry."

"No, it's easy. One basic fact, okay? Landing. I'll land at the Busted Spur, out in that meadow, or maybe, if I can get over that other ridge, I'll land right out here. Right out here in your parking lot. That'll show 'em. You'll probably be off work by then."

"What? Show 'em what? Show who? From up there you'd come here? That must be, how far is that? And what would you have to fly *over* to get here? The freeway? Power lines. A thousand ranchettes. Fly over all that? That's not going to be wise, honey. Please. The whole idea is just. . . ."

"Hey," said Ed Plapp, "All *riiight*. Let's show 'em. I'm in." He had rallied remarkably.

"Sure," said Tenon. "In for what?"

"Whatever you're doing."

"What I'm doing I can't discuss. Exactly. Taking a ride, really."

"What do you think I am?" asked Plapp. "If you had to guess, what would you guess I do?"

"You sell insurance of some kind," Vida said. "Noah, do not get this guy involved. Mr., what was it? Ed? You've been here all morning. He says he wants to go on his own—good enough. Let him. I can never talk him out of anything, but he doesn't

SURVIVORS SAID

have to get you involved. You've been at it pretty steady, and you're in no shape to be . . . involved."

Plapp tucked his chin, affronted. "Give me one to go, and we'll just see. I'm up for a little sport, you bet. I'm in accident and life—heavy emphasis on the life. Creepy, huh? Sad. But, *hell* yes. I say. . . I could use some. . . . Is it illegal?" His right cheek bore the imprint of his knuckles, he had leaned so long against them.

"Sure," said Tenon, "you can come along if you want. But no more for the road. You might need to collect yourself a bit."

"Look at what you're wearing," Vida told the salesman. "Do you have any idea where he's going? Do you have the slightest idea what he's got in mind?"

"I do not," said Plapp. "Which is the beauty of it. *And*—I am very well insured." He pulled himself deliberately to his full height, and said. "Let's go."

Tenon had calculated on his map that the straight-line distance from Point Nine to the Angel's Rest Inn was under fifteen miles. As the crow, or as even Noah Tenon might fly, fifteen miles. The distance overland, though, from the bottom up, was a very much longer trip along winding, and climbing, and sometimes sparsely marked roads, and because Tenon had never previously been to this mountaintop he had to regularly assure his passenger, and at times reassure himself, that he'd taken the right roads. "We better be there," warned Ed Plapp. "We better not be lost, because if I get real, real sober that's when my instincts start to fail me. This is quite woodsy, isn't it? A person never realizes—the trees. There's like a world of trees once you get up in here. But, what was the plan again?"

A gate eventually validated Tenon's navigation. They came to a length of four-inch steel pipe that had been painted brown and striped with day-glo orange and hung by a cable arm across the road, about three feet above it. It was padlocked and plac-

205

arded, "Absolutely No Unauthorized Entry."

"This," said Tenon, "is where it starts getting illegal."

"Can't you drive around it?"

"This is what I'd call the hard part."

"What am I supposed to do?"

"Whatever you feel like. Probably drive the jeep back to your car, but whatever you want."

"Oh, thanks. So, what am I, the Donner Party? I'd be completely lost."

"Follow the road back. There's a road. How did you think you were getting down?"

"I was lit. I didn't think about it. There were a lot of roads. A lot of 'em. Oh, man, don't leave me here—I guess I might as well see the top as long as I've come this far. How far is that?"

"Not sure." Tenon slung the Roc onto his shoulder so that it was balanced fore and aft. "You could carry my helmet and my harness if you wanted. I can strap 'em to my wing, but this thing's already seventy pounds, just the glider alone. She's hell for stout, but heavy."

"Give me a second," said Plapp, "I'm—it's this being sort of lost—I might have to puke."

They walked up the road forbidden to them, the best groomed road they'd traveled so far. They climbed gradually but continuously and they didn't talk or try to do anything more than climb and keep breathing. Tenon shifted his glider from shoulder to shoulder as it wore on him. A half-hour of this yielded the top, and Plapp sat cross-legged in the road. He had carried the water jug as well, and now, grimacing at the chemical taint, he drank from it. "Where is this, did you say? Where are we?"

"You've seen it a thousand times."

"It's that . . . when you're coming in from Spokane you see it up there?"

"Or coming in from Kalispell, or the rez, or anywhere from that direction. This is Point Nine. It more or less looms over things. If you're looking for it."

"I guess so. I've got, oooh, there I go getting some vertigo, whoo. We are hellaciously high, aren't we? I'm not sure if I like it, to tell you the truth. You kind of feel like you could fall off—which is ridiculous, but—like you could almost . . . fall off."

"Oh, but you can," said Tenon. "That's the whole idea."

The low clouds of that morning had coiled and twisted and become columnar in shape, boiling pillars of humid air spiraling up to the dew point. On the exposed face of the mountain this weather was expressing itself in winds that came in fits and starts, blasting, subsiding, renewing from another direction. "This'll be tricky," said Tenon. "When the air's so squirrely, it doesn't hurt to have some help. I'm glad you came along."

"I am sober as a *judge*. Which is not exactly what I wanted to accomplish. Canada would be off in that direction, wouldn't it? *Whoo*. This might not be the top of the world, but we're as close as I ever want to get."

Tenon turned the Roc on its back in the road, unzipped the bag, and pieced together the triangle of his control bar; he rocked that up and attached the forward flying wires to the nose plate. He turned the glider over, stood it on the control bar, raised the king post, twisted out the cross tube and spread the wings, a wide spread of Dacron sail that flapped cracking in the wind. Tenon told Plapp to seize the unruly thing by the nose, which he did with much misgiving.

"Try to keep it headed into the wind—I'll point you that way as it changes. Just keep the nose into the wind and that same angle of attack, about your eye level, a little higher. That's good. That's all there is to it." The power in so much spread of sail was too apparent, too loud in the huffing, galling gale, and Tenon had often to instruct his nervous groundman. "Don't let the nose up too far or you'll lose her. No, that's fine. You're doing all right. You're doing fine."

Tenon slipped the Roc's ribs into its leading and then its trailing edges. He attached the winglets and nose cone and connected the system of cables that would let him flatten the wing in flight—variable geometry. He connected sprogs and tensioners. In its particulars an assembly of soulless aluminum tubing, Dacron, Mylar, steel cable, steel and plastic fittings—the Roc, when assembled, lived and breathed, and Ed Plapp held by its nose a dancing, willful creature resembling in its shape and musculature the wings of an immense albatross. Plapp's eyes were huge.

"If we'd been able to drive up, I would've brought the instruments and the oxygen, but that's okay. Soon as you hook in, you've got a nerve that runs right up into the wing, tells you everything you need to know."

"Come on," said Plapp. "This thing wants to take off, with or without you."

"Here. Take my gloves. You've got to hang on to those nose wires a little while longer."

Tenon drank from his jug, urinated, and drank some more. He put on a down jacket and walked once entirely around the Roc to see that all connections were secure and no cables had twisted, that the ribs were symmetrical and properly cambered. She was in perfect health and unhappy on the ground. "Hurry," said Plapp. "This is not easy."

Tenon stepped into his harness, and it was like the long thorax of a grasshopper, but hinged at the waist, tipped forward there so that his legs were free for takeoff. He arranged the several lines that would support him from his shoulders to his feet when he lay down, and he gathered them into a single carabiner that he clipped into his hang loop. He touched his parachute, his clasp knife, the closure on the carabiner, and then Tenon lifted the glider onto his shoulders and told Plapp, "Just keep hold of those nose wires 'til I tell you. Let's walk her forward a little bit, right to the bank there, and hang on."

The wind had increased in power and whimsy, and the tails of Plapp's brown silk tie were flying around his head; he was cursing continuously now at Noah Tenon. The Roc rared and bucked.

Tenon had spent very little time surveying his launch or possible flight paths, and he attended to these details very quickly now that he'd hooked in: The bank just beyond the edge of the road dropped steeply for about forty feet, but beyond that was a long and very gradual slope of car-sized, faceted boulders, and beyond that for five or six miles there was only timber or vertical rock face. Barring a bad miscalculation, or mischance, he should easily be able to clear the trees, and he knew of wide open meadows in the valley beyond, but he could not see them from where he presently stood.

When the wind turned to blow straight uphill, he said, "Okay."

Plapp released one nose wire, but tripped then, and stumbled backward, and to save himself from falling he held tight to the other side. The free side of the glider began to lift like a gate; it lifted Tenon onto the tiptoes of one foot, and the Roc was about to ground loop, one side of the wing fly entirely around the other to slam back onto the road, when Tenon urged, "*Let go.*"

Plapp dropped away, and Tenon, having been drawn over the bank, had launched in a mild stall and was sliding sidelong toward the rocks. He lay out in harness and pulled himself to the high side of the control bar, and he got flight speed at once and stepped into the stirrup of his harness, and he straightened his legs within it to close the cocoon around him. Snug and airworthy and aerodynamic, Tenon turned to see what had come of his groundman. Plapp was sprawled on his back on the road, and gravely he extended his arms and then his middle fingers. Grinning or grimacing, and still not completely convinced of it, he called, "You are *flying*."

Yes, but in a whirligig. Tenon dropped into a sudden pocket of sink to find himself twenty feet off the boulders. He pulled at the bar, an inch, and sleek and heavy the Roc sliced through the turbulence, and out over the boulders with the rigging and the air frame whirring purposefully. Out over the trees. He was cleanly away, but low. There was a window of open air before him, but the timbered mountain was behind, and timbered and steep canyon to either side. He had intended to be above all this. He had expected to soar today.

He crabbed to his right looking for wind surging up and over the canyon wall, and he found that if he kept that wing tip within thirty feet of the face there was enough ridge lift to sustain him in level flight; he edged closer and was carried up and over the ridge, and he worked back and forth over its spine, gaining a little with each pass; the Roc's shadow passed over a black bear scooping grubs from a rotten spruce. The sow flinched, ducked, wheeled away and loped, then plunged downhill to roll end over end. Finally it paused to look up at him and sneeze. Tenon worked the ridge until he had equaled his altitude at launch, then, as he cruised out over the valley the high ground dropped away, and now he had beneath him a pillow of thousands of feet of buoyant air.

He might fly back to the point, but Tenon could see no advantage in it. It seemed the whole sky hereabouts must be rising, and he was no longer dependent on the mountain for lift. He was much more than high enough to make the Angel's Rest, but Vida had successfully belittled that weak stunt, and she was correct in pointing out how bad the scenery was that way. He flew in wide circles and soon enough Point Nine was well beneath him, and he believed he might very well be able to reach any place that he could see from here, and he could see into the Jocko, down the Bitterroots, see the mouth of the Hellgate, see the granite crags of the Missions taking lightning strikes. Squalls were all around, the sky blown apart, but Tenon had flown into some vast bubble that carried him up without incident or interruption. Now he regretted the lack of an altimeter to give him his altitude, a variometer to give him his rate of climb; at this elevation such observations were made only vaguely, if at all, by his senses. He knew he was climbing pretty steadily, given the view. He missed his gloves. Flattened by perspective, Point Nine became a smudge in the carpet below.

• • •

In his fondest boyhood dream, the one from which his mother had so often awakened him, young Noah was aloft with no apparatus but his desire to sustain him, drifting as a matter of sheer preference over the dreamscapes of his juvenile subconscious, and as luck would have it, he was still a young man when a breed of aircraft was devised to reprise that very sensation. Thought to be a willful boy, then and now, Tenon had long maintained that on the right day, with the right glider: What? Not so little as a thrill, but what? Apparently he had arrived. He was so high above his planet's noise that the rush of the Roc through the air was, in the absence of any other sound, a soft roar.

The quality of his headache suggested altitude sickness. Was he thinking well? Tenon thought it best to crank himself down to an elevation where he might repay his oxygen debt, and so he twisted into a series of wingovers, high, steeply banked turns that he entered with insufficient speed so that he would fall out of them, pitch the glider almost onto its back, and fall for a time before recovering. At the bottom of these maneuvers Tenon had for several seconds to press half again his body weight at the control bar while the harness pressed back at him with equal force, and he had not romped for very long in this exhausting way before he decided he was losing no altitude by it.

How long? No watch. His knuckles, nose, and feet suffered and then were numb. How long? How high? No watch, no gauges at all. His temples throbbed at the foam in his helmet. Neither sufficient nor insufficient now, but only a diminishing dot, Tenon set his airframe for top speed and aimed for the nearest squall, for the underside of an angry cloud, the heart of a rainstorm that may or may not be felt as far below as the ground. To follow it down.

WITH FREE DELIVERY

A half day early to his conference, small suitcase in hand,
Lozeau crossed the oatmeal and butter lobby of the Autumn
Hotel. Slow down. In an adjacent room, behind steamed glass,
an overripe woman in a red bikini guided a little boy around
the perimeter of a pool. The child wore bladders, also red, on
its arms, and an older boy stood hip deep in the pool, splashing.
What's your hurry? Lozeau joined a short line of guests at the
desk and eavesdropped on the clerk's honeyed interrogations
of other travelers. Nothing awaited him but the boredom of his
room. Shifting foot to foot, he was consumed by the question of
whether to put his suitcase down or continue holding it, and he
prevented himself from checking his watch against the clock on
the wall. Before him in line stood a short man under a lustrous
cap of bronze hair, heavily cologned in the chlorinated air, and,
just as Lozeau had feared he might, this person turned to pass
the time of day.

"Nightmare."

Lozeau could only agree.

"Travel anymore."

"Mmm. Terrible."

"I mean, only if you absolutely have to, right? The wife's got
me running around seeing specialists, and they're everywhere.
All over the place. You wouldn't believe how many specialists
there are."

"Oh?"

"Just for my specific condition," said the stranger. "Just for
pancreatic cancer. There's dozens of 'em."

"Ooh," said Lozeau.

"She thinks somebody'll pull a rabbit out of his hat. Save me."

The stranger's current complexion was more sanguine than his own; apparently the man hadn't started dying in earnest. No word or soothing noise suggested itself to Lozeau. He nodded again.

"Quacks," said the sick man.

Relax, Lozeau told himself.

As a loyal, long-time employee, he was rewarded every year or so with a trip to some new city to convene with other warehousemen, a generally unsociable lot whose profession, they always found, bore little discussion. Have fun, the supervisors would insist, and Lozeau would be off to a locale with slot machines he wouldn't play, or water slides he wouldn't slide on, or jet skis that started howling every time he attempted a nap. Have fun, they'd say, as if he still knew how. Make some connections, they'd say, as if there was really anything to share. He didn't do well on vacation. Lozeau had let himself become a creature of his work, of wan light and pasteboard corridors and an order he himself maintained with nothing more than a clipboard and a forklift; on vacation he often felt like a mole forced blinking into the sun.

He rode a creamy elevator, walked creamy halls. On reaching his room he called Denise to let her know, and Denise sounded overhappy, as if his arrival here had stood in some doubt. She didn't miss him at all. "Is it nice?"

"Pretty nice," he said.

"Well, good. So try and enjoy yourself a little, okay? Loosen up. You might as well."

"Okay."

"Mainly, though, don't get in a bad mood. And you don't need to start eating like a teenager just because I'm not there to keep an eye on you. Go see that museum they mentioned."

"All right," he said. "Love you."

"Love you, too."

Lozeau's next call was for, "I'd like your, oh, how about your double-meat, double-cheese, jalapeno? The fourteen-inch. And two of those big root beers. Breadsticks? Mm, no. No, I'd better not. Room four-eighteen, I'm over on the freeway side of the building, if that helps."

Waiting, he opened the curtains to see himself vaguely in another glass wall that overlooked his bit of balcony, a large parking lot, and beyond that an assembly of weeds and grade stakes and earth movers. Nothing moving. He saw it entirely in five seconds. Do not, Lozeau told himself, do not turn on that television. Once he opened the blue beam, he knew, he'd be impaled on it until he checked out late tomorrow, and it was hard to think of a desolation more complete. Night and day. What else to do? What did it really cost him? He reclined on the bed, remote in hand. The quiet pressed down and down, the whole of life, it seemed, with its always unexpected capacity to become even lonelier. But he did not turn on the television.

Eventually he startled himself with the rip of his own snoring, and then he settled into an easier wheeze, and then a cotton-headed sleep, and time passed cooperatively for a while. When the knocking came, later, it had gotten pretty brisk before Lozeau could come to himself enough to remember where he was, to be embarrassed. "Coming. I'm coming." Pushing up, no longer even slightly hungry, he happened to think that if he hadn't arranged for this interruption he might have slept around the clock. Which might have been the wisest thing. "Sorry," he said at the door.

The girl had no food. Arms folded in a lavender business suit, one needle toe thrust well forward, she said, "Carson? Or is it supposed to be Mr. Carson?"

"I? No."

She had done something Egyptian with her eyes and powdered her face to make herself look shopworn. She was not very old. The girl glanced often and urgently down the hall to her right, and when Lozeau leaned out to see what was troubling her there—nothing, as it happened, nothing that he could see, or no one— the girl slipped by him and into his room. She stood near the bed, hands on her hips, instantly bored. "Come on, Carson. Don't get squeamish now."

"Squeamish? You're not with the hotel, are you?"

"I am, as much as you are."

"But not an employee? Or an intern? And you're not with Stageline?"

"No, I'm with *Sun*shine."

"Pizza?"

"Don't be an asshole." Her hair was drawn back so fiercely it had distorted her face.

"There's been a mistake," said Lozeau, who thought he sounded convincing.

"No," she said. "This is room four-eighteen. This is where I was sent."

"I'm sorry, but no. I was very specific."

"You can't always get exactly what you want. I'm what they had, so they sent me. Sorry you're so disappointed, man. It's my executive look, and I like it."

"They send?" Lozeau wondered. "Who *sends* you?"

"You do, honey. I'm so happy you called."

"Again, and I really have to emphasize this, young lady, there's been a mistake."

"No mistake, Carson. I'm on a job. I work. Now I have to get paid. I *have* to get paid. Okay? Let's understand each other." She wore her successive attitudes like an actress in a high school play, but this one was authentic.

"I didn't ask anyone to send you."

"There's only one room four-eighteen in this whole hotel."

"But I'm not Carson, or Mr. Carson, or anything like that.

That's not my name."

"You're here," she accused. "What you're calling yourself at the moment doesn't really matter."

"The thing is," said Lozeau with finality, "I don't have any money. I mean, a twenty and a ten, I think, in my wallet, and I won't have those for long."

"You better be kidding me." She sat on the bed, unintentionally prim now, her hands folded in her lap. "This could be—bad."

The only satisfactory solution to the mystery of this child would be to get rid of her, and this, Lozeau thought, should be very easily done by way of a simple and reasonable request, but there she sat in her weird severity, and he didn't think she'd be open to suggestion. "Look," he said, thinking what to say, and just then there was another knock at the door, a stout rap, and the girl flinched, and her kohl-lined eyes opened wide in her taut little face. Lozeau thought she might be trembling. "It's just my pizza," he said helpfully, hopefully.

The sagging box was well infused with grease, and there was no charge for the delivery because it had taken so long. A little sickened by it, Lozeau carried the thing ceremonially into the room and placed it on a ridiculous table suitable only to a pizza or to a two-handed card game. "See? This is what I ordered. You want some? I guess it's about all I can offer you. For your trouble. Want a soda?"

Now the girl went to the glass wall to look out, and she looked much longer than the view warranted. She seemed to reach a conclusion, and she turned to him and said, "It's really way better when I'm only just disgusted. I can live with that." Her head was very small, her shoulders slight.

"What's worse? Not that it's any of my business, but. . . . Well, I'm wide awake, anyway. Hey, this wasn't your fault. As you say, *they* sent you. Wasn't it *their* mistake?"

Not tall and not steady on her high heels, she said, "I don't know how it is in your business, sir, but in my job a person just has to take personal responsibility. That's the deal, and you can't get around it."

PUNTA COYOTE

Babies and a piglet made night sounds aboard a second-class bus bound from Cabo San Lucas to Tijuana, and Katy Barnett, seated well to the rear of the airless coach with mescal dripping from the luggage rack onto her lap, wondered, How do these people sleep? Sagging bodies enclosed her. Shame mingled with a loathing she had begun to conceive for those more practiced in their misery. From somewhere near at hand, what she took to be love songs issued through a cracked speaker, forlorn, for hours, at all tempos, and the Sea of Cortez would reappear from time to time gliding quicksilver in the window to her right.

According to her guidebook, the Chinese had come to Baja as traders, the French to mine copper, mestizos to do what they had always done on the mainland, farm and raise children in the bosom of the church. Before that there had been those lost tribes who were now nothing but caches of bone all up and down this spiny peninsula, waiting to powder at a touch. The Barnetts were here because Katy had for some years been waging a campaign against the cloying familiarity of everything they'd become. She had insisted and insisted on some small, even if momentary, change of scene. Change of routine. I know we can't afford it, she'd said, but we can't afford not to. Something. Anything. Hanging arid and profuse in the skies north of Loreto, the stars suggested hoarfrost. Gently she set her hand on her husband's knee. Gently she removed it.

Those few conversations the Barnetts managed with fellow travelers had all worked around to the subject of Highway 1. A young man from Milwaukee with terribly tender flesh told them one night in a bar that "it's just twelve hundred miles of ugly-ass blacktop. They can get the big refrigerator trucks down here now, and that's all right, I guess. Truck in frozen orange juice. But I liked it better when a guy could come down here and get completely away from those Coupe de fucking Villes."

The Barnetts had pretty often encountered the implication that this had been a more authentic place before the advent of tourists like themselves, before the road was paved. Still, Katy thought, it was well that there was at least a line of asphalt available to the headlights. Highway 1 was awash in sand drifts, and had been for hours, the bus bursting along through them like an overland speed boat. The drip from the luggage rack slowed, stopped, and her pants dried quickly, but smelled then as if she had been urinating in them.

The sun rose reluctantly over Bajia Fertilidad.

In the seat across from Katy's, and wedged in the aisle between them, there was a family of four. As the waters of the bay shaded through steel to royal blue, Katy heard the woman of the family, in fact it was just within the threshold of her hearing, murmuring to her sons, her husband. "Tsst, Mardo. Ruben. Viejo." The woman's sons had slept standing, and when she roused them their weight came away from Katy's shoulder. Katy envied the reverence in the whispers that passed between this family. Similar intimacies were beginning to ripple through the coach, the odor of humanity was also swelling, and Katy could neither ignore nor accustom herself to her own rich contribution. As she was wondering where the old woman had got so much tenderness, so much authority, Katy saw from the corner of her eye that the boy who had been called Mardo was fingering her hair.

She forced herself to look up. What to say? In any language? She thought it might be best to be a little afraid, but the boy was so smooth of face and so obviously witless. "Art," she said. "Art, wake up." The hand withdrew from the margin of her vision.

Her husband jerked and opened his eyes; he moved his head from side to side, taking stock of the situation, sucking air in through his teeth. Art was cut spare, his profile suggested more hardship than he'd ever really known. He winced at a catch in his neck. "Where are we?"

"I think it's still a long way to Tijuana. A long way. I wish we could pry one of these windows open."

"Well, we can't. If we ever go anywhere again, we're flying." Cautiously he rotated his chin. "See the country? Here it is. Satisfied? You and your bargains. Cheap. See the country, take the bus."

"I really have to use a restroom. Almost any restroom, except the bus-stop ones."

His head moved mechanically, left to right, testing a limit. Then, when there was light enough, he returned to the study of a phrase book he had come to detest. "'When does your chef return from Barcelona?' In my entire life, is that a sentence I'm going to say even once? *Quando? Quaaando.*"

Mardo looked down. "*Pronto*," he said. "*Ahora.*"

His brother, or the slighter boy standing just beside him, said with long, lewd emphasis, "*Ahorrrrittah.*"

"Oh," said Art.

Katy nodded her vague approval. "Do you think they're telling us where we are?"

"Look out the window," her husband said. "We're nowhere. This is nowhere. We're in nothing."

Katy didn't want to be goaded into a fight. They didn't often fight, and they weren't very good at it. This trip had forced them to improvise a lot of things, and they hadn't been good at any of those, either. It seemed that she had proven something she'd set out to prove, which left them, just as Art had said, nowhere.

• • •

The Baja Peninsula is a continental afterthought; buff and
russet cordilleras twist down its length, evidence of a tectonic
birth. Between two of these ranges the flows from several
springs converge in a river that bears various local names and
empties into Bajia Fertilidad. At one point along its banks a
thousand acres of date palms flourish, and among these, less
abundantly, is the village of Proviso. Proviso was where the
Avellanos, their murmuring neighbors in the night, intended
to get off, and as soon as Katy understood they were preparing
to leave the bus, she determined that she and Art would also be
offloading. She could not and would not qualify her decision:
They were getting off.

Before the Barnetts' luggage could be tossed down to them
from the top of the coach, the Avellanos were rounding out of
sight, moving single file and followed by an apparently feral
dog along a path through the gravel hills. Mardo looked back at
them, thickly, and waved goodbye. The highway ran along a sort
of terrace above the river, and a lesser road ran down to follow
the river bank. Both roads were already radiating heat, and once
again the Barnetts' feet were roasting in their shoes. Still so early
in the morning. Just as the bus hit third gear, Art remembered,
"Mike's som*brero*. God darn it. Well, let's just hope *some*body
gets to enjoy it. You'd think one of us would have remembered.
Do you know how long it could be before the next bus comes
along? Katy? We should've looked. This was, this looks like a
pretty bad idea."

Katy nodded toward the Pemex station a quarter mile
away, down in the village proper. They hefted their remaining
luggage and started off. Three grinning curs loped in sideways
to join them—why so many dogs?—and a girl child stood
slack-mouthed and barefoot by the road, an infant in its arms.
Gnats clustered unheeded, drinking probably, on the children's eyelids. "Boy," said Art despondently. Down among the

date palms, along the river, the air turned insufferable.

At the gas station there was a cooler chest, Coca-Cola red, with pop bottles suspended from a rack in nearly frozen water. Art used the last of their pesos to justify Katy's use of the station's nice lavatory and to buy them two bottles each of some violet concoction. Katy was so thirsty the first bottle seemed almost to vaporize in her mouth before she could swallow it. They crossed over a stone bridge into the old village, a squat adobe square. Adobe and stone and terra-cotta tile, a mission-style church. There was a gazebo in the square, and the Barnetts went under its shade. Their companion dogs became bored with them and went off, and then there was nothing and no one moving in the square, and in the same moment Katy realized that their camera had been whisked away with the sombrero; she thought it just as well. She must remember this. It was not a picture to be taken. The brave things people do with mud. The lives being lived in this village now were no more evident than lives led here, and concluded, long before, and Katy was haunted and quite happy with this arrangement. She must remember it.

"Now what? We can't just wait up on the highway for the next bus to come. We really did not think this through."

"I feel a lot better," she said. "Thank you for asking."

"I know you do. I know we had to. . . . But, I don't know. I mean, I don't see any place here where we could stay, or wait, and we don't know how long . . . don't know who to ask. Or where. See what I mean? You have to admit this is not real well organized, and maybe we should have stuck with the original plan, but, oh, look. *Helados*." The word was written in a fading arc of block letters above a bright blue Dutch-door. "Remember that cart in Cabo? *Helados*, that's ice cream. If it's, if they're open. Of all things. I wonder if they'd take American?"

They had meant to travel light, still their plaid luggage weighed like real wealth, and Katy felt conspicuous crossing the abandoned square, though it seemed there was no one to notice them, and she felt new but not rejuvenated. Where was everyone? It was a village that might have been depopulated by firing squads.

But when Art tried the blue door its upper half swung open, and an aproned woman came scurrying to open the bottom half and invite them in. They were welcome. They learned at once that their dollars would be very welcome. The proprietress, wringing her hands, showed them to a glass table and chairs of baroquely twisted wire. Katy's eyes enjoyed the lesser light and what remained of the previous evening's cool in the room. So that's where all the citizens had gone. Inside. Their server named for them her many flavors, and among these Katy recognized *vainilla* and *chocolate*, but could only wonder at *aguacate* and *datil*. "Water?" she asked. "Could I just have some *agua*?"

"Go ahead and get some ice cream," Art advised, "I'll eat yours, too, if you don't like it. I want to spend some time in here. Think things through. Rest." The woman awaited their decision too patiently; in her smile were several teeth capped with a metal that bled blue onto the white of their neighboring teeth. The woman waited upon them like an animal bred and trained for a single trick, which embarrassed Katy, whose mention of water had instantly resulted in two glasses of it at their table. Katy drank both of these and they were instantly refilled.

Art finally ordered by pointing to the menu on the wall and smiling back at the woman. The woman responded at once by bringing them two deep, chilled bowls containing many scoops of the specialty of the house, date ice cream. Large fragments of date were in it, and in these Katy saw an unfortunate resemblance to cockroach husk, but she had come to try new things, so she braved it. The new flavor was as repulsively sweet as pecan pie.

"Ooooh," said Art of his, "You wouldn't think, but. . . . This must be hand-cranked, that's the only way you can get it like this. This texture."

"You can have mine. Too rich. I'm sticking to water."

A tall man with a massively, greasily bandaged foot came limping into the shop cradling an empty parfait glass in his fingers. The man presented this to the Good Humor woman along with quite a lot of instruction. He wanted ice creams entered into it, and nuts and syrups in a certain order, and in certain amounts, and the woman of the ice cream shop tried hard to please, attending him closely, measuring elaborately, but still she fell short, and when at last he got the finished confection in hand the man was too obviously unhappy.

Though Art had no idea what the man was saying, and though the man's lexicon of facial expressions was also foreign, he knew him for a "cheapskate. Katy, I think he's trying to beat that poor woman down on the price. What a. . . ."

The man turned to them. He was about sixty, pouch-eyed and freckled, and his glistening hair might have been marcelled. He shook his finger at them, a showman's gesture. "I've got you. Doesn't take me long, does it?"

"Got?" said Art. "Me?"

"California," said the man. "Central California."

"I?"

"Your accent. I've lived everywhere, so I'm great with dialect, dialogue, whatever it is. I've got a good ear. You're from Central California."

"Nebraska," said Katy. "We're from Ordella. I doubt you've ever been there."

"Ordella? Grain elevators? There'd be a two-story high school at the end of Main Street? Some Methodists? I think I may have visited. What brings you to this sad state of affairs? Do you know someone here in Proviso?"

"Is that what they call it?" Art said. "No. We're new in town, which is obvious, I guess. This lady's shop could turn out to be my favorite thing of the whole trip, but we sort of got a little farther off the beaten track than we meant to. I think you could safely say we don't know what we're doing."

"We probably could use some advice," Katy conceded. "Or information, I'd say. Would be good."

"I'm sorry," said the man, "you forget your manners living down here." He spoke his name as if to instruct them— Da-*beed*, it was to be, Da-*beed* Eegnathio. He wore a lavender kerchief round his neck. "Go for months on end," he said, "with very little use for the social graces. And you good folks are— from Nebraska? And?"

"We teach," said Art.

"Your names?"

"Oh. I'm kinda . . . myself. I'm Art, and this is Katy. Barnett. We don't get out much, as you can probably tell."

"Then you've really outdone yourselves this time. Because you are a long, long way from Nebraska. You're a long way from anywhere here."

"That's sort of what I was saying. Don't get me wrong. We like it here, but we, we don't exactly know how you'd get out of town. We're winding up our vacation, so we'd like to do that pretty soon. Get headed north again."

"We're fine," said Katy. "We're doing fine—if my husband hasn't given himself diabetes. But, is there anything like a bus schedule? I noticed there was no bench or anything where they let us off, so I know it's pretty informal, but."

"You might as well hitchhike. It would be faster and just as reliable."

"Is that legal?"

"Legal?" Ignacio was touched. "You haven't been down here very long, have you? This is all new to you."

. . .

David Ignacio guided a spring-shot Buick, the heaviest ever made, along a little riparian road. He could not with his bandaged foot be subtle on the accelerator or brake; a tail of roseate dust plumed out behind them. He had told them he was the manager of something like a hotel, that he found them intriguing, that this was their lucky day—they'd stay for free if he had his way. Maybe for once there'd be some civilized conversation, some news from outside Mexico. "Viva," he said. "It's viva this and viva that, but really, this whole country is just one appalling cult of the dead. I have to say in all honesty, give me Dayton, Ohio, every time, awful as that was. Give me the good old gringo way. I was in retail, married to a Polish woman. This was the wife after Graciela. I like America. It's ruthless, of course, but generally very sanitary."

There were fishermen's dwellings at intervals, ingenious huts walled and thatched with palm frond, but near these places it was the local practice to clean each day's catch. A reek of hot fish guts poured through their windows with every habitation they passed, and Katy could not recall ever before giving so much thought to sanitation. The road was not promising, the river remained sluggish even as they neared its mouth. Hotel? She was afraid this Da-beed might have a tendency to overstate things, but it was her habit, not always wholesome, to try to think the best of people. This had been a simple choice. They had nowhere else to stay; her bowels were more and more fretful.

They rounded a turn at last that confronted them with the bay, bottomless blue and shimmering. "Wow," said Art. A hundred yards up the beach a compound rose from the litter of crushed shell and sand and sea globs, a dull white monolith, the destination of this road.

"Home," said Ignacio with negative enthusiasm.

"Wow."

"Okay, great," said Katy. "But let's kinda hurry."

They left the Buick standing in the desert and went in through an arched portico that led to a flagstone courtyard with a great planter in its center, date palms rising out of that. The shaded flagstone was cool under foot, and they were encircled by two tiers of small rooms without a single visible window, and this seemed a sort of inverse wedding cake— two rounds of doors set awfully close together.

"Is this a monastery or something?"

"Prison," said Ignacio. "Or it was. I'm told the inmates maintained quite a garden. They were provided nets and hoes and buckets, and many were supposedly happy here. Which is . . . mm. I'll find Mrs. Yee and have her get something ready for you."

"Would it have a bathroom?" Katy asked.

"All the deluxe cells do."

"Ooooh, God," she said when Ignacio had gone off. Her digestive tract writhed along its whole length, the creature within. "That lady had such cold water, it just didn't seem like it could be, I might need some I-don't-know-what."

"We'll be okay. As long as we stay out of that sun. Won't this be a story, though? Kind of colorful, if you think about it. At least we'll get one good story out of the trip—our night in a prison."

"I don't think I'll be wanting to talk about it too much. I think it's going to be a little embarrassing before I'm done."

"You know you kind of asked for this. In a way."

"I know," she said. "Oooh."

• • •

Her cot was narrow, but it was her own. For some days, Katy lost count, she rarely rose from it. Art brought her beer or wine from time to time, the only liquids she would risk, and Mrs.

Yee, a bird of a woman, came bowing with bananas and rice
and brittle chunks of chocolate laced with cinnamon. When
Katy mentioned her boredom to Art, he brought her an edition
of Black's Law Dictionary. Alone with the cot and a straight
back chair and her thoughts, she was soon unable to arrange
herself comfortably with any of these things, but she wasn't at
liberty to quit her room, her heroic commode, so to keep from
fidgeting or thinking too much of her gut or her aching back,
she browsed the book Art had brought, the only written English
to be found in the compound.

Corrections, house of. A prison for the reformation of petty
or juvenile offenders.

She was in error. In her cell this had become apparent.
Along with so much else she had evacuated her good opinion
of herself, and try as she might, she could not be convinced this
emptiness was only boredom or sickness.

Corpus. Physical substance, as opposed to intellectual conception.

They had been good, she and her husband. Good generally, and good to each other for all of their adult lives. They'd
raised a sound, reasonable child, maintained their own health
through regular habits and moderation and solid citizenship,
and they'd avoided serious debt. But more than anything,
they'd been kind. What in the world could be wrong with that?
The reproach that sat on her in her cell would not announce
its reasons, and it would not relent. The walls were near and
bare and very tall around her. Never before in her married life,
which had come to seem all of her life, had she slept alone.
Eaten alone. Been alone.

Omnis actio est loquela. Every action is a plaint or complaint.

Omnis exception est ipsa quoque regula. Every exception is
itself also a rule.

. . .

A saffron rust coated her forearms the moment she leaned on
the railing. Rust dusted her shirt. Katy Barnett leaned weakly to
look down from the upper tier and she thought the tilt of the
sun into the courtyard might mean it was afternoon, but this
was proximate. She had lost all her bearings. Where would Art
be? No idea. Until just now, she hadn't done more than wonder
when he might be coming by with her beer. That beer had saved
her, and he seemed to enjoy bringing it, and she'd barely given
him a moment's thought between times. But where had he been
keeping himself?

What was this?

The planter in the courtyard contained a small park with
shade-loving flowers, and there was a hammock strung between
two of its date palms, an old man's huaraches protruding out the
high side of the hammock. From Katy's vantage the man's head
was only a nimbus of white hair and white beard; he was turned
from her so that she couldn't tell if he was sleeping. The silence
of her cell had followed her outside, this was the stillest place
she'd ever known, and when a fallen date struck the flagstone
with a bright, wet pop she was so startled as to tremble, and her
first question was answered: She wasn't well enough to travel.

A Siamese cat strode out across the courtyard, leapt up onto
the planter and crossed that to leap onto the chest of the man
in the hammock, where it was petted. They hadn't noticed her
watching them, and Katy hadn't a thought of announcing herself. She was among strangers. As usual.

. . .

He seemed a guest now, her husband, there at the foot of her
cot, in her chair, leaning at her, the tan benefactor. He looked at
last like he'd had a good vacation. "I was really worried."

She nearly apologized, but didn't. "I'm getting stronger. We'll be out of here in a day or two. I'm glad you dodged it, whatever it was. This has not been fun."

"There's no hurry. I'm in no hurry."

"You must be going out of your mind. There can't be a whole lot to do around here."

"Oh, they've had me puttering."

"They?"

"The owner. Mr. M, as I call him."

"He give you a hoe and a net?"

"Motors. Outboards, inboards, they're running quite the little marina just a little way up the point."

"Oh. Well, good. I guess. So, what is this? What goes on here? It is *not* a hotel. Or not a very busy one."

"Well, it's his place, and . . . I don't want to spoil it. You'll be hearing all about it. You sure you'll be up to coming down to dinner tonight?"

Her husband was become a weird echo of the avid boy who'd asked her to the prom. "I think," said Katy, "if I take about twelve showers I might be presentable. I have to say, the plumbing here *is* deluxe. I mean, to look at the place, you wouldn't know what to expect, but you certainly wouldn't expect all this hot water. So I'm wondering."

Art smiled a new smile—she remembered something tamer. "It's quite the story," he told her. "Wait 'til you hear it all. With some surprises, too. We've got some surprises for you. Why don't you go ahead and get some rest, and then when you . . . maybe you'd wear your nice dress down?"

"I'm sure that's pretty wrinkled by now. But as long as there's beer."

• • •

A card table had been set up in the courtyard, draped with checked linen and set for four and a stand of guttering candles stood nearby, reflecting off the oily water in a bird bath. She was on Art's arm, preposterously, but he had insisted. David Ignacio rose from the table at their approach, as did the man she'd seen in the hammock, and Katy Barnett did not recognize herself as a figure in such a scene, but there she was, floating along.

"Katy," said her suddenly pompous husband, "I'd like you to meet Sean Maldonado. Señor Maldonado, I'd like you to meet my wife. We practically owe you her life."

"We do?"

"Señor Maldonado," explained Ignacio, "owns the Sentinel. I'm sure he'd want you to call him Sean."

Art had withdrawn her chair. The other men were still standing. Not Nebraska. "Well, good," she said. "Nice to meet you, sir. And thanks." She offered to shake, but he took her hand and bowed at her. She felt a chill gusting off old Maldonado's formality; he was short and thick and wore immaculate campesino's clothes, also white, and her hand only just rested in his, but she had the sense he might crush it. When he raised his gaze to her it was pointed, and his eyes were improbably gray for his complexion, and he said something to David Ignacio, who said, "Sean says he regrets how poorly equipped he is to express his pleasure in having you here."

"That's very nice of him. Considering. Thank you, sir."

The old man's basso Spanish issued again. Ignacio translated. "Our lives are changed forever."

"Oh," she said. "Well, please, let's all sit down."

Until now, it had been her experience that strangers were generally polite enough to remain strangers to her. She'd not been a guest of honor this way since perhaps her eighth birthday. They were all examining her, probably with the best intentions, but examining. "So," she said. "I'm not sure I understand. Is this an inn or? Or what is it?"

"A retreat," said Ignacio. "I think you could call it a retreat. *You*, certainly could, Mrs. Barnett."

Señor Maldonado loosed a loud rebuke to someone out of sight.

"When this was a prison," Ignacio explained, "Sean was a guest of the Republic. He not only managed to escape, which wasn't actually all that hard, but he also returned and bought the thing. The right revenue in the right hands. He belonged to it, now it belongs to him."

"But why would you. . ? If you don't mind my asking, sir? Can you under. . .?"

"*Porque no?*" was the old man's answer; Ignacio didn't bother to translate.

Big deal. Katy saw it as possibly a larger accomplishment than she'd ever do, but big deal. It seemed an odd thing, a male thing to have returned, to stake such a claim. "Who comes?" she said. "To these retreats?"

"The Barnetts, so far."

"So, it's a new thing?"

"Oh, we've been thinking of it for a while, but as you might imagine, word of mouth just doesn't escape Punta Coyote all that often, and it is *very* hard to try and put together any kind of staff here. The locals aren't drawn to this kind of work."

"I thought you said it was Sentinel. The Sentinel or something."

"That's the name of the facility. It sits on Punta Coyote, this long spit we're on, most of which Sean also owns." Ignacio glanced pretty often toward the older man, as though to continue conveying his thoughts.

"What kind of work? Aren't locals drawn to?"

"Anything domestic," said Ignacio. "It's not hard to subsist by the sea, so it's not a hotbed of ambition. That's what the true American never understands."

"Well," she said, "the bay is very beautiful, and I guess you must have everything you need. All this everything, the sea and. Yeah." The owner looked upon her with what appeared to be grave, considered approval. "Congratulations, sir. Once you *chose* to be here, I suppose that would be different." He beamed at her, Señor Maldonado, with what seemed gratitude, and then he turned his head just a few degrees and bellowed at an unseen servant. It had been so quiet before. Her husband, a glass of the table red already in him, acted the hapless, haggard pup.

A boy with a big forehead hustled out with a platter so large that the diners were obliged to take their plates into their laps when he set it on their table. On the platter was a great fish and it smelled of sage and lemon and still of the sea. The boy, constantly harried by the old man, and by David Ignacio who called him "Bobo," carved the fish into cutlets and distributed these to their waiting plates. In the candlelight—they ate so late here—the old man's eyes kept returning to her. The escapee's old eyes. Mrs. Yee came with a stack of hot tortillas, and with fried onions and peppers, another bottle of wine, and then at Maldonado's stiff command she came back with a mug of beer for Katy.

Not Nebraska. Art had not said grace, but said, "This. You never really believe you'll be in the right place at the right time, but then—this. I mean, who would have ever believed?"

"Well," said Katy, "you won't hear me complaining."

"And you don't know the half of it yet," said her husband.

• • •

He claimed the light was only right in the morning, a sort of misfortune because he hated to rise before ten. David Ignacio had brought to the beach his easel, palette and paints, and Katy his hesitant model. He fussed and fussed to get her turned just so, standing with her back to the bay, and the wind blew her hair into her face, and Ignacio's easel blew over, and he dropped his palette as well, wet side down in the sand; he maneuvered around his lumpen foot, cursing in other tongues. Then, when he'd given up, they sat side by side on the beach and looked out from their befuddlement at the tossing water and into the damp breeze.

This had been one of Art's surprises for her. The Barnetts were to stay on for a while. Katy was to have her portrait done. The broad, pink image of her face was reliably enough fixed in her mind's eye that she saw no need to further memorialize it. She knew what she looked like, and so, now that it seemed that the portrait project had been scotched, she was relieved.

"Charcoals," said Ignacio. "That's the more dramatic way. Maybe an interior setting. Why deal with the elements if you don't have to?"

"You don't have to do it at all," said Katy. "Everyone's being so nice and everything, but. Really."

"If I want that commission, and I do, I have to do it. Or . . . not that I *have* to, that's not the point. It's art."

"I thought it was Mr. Maldonado who wanted it."

"No. I mean for the sake of art. *My* art."

"You've got these seascapes," she said, "all these interesting country folks out along the road, out in their boats—that's what I'd be painting if I was here."

"You are here."

"I mean, yeah, but. . . . I don't know what Art's thinking. I'm happy to see him happy, but I don't know what he's thinking. I mean, it's the end of summer. It's getting kind of late. This is, we've already been gone longer than we intended."

"Everyone gets sidetracked from time to time."

"We never have. We're about as predictable as . . . predictable."

"You're in a different latitude now."

"You don't like it here, do you? Very much?"

"That is beside the point."

"It is? Why would you stay?"

"I'm committed," Ignacio groused. "This property, all of it, happens to be in my name, because I happen to be the Mexican national."

"Then what's Mr. Maldonado? That Sean?"

"He's the money. He has resources."

"Yeah, but if he's not Mexican, what is he?"

"I don't know. He doesn't mention his life before he came here."

"And what did he do to get here? In prison? I mean, the first time."

"He doesn't get into those specifics, and I'm sure I'm not interested. His life started here, to hear him tell it. I think he fancies himself the Count of Monte Cristo or something."

"You don't know what he did? Where's he from?"

"I met him at a party in the Zona Rosa. More than that, I couldn't tell you. I suspect the Sentinel—this place really isn't too typical of the country's penal system—I think it might have been for political prisoners. The isolation. But I don't know. No one left any brochures lying around. All I know is, I'm here, and whenever a certain ridiculously healthy party chooses to leave, then it's mine in more than name only. I *do* know how old he is. Of that I am quite certain."

"Gee," said Katy. "That was a favorite of mine. I loved that book. In the book, though, the man just breaks out; he doesn't come back. Dantés. That's what I find odd about this whole deal. And you. What if he is gone? What if it *was* yours? Then what? You don't even like it."

"You should have been with the police," he said. "You would have made a fine interrogator."

The desert continued to the very edge of the sea. They sat on hot sand, their arms wrapped round their knees, looking out at the water and the far shore, a chalk mark along the horizon. Even more Mexico. In Mexico, she thought, she became a smaller particle. She was as out of place here as a maple tree. "Can we go into Proviso now? Before it gets too hot?" Ignacio had promised to take her to a telephone exchange in the village where it would be possible to call home. The time had definitely come.

If she was honest with herself, and that had lately been hard to avoid, she had been giving scant thought to their son. Michael, alone in the house, and more than capable, and probably very. . . . she preferred not to think how happily self-sufficient he must be alone. Alone. She'd been thinking of no one but herself lately. But here she was, wasn't she, returned to doing the right thing, and she was having to hear more of Ignacio's sad history to do it, and he was such an awful driver. Those fish guts again, putrid here and there. Ignacio, mentioning his art again, and a car dealership in Daytona Beach, and something about contract bridge.

"Whoa. You need to pay attention to the. . . . Da-beed, please, that is just . . . whoa!"

"It's fine," he said. "Not the most responsive steering, but . . . and the Colonel would fly in from anywhere in the country, any time there was a tournament. We were almost unbeatable."

"*Whooop!*" she said. "That's the edge right there, so." They were a long while covering the short distance to Proviso. Ignacio spoke of bidding, finessing, and a local tribe only recently extinct that was said to be so primitive as to eat the seeds from its own excrement. She listened, but only because it seemed the best way to keep him from wrecking them in the river.

The telephone exchange was only slightly bigger than a phone booth, and it was necessary for Katy and Ignacio to crowd into it with a phone clerk, and it happened more than once in the ten-minute course of placing the call that all of them were speaking simultaneously. When at last she heard it ringing, Katy felt too tired and jangled.

"Hello?"

She found herself talking over someone again, trying to be heard over the operator's opaque questions. "Michael. Michael. Accept the charges. She's asking if you'll accept the charges. Say, 'Si'. Michael."

"Si."

"Are you there?" She continued to yell into the receiver. It seemed the thing to do.

"Mom?"

"Hi, honey. How are you?"

"Great." Michael yelling, too. "How are *you*? *Where* are you?"

"We're still down here," she said. "South of the border, as you might say. They do have a real slow pace of life. We kind of got stalled."

"Great. Good for you guys. Could I take some more money out of the bank? I've still got that other check left."

"Sure. You might want to make it for a little extra. If you head off for school before we come back."

"What about your school? How does that work? Yours starts before mine, doesn't it?"

"I got a little case of the *turista*," Katy said. "We've been held up. But I'm feeling a lot better now, and it shouldn't be long. Feeling a lot better."

"You want me to call Mr. Roth? Tell him you might be delayed?"

"No. Don't do. No, that won't be necessary. Did Darla bring that little refrigerator by for you?"

"Is there any way I can get in touch with you if I need to? If I need to lock up the house?"

"Ah, noo," said Katy, and she realized it only as she said it. "No, I guess there wouldn't be. But we'll be back, honey. We'll be back soon."

"Are you all right, Mom?"

"I'm getting there," she said. "Eat those pork chops, why don't you? Before they get freezer-burned."

"Mom?"

"Can you hear me? I love you, honey."

"Mom?"

"So much."

"Mom? Is that? Mom? Still there?"

"Bye, honey. Bye. See you very soon."

• • •

"I don't know," she told her husband. "I think I've had about all the surprises I can take for now. Would it be real impolite if I just skipped dinner tonight? I could say I overdid it today, and I could say that in all honesty. I'm tired, Art. I just want to go home as soon as I can. Could we start looking into that? Figure out how we're going to do that?"

"That'll be easy. That'd be very easy, but there's so many other things to talk about, things I want you to see."

"Motors?"

"Among other things. All I ask—try and stay open-minded. I mean, the food's good, isn't it? Maybe we can get David to shut up. Maybe we can get Sean to say a few things to you. He can, you know, but he's shy."

"He's *shy*? Art. Holy smokes. *Shy?*"

"In his way. About certain things. We're having pork. They've had a suckling pig in the pot all day, and I even got Mrs. Yee to lay off the garlic a little bit. Just try and stay open. The best is yet to come."

And so there was another dinner, she was too weak to resist, and another late night with beer. The gray eyes again, and tonight the old one dictated almost constantly through David Ignacio, who bore the duty poorly, preferring always to speak of himself. Señor Maldonado, as she understood it, had the deepest respect for what Ignacio expressed as, ". . . a woman's graciousness and pure motives."

"I," she said. She did not know what he was talking about. She had been mistaken for someone else. Even Art had now mistaken her for someone else. "Yeah," she said. "Well. I don't know. I'm just kind of a homesick person right now. More than the other kind. Of sick."

The old man went on. He was too clean for his clothing or for anyone's clothing. His hair and beard were white as cotton balls. He went on and on through poor Ignacio, and it seemed he meant to have the last word on every last subject before they'd finished their salads. He did not like communism. He did not like socialism or organized crime. He despised Dow Chemical. One's niche was narrow, wouldn't she agree? One's little place of repose? What did Mrs. Barnett prefer? What would she wish for in her most perfect world?

"Good manners," she said. "I used to worry about hunger. People being hungry. Anyone, anywhere, but, and I don't know why, it doesn't seem such a big thing anymore."

"Sean says he knew you'd be in deepest agreement, or sympathy, the moment he saw you, even when you were so ill. Good manners. He likes that."

"There's not all that much to agree with. Or disagree with. On most things I'm fairly neutral. No opinion."

Maldonado made a word that Ignacio changed to, "Wise."

It was clearer and clearer, she'd been mistaken for someone else, and it was taxing, and dinner scrolled out brutally again and then was punctuated by yet another surprise. Over coffee, and coffee was new for him at any time of day, much less midnight, Art could no longer contain himself. "Katy," he said, "I should've waited for Sean to bring this up, but we've been talking over a business proposition."

Maldonado said something long and complicated and florid. Ignacio compressed it for her. "A corporation. He's talking

about a corporation. Which is not a bad idea. They're thinking of you for the chief executive officer or chief stockholder,
whichever you prefer."

"They are? Art, this is . . . *your* idea?"

"It is now," he said. "And I'll have to admit, it is new. So,
like I said, keep an open mind. What would you think about
staying on?"

"Here?"

"There are a lot of things we could do with this structure.
Great things. Knock out a lot of walls. Upgrade the generator
system."

"Why?"

"To make it a little more livable."

"Here? You mean?"

Maldonado said something.

Ignacio said, "For any chance of success, the corporation will
rely on the opinions and judgment of a shrewd woman. I think
he's right about that, by the way."

"Well, that wouldn't be me," she said. "In fact, I'd say right
now I'm the one who's pretty darn slow to notice things. Cor-
po*ration*? To do what?"

• • •

One symptom of her recovery was that she could no longer
steal the briefest moment of comfort on the cot. Only when she
was fairly sick had she failed to notice how very hard it was. She
smelled nicely of the sandalwood soap she'd found in her shower
stall, and she was full of pork and some leafy green like chard, but
something had happened to her husband, and she knew herself
to be responsible, and she wouldn't be sleeping any time soon.
Stay on? Not a mention of their home, or their son, and what was
to become of those incidentals in this scheme of his? This was the
first year in many years that Art had not spent some part of Au-
gust varnishing desks or conditioning the football field. Just for

a little extra, he'd say, and a portion of even this small pay would find its way into their retirement fund. And Art would varnish, and Art would teach, and Art would put up storm windows in the fall and bed the garden for winter. Without comment he carved their holiday turkeys and hams. That was Art, and if his personality was a small territory, he'd always seemed so at home in it, and she'd envied him his simplicity, and now, too late, she thought she might miss it if it had been broken or stolen or compromised when she wasn't paying attention.

He was calling it "my marina" already. Tomorrow they'd go and have a look, and take a snorkel—he'd been learning to dive—and then, she'd been told, she'd have a lot better idea of what they had in mind. But no one who'd washed up in this place seemed reasonable about it, or in any sane way happy here, and Katy couldn't begin to understand how these men had gotten into its grip. What was the attraction? She wouldn't see anything tomorrow that would change her mind: Here was here, and she already understood to the bottom of her being that no part of her curtained little soul was ever going to love it. It was impossible to know whether it was night or day without igniting the bare bulb and consulting her watch, and she waited and waited, and then it was two-thirty with a gecko on the wall. She let it be dark again and waited.

This new Art. Art the optimist, with his drinking anything at all hours and his appreciative chuckles for the many phrases he didn't understand, his zest for the next thing. Not Art. Not Nebraska. More than homesick, she felt as if she were watching the approach of a funnel cloud. It was four-ten. What were her thoughts to be if she was ever too long alone? The cocoon that had chafed her so had been safety, after all, and how dare she question the good in simply hanging on? Was there no wisdom in her? At four-fifty-six she concluded that she'd stranded herself at the wrong end of a hissy fit.

At last she smelled bacon. Katy went out of the cell and onto the narrow walk way circling the upper tier. It was steel. So much of this was steel, the walkways, the doors, the stair, and it would have been a clanging place with anyone here, with its inmates. This was a prison, she thought, and could never be anything else. Katy hadn't slept at all. She went down the hard stair, careful not to bang it in any way, and she went to the door from which she'd seen Mrs. Yee and Bobo emerge with meals. On the other side it was well windowed, and there was a row of deep sinks and a naked chicken and a garland of garlic hung in slant morning light. A diesel generator hummed just the other side of the wall, and a portion of the room opened onto a terrace. "Good morning," she told the startled Mrs. Yee. "*Buenos dias.* Could I make coffee?"

Mrs. Yee nodded constantly, but never with comprehension, and because Katy didn't think it right to nose around in the woman's kitchen she found a chair and sat down. It was warm in the kitchen, not that she'd been cold before. By turns Mrs. Yee brought her bacon, and melon, and eventually coffee. Bobo in the midst of his morning chores was diverted by the unexpected gringa, and made a game of peeking round at her from here and there. A funny old gringa she must seem to the boy. Mrs. Yee's kitchen was a splendor not at all foretold by any other part of these premises, and if nothing was settled then nothing could be unalterably wrong. Could it? The coffee, though there was chicory in it, was proving helpful.

• • •

A single naked bulb—there must be one in every cell—was the sole source of light in Ignacio's studio where oils leaned garishly along one wall and charcoal sketches along the other, so many of these, childish in conception and in their petulant incompletion, that there was only just room to stand among them; Ignacio with his slight craft had at least learned to express the pitiable, and the artist had finally succeeded in making her feel sorry for him. With that pity and the unventilated acetone in the room, she felt a little dizzy. "We went to town one year," she said, "and there was a guy in the mall, and he had these, oh, crayon thingys, and he'd do your portrait. Take him about ten minutes, and he charged twenty-five bucks. People were lined up for that. He just did the basics, but. . . . No. I didn't mean to offend. I know that's not *art* art. Not *real* art. But it'd sure be good enough for me. Since I have to get going anyway."

Ignacio was already in a huff because he wasn't to be involved in the day's field trip. He couldn't wade out to the launch without saturating the mass of gauze round his foot with seawater. "I hate being alone here," he said. "Under the best of circumstances it's usually just, well, Maldonado and staff, but that still trumps being completely alone here. You know, the whole idea, for me, is just to get some people to come. Some more people. Not these priest-ridden villagers and thugs, but people. Believe me, when it's just you and the bare walls around here, then you find out what you're made of."

"I can imagine."

"That's why we need new blood. More blood."

"I'm sure you do. I've been meaning to ask, though, what happened to your foot?"

"More ideas. Fresh ideas. That's why we're all hoping you'll change your mind. Or at least wait and see what they've got to show you before you decide."

"I'm not an idea person," she said. "Maybe just a little arts and crafts. But I have a job. We both have jobs. Among other things."

"Home economics? Industrial arts? I know you do, but you must know you can do better. There are certainly other jobs in the world. I can't think it would be all that difficult to find more interesting ones."

"Maybe, but. Maybe we're not that interesting. Someone has to teach those girls how to make something other than Cheese Whiz. Sorry if that was a sore subject. About your foot."

"Dream the dream for once."

"Which dream was that?"

"You'll see."

• • •

The launch was buffeted by quartering seas. Quartering seas, that's what Art called them over the engine's high droning. To their right that great stretch of water, to their left a desert beaten nearly featureless under the sun. How far might they have to pound along the coast, Katy wondered, before they came to anything that might sustain human life? Bobo and Mrs. Yee were with them, and they'd brought the hamper they'd been filling that morning in the kitchen. Art at the tiller, happy as a clam. And Maldonado. All of them looking forward into the onrushing air like dogs in the back of a pickup. Half an hour of this brought them to a lagoon with a stone breakwater; another effusion of date palms on the shore and a wild ass sprinted away from these and into the desert at their approach. On the shore there was a system for dragging boats out of the water and a hut containing other greasy equipment. Art swung the launch in behind the breakwater and then mercifully killed the motor. He hefted an anchor over the side. "Well, honey, now what do you think?"

Her ears were ringing. "I'm not sure," she said.

Maldonado said something and the Barnetts looked at him.

"The location?" Art asked her.

"Oh, well . . . it's scenic in a way. Fairly scenic, I'd say."

"Can you see it, though? Boat rentals. Boat repair. Diving. Eventually a tour boat so we could go out and see the whales."

Maldonado said something else.

"That might be nice," she said. "But who would come? Here?

How would they get here if their boat wasn't working? You couldn't even get here in a bad boat, could you?"

"I know it's a lot to throw at you all at once, and there's a lot of details to be worked out, but let's just go for a dive and you'll, then you can really appreciate what we've got."

"We've got?"

He seemed so young, so good whenever he got his hands on any kind of equipment. There were masks and tanks and a regulator and flippers and her snorkel tube, and he was in his glory explaining these things to her. Back home they were a long way from water, but it was just like her husband to have acquired this arcane knowledge and lingo. He brought them a bit closer to the shore, and they lowered off the side of the launch, so that Katy could take instruction. Simply standing in her flippers was almost impossible, and she was near to panic at the thought of planting her face in the water. "First," he said, "spit into your mask and rub that around on the lens. Keeps it from fogging up. Okay, now get a good seal. Take your snorkel in, and—you don't have to bite it. Hands at your sides. At your sides, honey, I've got you. Now just lay forward, here in my arms, I've got you. All right. Put your mask in. Go ahead."

She pushed her face down into a world as fecund as the desert was barren, and her dread yielded at once to fascination. Kick, she heard him say. He told her to wiggle her flippers, and she hardly noticed that he'd taken his arms from under her. Her breath sounded in the tube. She was an aquatic thing, gliding over the sand in company with schools of fish that were hardly more than points of light, and a corpulent bottom feeder with feline whiskers, and sand sharks, and things that might or might not be vegetation. He'd promised surprises. To glide, that was the thing. She could recall nothing so delicious, and she'd suspected none of this while looking out upon the surface of the sea.

Eventually she slid out over a shelf where the sand dropped away, the inevitable edge, and she was in much deeper water, the bottom shading off quickly into gloom. Her companions were fewer here but included a supremely confident little barracuda and then, invisibly, jellyfish. The first sting hit her ankle like a jolt of household electricity, but with a more enduring pain, and in turning to it Katy scooped water into the end of her snorkel. She breathed some of this and came up sputtering, flippers flailing under her as if to drive her shoulders up out of the water. Blinded each time she exhaled through her nose, she was stung again on the arm, and the cry that hummed through the rubber tube seemed to come from someone else.

You asked for this. Calm down.

Katy looked back toward the beach for Art, but he'd gone under with his equipment, so she set out to swim to the launch with the wretched crawl she had acquired at their municipal swimming pool, and she was stung once more along the way, a shot to the ribs that she felt transect her bumping heart. With her stroke none too efficient and her fancy equipment only in the way now, she was a long time reaching the others, but by the time she'd got there she knew for certain that water is not a prairie gal's medium, and she could walk back to Nebraska if necessary.

Maldonado's arm came over the gunwale, he'd made a hook of it, and he slapped at the crook to demonstrate she should take hold there. She grabbed round it and, ancient as he was, he lifted her smoothly aboard.

I've lost some weight.

The four of them sat mute. There wasn't a scrap of shade anywhere on the launch, and it was coming on noon. Art stayed under, and it was hard to measure time, but it seemed too long after a while, knowing some of what was down there with him. He could hardly be more than a novice himself, underwater.

The others were better with the sun; Mrs. Yee had unveiled her broad-brimmed hat. Katy, the crook of her hand pressed almost continuously to her forehead, looked out. Her husband was under the sea. No one was saying anything. Not even Maldonado. Were they waiting? Wondering? Bobo after a time began an infant's game of hide-and-seek with her, glancing her way, glancing away and giggling. He would be about her son's age, but was so much younger. Mrs. Yee, with no task presently to hand, had folded in on her tiny self to wait, and to endure the heat, and Katy felt things had crawled to an absolute, melted halt when Maldonado suddenly exploded at the boy, "*Tonto*," he said, and he crossed the boat in a single step to deliver a round-house slap to Bobo's upturned cheek. He slapped him again, and the boy grinned hopefully through bloody teeth. "*Tonto*," Maldonado said again, and then to Katy, "If I can say it, I am . . . regret to you."

"Oh, please," she said. "Let's have no more of that. Please."

Maldonado, mistaking the source of his guest's distress, gave Bobo's cheek another great stroke.

• • •

"Get packed," she said. "Let's just get packed and get out of here."

"What happened?"

"Come on, Art. I am not even sure, or I probably couldn't explain it. Let's just go."

"Well maybe it isn't that easy," he said. "Maybe it isn't what I want. To leave."

It was her first visit to his cell. There was nothing in it but his cot. "What *do* you want? This cockamamie *thing*? It's impossible, honey. I'm sorry, but it's ridiculous."

"What do I want?" and her husband considered a moment. "Well, one thing for sure—I would like to be somebody, for once, who didn't bore you. I mean, did you think I didn't know?"

. . .

The only way she would accept the use of the Buick was if she drove them, and she drove them to Santa Rosalia. Saguaro stood everywhere waving hello or goodbye as they do to the eventually hypnotized traveler, and the big cacti seemed to suck all the life to be had from the improbable ground. Nothing else grew here. Katy Barnett was headed north again, intending to catch the ferry to Guaymas by noon, and among other injustices, she felt that Ignacio had defamed this noble car. "This thing seems to do okay, considering what you put it through. It could use some air in the tires, though."

"That's why I thought we should bring Bobo along. To handle things like that."

"No Bobo," she said. "Poor thing, but I've got enough on my hands."

"You're being hasty," said David Ignacio. "Is that really like you, Mrs. Barnett?"

"Katy," she said. "Haven't I said? It's just Katy, please. Out of school."

"Stubborn, too. What can this mean for your marriage?"

"Beats me," she said. "I guess we'll know soon enough."

To pass the time he enumerated his five marriages to date, named each of his wives, recounted unhappy endings with avaricious women who'd cleaned him out in Cleveland and Mexico City, and he said his heart had been broken even more times than he'd been married, broken with great regularity, but in the end, he said, "I can't shake my faith in love, Mrs. Barnett. What about you?"

"Love?" she said.

"Do you still believe?"

"Yes," she said. "And no."

TACOMA

The rooming house where Leonard Diehl was born had been replaced by a cinder block building with no windows and no apparent purpose. He stood behind a curtain of sliding gray beads, rain dripping from the awning of the Peerless Luncheonette, and he remembered a Victor Avenue of chipped white paint and flower boxes, the smell of soap being made from lard. Leonard folded a trench coat into the crook of his arm and watched himself walk up and down the street. Newly fitted in long pants, he carried a growler of beer home to his father and a gaggle of freeloading uncles; an older child, a walking hard-on, humiliated himself haggling with a frowzy Armenian whore; the sailor home on leave swaggered once more into the lobby of the now absent Empire Theater, a stain blossoming rose-like beneath the USS *Roanoke* patch where a shiv had nicked. A rosy glow on the whole damn neighborhood. The old life looks good because you were young in it.

Leonard, at fifty-seven, was a small, squarely made man wearing a summer suit, a suntan, a pair of wingtips soaked to the laces. That, he reminded himself, had always been the essence of Victor Avenue. That obstinate chill in your feet. He went into the luncheonette. Steam misted stainless steel behind a vacant counter. A waitress pushed through the swinging door from the kitchen and told him, "You better sit at this end of the counter. There's a draft down there." Nearly fat, nearly pretty, she approached him as if she had been sentenced to do so. "Slow today," she said. "I get really lazy when it's slow like this."

"I can't believe what passes for summer here," he said.

The waitress tore two sheets from a roll of paper towels and suggested he dry his hair. Leonard ordered a cup of

Sanka. He waited with a cigarette, the column of ash burning toward his fingers. The kid isn't even curious, he thought. The kid isn't a kid.

• • •

A week earlier Leonard had received a note from his attorney saying, "I don't know who sent this. There was no return address. Assume it was meant for you." Paperclipped to the note was a slightly brittle scrap of newsprint announcing the death of Karla Diehl. Leonard sat down. Her time had been brief and his would be too long. An insistent justice. He would never be beyond her reach. Listed among her survivors was a son, Joseph, also of Tacoma. It would have been Joe who'd sent the clipping.

That was Saturday. On Sunday Leonard drove to Del Mar where he lost a hundred and fifteen dollars at the pari-mutuel window. On Monday he called his secretary and cancelled his appointments. The vacation extended day by day, a chastened Leonard letting the other fools bet, leaning on the rail, drinking iced tea, breathing the dust the ponies raised each time they rounded for home.

By Friday the sporting life had also staled. He woke that night faced with a test-pattern Indian, the cuffs of his trousers pulled up around his knees. To clear his head he stepped out onto the sundeck, into a gentle San Diego evening, and he asked himself, What kind of a guy strings this dime-store crap all over his own back yard? His Japanese lanterns—fatuous, undulant, still lit at three in the morning. The hours before the paperboy's delivery were predictable. He felt himself turning down that corroded corridor in his imagination through which Karla and the boy, or their vapors, made their endless retreat.

Leonard showered, spent a good deal of time examining himself in the bathroom mirror. Without being particularly hungry, he made himself breakfast. He drove to Lindbergh Field. Within an hour he was on a flight north, drinking brandy and eating cashew nuts. He ate a second breakfast at SeaTac International. His stomach was in an uproar. He had survived into a too efficient age. What next?

At an airport gift shop Leonard bought the trench coat and a tin of aspirin. He wandered into a tiny arcade and invested five quarters in a video game. The machine spoke to him, taunting his ineptitude. Enough of the airport.

A frail old cabbie drove him to town and reported that his first choice of destination, the Elbow Room, had burned. "I believe the Democrats were still in then," the man said. "Long time ago. How about the P&Q?"

"When we hit town, let's just drive around a while, see the sights."

"I get off shift in ten minutes," the cabbie said. The skin on his cheekbone was taut and shiny.

Leonard rode as far as the Diamond Cab Company's garage. "There used to be a tailor in this building," he told the driver. "Maybe that was next door. Made my old man's shirts. Had his whole family in there, sewing, and no heat."

"We've got a stove now," the cabbie said. "Things are better that way. But you couldn't get a shirt made any more for less than a hundred bucks. Hey, I wish you'd change your mind about walking. It's nasty out there, and my relief would be happy to take you anywhere you want to go."

"What's a little rain?" Leonard asked him.

A church bell joined briefly with the clanging against a pierside hull as he got out of the cab; paper torn from shipping crates dissolved to pulp in the gutters. Ships at anchor. He had once believed every rustbucket to leave this port would find some wonderful tragedy, a boarding party, an oriental reef. Leonard found a phone booth, walked past it, then came back. The directory had been torn from its cable. He called information.

"Yes," said the operator. "It's a new listing under this name," and she intoned a familiar number. Leonard dialed it. The phone at the other end rang several times before the receiver was picked up, dropped, picked up again, and a deep, sleep-thickened voice said, "Hello?"

"Hello," he started. "This is Leonard. Leonard Diehl."

"Who?" The voice incredulous or stupid.

"I'm Leonard. Your . . . you know. Leonard Diehl. Is this Joe?"

"Yeah."

"I'm. . . ."

"I heard you."

"I'm in town," Leonard said.

"Oh."

Leonard heard himself turn ridiculous. He invented a story about a business trip and the failure of a rental car. The words seemed to move sideways up his throat. "Probably water in the gas line or something. So I called the office, and what do they say? They'll send a wrecker. 'Try National,' they tell me. National won't take my goddamn gold card. So that leaves me. . . . So I was wondering, if you're not too busy, maybe you could give me a lift to the airport?"

"Where are you?"

"Victor and . . . Third. Why don't I meet you at the Peerless Luncheonette? That's still open, isn't it?"

"How would I know?"

"I can be there in five, ten minutes. Okay?"

"All right," Joe had said.

• • •

There were filters in his ashtray and a small pile of empty sugar packets on the counter. Leonard had become the waitress's only interest. She eyed him from behind a rack of cereal boxes. He tilted his chin toward his cup and told her, "I've got Sanka dripping out my ears. Is there a phone in here?"

"On the wall between the restrooms."

"Passed it twice," he said. "Didn't notice."

"It's a quarter."

He smiled at her indulgently. He knew the cost of things. Leonard left without using the phone.

Outside, the rain had stopped, having left behind a curious organic odor. Another little walk. Because his legs were heavy, Leonard bent at the waist as an athlete might, stretching himself.

A small orange car came around the corner, slowly up the street, and stopped in front of him. A Toyota. It was Joe. He wore a quilted black cap. His window slid open. "Hope I didn't make you late for your plane."

"No," Leonard said.

A huge man, Joe unfolded from the car. "You'll have to get in on this side. The other door's wired shut." Much of his face was obscured in a sparse web of beard. A fleshy face. But the nose— the nose was Karla's on a larger scale. YMCA stenciled across a stretched sweatshirt. Joe. "How'd you wind up in this part of town?" he asked.

"The old stomping grounds," Leonard said. He slid under the steering wheel, into the passenger's seat. "Your mother and I lived here, too. When we were first married. Before you were born."

"I knew that. Where's your luggage?"

"Don't have any."

"Not even a briefcase?"

Leonard thought that Joe's suspicion had a glossy, well-used quality about it. "Is there a steakhouse around here? My plane doesn't leave until eight."

"You know she's. . .?"

"I got the thing you sent."

Joe said that she had been sick a long time, hospitalized for some months, but that her voice had remained a foghorn until the end. Leonard had forgotten her voice. She was, he learned, four months gone. The tires skiffed occasionally through standing water.

"I can't afford to eat out," Joe said.

"It's covered. Think I'm cheap or something?"

"No, I've got some hamburger that has to be cooked today."

They continued toward a better part of town along tree-lined thoroughfares. Leonard's first ambition hadn't taken him far. Only ten minutes by car from Victor Avenue, South Florence had once offered space and comparative quiet to those escaping Tacoma's tireder addresses. The neighborhood was so much what it had been during Leonard's time there that the cars in the driveways, the bikes and tricycles, everything of recent origin seemed out of place. They came to the 900 block and a dormered bungalow. In 1955, Leonard had considered the dormers a very classy feature. Ridiculous to a more experienced eye. A lot of trouble to fill an attic with natural light. The glider was missing from the porch.

"Pink? Who painted it pink?"

"Peach," Joe said. "I'm trying to sell the place."

As there was no place to sit in the kitchen, Leonard waited in the living room while Joe cooked. The room had been partially stripped, various pieces of furniture commemorated by dents in the carpet. It was smaller than he remembered. Under Karla's influence the place had been airy, neat. The curtains had been thrown open every morning. Now her flock of porcelain sheep grazed the dusty surfaces of a Hammond organ among empty beer bottles, bills, and a framed graduation picture of Joe that Leonard considered stealing. The kid had been fairly handsome without the beard, more alert looking.

Joe joined him on the couch and set a plate of hamburger smothered in catsup on a footlocker, his table. "I thought you said you were hungry."

They sat in a pile of blankets that gave forth a stale smell whenever it was disturbed.

"You're living here alone?"

"I moved back in a few months before Mom went to the hospital. It's been kind of strange. Beats paying rent, though. You thought somebody else lived here?"

"You're still single, then."

"Couldn't be singler."

"That's good," Leonard said.

"It is, huh?"

"What kind of work do you do?"

"Machine shop. Welding, mostly."

"You're like your mother, good with your hands."

"What's that supposed to mean?"

"Nothing. I'm just saying it's best to have a trade. That way you're never out of work."

"I've been laid off the last six months."

"Don't worry about it. You'll find something. In your field...."

"I'm not worried."

"It's better to keep busy," Leonard said. "Keeps you from going nuts."

A tablespoon at rest in a pool of grease on a cracked plate. Joe had finished his lunch. He lay back, closed his eyes, laced his hands on his stomach and let them fall into the peaceful rhythm of his afterdinner breathing. His right cheek bunched, curling that half of his mouth ambiguously. The expression was something else he had inherited from his mother. "You know those checks you had your lawyer send us? Mom put half of every one of those into an account for me."

"That's what she was supposed to do."

"You wouldn't have known any better if she didn't. Anyway, she wanted me to go to school. I could have, too. I had the grades for it. But I bought a pickup and took off. Worked a rig in the gulf for a while. Got married in Shreveport. Two years later I was broke. And divorced. So I wasted it, okay?"

"If you didn't, I probably would have. I never remarried, you know."

"Neither did Mom."

"She should have," Leonard said.

The kid had a certain limited genius, control of several painful facts. Leonard excused himself to go into the bathroom, sit on the lip of the tub, and light a cigarette. What did you expect? Left this house eighteen years ago with a pasteboard box under your arm. So what did you expect?

He had gone into Joe's room. The very last thing he did in this house. He'd gone into the boy's room and crouched near his bed. His hand on the little boy's back—sweaty flannel. He'd whispered again and again, "What has she done to us?" He knew now, as he'd known then, that the child had no answer for him, and that, even as he'd loved the child, he'd faked love also. Slobbering old bastard, whispering mean mysteries in the dark. "My boy. My little boy." Then the boy had had enough. The child Joe rolled over to show that he was awake, that he'd been awake all along. He asked nothing, said nothing. He did not cry. Joe had just found and held onto his father's forefinger.

• • •

"You want to go somewhere and get a drink?"

"I could run down to Donatellos for a six-pack," Joe offered.

"Nah."

"TV?"

"I hate TV," Leonard said.

"How about cards? You play cribbage?"

"Sure."

Joe produced a deck of cards, some wooden matches for pegs, and a cribbage board cut from white oak to resemble a sea bird. The peg holes were drilled into inlaid strips of something he called whalebone ivory. "I made ten of these. Thought I might be able to sell a few."

"I'd buy one," Leonard told him. "I might buy a couple. They'd make nice presents."

"I'm not sure where the rest of them are now."

Never in any competition had Leonard met so luckless an opponent as Joe. The kid's game was resignation. "Fifteen-two, fifteen-four, and a pair of jacks for six." They ground away at the afternoon. Leonard wondered what things might have been like if they'd met at random, just two men trying to dispose of another day. Joe was a poor companion. A thief's or a suitor's tremor ran through Leonard, kept running until it wore him out.

Eventually Joe looked him over coolly and said, "You're not much different. You don't look all that different. You must take good care of yourself."

"I use a good grade of mouthwash," said Leonard.

"So what's your livelihood?"

"My job? I sell real estate. Commercial properties."

"I thought it must be something like that. You don't look like you work for a living."

"I did my share of stoop-and-grunt," Leonard said. "Now I make money." And he was nothing if not a practical man. "If you're serious about selling this place, there's a few things you ought to do. Varnish the wainscoting. Open a window once in a while."

"I can't afford to make any more improvements."

"You can't afford not to make improvements. Everything you put into fixing the place up, you triple that and add it to the asking price. The more a place costs, the easier it is to sell. It's a quirk of human nature."

"I'm broke," said Joe.

"No, I invest in deals like this all the time. I'll float you a loan, and when. . . ."

Joe stood. "You think I'm hitting you for money?" He cleared a stack of dishes from the footlocker and went into the kitchen with them. Leonard heard them rattle in the sink. He followed.

"I'd also take up this linoleum. It was ugly to begin with."

"Maybe you're not getting my drift. I don't want any more of your money." Joe rinsed a bowl. "What time is it? You want to listen to some tunes?"

Joe's music prevented further conversation, but that was the best that could be said for it. They sat at either end of the couch so that it was not difficult to avoid looking at each other. An adenoidal folk singer detailed his losses; there followed a number of recordings that sounded to Leonard like religious zealots meeting in an assembly plant. The muscles in his back constricted. Was this polite? Joe stared into a middle distance, did a little drumming on his thigh. Leonard played solitaire and smoked. Finally, he got up to lift the needle from a particularly quivering guitar solo. "Stuff's driving me up the wall," he said.

"It's about that time, anyway. It's almost time for you to go, isn't it?"

Leonard's foot had gone to sleep. He limped to the window. "You'd think we'd have more to talk about."

"We don't have that much in common," Joe said.

"Well, maybe more than you. . . . I think I came up with a pretty good idea while we were sitting here." Leonard fingered the leaves of a sagging coleus and filled his lungs with rancid air. "You could use a job, couldn't you?"

"A job?"

"I've been wanting to open a new office in Escondido. Things are hot as a pistol down there, but I haven't been able to find anybody I trust enough to run an operation like that. If you got your license—and a shave—you could make out like a bandit. We both could."

"Shit."

"You've had a better offer?"

"What do you want from me, Leonard?"

"Do me a favor, don't call me Leonard."

"What do I call you? Daddy?"

"I wouldn't mind getting to know you, Joe."

"I can see it all now. Get out there and throw the old pill around. Go to the zoo on Sundays. Why don't you just rent one of those African orphans?" He pulled out his key chain from his pants pocket. Pennies dribbled out.

Leonard got his trench coat and followed him out the front door. On the stoop he caught at Joe's windbreaker. "You know why I left?"

"I know. Come on. Sometimes I have trouble getting the car started."

"You know that kid I used to call ratboy, what was his name?"

"Jay Heeny?"

"One night I came out here to call you in for supper. The two of you were over there in the Sundvolds' yard."

"We don't have time for this."

"Oh, I've got all the time in the world, Joey."

"Well, you can use it. . . ."

"He was giving you a hard time," Leonard said. "Shoving you around. I felt like going over and twisting his head off. But then you grabbed him by the wrists. Man, that was great. You were really strong. You had him. Kid didn't know whether to shit or go blind."

Joe toed a loose chunk of cement at the corner of the step. "If there's a point to this, why don't you get to it."

"You had him by the wrists. You remember what you said?"

"I barely remember Jay Heeny."

"You said, 'Please.' And you let him go."

"And?"

"That's when I knew," Leonard said quietly. "That's when it hit me."

"That I was. . . ."

"I knew she'd been with another man. That's when I knew you weren't, you weren't mine."

"I don't get it. You must have suspected something before that."

"You were such a beautiful little boy."

They crossed the lawn and got into Joe's car. Joe set his hands on the steering wheel and stared at the dash. "You had to suspect something before that."

"You don't see what you don't want to see," Leonard told him. "It's like cancer. You pretend it isn't there, then it gets to where you can't ignore it anymore. By then it's too late, too big to cut out. In a way, it didn't have all that much to do with you."

"I always thought she told you about it."

"She did, when I threw it in her face."

There was a freeway now just a few blocks north of Donatello's market. Once they were on it, Leonard lost his bearings.

• • •

The sky had cleared and it was a long dusk. They stood in a lounge, watching broad puddles shiver in the wind across the runways. The quality of Joe's silence had changed. Though he wasn't sure he had reason to be, Leonard was ashamed of himself. He knew that he was expected to say something else. Through a whining microphone the passengers of United Flight 63 were asked to begin boarding. "Thanks," he said. "I would have been stranded."

"That's all right. I wasn't doing anything else."

"And thanks for letting me know about your mother. It was. . . . She was a good woman."

"Too good," said Joe, certain on this point.

"You can't be too good."

Leonard offered his sweating hand. It was accepted.

"I just came up with another one of my famous ideas. No, hear me out. This is a good one. I've got a friend with a place in the desert. A cabin. He says I can use it any time. I know another guy who can get me champagne at wholesale. So I was thinking—if you could get free around Christmas, maybe you could bring down some smoked salmon or something. We could have sort of a desert Yuletide. It's just something to think about."

Joe nodded, started to say something, then simply nodded again and turned to walk back down the concourse to the main terminal.

Leonard moved forward into the boarding tunnel with a crowd of cologned, southbound travelers. He took his seat. A stewardess gave him a condescending smile, a pillow. He closed his eyes and tried to nap.

At thirty-five thousand feet the 737 began to level off and Leonard watched the leading edge outside his window slice into a feeble string of lights along the coast, then into an apparently endless blanket of darkness. The waters below him were well charted, the tides timed, the various currents almost predictable. He couldn't see the Pacific, of course, but he knew that it was there.

GRAY KITTY

Dear Athalie,

I have been installed here in a cottage that may have once been a carriage house but was more probably a garage, a tiny, blue-trimmed thing that sits well off the street behind a copse of shaggy fir trees and reminds me (the color scheme) of your mother's blue willow plates, and this is typically odd. I've always been easily fogged by reminiscence. She is gone, she is not gone. I continue to experience her absence as a snapping shutter. Bad digression, though, when I am really writing to tell you I'm doing pretty well. As you say, I am the remnant of a great romance. This business of surviving her has proven entirely un-romantic. I've discovered in myself a rat's fortitude. One simply goes on. That's what I'm doing.

The night air here is not nearly as sedative as I'd been led to expect, and I had to drive over to Fort Morris the other day to supplement my pharmaceuticals, and I remembered on the way back that you'd asked after the local sights. Thought I'd drive around and see some. It's corn, though. An ocean of corn with a few farmsteads adrift on it. Some of the fields roll a bit, most don't, and you hate to dismiss a new place as bor-ing, but I'd have to say the farmers hereabouts have gone out of their way to make it so. Found myself in a seething green maze, NO vistas, and then—you must have such fond memories of my navigational skills—I got lost, and it was a good thing I'd thought to absorb some chemical composure before I detoured through the wilderness.

So I came upon a man walking the roadside in overalls. At some point he must have been broken in body and spirit because he walked like something underfoot at the beach.

I coasted up beside him and asked him where I was, and I regretted the conversation even before the man revealed his interesting teeth. His beard consisted of quills, and he didn't seem to belong in such a prosperous spot, but I was also out of place, so I put my question to him, a real mistake. Can you tell me where I am? Where are you? Why, it's Johnson County, where else? Where else, indeed. I was about to speed away, with or without the usual pleasantries, when I noticed a burlap sack he had in hand. It was writhing some, and I could only be curious about it, and I can't tell you how little this man seemed to appreciate my curiosity. Kitties, he said. They were the last of a dozen fresh barn cats, and he was on his way to drown them.

So I found my way home without the man's directions but with the kittens, and what a steamy experience that was, the windows up tight. My new roommates are calico and gray. Both female, I think. Full of swagger. I am smitten by them and would be insufferable, I'm sure, if there were anyone here to see it. But the little ones aren't complaining. They've been taking nearly hourly doses of canned milk that I drip into their mouths like they were little sparrows. Feels almost as if I'm being suckled. But enough of that.

For my studio I have been given what was until last year the home of the school's modern dance program. Would there be such a thing as post-modern dance? Anyway, I've got a huge, reverberant space, and it should flatter my students very much, and maybe they'll think I'm responsible for giving them their big new sound. Meanwhile, I see myself from every angle, completely surrounded by mirrors, and my work day, when I pay any attention to it, seems like I am starring in fractured scenes from the French cinema. I lack élan for the role.

I have resumed playing at last and can report that the tremor is only evident in very technical passages. It is so hard to cede anything to age or infirmity, especially something so hard won as technique. There are certainly no guarantees. These fingers were so cooperative for so long.

Dined with the head of the music department last night. At his home. With his family. Another ordeal. Dean Phillips raved as before about having been a fan, having seen me concertizing at some of the nicer seaboard halls, twice during my tour with Dmitri, but this time the Dean shared his enthusiasm with his wife and teenage sons and bored them all comatose. The man sustains long soliloquies in what I would guess to be Italian. He makes his own beer, and it is salty. I cannot imagine that was his intention. There were prawns on the grill, and an awkward little grace before the meal, and we had a salad of the summer's last garden greens, so it should have been pleasant. I know it should have been.

You'll be amused to hear that I have a standing offer to join the Dean's bible study group. Only if they show movies. This dates me terribly, but I remember when Victor Mature slew a host of feckless extras with the jawbone of an ass, *Samson and Delilah,* that's my idea of bronze-age fun. I like to think I would have been the ram's horn player in those days—there were just the two tones to master, rehearsal would have been minimal, and you'd be calling the people to devotions and to war, so your audience would have been everyone. There were probably no union dues.

Gary should soon be receiving the school's official tee shirt. Smallest size I could find. BULLDOGS. Though the student body has yet to arrive in force, these garments are ubiquitous anywhere near campus. There is a strong commitment to wear the copper and green, and it all seems pretty horrible to me. My education was nothing like this. At the conservatory we knew no such patriotism. We wore mufflers, thick glasses, and our talent. You say I have lived apart, lived in my rarified environment. Mea culpa, but was it as bad as you sometimes make it seem?

Dad

Dear Athalie,

Seems I'm not such a complete bachelor that I can't manage a bread and butter note, so—thank you. I gained seven pounds at your table, and I will carry it, it seems, on my abdomen like a gourd. The weight does not flatter, but I ate continuously for the whole week I was with you, so I suppose I should have expected some repercussions along the waistband. Is there a food more unlikely than turkey? Giblets? I ate everything, dear, all that you placed before me. Thank you. I'm writing from my recliner.

Still eating, actually. I've discovered Billy Woo's with his bamboo everything, and they stage a poor man's Chinese opera constantly in the kitchen. It's a jangling language, wonderfully discordant to my ear. Oh, and another odd food. Rice. I don't care if it's staple to more than half the world, it is, if you think about it at all, a very peculiar thing to eat. But I do eat it. The things we eat, the things we won't eat. Our preoccupations. What I've noticed upon coming home, or coming here again where I apparently live, is the very low wattage of a single personality. I burn none too bright on my own. There's a silver lining though—I don't mind.

Remember those walks in Calchet Park? The swans?

Midterms are upon me. My students are performance majors, and so I'm expected to require rigorous performances of them at intervals, and the first of these tests are looming. The poor things will be wanting my early opinion of their ability. If they get it, honestly, then I'd probably end up sending every last one of them off to their rightful careers in meatpacking plants. But I'm sure that wouldn't do, so it's an ugly, unmusical job of work, this pedagogy. The paychecks, if I hadn't mentioned it, are astounding.

I've decided not to come for Christmas. I know your offer to be genuine, and I know it to be overgenerous. That little family of yours is like a tripod, very stable on its three legs. Also, my cats have made it very clear I'm not to leave them for any amount of time. There's no one here I know well enough to look after them while I'm gone.

The Department, as my colleagues call it, the music department is a hermetically sealed world. I was recruited for my name, in these circles I have one, and I'm a celebrity here, esteemed for something I used to do, a capacity I used to have. Deplorable. I'm blowing long tones well enough, but I'm really only good for lullabies and cool blues, certainly nothing up tempo, nothing very complex, and I bore myself and am bored by this cozy veneration. I had not meant to whine. Sorry. What I meant to say, and what I hope I've said, is thanks so much for having me and indulging me.

Dad

Dear Athalie,

A strange, sad incident to relate. Earlier this week my gray kitten upset a broom I'd leaned against the wall. The handle fell, and she tried to outrun it, but it caught her right on top of her head, a really serious blow, and I believe she may be brain damaged. She was doing so well. I'm not sure what to make of her now. These cat episodes have caused me to reflect on what a muddled parent I must have been. When you were very small and just learning to walk, I noticed that your head was exactly level with every hard object in our home, and you'd gouge your eyes out on the coffee table. I have continued to regard your progress through life with the same constant dread because you are too precious to me. It's just that I adore you.

I am guest conducting the faculty orchestra. Sort of a tyrant about it, which surprises me unpleasantly. But they seem to want me stern.

Does Gary enjoy his midget marimba? I wasn't sure if he'd be too old for it, or too young, or that you'd want me delivering a machine capable of making that much noise into his hands. Music. Music for everyone. From everyone. I'm becoming more democratic. This should do me no harm. It should be fairly easy to mute those mallets with socks and rubber bands.

I did end up joining a fellowship, Unitarian, no one is especially encouraged to believe anything. We do our studies. Solomon has been very popular—Thy son, hear the instruction of thy father and forsake not the law of thy mother. For they shall be an ornament of grace unto thy head, and chains about thy neck. As I'm writing this, my gray kitten is shredding this house. I think she's badly damaged. Solomon also has this to say—All is vanity.

Dad

Dear Athalie,

I wish you hadn't shared my phone number with your aunt. Now I've had to get the thing disconnected, but then I really only used it for ordering takeout.

I was at fellowship recently when a very old memory some-how emerged, one of your grandmother's enthusiasms, a certain Reverend Gilhoover. He'd have been a presence when I was about ten. The man had a towering odor, a certainty about him, and he was avid after my mortal soul. I remember him at a picnic in a coal black suit. Perhaps I'll take up bowling now for my social life.

The phone is also a casualty of my remarks to Ted. Our misunderstanding. Tell him again I meant no offense. But if the man finds baseball intriguing and Brahms dull, I can hardly help it if my perspective may at times seem skewed to him, and if he resents my contributions to your household economy, then he should contrive to sell more flooring.

No phone will be all for the best, don't you think? Love. Dad

Dear Gary,

This is a picture of your grandfather and his cats. How do you like our scary red eyes?

Grandad

Dear Mrs. Hendrickson,

It would have been more neighborly if I had just gathered my courage to come over to talk to you face to face about these issues. I'm not sure what opinion you may have formed of me, and I wouldn't be surprised if it was pretty bad. Maybe I thought it would be easier to assure you in writing that I am actually a fairly decent human being. I know some of the things you have seen, and many things you may have heard from my house could cause you to think that I am not in control of my emotions. If you have reached that conclusion, you are of course correct, but I would prefer it, and the police would prefer it if you didn't call them anymore. There's nothing they can do.

I hope you'll recall that when I first moved in, when I was living here alone, I was not a merely quiet neighbor, but a virtually silent one. I hope you don't imagine that the cacophony in my household is at all customary for me, or anything I enjoy. I'd go so far as to say it has been hell, thus my sincerest sympathies for anything that has come to your attention. Obviously, I am not good with animals, but I only recently became aware of it. I don't know what to do, but please know when I tell you I am sorry, that I am sorry from the bottom of my heart, and I am trying very hard to bring this situation to some acceptable resolution.

Sincerely,

Evan Nasciemento

Dear Athalie,

Let me begin by apologizing, I'm doing very little else currently. I've not been sulking, and I haven't been particularly busy with school, and I'm not playing at all these days, but I have been extremely preoccupied. I've been at a loss to know if I should, or if I even could describe the situation here. You'll remember last fall before I signed off, so to speak, I must have written or mentioned my cats in a sack. I acquired these kittens. A good thing, I thought at the time. Something to take me out of myself. Kittens. Adorable. I personally supplied them with a couple of their nine lives. What could possibly go wrong?

And they were wonderful in the beginning, puffballs, daredevils, scofflaws where it came to the laws of physics. They were fun. They were sweet. Acey and Deucy, Acey being the calico, Deucy the gray. There were indications, of course, right away. Their personalities were apparent as soon as I'd got them healthy enough to have personalities, and from the beginning it was clear that Deucy was somewhat different, but she was only an odd kitten until the accident. They were a very pleasant choice I'd made. I think I wrote to you of the moment with the broom, brutish, mechanical fate, and how my poor gray thing hurt her head. Who knows what she may have seen on the farm before that? Believe me, I managed to sustain quite a lot of sympathy for this cat for quite a long time. An absurd amount of time. Take whatever fondness is, and invert it, and that is what I feel for her, and my loathing is more than justified.

She took some additional mending after she was hurt. She slept all the time and was too lethargic to eat unless I started feeding her again, which I did. The light was pretty literally gone from her eyes, and I just kept feeding her, caressing her in the hope that it might be of some benefit. After a while, she rallied again. She has great recuperative powers. As soon as she returned to health, though, her health sort of spiraled out of control. She became an anxious predator overnight. The songbirds that had attended my cottage were soon gone. I tried to keep her in to prevent it, but Deucy introduced me to her scream then, that sound they usually reserve for fights and breeding. She wanted out. She wants what she wants, and she invariably gets it. Acey is long gone because Deucy wanted every scrap of available food in or near this house, and she was happy to be vicious for it. She ran her littermate off. She's crippled at least one neighborhood dog. Now it's the two of us, Deucy and I.

We have been alone together for several months. All through the end of winter. Spring finally arrives here, but I can't open the windows. It's very complicated. I have hesitated to try and explain something I can't pretend to understand. She has a diamond face, tall ears, and the coat of a true omnivore, sumptuous and glossy. It's not too hard to imagine Deucy dripping from Nefertiti's lap. Imperious. She wants what she wants, and what she wants more than anything is me. Those caresses I mentioned, she can't seem to get her fill of those. When she requires my attention, she climbs onto me, climbs up me if necessary, and curls like a sable stole round my neck. I might be sleeping, or trying to sleep, cooking or trying to cook. I might try and attend to my toilet. But whatever I am doing must accommodate her need, because when she snuggles in there's no removing her.

That scream. It continues to raise the hair on the back of my neck no matter how much I've heard it. Her unholy note. Her claws. She clings. There are times of relief when she's off hunting or policing her territory, but she always comes back, and she screams if I won't let her in, then screams if I try to prevent her from attaching to me. The texture of her fur. At times, I suppose, it's welcome enough. She screams as she finds it necessary, and sometimes I scream back, but with no effect.

So that's the news from this end. How are things there?

Dad

THE MELODIST

At birth she was red and wrinkled and hideous, but she was an only child and soon enough became that solemn little girl at Easter service holding the bail of her wicker basket so primly in both hands. In those years you would have thought her a packet of confectioner's sugar done up in ribbon and taffeta, but a more privileged glimpse would give you to understand that you had encountered a lily of the field. Imagine the end of a fall day; leaves are kiting down to tawny lawns and in the air a sense of sweet inevitability, the scent of fried onions. Knockkneed as a marionette, she runs along the sidewalk toward home, five minutes late for supper, utterly happy.

. . .

Lyla sighted down her legs through the vee of her saddle shoes, thinking, "No." "No," as if by an effort of will she could make the car change course. She never thought to appeal to the driver. The driver was her mother who was often disappointed in her. "No," thought Lyla. "No." Sun streamed through the maples, dappling the road before them. They passed a baseball diamond, a game in progress, and she placed herself deep in right field, heroic out there. Lyla did not in gross reality play baseball at all, but so long as she remained in her mother's finny Plymouth there were few inhibitions to her secret life. A block later she had them in a small boat on a tossing ocean, but it was hard to sustain that scenario in a car that moved more like a barge. Voices welled from the radio, celebrating love regained. They passed a school ground, the park where Lyla had once fed some ducks, and then they were in a different part of town. They rocked to a stop along a block of brick row houses.

People lived here without lawns. There were brave flower boxes in some of the windows, but these only made her sadder. It was no place for children. "Now I've probably got that pain again. I probably can't stand it."

"This is not life and death, it's a piano lesson. I wish you wouldn't be so dramatic every time."

What would happen if she couldn't get out of the car, a mechanical problem or paralysis, or if she could somehow generate a fever? Her illnesses never came when she needed them.

"Honey, not so tight. You're hurting my hand. In fact, let go."

Miss Smith's door was black with a brass knocker that her mother knocked. A thick door, but through it they could hear the rustle Miss Smith made, coming to answer, and Lyla's stomach turned—diarrhea, would that be enough to get her out of this?—and then there she was, Miss Smith, smiling down. "Well, aren't we pretty today?" Her hand came to rest on Lyla's head, and Lyla could not prevent herself from shrinking away.

"Would you mind if I'm a little late picking her up? I promised her father I'd deliver some linens downtown."

"She's my last lesson today. We can make great use of a little extra time, can't we, dear?"

Lyla's mother knelt before her. "Now, just relax. You'll do fine. You always get so anxious, but you know you'll do just fine. Won't you? My little perfectionist."

"Would you like to come in? You girls look fresh, but I need my air conditioning."

All at once her mother was gone, and Lyla was in the dead cool air inside, being shoved through the vestibule by Miss Smith who seemed always at the point of bursting through her poor, strained dress. Miss Smith gripped Lyla by the shoulders, right at the neck, and pinched just a bit at the strands of muscle there. "Perfectionist? Where on earth did she come by that idea?"

There was an odor about Miss Smith's house; Lyla had never

identified its source, but it smelled sweetly yellow to her, or brown. This was very heavy air to breathe, and perhaps the effort of breathing it had made Miss Smith so strange and large.

"Well, we do have some time, dear. What would you say to some milk and cookies first?"

"I like cookies but not milk. I'm actually allergic to milk."

"Oh, you are not. No growing girl can possibly be allergic to milk."

"Really," said Lyla. "I am."

"Now. Remember what we had to talk about. About telling the truth."

"I'm having some problems in my stomach, too."

"Come on into the kitchen."

Lyla could not remember that she had ever swallowed any milk, but instinct told her she had every reason to expect a bad reaction. She very well could be allergic, and why find out for sure? Lyla knew, however, that all these points would be wasted on Miss Smith, and the truth would be of no use: She just detested the whole idea of it, in her mind it was something greasy, clotted, and a little rotten, and she hated even to think of it in the same refrigerator as her food. But Miss Smith had her own ideas. Miss Smith always thought she was so completely right. She set Lyla up at her table.

"Chocolate chip, or peanut butter? Or both?"

"Both, please."

"And you're not going to try and tell me you don't drink your milk when you're at home. Are you?"

"No. Water. Grape juice. I like water best. Not milk."

"Well, in my house, young lady, you will drink your milk. I wonder if you're malnourished. That could explain the problems you seem to have with concentrating."

"They say we came from Norway," said Lyla. "Some of our ancestors did."

It arrived in a tall glass. This, when she forced herself to touch it, was not even cool to the touch, and Lyla's throat was in full rebellion even before she brought the glass under her nose and caught a grassy whiff. She closed her eyes, pinched off her nose, and grimaced, but she could do no more. Not in a million years.

"My, what a performance. Don't think that lets you off the hook. How do they provide you your calcium? Your vitamin D?"

"From soup. I get everything from soup."

"Drink," said Miss Smith. "It's good for you."

She had returned the glass to the table, and just the act of reaching for it again was enough to make her gag. Impossible. Don't accidents happen, though? Aren't children known to be clumsy? "Ooooh." The glass tolled once, striking the table, and milk raced evilly over gleaming wood.

"Lyla! You . . . that was no accident."

"Sorry."

"That's what makes this hard, Lyla. I'm always so angry with you. But this is the worst. That was a very bad thing to do. I'm inclined to tell your mother."

"Do you have any paper towels?"

A frail old woman scuffed into the kitchen in a brocade housecoat, and she heated some water for instant coffee, and Miss Smith bustled around mopping, drying, spraying polish on the abused table, and buffing it. The two women did not look at each other, and neither of them looked at Lyla. It was an invisibility pact. The veiny elder retired with her cup to wherever she'd been before, and Miss Smith stood over Lyla and said, "One piece of advice, young lady: You never want to make people think their kindness is wasted on you. Come on. Let's try and get something done."

They went into the alcove, to the waiting piano. Miss Smith sat beside her on the piano bench, and Lyla had always to lean a little away from her, and this was just the first of many discomforts. Miss Smith seemed to pulse beside her. She was still angry. She was always angry. Lyla smoothed her exercise book before her. It had become willful, its pages unwieldy since she'd got it wet. Miss Smith sighed to see it so.

The song was called "March the Step Away," a scattering of eighth notes across the page like starlings on telephone lines.

"Begin."

Lyla placed her hands on the keyboard, the one thing she had learned to do properly. This, unless she was very lucky, would be the top of her performance. She could not even name the notes, much less strike them coherently.

"I'll count you in. One, two, three . . . Lyla?"

Already out of rhythm, she touched a chord, and it wasn't terrible.

"No. You haven't looked at this at all, have you?"

"I sort of sprained my thumb."

"No. Lyla. Lyla, why?"

"I fell off a fence."

"You have to practice. If you don't practice you're just wasting your parents' money. And my time. Now, is that fair?"

"No." But Lyla also felt that it was not fair to be confronted with the fact that it was not fair. She did not care for shame. "I'm ready now."

"I highly doubt it, young lady, but we're going to walk you through this in tiny little steps, and you're going to learn it despite yourself. You will be playing *some*thing at your recital. Your parents are entitled to that much, don't you think?"

"I'm ready," said Lyla, though she was not.

"Put your right thumb on middle C. No—there. Good lord, Lyla. We're right back at the beginning, aren't we? C-E-G, can you do that for me?"

Lyla was not accustomed to think of her fingers as individuals with responsibilities. And the notes. The notes. They went up and down, side to side. They were moving targets. When she was diligent she was never diligent for very long before she remembered the problem. This was beyond her. The idea was to see these notes, and then they were supposed to tumble out of her fingers in a certain, pleasing order, and she was all for it, but while she favored music, she could not seem to comprehend it. A wall rose up when she tried.

"One. Two. Three. Do Mi Sol, Sol Mi Do. One. Two. Three. *Threee.* It's in threeee, dear. Remember? That phrase with your right hand. Do Mi Sol, Sol Mi Do, One. Two. Three. Do Mi Sol . . . that's . . . nearly. Do Mi Sol, Sol Mi. . . . *Nooo.* Almost. Let's start again."

"March the Step Away" was illustrated by a line drawing of a drum major in a high hat, his baton and one booted leg aloft, and behind him a file of frolicking farm animals played their band instruments. Children, Lyla knew, were supposed to be charmed by this kind of fraudulence. But she was grateful for any diversion. Notes. She could not equate them with what her hand was doing. Up and down in dismal pursuit of C-E-G, G-E-C. Miss Smith breathed by her side, and she sighed and sighed, and maybe she would at last come around to Lyla's opinion.

"Lyla, now I just know you can do this if you'll only try. But you have to pay attention and give it your best effort."

"At the same time?"

"You just have to try. You have to be here in the room, and try. Really, really pay close attention, and not go drifting away. So, I'll count you in, and, One. Two. Three. . . ."

She'd been told to think of her fingertips as hammers. Lyla had been told she needed to learn attack from the beginning. C-E-G, G-E-C.

"Keep repeating that. Just that, until you can do it smoothly and evenly. Then do it some more. Until you can do it in your sleep. I have to visit the lady's room." Miss Smith departed like a cloud sliding from under the sun, and in that moment Lyla got better. The exercise began to yield to her effort. She was really going to try now. She was going to do this *very* well, and Miss Smith would be surprised. C-E-G, G-E-C had become more like jumping rope than thinking, easy, and so Lyla began to hum it, too. What a surprise. There was something in her. C-E-G, G-E-C, proficiently. Why not the left hand now? Before she got bored? Before her mind might wander? All on its own, the left came into play, settling down into some bottom, and she pumped this blustery chord under C-E-G, G-E-C, which was beginning to lope a little. Something was in her. Lyla had never thought to play loud before. It made all the difference.

Louder and louder, then. She was the master of this theme. Full of understanding. She felt that this poor piano had been mistreated until now, by her, by Miss Smith, by Miss Smith's miserable students. She'd established a bond with the thing, G-B-D, D-B-G, and they were both to be liberated. Their sound was big, getting bigger, and it didn't need to be pretty. Her fingers were hammers, but welcome where they pounded, and Lyla smelled Miss Smith's return before she saw or heard her; Miss Smith was wearing sharp new scents since she'd gone away, and she came and stood behind Lyla, her arms folded, her face slack, and all at once the weight of her head overbore her weary neck, and her head rocked back. With nothing much to look at above, Miss Smith closed her eyes.

ANOTHER QUENTIN HOULIHAN

You get a million guys come home like that, all at once, and a million women waiting, and whattaya think will happen? It's hot times in the maternity wards, and up go your suburbs, and up go your freeways, and whoopdeedoo. There for the first ten, twelve years after the war, about all I ever did was swing a twenty-eight ounce framing hammer. This was out in Bremerton, Longview, out on the coast where I happened to be for no better reason than that's where I'd mustered out of the Navy. Your postwar economy was an awful sweet deal for a man who'd managed to avoid that matrimonial bliss, and I was driving a two-tone T- Bird, the Town and Country model. Built my own hi-fi out of parts I got through a mail-order catalog.

We'd throw up one of those GI-financed crackerboxes, frame it at least, about every two or three weeks, and I was known as a guy who could sink a sixteen-penny nail, run a transit or whathaveyou, finish cement if it came to that, and so on it goes, and I'm building. Only time in my life I ever made more money than I could spend. Course, I had my diversions, too, couple of bad habits. Drank quite a bit, like everyone did back in those days. Tried golf for a while, if you can believe that. Like Ike. Mostly, though, it was work. Oh, every once in a while I'd get a wild hair and run my Ford out into some desert or wheat field somewhere, put my foot down and open up all four barrels, and, whoosh, cheap gasoline just pouring through that carburetor—man, how I loved that particular V-8, what a mill—and you watch the needle swing right up to one thirty-five, watch it hang there. You got the top down. I knew a few girls, too, and almost every one of 'em liked to cruise. That Philco was the best radio ever made, and here's a blond with a big, boozy grin, sitting right next to you, maybe a few bugs in her teeth. You get the picture. I had forearms on me like Popeye, had a little bit of a savings account and a brain no bigger than a walnut, and, all in all, I was doing okay.

Then one day Mrs. Schaeffer grabs me as I'm coming in from the greengrocer's or whatever, and she directs my attention to that oak stand she had out in the hall where she'd leave the mail for her upstairs tenants—she knows I never get anything from the post office, not even bills, so she knows I'm not likely to look for it, and so she shows me something's come from Miss Moira Houlihan in Elisis, Montana. It's addressed in pencil, in letters so tiny they look like hieroglyphics; must've taken Moira about an hour to do this, and the end result is that you've got to squint real hard just to read it, and that's her signature, really, some strange shit like that. She knew where to get me 'cause I used to send her a check every Christmas and a note every time I moved, but it'd been at least a couple years since she'd bothered to write back. I didn't mind. I rarely called her anymore—you'd call her and be tired for a week after. See, my sister was demented. I knew she couldn't help it, but she was goofy in ways that had started to kind of irritate me. Can't help it, and she can't help it, and so forth—what good is that?

So, with Mrs. Schaeffer standing right there—she'd be long gone by now—I open this deal. And it's not a letter Moira's sent, in fact I don't get so much as a note to explain it; no, what I've got is a birth certificate, an original birth certificate, stamped and sealed; and what does it certify but the birth of another Quentin Houlihan on the seventeenth day of April, nineteen fifty-five? Mother: Moira Houlihan. Father: Unknown. They stamp the baby's footprint on those things. That's what got me first. That little footprint. Looked like a seashell to me, the way it was turned in on itself, the way it was, you know, perfect.

So I went down to the pay phone on the corner and tried to call Moira and congratulate her. Maybe congratulations are in order, maybe not, but I better call. So I call over and over for about a week and never do get an answer, so then I think to call Potter Blixt, who I haven't seen or heard from since the day in forty-two when we shipped out in different directions, and I ask him if he knows what's going on with my sister. He tells me he thinks Moira's still in the old place, but he hasn't heard anything about a baby. So maybe his information is not too current. Says he only sees her a couple times a year. They live in a town of five hundred people, and I remember Potter as a very sociable sort, too, so I'm wondering. I'm wondering, among other things, what is the deal with this baby? Pretty soon, her phone's not ringing at all.

I let that eat at me, and it's hard to even believe it now, for a good solid year before I finally decided to take a drive.

Back when we were growing up, back when the sawmill was still running, there were four saloons doing good business here in town. We had Doty's Grocery and Feed, and those four saloons, and the auto parts store. My folks owned the Aces. Somewhere along the line they'd got to be their own best customers, and a lot of times they'd sleep down at the bar. They'd come home to shower, Mom to pick up that week's issue of *Look*. As far as anybody raising Moira, I suppose that was me. Afraid I did a poor job of it, too, the way things turned out. We had a pretty good time, though—I think—when it was just the two of us in the house. We'd get ourselves up and off to school, fix our own breakfast, fix our own supper. I'd even read to her sometimes when she was still tiny. We didn't mind being so much on our own. Mind? We liked it. Moira was Suzy Sunshine in those days. Really. Sweetest person I ever knew. I think it was right around the time she got her first period, though, that she started getting ringy—her whole problem might've been one of those female things, who knows?—and not too long after that I'm off in the service, and then I'm deployed out on the South China Sea when I get the news that Mom and Dad have passed, one right after the other, like they loved each other.

I think Moira must've been awful lonesome for an awful long time. And I don't think she was made for it—course, who is? She was too screwed up to get out of town or to find somebody to treat her good, and so there she was, waitressing at the Stop N' Eat for years. Worked there, I guess, until they finally closed the doors, and that place was a greasy spoon at best. Back when I first started calling her, I'd ask about boyfriends; she still had her wits about her enough then that you could talk to her and even tease her a little bit, but she never claimed to have any love life, and after a while I quit asking 'cause I didn't want to embarrass her. Later I get the lowdown and find out she'd had all kinds of boyfriends. About half the males in Elisis have been her boyfriend for twenty minutes or so. She should've at least charged for it, but I guess all she wanted was the attention. By the time I got home she'd even run through that phase, and she was too used up to be a fallen woman anymore, or a harlot, or whatever you'd say.

Home. That's me, calling it "home" now. Jesus H. Christ. This is the last place I ever thought to be found, and I remember rolling back into town—hadn't laid eyes on it since Ensign Taylor took me to Butte for my physical—and you're away from Elisis any amount of time, just any amount of time at all, and all you'll see by way of change is what's collapsed or caved in since you left. Oh, I guess they'd built the new grade school by the time I came back, but that thing was ugly to begin with. There's no improving Elisis, that's what I thought— you might fix up cities that've been bombed to brick and ash overseas, but there is no fixing what weather and neglect do to this town; and we sure never got the relief they sent to Germany and Japan.

You know, we've got forest for hundreds of miles on all sides
of us here, but right here, right here in this valley it's just high
desert. Sage brush and cheat grass in clay. Lot of nothing, really.
Even so, this is country you can develop a taste for. But not
for Elisis. Elisis—god-all-Friday, this town is a firetrap. It's an
eyesore and has been forever.

So, in spite of my better judgment, I came back. Certainly
hadn't come to stay. And I drove up Aeneas Street to the Houlihan household, scene of my odd little youth, and I saw it was
still wearing the same coat of paint Dad stole from the WPA,
which I remember as gray, and the siding's twisting, and cup-
ping, and pulling away from the wall, and on the porch I find a
box trap with a cat and a porcupine in it. They're dead. They're
reeking. Immediately overhead of you, just under the eave at
the gable end, you got a wasp nest as big as a basketball. And
it's busy, and I am ready to turn tail and run and not look back.
But I don't. I knock at the door, I call in. I crack it open and call
in again. Nothing.

Then the wasps drove me inside.

So I'm in. I step through the mudroom and on into the
house, and there's Moira, she's been sitting there in her recliner
all along. I get around in front of her, and she's awake, seems
happy enough to see me, and I wonder if she's gone deaf and
that's why she wouldn't answer the door or the phone, why she
let it get cut off that way. A couple words, though, and I can see
she understands me. She just doesn't feel like saying anything
yet. But she did want to hug me. She got up out of that chair,
and when she did I saw where she'd left a little trench in the
Naugahyde, it's an impression of her spine. Moira was bony,
skin around her eyes looked like bad fruit. She wasn't thirty
years old, and already every tooth in her head's been pulled,
which I happen to notice 'cause she can't for the life of her keep
the plates stuck to her gums even just to breathe quiet or try a

smile. She does want to hug me, though. Wants to kiss me on my cheek. She always was sentimental.

But I was there to see about the kid, and he was nowhere in sight, and what I had seen so far was not real promising; so we don't get too much hugging done before I ask her about her boy. Is he here? "Nap," she says. It's the first word out of her mouth, but it's enough to get her started, and then she's off on the subject of poison. There's poison in every innocent thing: potatoes, and rhubarb, and fish, and anything, critter, fruit, or grain, that was harvested after noon. She tells me there's poison in the municipal water supply. Few minutes of this and my brain is Jello, and we never did get around to "hi-how-are-you-how've you been?—how's old so-and-so?" Just Moira and her theories on bad air. Wonder anybody's survived at all as far as she's concerned, and she goes on about it seems like forever, and the whole time I'm getting more and more wound up about this kid; I didn't think at that time it could be healthy for a child to be sleeping so much during the day. I didn't know about naps. Didn't know about children generally. Knew they were loud and I liked to avoid 'em. But I can also see my sister is way around the bend, and I can see that she must make for a very uphill mother.

So it's a relief, a big relief to me, when the little bugger finally swaggers out of the bedroom. All two feet of him. He falls down every other step—just, plop, on his butt—and it hardly even slows him up, and I didn't know that he'd be able to walk, or what he'd be able to do at that age, and I certainly didn't think he could be much of a person yet, but he makes straight for me—kid's already learned to mostly ignore his mother—and, he makes straight for me and he puts his fists on my knees. He's got fists like dough. And he looks me up and down as much as to say, "Who the hell are you, mister?"

This was an above-average baby. He sure had my number.

• • •

I was once a hero, don't you know? They gave me the Bronze Star. For valor, no less—I'm twenty years old, about as useful as a blister, and I happened to wander on deck one morning to throw some garbage overboard, see we weren't stowing garbage at that time because the enemy already knew where we were, they knew exactly where we were and they didn't like it, and along comes a flight of Jap fighters and strafes Manley off the aft twenty-millimeter guns; they smeared the poor guy against a bulkhead, and since we're in convoy we've got air support, and our boys get right after those fighters and run 'em off, but they're no sooner out of sight than we've got a pair of kamikaze coming at us from out of the sun. So there I am on Manley's gun, and I'm firing. They come at you from behind, you're sitting on a hundred and forty thousand barrels of aircraft fuel, you're north of Okinawa, steaming for the Imperial Palace as far as they know, and if they manage to get even close to the *Guadalupe* before they blow up, then up she goes, too, and it won't be down with the ship, it'll be up with the ship, and not a glob of grease left of her, or you, just flame and black smoke. Those oilers ride low in the water when they're heavy. What a fat target we were.

So I'm firing, and my first burst takes one of 'em out, but the other one is all over the sky, and I just can't find him, and what I've been for the last cruise and a half is a messman down in the scullery, a greasemonkey in the hold, and this is my first firefight—I remember my old training a little, remember I'm to stay off the trigger 'til he's in my sights, I'm supposed to fire and let up, fire and let up, keep the barrels cool, keep the mechanism from jamming, but I can no more stay off that trigger than . . . and I'm firing; and he's all over the sky 'cause they don't give 'em any flight training to speak of, don't even teach those boys how to land, and I'm firing, and his propellor has that same oily shine to it as a dragonfly's wing, and the kid's got

no ammunition, nothing but himself and that plywood airplane and the fuel in it, but he's coming, and I'm firing, and he's
coming, and then he's spinning ass-over-teakettle across the
ocean, and he sinks just short of us.

So the next day I'm at sick bay with what I think is the worst
case of strep throat I've ever had, but the corpsman happens to
know I've been in combat, and so he tells me my throat's just
raw from the screaming and the smoke. Screaming? I wasn't
screaming. Sure, he tells me, everybody does it. Corpsman
asked me if I'd shit myself. Well, I did not shit myself. I did what
I had to do when I had to do it, and I got promoted back up
to petty officer again, and I got that medal, which I still have
somewhere, I think, and all of it together was pitiful little to
show for being twenty-three months seasick. I was not much of
a sailor, and I'm still not much of a patriot. But, there you have
it. You do what you do. I got to Elisis, and Moira really gave me
no choice in the matter. That boy left me no choice at all.

Nowadays, I imagine, there'd be a pill for what was ail-
ing Moira, but in the fifties you really didn't want to make a
big thing of it if you thought somebody was a little off, 'cause
they were taking out pieces of peoples' brains back then. Had a
gizmo they'd run up through your nose, and—snip-snip—nobody's home. That, and they were shocking 'em damn near to
death. You had some hard, mean psychiatrists around in those
days. And I'd have to say, can't help but freely admit it—Moira
was of no earthly use to anybody, but she was also harmless, so I couldn't see her as a ward of the state. You hear how
Warm Springs is really pretty nice. A nice setting for it. Bullshit.
There's wire over the windows, and I don't care how pretty the
mountains are. Oh, but Moira had turned spooky, especially
when you weren't used to her. Spooky, and that's putting it
mildly, and I just knew if she was left on her own for very much
longer then she'd fairly likely end up in the booby hatch. Or

somewhere. And in the meantime she'd be that baby's whole world, that's what I couldn't hack—the thought of my sister talking to that boy all the time about thalidomide and arsenic and nuclear winter and whathaveyou—Jesus wept—even I could see where he'd need some better stimulation than that. No kid should be so unlucky, I knew that much.

I went back to Washington where I could get a decent price for my car, and I sold it. Sold my truck, too, and bought a better one, a panel truck this time, and I rounded up all my tools and headed back. I had the idea I'd get things sorted out. The first thing I did, my first and worst mistake, was to buy that Zenith television, big old console model; we got the one channel off some crummy airwave, picture and the sound were both like something they poured through sand, all static, and that thing was on from the farm report in the morning til they played the national anthem at night. Then she'd be staring at that test-pattern Indian. So you'd switch it off, empty her tray, clear her mess away, and throw a blanket over her. She didn't ask for much; you could never call her demanding, but you damn near had to dust her. After that TV came in, Moira was there and breathing, and that was about it.

· · ·

So what I did was get us a paper route; that was me, a grown man with a paper route. Had my panel truck and the contract for delivering *Missoulians* from Dog Lake to Hog Heaven, rural delivery, and there wasn't much money in it, but it wasn't much work, either, except in bad weather, and we generally made our little bit every day of the year, that's how many issues they printed. In those days people relied pretty heavy on their newspapers, and that's why we got no vacations, no vacations at all, but I never figured I needed any—the job had one big advantage—I could take Quent along. We rode right around a half million miles together in that panel truck, quite a bit of that at thirty miles an hour, and, but for the money, it was the best job I ever had. You're up in the timber, you're out in open country, you're all over the place every day, and in winter you got your tire chains going ching-ching-ching, and in summer you throw open the windows and smell the rain in the sagebrush. About as much as I ever wanted, and I believe Quent kind of thrived on it, too. We had the radio, of course, and he taught himself to sing, and sometimes he sounded like what I called him, "Itty Bitty Conway Twitty." Or that kid could sing like a couple English choir boys, he could make the sound of a French horn. That's the kind of traveling companion he made. Taught himself to yodel, too, which, if that'd been anybody else in there, that would've drove me crazy.

Thing I liked about him, one of the things, was that Quent was a real quick study. When we first started the route he was still in diapers, and so we had that godawful diaper bucket, and sometimes toward the end of the day when the diaper bucket's half full and the heater's going full blast and the windows are up, that'd get a little ripe in there, give you a headache. Wasn't too long, though, before Quent could hold it better than I could, and those diapers were long gone, course Quent wasn't sucking coffee from that thermos like I was. Between coffee and gravel road, a man can piss up to twenty times a day. But the point is, I liked it. We got used to each other, and when you get to where you're easy in somebody else's company, always easy, that is a rare thing, and there you are, you're living the best couple years of your life, and you don't even know it yet, but you do know you're having a pretty good time. I remember him poking newspapers into those yellow *Missoulian* tubes when he was still so little his whole arm'd completely disappear up in there.

Then, before you know it, it's kindergarten, for Christ's sake. Man, how I hated the day I had to turn him over to Mrs.

Whatshername. What was her name? Anyway, the old girl led him away very gentle, she must've done that for the little ones many hundred times, and there's all the other children, lot of 'em scamps, running around in their socks, and Quent's looking back at me, and he's fine—I'm not, though, I am not at all fine; I know he'll show 'em what-for, I know he'll shine, but up to now he's been shining just for me, and I am every bit as jealous as a mother might be, and I've got no desire at all to share him. None. I like it best when he's mine-all-mine, and even though I know it's kind of ugly of me, I can't help myself. Mine-all-mine. That couldn't go on but so long. Just as well, I guess. But I'll tell you this much, after he started in school and got among other people, Quent never sang another note that I ever heard.

So then it was the Christmas pageants and the plays and the concerts and the May Days and the two hundred other deals they liked to put on every year, keep everybody busy and distracted, and I'd talk to his teachers every so often, and I'd bake cookies and make fudge, and of course this routine really put the kibosh on that paper route, so I dropped that and put together the cabinet shop. I did cabinets and upholstery. Built the shop just behind the house, that way I could be covering a couch and have bread in the oven, too. Betty Crocker had nothing on me in those days. Also, I wanted to be handy when Quent came home from school. The business really took off then, maybe even more than I wanted, but it kept us afloat, and then I did good enough that I could knock down the folks' house—what a mausoleum that was, bat shit six inches deep in the attic—and then I built us a new windbreak on the old foundation. At least I put em in a decent house. Anyway, with Quent in school, I just went back to work. It's what I do. It's what I am, and some I know are proud to be this way. But I . . . you're kidding yourself if you think you're ever getting anything done.

Quent had quite the little motor in him, too. He'd be at one thing or another pretty hard all day. He ate like a ditchdigger and burnt it all up. Kid could get himself around six of my big caramel rolls all at once, no sweat, and he's lean as a whippet. He never had much use for toys, never had many friends, not when he was a little guy. I bought him a bike, but he liked better to run, and he'd be up Skunk or I'd hear he'd been seen way-the-hell-and-gone up in Mill Pocket. That Quent. Had a range on him like an elk or something.

About the time he hit the third or fourth grade he started to look like what he'd be as a man, and that's when the daddy mystery got cleared up: he is the spitting image of Delbert Oslavski, got exactly that same quarterhorse build on him, same face, same hair—from the physical side, anyway, he's picked himself a good sire. I'm sure I wasn't the only one to see it, but no one ever said a word, at least not to me. Not to Quent, as far as I know. And I wonder if it was too obvious to need saying or if. . . . I just know that I myself never said a word.

You'd pass the guy in the street, run into him at a game or a rodeo or parade or somewhere, run into him all the time, and you're with his son, and the man doesn't even have the good grace to be embarrassed, or try and look away. Nope, Delbert knows he's got a catch colt, and he doesn't care one way or the other. I might've been afraid of him. Maybe I was afraid of getting carried away and getting my ass kicked. Oslavski wasn't much of a man until he was in a fight. The thing to do was shoot him, really, but that would've been beside the point.

But, anyway, Quent was a restless boy. At times it sort of hurt to see it. He wasn't like one of these mutts who can't concentrate; you could slow him up with food, and now and then he'd stop to read, and once he got fascinated with rocks he'd stop anytime or anywhere to look at one, he probably knew the name of every rock in the ground. But when you think of him, the way he was as a boy, or always, I guess, in your mind's eye he's on the move.

Except I also remember how his mom would wave him over to her chair. She'd glom onto him, grab his hand and hold it, and then he'd stand there beside her, kinda have to lean in sideways the way she'd get him, and she's hanging off him, and she's got her mouth half open and she's glued to *Green Acres* or some happy horseshit. Quent'd stand there for as long as she wanted him to, never complained or even fidgeted. He'd just stand there, and, man, that broke my heart every time. Sometimes he'd brush her hair.

She had the prettiest, healthiest head of hair. Moira did at least keep herself clean, and for that I was very grateful. Imagine if I'd signed on for that chore, scrubbing her. No, but she kept herself clean, and even kept herself kind of nice for as much as she'd wasted away, and I have to give her high marks for grooming, I suppose. I always wanted to forgive her, but I couldn't. There was nothing to forgive, so where does that leave you? Most of the time I think I must've treated her like a piece of expensive furniture, cause, you know, I just couldn't muster any more feeling for her than that, and I didn't want to give her an opening to get off onto fluoride or one of her other topics. She hated anything she considered chemical. But Quent's growing up; Quent's off running or at school or in his room, and pretty soon I'm Moira's company most of the time, and she's mine—I gotta say, there were some long, long Sunday afternoons with my sister. You wanna be kind or pay attention or something, but why? After a while, what's the point? She was just as happy to be ignored, and she took very little interest in me, I can tell you.

So I had my stack of *National Geographics*, and I read every page of those many times. Guys with hoops in their noses, you know, fishing with blowguns—I had that. Had my magazines, my soldering gun, that stereo I built and built on and never did get it to play right—thin soup, pretty fucking thin. And poor Quent built himself a trestle bridge out of popsicle sticks, that thing eventually took up two whole walls of his room. One Christmas I found a locomotive, took me some finding, too, it was a very narrow gauge, and we put that up on top of the structure, damn near to the ceiling. He had his chin-up bar and his dumbbells in there. You'd look in on him, and there he is reading that *War and Peace;* he read that book all one winter, which, I tried it and was snowed in thirty pages, completely flummoxed by those people's names. Names and titles, not for me. Anyway, unless you liked your television, and you liked it going full blast the way Moira did, you kinda kept to your room. Wasn't long before that arrangement made us strangers. I never especially intended it when I built 'em, but somehow I'd done a good job of soundproofing the walls in that house.

• • •

I could go the track meets, and I could go to basketball, but after a while I couldn't stand to watch him play football anymore. You'd see Quent rock up onto his toes, and you know he's about to fly. Out on that field he'd make those other boys look tired, make 'em look like they came to watch. He was so much faster, and shifty. You just knew those little sonsabitches probably wanted to hurt him. The ball is in his hands every play, and I'd want to go down to the sideline and yell at his coach, "Give him a break, would you? Don't you know he's just a kid?" Course, that wouldn't exactly do, so I stayed away instead. I was scared they'd hurt him or wear him out, but they never did, and I'm told I missed some real exhibitions; they tell me he never did take a solid lick. I was all right with reading about it in the newspaper the next day.

So now he's popular, but since he's every bit as shy as he's

ever been, all these new friends are no boon to him. If it isn't
a girl on the phone it's a recruiter, and Quent'll be nice to 'em,
he's pleasant enough, but he's never on for too long. What'd I
call him, elusive? He was alone whenever he could be, and I saw
less and less of him all the time, and here it is getting closer to
graduation, and I've started to wonder, way too late in the game,
I'm wondering a little bit, "What have I got myself into?" I am
not looking forward to the me and Moira show. I'm getting the
preview—in many ways Quent was gone before he ever left.

You know, we stood two years there of visits from assistant
coaches, and head coaches, and alumni, and a whole herd of
people who probably never before or since set foot in a class C
town. That was hell for all of us. There you'd be, trying to be
polite with some poor guy at the kitchen table who's been sent
to get himself an athlete, and the guy's eyes keep flipping over to
that specimen in the living room, and some of 'em even try and
sweet-talk her. That must've been real strange duty; plenty lined
up to do it, though. So it was a little odd, after all that, that Quent
gets a scholarship at Berkeley, California, a full-ride scholarship,
and just for a score he got on some test. For years they've been
telling me at school that he tests out unlimited—unlimited
potential, they say, if he ever breaks out of his shell. So he tells me
he's decided to go down there and study Anthropology, which
I've heard of in my *Geographics*, but I'm not real sure what it
is, and I'm still not sure after he explains it to me. They study
human beings? The nature of human beings? Can that be right?
Anyway, anthropologist was not everybody's idea of local-boy-
makes-good. They all wanted to see him play ball somewhere.
People around here were a little ticked off at him because of
that—like it was any of their business what he did or didn't do.

Then, and I don't think it was even two weeks after we got
news of that scholarship, Moira died. Just died for no particular
reason. I came out one morning and there she was cold in her

recliner, and she must've had about the gentlest death there ever was, but she was still dead. We took her out to Lonepine and planted her next to Mom and Dad; we took the recliner and the Zenith, which was still going strong after all those years, we took those out to the dump, and that was that. Came home to a big hole in the living room. That living room was still Moira's territory for as long as I lived there, but, let's face it, I wasn't exactly overwhelmed with grief. Don't know how Quent felt about it; he never said, and that's not the kind of thing you ask somebody, but I knew the next time I had to let him go, he'd be long gone. I wouldn't have had it any other way.

That last spring he spent with me he was running track for the pure hell of it, and he was far and away the fastest schoolboy in the state. He was running the hundred-yard dash in under ten seconds, seemed like he took about ten yards a stride. You watch those sprinters, when you watch 'em from up close, you see how their faces quake every time they hit the ground, they hit so hard, and most of em look quite grim, like it really costs 'em something to go so fast. But Quent would smile. Might be a little harder to spot it when he was really hauling, but he always smiled when he ran. Smile and pull away, and it was the greatest thing I ever saw. Course I also had the walking pneumonia that spring, and those track meets did not do good things for it. I was sick that spring, sick all that summer while Quent was off fighting fire, sick when he went down to school. I stayed sick for about a year there, miserable and puny, and just barely able to work. Geeze, I felt like a plowhorse.

And I'd got into some trouble with the IRS.

Many years earlier I'd made a mistake in my book keeping, an honest mistake, and I'd underpaid my taxes, but not by much. Never mind that it was an honest mistake, and never mind that it was a small one and they took their own sweet time finding it—with penalties and interest, it turned out to be a very substantial sum, and then I made it much worse, much, much worse, when I got my back up and hired a lawyer, a guy who told me from the start there was nothing he could do about it, but I made him waste his time and my money trying, and meanwhile that interest is compounding, or whatever it does to make it get so far outta hand, and before I was through, I owed 'em everything. Bless their hearts, they agreed to settle for everything I had. I managed to hang onto the house until that next summer when Quent came home for a bit.

He looked like a gypsy. He's grown himself quite the hank of hair, and it's tied up in a silk rag, and he's relaxed in some new way. I think maybe he'd found out down there that being smart wasn't exactly a character flaw—and he's got some girl with him wouldn't dream of wearing a bra or, you know, disappointing him in any way. He tells me that now he's gonna travel. It's independent study, he says. He's with a traveling collective for independent study and community development—which is to say a bunch of footloose hippies, and one of 'em hasn't got his scholarship anymore.

He stayed—they stayed—about a week, and then they went south, and I have to admit I was so embarrassed about losing the house, and about not having any way to help him out down there at school, it wasn't all that bad for me when he became a college dropout. That's when I should've got out of Elisis, too, that was probably my best chance, but at the time I told myself I didn't have the oomphta or the cash to go anywhere, which was really pretty true, and I got set up in my little trailer out by the highway, one of those things like a guy might take up hunting, about as big as a two-seater outhouse, and it rocks every time a semi goes by. Was I feeling sorry for myself? Yes. But I did have the same post office box, and I had phone service with the old phone number, and at least I was where Quent could get in touch if he needed.

Eighty-eight-oh-one. One Houlihan or another has had this

same number here ever since the Elisis Telephone Company was formed. Big deal. All it shows is a lack of imagination. I think that's what kept me in town, I could never come up with a clear idea of anything better. But, little by little I put myself back together. For quite a while there I lived on macaroni and postcards that took months to get here. He's in Honduras, he's in the Yucatan. At first he'd just tell me where he was at, and how the food was, and once in a great while I'd get a picture, but it was never a picture of him. After he'd been down there a while he started to throw in little bits about imperialism, and this-that-or-the-otherism, and I am just praying I don't catch a whiff of Moira in this stuff. Police states, he says. He don't like 'em. Who does? So why would you go so far outta your way to go be in 'em?

At least I'm getting my postcards.

He'd call every Christmas, but that was like shouting at each other from either end of a tunnel. I didn't ask what he was doing, and he never offered to tell me. I hoped he was doing nothing. Nothing, I think, that's his best option down there. I'd get mail from him, but I never sent him any back, never tried to, 'cause whenever I'd hear from him it was understood—wherever he was, he wouldn't be there long. After a while there was no politics in his letters, and he was back to telling me about the birds and the plantain and the way they made their local dishes, sometimes the fish in the sea, and these are some wonderful letters, but you can see where somebody's opened 'em already, they didn't even try to hide it, they'd just rip that envelope open and then, very half-assed, tape it closed again. So I'm wondering how he's getting by down there, and here I am rooting for him to be as shiftless as possible, hoping he's a drifter, and maybe that's all he's up to, but I don't think so, 'cause he's got a serious side, that damn-near saintly side to him, I've seen it a few times, and who knows what kind of Latin bullshit could happen to him on account of that? I read the news. I know how they are. Those bastards got a lotta jungle where they can hide their dirty work. So I had my heart in my mouth, a little bit, the whole time he was down there.

It was around in then that I got myself involved in a minor shack-up with Phyllis Comes Last. I was in the house on Pine by then, had a place to keep her. Phyllis was a Blackfeet gal, and she'd drank for many years on her looks; by the time I got to her she was drinking on her pretty laugh. She had a talent for convincing you not to take things so serious, and people liked to be around her. She'd walk out of the house with a nickel in her jeans, come back two weeks later and she's been drunk the whole time, even if she hasn't ate, and she's been to parties in three states. I never got in her way, so she liked me. We were actually a pretty sociable couple, considering I was half of it, and we'd go over to somebody's house for dinner and wind up sleeping their floor. My liver didn't handle that too good. Phyllis, I liked. The freight that came with Phyllis, I just couldn't pay. She was in Elisis purely by accident, and once I gave up on her she had no reason to stay. Eventually she was up in Canada—she was a Blood or a Piegan, I don't remember, but a part of the tribe that was eligible for their health care system up there. Last call I got from her, she said she was all worn out inside. She didn't seem to be too shook up about it, though.

In the meantime, I just went out and busted ass, an old man working like a young one. At some point your back gets to be a whole different deal, and it takes you about a day just to get over a day of doing rough carpentry. But that's okay. I built the Sherwoods their pole barn, remodeled a couple places that should've been torched. After Phyllis, I had few expenses, and I'm back at it, and, as I say, little by little I got well. Man, I sure appreciated eating good again; had a standing deal with Garney Fronapel to keep my freezer filled with grass-fed steak. Around in then was when I first started doing my carvings, too, and when they got decent enough that I could stand to look at em, I'd go to the craft fairs and sell 'em. I was doing a lot of bears' heads at first, and then I got on to my rowboats with the miniature oars; those were very popular. Sold those first few things for five, ten bucks apiece, and I thought I was making out like a bandit, to get paid anything for goofing off, sure, I'll take that. So, anyway, you'd have a lot of hippies at those events 'cause they've all got the same basic idea as I do, try and sell some kinda trinket, some harmless thing; and every so often I'd catch some kid outta the corner of my eye, some kid with a certain way of walking, kid with a mop like they wore back then, and that'd bring me up short. I don't know why. I had my eye out for him even when I knew he couldn't be there.

• • •

Eventually he worked his way north again. He was a longshoreman in New Orleans until he turned somebody in for cockfighting on the docks; he sawed logs down around Medford, and for a good while he worked a fishing boat out of Sitka. And if he still never stayed put for very long in any one place, at least I usually had a good address for him, usually he'd even have a phone—and you don't want to intrude, but you write, you call, you kinda wait to hear about what he saw down there in the tropics that makes him sound so old sometimes, but he doesn't talk about that, doesn't talk about much, really, if it has to do with him. I'd slip him a few bucks from time to time, and he always sent it back. Said he was probably making more than I was, which might've been true, but I'd been living so close to the bone for so long I had no need for any extra.

He used to come to see me in Elisis . . . well, I guess he came twice. Once he came with another one of those hippy girls, and the next time he's got a dog he picked up on the road. Crippled dog. He came to ask me how I'm doing, and, to tell you the truth, that gave me a little case of the yips. How'm I doing? How am I supposed to know? You want a bear head? You want a little boat, got some toothpick oars in it? Really, I'm just itching to ask him . . . what? I don't know. He is in some ways his mother's son, and you get the impression that for all his smarts and his big heart and everything, he could just up and drift away on you some day, and without ever leaving the room. I guess I wanna ask him, "What's eating you?" Strikes me he might be inclined to check out like Moira did.

So that's why I started to think maybe it's up to me, maybe I better do something. I didn't have the slightest idea what it might be, but one day I threw a war bag in the truck and drove out to see him. He was in Seattle, or close to it. Had a maintenance job at a hospital. Had an apartment. And what I didn't know til I got there—he had a new girlfriend. Rebecca. She's a doctor's daughter, and kinda full of herself, you know the type, and that whole apartment is just filled with clown shit—clown dolls, clown posters, got some clown shoes on the end table. Again I say, to each his own, but there's limits to that. Harlequins, she called em. Creepy. But she doesn't seem to be doing Quent any harm that I can see, she's even kind of a hand on the tiller for him. Doesn't matter if I like her or not. So we have dinner a couple times, and she calls us cowboys. We're both just mortified, but we don't say anything. I've stepped in heifer dust about twice in my whole life. She wants to know what he was like growing up. "Busy," I tell her. I'm not gonna tell her, "Sweet." Who knows how she'd take that? Who knows what she'd make of it?

She says they are very happy together, that they understand each other so well. She understands him? Well, bully for her. I'm thinking she might better understand how he tends to take off. Quent tells me he's saving money to go study computers, and that's practical, that's more of a plan than I've heard from him in quite a spell, and I should be pleased to hear it. He'll have all the work he wants, I suppose, and never dirty his hands. But I remember when he mentioned that computer thing I felt like I'd been kicked in the belly, and I remember when he said a couple months later he was off it, I felt good about that, too. But then he got a job fixing coffee machines. What in the hell? Seemed like kind of a step down for him. And *then* he tells me he's marrying Rebecca, and I wonder, "Does she know about this?" 'cause she doesn't seem to me like the kind of girl to settle for any kind of mechanic, much less a guy fixing coffee machines. It's *es-pres-so*, he keeps telling me. I'm not too impressed.

But here he is on the phone, and he says they're getting married. I could hear some kinda silly-ass chimes in the background—and he tells me he's asked her father for her hand. Her dad said okay. They're getting married. Well, whattaya do with that information? Got in the truck and drove on out to Seattle again. Rented a tuxedo, even had to rent the shoes, which, to my mind, that's about the same as wearing somebody else's underwear. Who knows who's been in them rented shoes? But I bought some black socks, and I went ahead and wore 'em. And at this wedding you got the groom's side of the aisle, which is me and the crew off a cod boat and some little dark gal who doesn't have a word of English, turns out she's a net mender, comes from Portugal—and on the other side you got Rebecca's people. A lot of 'em. These are people what we would've called swells in the old days, and the presents they brought . . . it was ridiculous. There was a lot of those envelopes tied up in silver twine, you knew what was in 'em.

They got married, and her dad, Dr. Merton Detwiler, gave 'em a cottage sitting on five acres of Vashon Island, piece of ground that looked out over Puget Sound. I gave 'em a toaster oven and went on home.

• • •

You get old, and you look back on your life, and you see where there's big chunks of it you can't hardly remember 'cause they weren't worth remembering. You're fifty, sixty, seventy, and so on, and you been stuffing your face and sleeping. And what else? Meanwhile, you got the rheumatiz, got your arthritis, and there's more hair growing outta your nose than grows on top of your head. You get ugly, is what you do. Real ugly.

Personally, though, I've been an artist, and I've got no room to bitch. An artist. Me. Just tickles me pink. I went ahead and put a lot of windows in my kitchen, tore those appliances out and put 'em in the basement where they belonged, and I sat down and started whittling pretty serious. Out come snakes and snowflakes. In time I'm doing hummingbirds and geese and about anything I want. My little discovery, I guess you could call it—there's this species of spruce up in the Thompson River country, and I can buy it a thousand board feet at a time, buy it as cheap as pine because I buy it raw. If I cure it right, cut off short cants and kiln-cure 'em, I can do almost anything with it; it's got a very forgiving grain; and then when you're finished, then a piece always colors up somehow and it takes on a life of its own. There's been a surprise in everything I've ever carved. So here I've sat, whittling, and you look down at your hands, and they're like your pals, the guys who actually know what you're talking about, and you can get just as lost in that as anybody ever got lost in liquor. I'll take it, though, believe me. I'll take my addiction over most others I can think of. Before I know it, my stuff's in the shops in Missoula and Kalispell and Bigfork, I mean the nice shops, and even in a few little museums, places where they really know how to light it so you look like a genius. And they give me good money to do this—who would've ever thought? Hell yes. I've just sat here, and sat here, and whittled away, and I've called no man boss—unless it was the tax man. I don't see where I can complain too much.

And Quent's done fine, too, I guess. Better than fine.

There was a time there where I just kind of let him alone while he was making a success of himself. Took quite a while, I have to say, before I figured out that's what he was doing. I didn't expect the thing with Rebecca to work out, and maybe that was wishful thinking, but you got a fart in a whirlwind and a rich girl—who would've been optimistic about the chances for that. I was wrong, though. They both proved me wrong. He started out fixing those machines all day every day, and this is a lot more complicated equipment than I ever thought it could be, and fixing 'em is top money; then he's got his own company, and he's training other people to fix 'em; then he's selling 'em; and then he's selling the damn things all over the world. He goes to Switzerland all the time. After a while I've got quite the collection of business cards on my corkboard, got some from Rebecca, too—card from when she had her dress shop, a flyer from when she ran for city council. They're busy people, so I leave 'em alone, and he's always saying to come out and see 'em, to come on out. But I don't.

After they had their kids, I started getting a steady stream of pictures, too, which is all right cause those kids are gorgeous, and I'd send the little ones their checks on their birthdays, fifty bucks a whack, which may be kind of a joke to them, or it will be soon, but I keep track of their birthdays, Christmas and Easter, and that's about as much of the year as I pay any attention to. "Come out," he says all the time, and I know he's proud of what he's got, what he's done for himself out there—and you can tell he's real proud of those babies—but I still never go. I got a camper and everything, and I go everyplace else, drove all the way up the AlCan and back, twice, but for a real long time I never got out to see Quent and company. It was silly, and I'm not too sure why I stayed away, but I have noticed that when you live by yourself it doesn't take too long at all before you're weird, and I was kind of an odd duck to begin with, and I really can't imagine anybody should have to put up with me. So he says "come," and I say I'll be out when I've got the garden put up, when I'm finished canning, which, to tell you the truth, I rarely do that. He says "come," and I tell him I'll come when I'm done fishing. I'm sure he knows it's always fishing season somewhere.

So there's a lotta phone calls back and forth, but, one thing led to another, and I never saw him for nine years. Finally he just sent me a plane ticket and a note to say he was sorry he hadn't thought of it sooner. That forced my hand, of course, and a good thing, too. I'm a little ashamed of the way I get. One way or the other, it's always been Quent who grabs me by the scruff of the neck and shakes me out of it. So there he was at the airport, waiting for me, and he's got a hundred-dollar hair-cut and all, but he's still got those same eyes he inherited from poor old Mrs. Oslavski; kind eyes, I'd call 'em. I won't even try and say how good it was to see him.

But then we get to Merton. He's brought his little boy with him, and the kid's a Houlihan through and through, except he's better looking than the usual run of us, and I guess I'm supposed to get that family feeling for him, or something, but I don't, 'cause in the flesh this kid is very hard to like. He's an asshole, this Merton, and that's about all I remember from the airport. I count on my fingers and figure up that he's seven years old. I don't remember anything at all like this from when Quent was seven. So we get in the car and I give Merton this chain I'd carved out of a single piece of stock—the thing's two feet long, twelve links, and these are all independent, free-moving links, and it's been a week's work for me to carve it. That chain hits the floorboard about as quick as Merton can pitch it down there, and then the kid's jazzing his little electric pin-ball machine, some little deal he can hold it in the palm of his hands, but it's loud enough you can barely hear yourself think in there. Quent asked him a couple times to turn it off or to turn it down, but the kid says no and keeps right on with what he's doing. He's a nightmare, if you ask me. Quent seems okay with it, though, and there I am, riding along with 'em, trying not to look disgusted.

We got on the ferry out to Vashon, and Merton wanted to stay in the car. He wants to sit there and goose his thingus 'til the batteries wear out, or until I kill him. Quent, of course, has to sit there with him. But I didn't have to, so I got out and went on up to the upper deck, as far away from Merton Houlihan as I could get on that boat, and I'm standing there, catching rain in my mouth. I can see where if that brat was mine, I'm not too sure we'd make many ferry rides before there was a little splash some night. I hadn't been missing a goddamn thing on the Merton score.

So then we get to the ferry landing and the kid's gone to sleep. I count my blessings. We do the ride to Quent's place without saying much. I make a few brilliant observations—it's pretty, it's green, and so forth. Whatta they call 'em now? Communication skills. I never had any. I just sit there hoping he's not mad at me 'cause I can't stand his kid.

Now, this property of theirs didn't look a thing like I remembered from way back when, when the doctor bought it for 'em. Quent tells me him and Rebecca unwind on the weekends by doing their own landscaping, and there's not an inch of their ground that hasn't been planted and pruned and prettied up. It's a little fussy for my taste, and a lot more yard work than I'd ever do, but you'd have to say it was nice. And that house. Somewhere under there was the cottage they started with, but it's been remodeled into a castle. Must be four or five thousand feet wrapped in cedar board and cedar shakes, and it's gussied up in some kind of copper trim that was new to me. I'd never seen anything like it before. Inside, you got your parquet floors and marble countertops and about an acre of windows looking out over the water. That one wall's like a great big movie screen, there's barges and whales and schooners and all kinda traffic in those windows.

Then Rebecca comes downstairs with little Daisy on her hip. The females of this family are something else, I tell you. I gave Daisy her angel, cause it was what I'd carved for her, and that angel's head goes straight in her mouth, and as soon as Rebecca's convinced there's not been any shellac on it or anything, that's where it stays. Drool running down her chin, snot running down her lip, and that little girl was still cute as a button. You couldn't hardly stand it. When her mom sets her down, she's off like a shot. Quent's been telling me this one might be the apple of my eye. He might be right.

So then we had a drink, or in my case a couple. Some kinda real pricey bourbon. Tasted so good and hit me so hard, I had to excuse myself before supper was ready, and I can see where they were making a production out of supper. I smell salmon on a grill somewhere, but even with my mouth watering, I'm not near as hungry as I am tired. So Rebecca shows me to my room, and she's got a funny little grin, and I'm thinking it's 'cause I can't hold my liquor and I'm acting like a tourist in their house, but she lets me in that room, and I get in there and see where it's been all set up for me. Everything they think I might like is in there, including a set of very fancy Japanese carving knives, and some pieces of cherry wood and walnut. There's a card on my pillow. Rebecca wrote it. This room's mine, she says. It's here whenever I want to use it, for as long as I want to use it. I got a lump in my throat so big I damn near puked. That was a fine note to pass out on.

That next morning I rode into work with Quent, and he apologizes that we have to take the ferry again. Hell, it's something he has to do every day, why should I mind? His business takes up the best part of a three-story building smack in the middle of downtown Seattle. You got your showroom on the ground floor, repair and fabricating over that, and on the top floor there's offices. We breeze through the whole deal, and it's, Mr. Houlihan this, and Mr. Houlihan that, and everybody's just delighted to meet me, like I'm just the most wonderful geezer they ever saw, and every place we go Quent solves some little problem for somebody, just fixes it on the fly. You can tell he's been good to these people. You can also tell he's in charge, which is a little different face than I've ever seen on him before. When the tour's finished and all the introductions are over, he takes me to his office and makes me the best cup of coffee I ever drank. No, he says, it's *es-presso*. Well, by now I should get this straight, I suppose. All I know is, I may have to start using that machine he sent me. No wonder he can work so damn hard. The stuff's like some kinda tasty rocket fuel.

Then he settles in to make phone calls all day. He apologizes about that, too. No problem. I take a little walk around Seattle. Got in the wrong part of it, of course, and some wino mugged me, and he damn near conks me over the head with a pipe before I can convince him, no, I don't have a credit card. Guess I'm the last guy on earth without a credit card.

Then it's back out to the island and another nice dinner. I get the impression they do this every night—you got pasta and a big old salad and a slab of pig in sweet and sour sauce, and the kids are set up with their own separate meal. There's a sound system that pipes that sticky dead-guy music to every corner of the house, which is not so tough on the ears after you get used to it. Rebecca opens up a forty-dollar bottle of wine like it was so much Kool-Aid, but I figure I better lay off the booze. Drunk or sober, I still don't have a thing to say for myself. They're trying so hard. I'm just wishing I had one interesting thing to say. Next day I stay home with Rebecca and the kids, and we're out in the yard, and I fix a gate for her, and then I get to playing hide-and-seek with Merton, and I find out I can stand him after all. He's still a house ape, mind you, but you get him outside and playing around, and he's a kid like any other kid. Then that night Quent comes home late and takes us out to a restaurant. They treated me like royalty the whole time I was there. I was wishing I'd done a little something to deserve that.

That was my last night there, and while Rebecca's off giving the kids their baths, me and Quent step out on the deck. The stars are out, kind of unusual in that part of the world. So I take the opportunity to tell him how proud I am of him. It's hard to explain, but here he is, he's made enough money to retire already if he wants to, and he's been all over the world and ate things I've never even heard of, and he's almost got his head down about it. This is what I remember about him— right from the beginning, nobody ever had a lower opinion of Quent than Quent did. He was always so terrible easy to em- barrass, and I remember that was one of the things that made me so tender about him. He's kind of a heartbreak, and neither one of us really knows why. So I tell him I'm proud of him. Tell him I've never been anything but proud. He tells me he wants me to come and live with 'em. We both know what the answer to that'll be, but I am kind of weak in the knees to get the offer.

After that I started visiting every so often. Watched those kids grow up a little bit at a time, and that was good fun. Mer- ton turned out to be a whizbang lacrosse player, and I caught a couple of his games before he graduated. Daisy just kept living up to her name. Meanwhile Quent's getting richer and richer and not a year passes when I'm not a little fonder of Rebecca. That whole bunch out there, they're the reason the sun sets in the West as far as I'm concerned.

But also . . . I don't know. I'm on the phone more and more

with Quent the older he gets, and more and more he wants
to talk about old times. Then one day he calls and asks me to
meet him out at the Elisis airport cause he needs to get in some
twin-engine time. He's been flying a few years now, and he's
just moved up to this Beechcraft. That's a damn short runway, I
tell him, and it's just dirt, but he says he'll be fine. Sure enough,
two, three hours later there he is, coming in over Baldy. He
makes his approach and sets 'er down on the apron, and his
brakes are locked up and smoking, but he finally gets stopped
with about ten yards to spare before he's through the barb wire
and out into somebody's pasture. Quite the little landing. And
he gets out, and he comes over to the hangar, and he tells me
he's got a confession to make, he really didn't need the hours
that bad. He just wanted to see me. What's wrong? Nothing, he
says. Nothing's wrong. Not exactly. Fine, then, I tell him, lunch
is on me. But he wants to know if I could do him a favor. Wants
to know if we could go out and drive some of the old paper
route. Well, sure. One thing I've got a lot of is time.

This country has changed a good deal since he was young
in it, or some of it has. Sprinkler systems. They managed to put
water on dry ground up at my end of the valley, and there might
be fewer people here than there used to be, but those who stayed
make a half decent living. They're not so godawful poor as
people around here used to be. There's a lot more cows on this
ground, I'll tell you that. So we swung by the graveyard to visit
Moira's grave, and then I thought I'd head up toward Niarada,
'cause that's about the same as it always was—except Niarada itself is gone. You got the same old gravel, same old sagebrush, but
no place to even stop and buy a Coke if you want it. It's empty
out that way, which is why I kind of like it. And we're riding
along, and it's just us and the coyotes, the way it used to be, and
I look over, and there's something about the way his head sits on
his shoulders, or something, I don't know. He's the same. He's

that boy who knew every tune, and I'll bet he knows 'em to this day. But he's also the man who don't sing 'em.

We rode out in the lonesomest country we could find. Rode out, drove around a while, and then we went home.

ABOUT THE AUTHOR

Matt Pavelich was born in St. Ignatius, Montana, and attended the University of Montana, the Iowa Writers' Workshop, and the Northwest School of Law. He is the author of the short story collection, *Beasts of the Forest, Beasts of the Field* (Owl Creek Press, 1990), which won the Montana Arts Council First Book Award, as well as the novels *Our Savage* (Shoemaker & Hoard, 2004) and *The Other Shoe* (Counterpoint, 2012). He currently makes his home in Hot Springs, Montana.

Clear Title: A Novel
by Grace Stone Coates
(introduction by Caroline Patterson)

Food of Gods and Starvelings
The Selected Poems of Grace Stone Coates
Lee Rostad & Rick Newby, editors

Grace Stone Coates: Her Life in Letters
by Lee Rostad

Notes for a Novel
The Selected Poems of Frieda Fligelman
Alexandra Swaney & Rick Newby, editors

The Pass: A Novel
by Thomas Savage
(introduction by O. Alan Weltzien)

Lona Hanson: A Novel
by Thomas Savage
(introduction by O. Alan Weltzien)

Splendid on a Large Scale
The Writings of Hans Peter Gyllembourg Koch,
Montana Territory, 1869–1874
Kim Allen Scott, editor

"The Whole Country was . . . 'One Robe'"
The Little Shell Tribe's America
by Nicholas C. P. Vrooman

Coming Home
The Historic Built Environment and Landscapes of
Butte and Anaconda, Montana
Patty Dean, editor

Frank Lloyd Wright in Montana
Darby, Stevensville, and Whitefish
by Randall LeCocq

Cass Gilbert in Big Sky Country
His Designs for the Montana Club
by Patty Dean